PRAISE FOR MELODY CARLSON

"…any story by Carlson is worth encountering."

—Booklist

"Ms. Carlson's characters are realistic and facing issues that relevant in today's world."

—Romance Readers Connection

"Melody Carlson's style is mature and bitingly funny, and her gift for connecting our heart to the character's plight also connects us to the complicated human condition and our need for one another."

—Patricia Hickman, author of Painted Dresses

StoneHouse Ink 2012
www.StoneHouseInk.net
Boise, Idaho 83713

First eBook Edition 2012
First Paperback Edition: 2013
ISBN: 978-1-62482-050-2

Book cover design Cory Clubb copyright © 2012
Layout design by Ross Burck

Published in the United States of America

StoneHouse Ink

BLOOD SISTERS

MELODY CARLSON

*Lovingly dedicated to the memory of
my original "blood sister."
I pray that we'll meet again in our Father's house.*

BLOOD SISTERS

One

LIKE A HEAVY WOOLEN blanket on a scorching night, the sticky
air pressed against her skin with a will more persistent than her own,
and the mercury in the kitchen thermometer pushed the red line
nearly to the top. "Unseasonably warm for June," the weatherman
had warned on the radio earlier this morning, and yet she'd left
the window gaping wide open, allowing the city's hot sulfurous
fumes to creep into her apartment as if by invitation. She pushed a
dirty strand of hair from her damp brow and reluctantly placed her
bottle of precious, blue pills on the dusty window sill, then closed
the window with a dull thud. Was this how hell might feel on an
unseasonably cool day? Perhaps it wouldn't be so bad after all.

Someone told her it took a lot of courage to live, but Judith
thought it'd take a lot more to willingly die—to bravely open that
door and then face whatever it was that waited beyond. She leaned
her forehead against the gritty glass and exhaled. Surely death was
better than this. How long could she continue anyway? Hanging by
this slender thread and all the while just waiting for it to break—or
more likely that she would simply let go, and float down, down,
down...

Clutching her bottle of pills, she stood straight, focusing her eyes on the window before her, yet only seeing its grimy surface and the gray blur of what lay beyond. She knew the scene well, too well. Busy street, four lanes of almost constant traffic, another identical cement apartment complex on the other side with rows of windows staring back at her with unseeing eyes. Varying shades of bleakness. Not unlike her life.

She turned away from the window and gazed across her small apartment, suddenly seeing it with unexpected clarity. Was this the way one perceives things in the final moments of their life? Everything suddenly grows clear and sharp, almost like an adjusted lens. Boxes still packed, their contents labeled in neat black felt-penned letters, and stacked evenly against the naked walls, almost like a fortress. Various pieces of new furnishings stored, not arranged, in the limited space, making the room appear more like a miniwarehouse than a place of habitation. But most of the time she didn't notice these things or even care

They had never meant to stay this long. It was only to have been a temporary stopping place—one of the small sacrifices that enabled Peter to finish law school. But it had become her prison and she had long since forgotten the way out. She sank into a chair and leaned her elbows on the scarred top of the oak table wedged tightly info a corner under the small counter by the kitchen. This antique table was one of the few larger possessions she had demanded they hold on to during their frugal, minimalist era. "Just wait, Judith." Peter had reassured her. "This apartment will soon be nothing but a memory. I promise you, honey, we'll buy a beautiful house—even better than our old Victorian back in Vancouver. Then we'll fill our new place with really fine things—no more of your mom's old castoffs or shoddy garage sale finds." He tossed her his lopsided grin. "Just you wait, Jude. Before you know it we'll be living the good life."

But Peter had been gone for a year and a half now, taking all her dreams with him. Since that time she had remained, trapped in this cruel time warp where the surroundings never changed. And now she couldn't imagine leaving. Still, she didn't blame Peter for her dismal circumstances. Not really. He'd never meant to abandon her like this. It was just the way life had happened. She sighed and tried to remember the last time she'd been truly happy. She knew she had been, once upon a time...

Was it only two years ago she had turned forty and their life had finally turned promising? After graduating with honors, Peter had joined the prestigious firm of Thompson and Baynes, Attorneys at Law. "I told you it'd happen." Peter had said with pride. "No more teaching summer school for you. I'm bringing in the big bucks now. I want you to go out and have some fun. Buy some new clothes. And start looking for that dream house, Jude!"

It was a joyous and carefree summer, with many weekends spent sailing with Philip and Amy Baynes. And by summer's end she and Peter had jubilantly discovered the perfect home on the high banks of the Willamette River. Not an overly large house, for by that stage in life they had decided they didn't need lots of room. But it certainly wasn't small either, and the view of Mount Hood was glorious. Peter had teased about how the deck would be ideal for a pair of rocking chairs as they gracefully grew old together, and Judith imagined quiet, intimate dinner parties watching purple sunsets reflected off the snowy mountain peak. In the fall, they placed a hefty deposit down, expecting to close the sale and be in their new home by November. Judith had already invited both sets of parents to join them for a festive Thanksgiving dinner to celebrate the new house and their reinvented life.

In late October, Philip Baynes had asked Peter to go to Central

Oregon with him to work on a corporate case, and Peter readily agreed. They left in the middle of the day, Philip flying them in his twin engine plane, one of the many perks of joining a small but successful firm. But an unexpected ice storm came in from the north and the small plane went down in the rugged Cascades. When Amy Baynes called and hysterically told her that Phil's plane was lost in the mountains, Judith remained amazingly calm, reassuring Amy that she was absolutely certain that both husbands were perfectly fine. Having no doubts of Peter's safety, she imagined the two fit men hiking away from the plane to find help. Because, most certainly, a loving God would not allow this to happen again to her—surely not twice in one lifetime. Nine years earlier, and also in the fall, she and Peter had lost their only son, Jonathan, to an unrelenting case of leukemia. "Tragedies like this don't happen twice," she assured Amy with stiff confidence, suppressing all other feelings deep within her.

After a long week of aerial searches, the plane—or rather parts of it—was finally discovered in the mountains. No survivors. Judith grieved in absolute numbness and partial disbelief. It was as if she were wrapped in layer upon layer of thick cotton batting. No feelings, no thoughts, no hopes, no dreams—just nothingness. Then, like a zombie, Judith continued the mechanical motions of teaching for the remainder of the school year, and she even taught summer school after the regular school year ended. And when fall came she began the endless cycle again, never pausing to face her loss. Never allowing herself the luxury of grief— for she felt certain that if she gave in, like a flood it would sweep her away and drown her. Besides, it seemed the demands of teaching in an inner-city school provided her with a floodgate of sorts. Of course, it was an escape, but it managed to distract her from the unrelenting ache that tightly entwined itself around her heart.

And now it was summer again, and she no longer had the strength to continue. She had declined to teach summer school and had no idea how to spend the next several weeks or even if she could survive them. It seemed her floodgate was down now. School had only been out two weeks and already she was a mess. She hadn't left her apartment for nearly a week, was existing on coffee and toast, and hadn't bathed in—well, she didn't even remember how long. On the table before her was a full bottle of Xanax. Prescribed by her doctor after Peter's death to calm her, she had never taken a single pill. Instead, she had saved them, like an insurance policy, for the day when she might *really* need them. And it seemed that day was today.

She took her eyes off the bottle and glanced around her dismal and cramped apartment again, as if searching for a clue—something to bring a sense of reason to all of this. But all she saw was the stacked boxes—her prison walls. Or perhaps her mausoleum. She picked up the bottle and carefully poured the pills across the table, such a soothing shade of blue, the color of a smogless sky. Was anything really that blue anymore? She pushed the pills into a small pile with her finger, wondering if there was anything left to live for. And even if she had the strength, why should she continue? Really, could hell be any worse than this? And what if there were no hell? Some of her friends believed that death was merely a pleasant and peaceful slumber. Wouldn't that be a welcome relief. She couldn't remember the last time she'd slept soundly throughout an entire night.

And yet, something inside her resisted the temptation to escape so easily. Buried deep within her, and nearly forgotten, was the tiniest fragment of faith. Like a lantern almost out of oil, it flickered just barely, so fragile a soft sigh could exterminate it for good. It was an old remnant of another era, another life, a time when unkeepable promises were made in love and desperation. She remembered now how God had quietly sneaked into her life when Jonathan had first become ill. It was, in fact, Jonathan who introduced her, and later Peter, to God. Their child's faith was unfathomable and indomitable, and his understanding of spiritual things far exceeded his tender years—it far exceeded hers, and even now it still mystified her. Despite Jonathan's pain and discomfort during his illness and frightful medical treatments, he had remained firm in his belief that his heavenly Father was taking care of him. Where did he get it? Even as the thin, pale boy stared right into the face of death, he had turned, looked his mother square in the eye, and said, "I'll be waiting for you, Mom. When you and Dad come to heaven, I'll be the first one to meet you there." And so, through many difficult years, Judith had learned to trust God too. It hadn't come easily. At first, she diligently prayed and read her Bible each day only for Jonathan's sake. But slowly and miraculously her formal and impersonal prayers transformed themselves into honest and often gut-wrenching conversations full of reality. And before she knew it, she was talking to God on a regular basis, and he really did became her lifeline. But then Peter died, and as if to retaliate, she ceased speaking to God almost entirely. Occasionally her memory had lapsed, and she caught herself actually praying. But rarely anymore. And now her lifeline, if it existed at all, was more fragile than a single strand of a spider's web. For more than a year and a half, she'd felt dead inside. She never allowed herself to think of Jonathan waiting to meet her in heaven anymore, nor of Peter, wherever he might be. And if there were a heaven, she certainly wouldn't be welcome. Not after today anyway.

She lined up the little blue pills in a straight row, then counted them, sorting them into five neat groups of ten. That should be enough. She knew the best way to do this was to take them one or two at a time, about a minute apart, allowing them to slowly absorb into her system without risking vomiting them all up. For if she was a failure at living, at least she would not fail in this. She went to the sink and filled a large glass with tap water and returned to the table. Then absently, perhaps only as a stall tactic, she began to finger through a week's worth of neglected and unopened mail splayed across the table right where she had dumped it each day. Mostly junk mail along with the regular monthly bills, still unpaid, even though there was plenty of money to cover them. Someone at the law firm would surely take care of those minor details. She rarely received personal mail anymore. But what should she expect if she never wrote? Even after Peter's death, she didn't bother to answer the slew of kind letters and sympathy cards that poured in. But shouldn't people understand these things?

She began to sort the bills into a neat little stack, largest at the bottom, smallest at the top. The junk mail she shoved off to one side. Then she noticed a plain white envelope partially adhered to a flyer selling vinyl siding. She picked up the thin envelope with only mild curiosity. It was so slender and light it almost seemed to be empty. Who would send an empty envelope? Her name and address were handwritten in lacy, scrawled penmanship, like that of a very old woman, but not the hand of anyone she could recall—certainly not her mother, who still wrote with the clear bold stroke of an elementary school teacher. Judith squinted to read the tiny printed words on the old-fashioned circular postmark. *Cedar Crest, Oregon.* She sighed with a faint stirring of longing. Cedar Crest, nestled quietly on the forested west side of the mountains. The bulk of her childhood memories were there— probably the most carefree, blissful portion of her life. Too bad the latter half hadn't gone so smoothly. She pressed her fingers into the postmark ink as if to absorb some of that old happiness, longing for it to send some warmth, some life back into the cold deadness of her withered soul.

Two

JUDITH HAD FIRST SEEN cedar crest in 1962, back when her mother accepted a teaching position in the sleepy Oregon mill town. They moved into a little yellow house on Pine Street in August, and Judith started first grade at Cedar Crest Elementary the following month. They had lived in the same little house right up until her freshman year in high school.

It had been a happy era—typical small-town life in the sixties. Rather uneventful, other than the usual growing pains and being the product of a single-parent home when everyone else seemed to be living like Ozzie and Harriet, at least on the surface. But the sweetest memories of Cedar Crest all seemed to evolve around her best friend and childhood soul mate, Jasmine Morrison. People often teased the two girls, saying they must have been twin sisters who'd been separated at birth. And they often pretended it was true, sometimes almost convincing themselves, except they could never quite explain how Judith had been born in Oregon and Jasmine in far-off Mississippi.

But then, after only a handful of delicious years of irreplaceable friendship, Jasmine's family had abruptly moved back to

Mississippi...*back to Mississippi.* "It's so unfair." Jasmine had said with tears in her eyes. "I don't want to go back there."

But Judith had tried to be strong. "We'll write," she said as the two girls hugged goodbye. "And don't forget our promise, Jasmine, our secret pact." Jasmine nodded. "Blood sisters." she whispered. "Blood sisters forever."

But after several years and several more moves, the friends eventually lost track of one another altogether. It wasn't until Judith lost Jonathan, that she had once again attempted to locate her old friend. But her letters always came back stamped "no such person at this address," and at last Judith gave up all hope of ever reconnecting with Jasmine again. In fact, she hadn't even thought of Cedar Crest or Jasmine in ages.

Now she fingered the still unopened envelope with a slight flicker of interest. No return address, only the postmark to identify its origins. She slowly opened it, almost expecting to find it empty, but a small newspaper clipping slipped out. She began to read, then dropped the paper like a hot coal. It was an obituary, and the name across the top in neat boldfaced type read: *Jasmine Marie Morrison Emery.* Judith's chest grew tight as she closed her eyes and took in a sharp breath. No, it could not be *her* Jasmine! She opened her eyes again, focusing them on the clipping on the table, almost afraid to touch it. She quickly scanned the words, hoping that it was another person, but when she got to the date of birth: May 15, 1956, she knew it was no coincidence for it was Judith's own birth date as well, a date the two girls had shared happily each spring. And when she read the part about survivors, listing Jasmine's parents' names, Judith had no doubt. Jasmine was dead.

Her hands shook as she poured herself another stale cup of coffee. Leaning against the counter, she took a sip of the metallic tasting liquid, and suddenly, in spite of the sweltering heat, she felt as cold as ice. Reading Jasmine's obituary felt strangely as if she'd just read her own. And perhaps it was only a matter of time. She sadly shook her head. Too bad it wasn't her obituary instead of Jasmine's. Surely Jasmine had had all sorts of wonderful things to live for—after all, Jasmine Marie had always been so much fun, so vibrant, so full of life. And now she was dead and gone and buried.

Judith sank into Peter's old leather club chair, the one piece of furniture *he* had insisted upon keeping. She leaned her head back; suddenly longing for Peter like never before—oh, to see his smiling face, feel the warmth of his touch, hear his voice! For the first time since his death, she allowed herself to remember him, to feel the sharp pain of her loss, to experience the crushing emptiness within her. And then she began to long for Jonathan— to wrap her arms around her son, to run her fingers through his wispy hair, touch the softness of his cheek. A sharp painful sensation burned deep within her—a longing that would never be satisfied. And now, on top of all this, she longed for her dear friend Jasmine too. All this longing could surely kill— for how much pain could one heart endure? How much loss could a person bear? Three of her most precious loved ones, all taken away, never to be seen again. Finally she was allowing herself to feel the full measure of pain that was hers. If she were lucky, it would kill her, once and for all, and she would finally escape. But her heart continued to beat steadily, and her mind remained clearer than usual as her thoughts raced forward.

She tried to imagine her childhood friend now dead and lifeless. But she could barely even imagine her fully grown into a woman. To her Jasmine would always be the sparkling-eyed, barefooted girl who ate banana and mayonnaise sandwiches and loved Elvis. Judith sighed and closed her eyes, allowing herself to travel back into time, back to 1963, to Cedar Crest, exactly one year after she and her mother had moved there.

It was the beginning of a new school year, and Judith was starting second grade. More than anything else on earth, Judith wanted a best friend. She had spent the summer with her mother at Nana's house over on the coast, but Nana's house was isolated, and it had been lonely with no nearby children to play with, so when she returned to Cedar Crest all she could think about was finding a friend—a *best* friend. On the first day of school she had worn the plaid woolen skirt that Nana had made along with brand-new saddle shoes that squeaked with each step. She felt very grown up that day as she walked to school all by herself for the first time. (Always before, her mother had insisted she ride in the car and stay in Mother's classroom until the first bell rang.) But this year was to be different.

Judith had known ahead of time that her teacher was to be pretty Miss Harper, who'd just started teaching the middle of last year when crabby old Mrs. Warner retired. Everyone in the school wanted Miss Harper for their teacher. She was young and brunette and had a beautiful smile just like Jackie Kennedy. Judith thought life was just about perfect then. Now if only she could find the perfect best friend. As she walked to school she considered the girls in her class from the previous year, and while they were nice enough, none of them seemed like real best-friend material. Just the same, she hoped to find someone who was very, very special.

In Miss Harper's classroom, Judith found her name printed neatly on a manila card that was securely taped to the left-hand corner of a square, wooden desk. She carefully arranged her school supplies and sat down to wait for the bell to ring. Then Miss Harper greeted the class and began to read the roll. Judith longed to look around to see who might become her new best friend, but instead kept her eyes straight forward on her teacher as she worked through the names.

"Judith McPhearson?" she finally said.

"Here." said Judith with her brightest smile.

"Jasmine Morrison?"

"Here, Miss Harper." said a sweet, lilting voice from behind Judith. But the way the girl pronounced the words sounded more like, *Hee-yah, Miss Harpah.* And some of the children giggled at the sound.

Judith turned in her seat to see who this new Jasmine Morrison might be and was pleased to spot a brown-eyed girl with nut-brown hair cut just like a pixie sitting only two seats away. Judith smiled at the new girl and was met with an impish but not unpleasant grin.

By the end of the day they discovered they had the same initials, identical saddle shoes, and hated beets with a passion. But the best discovery of all was that they shared the exact same birth date! By the end of the week they were indisputably *best friends.* And by the end of fifth grade, they became blood sisters, the same way Huck Finn and Tom Sawyer had done. By then they both wore their hair in the same short style, and because they both had brown eyes, they often pretended to be twins. Sometimes strangers actually believed them because they really did look similar, although Jasmine's face was decidedly rounder and, in Judith's opinion, prettier. And Judith had troublesome freckles.

⊶⊜⊰

JUDITH ROSE FROM PETER'S chair and picked up the obituary clipping again- She read it more slowly this time, searching for some sort of clue, trying desperately to recreate Jasmine's entire adult life out of a two-by-three-inch piece of low-quality newsprint. Apparently Jasmine had been married to a Hal Emery who resided in Cedar Crest, but it didn't appear they had any children. Poor Jasmine. She had always wanted to have at least eight children.

It also said she was survived by her parents who still lived in
Jackson, Mississippi, but gave no mention of Jasmine's little sister,
Constance. Jasmine had died only two weeks earlier, but no cause
of death was given, and the internment was to take place, most
likely had already taken place, in Jackson, Mississippi. Not a lot of
information to patch together the nearly thirty years that Judith had
been out of touch with her friend.

Judith stood up and began to pace back and forth across the
living room of her tiny apartment. She was well aware how in the
past eighteen months she had worn a path on the matted down
carpet, and sometimes old Mr. Ramsey downstairs would thump
impatiently on his ceiling when Judith forgot the time and paced
into the wee hours of the morning.

A multitude of questions rumbled through her mind, but two
seemed to dominate. First, *who* had anonymously sent this clipping
to her? But it was the second question that really bothered her. *If*
Jasmine had been living in the state all this time, why in the world
hadn't she been in touch with Judith? Judith still had a cousin
who ran the only beauty parlor in Cedar Crest. Goodness knows
how many times Judith and Jasmine had gone there for haircuts.
Surely Jasmine would've known that Polly could've easily reached
Judith's mother, who could've put her directly in touch with Judith.
It hurt to think that Jasmine, living only a hundred miles away, had
never even bothered to call. For all Judith had known, Jasmine
might just as well have been living in Tibet. Why hadn't she called
or written? *Why?* And now it was too late. Jasmine, like Peter and
Jonathan, was gone. Gone for good.

Without thinking, Judith went, over, picked up the phone,
and dialed information for her cousin's number, then for "fifty
cents extra" waited as the operator directly connected her. Judith
hadn't spoken to her cousin in years. Polly was really her

mother's cousin and about fifteen years older than Judith, but she was also an excellent source of information as almost every female in Cedar Crest eventually stopped by the little beauty shop for one thing or another. Polly had always loved both giving and receiving the freshest scoop on the latest morsel of gossip. "Polly's Hair Salon. Can I do a "do' for you?"

"Hello?" Judith felt her voice tremble. "Is this Polly?" "Sure is. What can I do for you?"

"Thiis is Judith McPhearson Blackwell—"

"Why, Judith Anne, it's been absolutely ages! How are you, darling? Oh, honey, I heard about your misfortune. Such a shame. And from what I heard your husband was a really great guy too. I'm just so sorry. I meant to drop you a card—"

"That's okay, Polly. Thanks for your concern. It's been kind of rough..." Judith paused, not quite sure what it was she wanted to ask. "Say, Polly, I wondered if you knew anything about my friend Jasmine Morrison—well, not Morrison, that was her maiden name. Let's see, I can't remember her married name off hand." Judith waited a moment, hoping that Polly would fill in that piece of information, but when the line remained silent, Judith stretched the phone cord over to the table and reached for the newspaper clipping then finally read. "Emery. Her married name was Emery—Jasmine Emery, Polly. And I know that she died a couple weeks ago, but that's about all I know..."

"Yes, I know of that person." Polly's voice grew stiff and formal, nothing like the friendly woman who'd originally answered the phone.

"Do you know anything about what happened to her? I mean, how did she die? And who's this husband, this Emery guy? And how long had she been living in Cedar Crest?"

"I can't really say."

"Do you mean that you *can't* say, or that you just *don't know?*"

"That's right."

What was wrong with Polly? Why was she acting so strangely? "I don't understand—"

"I just can't tell you much, is all."

Judith sighed. "Polly, I don't get it. Is something wrong?"

"No. I just don't have anything to say right now."

"Okay." Judith gritted her teeth, determined to remain calm, but the tone of the other woman's voice made her want to jerk the phone right out of the wall and scream.

"Anything else I can do for you, sweetie?" Now she sounded more like the same good-natured Polly, which left Judith feeling even more confused.

"No, nothing, Polly. Thanks for your time."

"I'm really sorry, Judith." This time Polly's voice sounded sincere. Almost as if she were saying something more, as though perhaps she was sorry about Jasmine too. But why couldn't she just say it plain and clear? Why couldn't she simply answer Judith's questions? It was all too baffling.

Judith hung up the phone and slowly shook her head. What was this all about? Why had someone anonymously sent her this obituary in the first place? She paced again, finally stopping at the window. She pressed her forehead against the glass, this time staring blankly at the lethargic city traffic in the street below.

"Dear, dear Jasmine," she whispered. "What has happened to you, my friend?" And then the tears began to trickle down her cheeks. It was the first time she had cried since that awful day when she had learned that Peter was dead. And even then she had only allowed herself to cry for part of the day. After that she had become very busy, bustling about, taking care of details, making lists and funeral arrangements, meeting with people. She had gone above and beyond what is expected of one who had just lost half—no more than half—of their life.

But today she cried with loud wailing sobs, not caring whether or not she disturbed old Mr. Ramsey downstairs. She cried for Jonathan. She cried for Peter. And she cried for Jasmine. And then finally, she cried for herself. For suddenly she realized that in many ways she was only a few steps behind them all. A fine line stretched between life and death, and she had been standing precariously close to its edge. But now this news about Jasmine had temporarily jolted her back into the land of the living again. How very like Jasmine Marie, the one person who had so completely loved living, that she could somehow manage to reach beyond the grave to give Judith one last firm shove towards life.

Finally her tears stopped, and Judith took a long tepid shower. For the first time in ages she actually felt the sensation of cool water running over her still throbbing head and down her thin body. She scrubbed and scrubbed, as if to erase all signs of death and decay. Because for the moment, she wanted to live. She wasn't sure what would follow. But for the moment, her curiosity propelled her.

She stormed her bedroom, jerking an old canvas suitcase from a dark corner of her closet and quickly filling it, paying little attention to what items she tossed inside. She had no idea where she would stay, nor how long she'd be gone. But one thing was crystal clear. Her destination was . Cedar Crest. Somehow she was going to find out what had happened to Jasmine Marie.

Three

FOR THE FIRST TIME since Peter's death, Judith was actually driving beyond the invisible boundary of the city limits. Teaching at an inner-city school had made it unnecessary for her to drive much anyway, and more and more her little dark green MG had remained parked in the garage below the apartments. She had been slightly surprised when the old car had started after more than two weeks of complete neglect. It felt strange and slightly frightening to be traveling so fast down along the crowded freeway. But then, why should she be afraid? Her life, in her opinion, had been nearly over anyway. What difference would it make if she were killed on the freeway? Except that now she had a mission of sorts.

This strange new urgency almost made her feel alive again. Almost. As if some inexplicable inner force now compelled her to find out what happened to Jasmine. For some reason, however childish, she felt she owed it to her dear friend—her blood sister.

Suddenly, and with startling clarity, Jasmine's young tear-streaked face forced itself into Judith's consciousness. There had only been a handful of times when Judith had actually seen Jasmine cry, and although this was a muddled sort of memory and one that

Judith had nearly forgotten, it seemed clearer than ever right now. Still, Judith tried to push it from her mind, for she knew it was tainted with unhappiness, and it wasn't a memory she cared to recall. But it was useless to resist, for the persistent image forced itself upon her in a haunting and powerful sort of way.

✽✽✽

THE TWO GIRLS HAD just celebrated their mutual twelfth birthdays and were making all sorts of exciting plans for when the school year would finally end. It had been a trying year, with other sixth-grade girls vying to squeeze into their tight-knit world and split the two friends apart in the way that only sixth-grade girls can do. But in the end their friendship remained stronger than ever. Until that sunny day in late May.

Unexpectedly, Eli Paxton had wanted to walk home with them. Which was fine with Judith because she and Eli had been good friends ever since she'd first moved to Cedar Crest. In fact if Eli hadn't been a boy, and Jasmine Marie had never moved to town, he might've very well become her best friend. Eli's family lived just down the street from Judith, and sometimes when Jasmine couldn't play, Judith and Eli would shoot baskets in front of his rickety garage.

But as much as Judith liked Eli, Jasmine had always remained distant to the boy. She'd never wanted to get acquainted with him, and sometimes Judith suspected that Jasmine was simply jealous of him. And even on that ill-fated day in May, Jasmine seemed slightly vexed when Judith invited Eli to walk home with them. But before long, Eli's imitation of Fats Domino had Jasmine laughing so loudly that her famous snort followed and threw Eli into complete hysterical fits. And so Judith had been hopeful that the three of them might finally become good friends.

She and Eli waved goodbye to Jasmine, who then turned off toward her house on the hill. But before parting, both girls promised to meet at the city park as soon as they changed clothes and did their chores, Judith boasting that she would be first since she had developed a scientific system for getting her chores done quickly.

As Eli and Judith continued toward Pine Street where they both lived, Eli asked Judith if the Morrisons were very rich. And Judith said that she guessed so since they lived in the biggest house on the hill. Then she and Eli said goodbye, and Judith hurried home to hastily change her clothes, make her bed, and do the breakfast dishes. Then she hopped on her bike and zipped to the park. Just as she expected, she was the first one there. She waited and waited at the park, but soon it was nearly five o'clock with no sign of Jasmine. Judith decided to ride up the hill and see what was keeping her friend. It was never easy to peddle her one-speed Schwinn up the steep hill, and she ended pushing it up the final block.

When she finally reached the white two-story house with its columned porch, she noticed that Jasmine was sitting on the front steps with her head bent down to her knees. Judith became worried. Was Jasmine ill? She dropped her bike on the immaculate lawn and ran up the walk calling to Jasmine. When she looked up her face was blotchy and red, wet with fresh tears. But worse than that was the dark, angry look in Jasmine's eyes—a look Judith had never seen. Then Jasmine actually yelled at Judith, telling her to go away, saying that they couldn't ever be friends again—*not ever!* Just like that! Judith froze on the walk unable to believe her ears. What was going on? Had aliens invaded and taken over her friend's brain? Then Mr. Morrison stepped out. He was a tall man with short-cropped blond hair and steely blue eyes. He looked down upon Judith as if she were a worthless piece of trash that some stray dog had just dragged in and deposited onto the front lawn.

"Don't you ever come around here again, Judith McPh-earson." he said with authority. "We don't allow nigger-lovers in our home. Do you understand me?" At first Judith didn't know what in the world Mr. Morrison was talking about. And then suddenly she remembered: Eli. His smooth skin, the color of polished bronze. Surely that was *not* what this was all about! She opened her mouth to explain, but before she could even finish her sentence, Mr. Morrison made it very clear that it indeed was Eli whom he was referring to. And then Judith climbed clumsily upon her bike, flying down the hill at breakneck speed with tears running sideways across her cheeks. When she reached the flats she continued to pedal toward home with wobbly knees and a broken heart. And when she told her mother, she noticed a flash of anger cross her usually peaceful countenance. Then her mother gathered her into her arms and kindly stroked her hair, saying, "I'm so sorry, Judith."

"Is Mr. Morrison right?" sobbed Judith. She'd been taught to respect adults and to believe that they were usually, if not always, right.

"No, dear," said Mother in a soft voice. "He is very sadly wrong. I'm so sorry."

The next day, Jasmine avoided Judith, her face a closed door and her eyes downcast. But finally, at last recess, Judith spied Jasmine sitting all alone behind the backstop of the baseball diamond. Judith walked over and quietly said hello, but Jasmine didn't look up or even answer. Just the same, Judith stubbornly sat down right next to her estranged friend, and after much persistent probing, she finally learned that Mr. Morrison had actually whipped Jasmine with a leather belt yesterday, and that he would do it again if she was ever caught anywhere near Eli Paxton or any of his kind.

And for the time being, even consorting with Judith was strictly off limits; Jasmine was grounded until further notice and maybe all summer if need be. It seemed that Mr. Morrison had been driving home at the same time the two girls were walking and joking with Eli, and he had seen them. He had met Jasmine at the door in a livid rage, his belt already removed from his pants. Jasmine said she'd seen her daddy's temper numerous times before, as had Judith, but never *anything* like this—at least not toward his own daughter.

Jasmine then tried to patiently explain to Judith how things were different in the South where she'd come from. White girls simply did *not* walk home with Negroes—ever! Fact was, they didn't even go to the same schools as Negroes, at least not until something called "bussing" came along, and she still wasn't completely clear on what that meant, but according to her daddy it was bad—very, very bad. And her father sure didn't like it that Negroes went to the same school here, even if there was only one family of them in the entire town. Then finally, Jasmine gingerly lifted up the back of her neatly pressed white blouse to show the awful red welts that had been put there by Mr. Morrison. It was then that Judith began to sob uncontrollably. She gently hugged her best friend, careful not to touch her tender back, and she promised that if that's how it was to be then she would just tell Eli Paxton that he couldn't walk home with them anymore. And they both decided that until Mr. Morrison cooled down some, they would just have to be best friends in secret.

That same afternoon, Mr. Jones had read to them from *Tom Sawyer,* and when he reached the part about blood brothers, Judith knew just what they would do. She stole a thumbtack from the bulletin board by the door and on the way home, beneath a maple tree and hidden behind the secure protection of a tall laurel hedge, she and Jasmine both jabbed the tack into their right forefingers and mixed their blood to become honest-to-goodness blood sisters. And they vowed to be best friends forever and ever, and to never allow Mr. Morrison or anyone else to come between their friendship ever again. But that childhood promise had long since been broken. First by time and distance, and now it seemed that death had come between them—forever.

Judith wiped a tear from her cheek, then exited the freeway and headed east. The road quickly became interesting with twists and turns, familiar bridges, and towering evergreens casting cool shadows. The small town of Cedar Crest nestled at the western foot of the Cascades, not all that far as the crow flies from where Peter's plane had gone down. It grew cooler, though it was still warm, as she reached the higher elevation. And then the air suddenly grew fresh and clean, pine-scented just the way she remembered it. She knew that anyone in their right mind would stop right then and there and lower the convertible top and enjoy the summer air. But she was not in her right mind, and this was not meant to be a pleasure trip. And although, she could almost admit to being alive—almost—she was not ready to feel good yet.

She pulled into town, hardly allowing herself to look around, although it was surprising how much everything seemed exactly and hauntingly the same. She parked right in front of Polly's Hair Salon and glanced at her watch. It was just half past four; Polly should still be open for business. The little brass bell jingled when she opened the door, just the way it had thirty years ago, and she was met by the strong smell of ammonia mixed with cheap perfume. An older woman with thin gray hair wrapped tightly in pink and green permanent rods sat contentedly behind a dogeared issue of *Glamour* without looking up. Judith glanced around the cluttered shop for her cousin.

"I'm coming," chimed Polly's voice from in back. "I just need to throw these towels into the washer and I'll be right with you."

Polly stepped out with a bright smile, and Judith was surprised at how little her cousin seemed to have changed over the years, although she must be pushing sixty. Her hair was still fiery red (she'd been dying it for as long as Judith could remember), and it was styled within the very limits of its life. With full makeup you almost didn't notice the extra wrinkles around her mouth and eyes. She approached the front of the shop in her soft, bouncy way, but then stopped in midstep when she saw who was standing there.

"Judith Anne?" she asked with wide eyes.

"Hi, Polly." said Judith evenly, hoping to sound nonchalant, as if she always popped into town unexpected like this. "It was such a beautiful day that I decided to take a little drive and get away from the city for a bit."

"How nice." said Polly dryly, glancing over her shoulder at the gray-haired woman who had suddenly laid down the magazine and was now watching them with unveiled curiosity.

"It was difficult to talk on the phone, and I hoped that—"

Polly cut her short, waving her hand. "Oh, I know, I know. Phones are just like that. But as you can see, I'm right in the middle of a perm right now."

"But I just wanted to ask you a few questions about Jasmine—"

"I know, Judith. It was just such a shock to everyone." said Polly with a firm mouth. She now rolled her eyes as if to signal that she didn't wish her overly interested patron to overhear this particular conversation. Although why it should matter bewildered Judith completely.

She studied Polly for a moment. "Well, I thought if you had time I could—"

"You know, Judith, if you have questions, you should probably just address them to Hal Emery," said Polly coolly. "He runs the hardware store right across the street. You see, I didn't really know Jasmine all that well."

Judith sighed. "Okay. Thanks, Polly. I guess I'll be seeing you then."

"Sure," said Polly without meeting her gaze. She turned back to check on her perm lady, calling over her shoulder, "See you around then."

Judith stepped out the door and sighed. What in the world had come over Polly and why was she acting so cold? She looked up to see the store across the street. It used to belong to Rich Carter, but now the sign said it was Emery's Hardware. But other than the sign, it looked just about the same as thirty years ago. Well, what did she have to lose? In fact, she'd like to meet Jasmine's husband. She had always wondered what sort of man Jasmine Marie would marry. Sometimes she imagined Jasmine married to someone exactly like Peter. Then other times she imagined her married to some rich, Southern gentlemen who looked just like Rhett Butler, a witty man with a quick smile and a great sense of humor.

Judith walked across the quiet street and stepped into the cool dark store. It smelled of old wood and metal, and the dusty crowded shelves appeared to contain some of the very same items that'd been there back in 1971 when she'd picked up masking tape to seal their moving boxes before she and her mother finally left Cedar Crest. She walked down several aisles wondering if Jasmine's husband, or rather her widower, would even be here in the store. And if he was here, what would she say to him?

"Can I help you?" asked a man from behind a long, glass counter. Judith looked up to see a slightly built, partially bald man with faded blue eyes. She stepped closer, certain that this was not, never could have been, Jasmine's husband.

"I'm looking for a Hal Emery," she said.

The man leaned against the counter, his pale eyes fixed upon her with keen interest, almost as if he recognized her from someplace, although she didn't recall him from her earlier days. By her estimation he was older than her by at least fifteen years, maybe more. Finally he spoke. "And why, may I ask, are you looking for him?"

"Apparently he was married to a good friend of mine. And as I'm in town for the day, I wanted to meet him. You see, I only just learned of Jasmine's death, and I am still so stunned."

He nodded slowly with realization, then sighed deeply. "I see. Y'all say Jasmine was a good friend of yours. But how long has it been since you last seen her?"

She knew by his accent he was Southern, and for some reason this caught her off guard. "Uh, well, it's been years and years." she stammered. "Actually not since we were teens. We both lived here back in the sixties, and then she moved away and we lost touch—completely."

The man smiled now, not a big smile, but just slightly as if her answer satisfied him. Then he extended his hand. "I am Hal Emery."

Judith felt her cheeks grow warm with embarrassment as she shook his hand. It was a slow, weak handshake, and his palm felt clammy against hers. She resisted the urge to wipe her hand on the back of her jeans when he finally released it. "Oh, I'm so sorry, Mr. Emery. I didn't realize that you were—I mean, I hope you didn't think—I just was so sorry to hear about Jasmine. May I offer my deepest sympathy to you."

"Thank you. And may I ask your name?"

"Of course. I'm Judith Blackwell. My maiden name was McPhearson—back when Jasmine and I were good friends."

"You know, I think I remember Jasmine mentioning you,"

said Hal, then he leaned over the counter and peered at Judith with raised brows. "It's very, very odd..." He didn't finish the sentence.

"Odd?" asked Judith, confused.

"How much you actually look like her."

"Really?" said Judith, strangely pleased at this. "When we were girls, people always thought we looked like sisters, and we liked to pretend we were twins."

"I can understand that," said Hal. "It's a striking resemblance."

"Not knowing her as an adult." began Judith, "it's hard to imagine what she may have looked like. You don't happen to have a photo around, do you?"

He shook his head. "I have some at home. Are you going to be in town tomorrow?"

"Perhaps," said Judith with uncertainty. "Actually, I came sort of spur of the moment. I'm not really sure how long I'm staying. But now that I'm here, I do want to look around some. Cedar Crest, and of course Jasmine, were a very important part of my childhood. I don't think I could leave without seeing the old sights."

"Well, if you stop by tomorrow, I'll show you some photos of Jasmine," promised Hal.

"Thank you. I'd really like to see them. I only wish I had known she was back in the state. I would have loved to have seen her before—"

Hal looked down at his hands in silence.

"I'm sorry." said Judith. "I know it must be very difficult for you right now. In fact, I know just how you feel. I lost my husband not too long ago..."

Hal looked down at the wedding ring she still wore on her left hand and then up to her face. "Yes, it's not easy, is it?"

"I'd like to say it gets better with time, but I'm not a very good example of it. I'm still dealing with the whole thing myself."

"I expect you never completely get over these things," said Hal, again without looking up.

"Maybe not completely, although one would hope that it might get better with time." Judith glanced uncomfortably at her watch. "I expect you're ready to close up shop now. Thanks for taking the time to talk to me. I'll look forward to seeing those photos."

He nodded. "You bet. Thanks for stopping in, Judith. I "spect I'll see you tomorrow then."

She stepped back out into the sunshine and instantlywished she had asked Hal more questions, like how long had they been married, or how had Jasmine died, or why was she buried in Mississippi. But the strange little man had just taken her so completely by surprise. How could someone like *that* have possibly won the hand of someone like Jasmine Marie Morrison? Of course, he seemed a nice enough man, and she shouldn't judge him too harshly while he was still grieving. She of all people should understand how grief might alter a person. People who had never known Judith before losing Peter would probably think she was a mousy, boring person too. But at least she hadn't *always* been like this. Even so, it seemed as if the old Judith had been permanently lost, never to be found again. As if a part of her had been buried with Jonathan, and the rest with Peter.

She sighed and walked across the street to where her MG was still parked, pausing to study Polly's little shop again. Still the turquoise blue canvas awnings over the windows, faded and shabby with age and sun. She glanced up to the second floor, which used to house the little apartment that Polly had inhabited when Judith was a girl. She wondered if Polly still lived up there. For someone hit with a lot of hard luck, including at least two bad marriages and numerous unhappy romances, Polly somehow managed to emerge a survivor, and her normally sunny perspective usually spread happiness onto the lives of others. But not for Judith—at least not today. It still bothered her that Polly had acted so unexplainably cool, almost to the point of rudeness, but there seemed nothing to be done about it. And even though the shop was still plainly open, Judith felt fairly certain she wouldn't be welcome inside. So she climbed into her car and wondered what to do next. Where to go? She really hadn't planned this mission very well.

Four

POLLY WAVED FROM THE open doorway of her shop. "Hey, don't you go off and leave already, Judith Anne! I haven't even had a chance to talk with you yet."

"Are you sure you want to?" asked Judith, as she climbed back out of her car and cautiously followed Polly into her now-empty shop.

"Of course I do. Come on in here right now." Polly pointed to a lime green vinyl-covered haircutting chair. "Here you go. Have a seat, honey." She was sounding more like her old self, but Judith still wasn't sure.

Just the same, she obediently sat in the chair, keeping a perplexed eye on her cousin. "What exactly is going on here, Polly?"

Her back to Judith, Polly began to fiddle with combs and scissors on the counter. Then she abruptly turned and smiled brightly. "Say, honey, I'm still open for business. How about a cut and style?"

Judith frowned. "I didn't drive all the way down here just to get my hair done."

Polly spun the chair around so that Judith could see herself fully in the well-lit mirror. "Well, just look at yourself, sweetie. It's not like you couldn't use a little sprucing up."

Judith stared at her reflection as if seeing herself for the first time in a very long time. Her straight dark hair fell limply over her shoulders and down her back. It was held tightly back from her forehead with a tortoiseshell hair band, the same she wore every day. Not a very flattering style for her thin angular face. Her dark brown eyes looked like burned out holes, contrasted by her overly pale complexion which was, as usual, void of makeup. Even her freckles had long since faded away. Her hand reached up and touched her cheek as if to see if the haggard-looking holocaust woman in the mirror was truly her. Unfortunately, it was.

Judith sighed. "I guess I've let my appearance go a little..."

"I'll say." said Polly without mercy. "But, honey, don't you worry. You've still got a lot going for you." She fingered Judith's hair. "Still good texture and thicker than it looks, and not a trace of gray, you lucky girl. And just look at your skin! It's still flawless, and I don't think you've even got a single wrinkle. There's nothing here a little TLC and a few good meals won't fix right up."

"Honestly, I really didn't come here just to get a makeover."

"I know, honey," said Polly, glancing nervously over her shoulder and out the plate glass window to the street beyond. "But, you see, I'm open "til six, and I don't have any appointments right now. And besides, I always talk better when I'm working with my hands."

"All right," agreed Judith, suddenly realizing that perhaps this was the only way to extract any information from her. "Then go for it, Polly. Do whatever you like. But just keep talking, okay?"

Polly had already tied a pink vinyl haircutting shawl over Judith's shoulders and was now wetting her hair. "Okay, honey, you ask the questions, and I'll try my best to answer." She reached for her scissors. "Just one thing though."

"Yes?" Judith looked at her cousin's suddenly serious reflection as she began to comb through the dampened hair.

"If that door opens, we immediately change the subject, you hear? That is, unless you want your hair cut in a Mohawk—not that you'd notice running around looking the way you do."

"Whatever you say," agreed Judith. When Polly turned her chair away from the mirror, Judith suspected it was to keep an eye on the door.

"I hate to take too much off," said Polly as she continued to comb. "Your hair really would be pretty if you'd only give it a little attention with a styling brush or curling iron."

Judith pressed her lips together, concentrating on where to start with her questions about Jasmine. "How long had Jasmine been living here in Cedar Crest?"

"Well, I'm not real sure exactly when it was that she moved back here," said Polly as the scissors began to snip steadily. "When I first saw her again, she was already married to Hal. No one had ever heard about them getting married that I know of. I heard they might've got hitched in Reno or someplace down there. And then after that I think he kept her holed up out on that run-down old farm of his. But the first time I saw her was almost a year ago."

"So they haven't been married all that long?"

"No, probably less than a year, I think. Hal had been married once before. A real nice lady named Beth, but she took the kids and left him fifteen or more years back. I used to do her hair, and she never came right out and said it, but I always got the impression he was a real jerk. They moved here from somewhere down South—Mississippi, I believe Beth said. I think she was right smart to get away from him. And I'll tell you, I was real sad when I heard that Jasmine and he had got together. I bet you anything Mr. Morrison had a finger in it. But, I'd better watch my tongue, Judith."

"Why?"

"Because there's things happen in this town, that's why. People got to look out, watch their backsides, if you know what I mean. And just for the record, I don't want you repeating any of this to anyone. I'm only telling you because you're kin. And the fact is, you can leave, but I gotta live here."

"I appreciate that you're even talking to me. Did you see much of Jasmine, Polly? Did she ever come in here?"

She shook her head. "Not really. Well, she *almost* came in—two separate times, as I recall."

"Almost?"

"I know, it sounds weird. But one time she walked right in that door. The shop was pretty busy, and she looked right at me just as I was touching up Mrs. Babcock's roots. Well, I nodded at her, and said "hey' but the look in her eyes." She stopped snipping. "Why, Judith, she looked just like a frightened doe. That's just what I thought when I saw her standing there—just like a frightened doe caught in the headlights of some big old Mack truck. And then she just turned and left. The next time she came by was several months later. But that time she just paused and looked through my window. It wasn't even busy that day. And I waved at her to come on in, but she just stood there and stared for a while, then she glanced over across the street, over toward the hardware store, I'm guessing. Then she just kept walking with her head down."

"Poor Jasmine," whispered Judith. "That doesn't sound a bit like the girl I remember."

"I know just what you mean. She didn't seem nothing like that little bright-eyed imp that used to come bopping in here with you to get her hair cut. You two were so cute back then. You know, the first time I saw her after she came back to Cedar Crest, I actually wondered if she might be on drugs or something. She just seemed like such a totally different—"

The little bell jingled and without missing a beat Polly continued, "Yeah, Hank down at the gas station says that we're supposed to have a real hot, dry summer. Says this could be a bad year for forest fires again."

"Hey, Polly." called a young woman from the counter. "I see you're busy right now, but do you think you can squeeze me in for a weave and a hot-oil in the morning? I've gotta be in a wedding this weekend."

"Sure, Karen, I just happen to have an opening at eleven."

"Great, see you then." The bell jingled again and the door closed.

"Seems so strange," murmured Judith.

"What's that, honey?"

"I used to know almost everyone in town. And other than you, I haven't seen a single familiar face today."

"Lots of the old-timers have left," said Polly sadly. "Don't blame them none either."

"If you feel that way, why don't you just leave too?"

"Stan, you never met him, but he was my third husband in a long line of losers— you know, I never was a real good judge of character when it came to men. Anyway, Stan wouldn't hear of us leaving this place. I begged him for years. Then the dirty dog ups and leaves *me* for a girl barely out of high school. It was all I could do to just hang on here and try to make ends meet after he left me with a bunch of bills to pay. And beauty shops aren't selling for a whole lot in Cedar Crest these days. I still think about leaving sometimes, but I'm no spring chicken, Judith. And I do like my little shop." She spun the chair around so Judith could see her reflection.

"Oh, Polly, that's so much better." Judith touched the layers that now gently framed her face and curled onto her shoulders. "Thanks, you're a miracle worker."

"Now, hold still there for just a minute while I put a little color on that face, and maybe people might not mistake you for a corpse or a ghost or something."

Judith sat quietly while Polly did her thing. It looked like she still sold the Suzy Lee makeup line she'd started with back in the sixties. At last, Polly spun her chair back around again to see. "I guess that's an improvement too," said Judith with reservations. "Although it's a little shocking after months of being a plain Jane."

"You don't mean to tell me you went to work and everything looking like that?"

Judith nodded. "It's been a tough year and a half."

"Oh, sweetie, I am sorry." Polly pursed her lips thoughtfully. "I'd say I know just how you feel, but the truth is I was never anything but glad after my men left me."

Judith forced a smile, but it felt stiff and awkward, as if her smiling muscles were out of shape. Even her fifth-grade students this past year, although they seemed to like her, had often commented on how rarely Ms. Blackwell smiled.

"And now," announced Polly as she flipped over the sign on the door. "It's closing time. Hallelujah!"

"How much do I owe you?" asked Judith, reaching for her purse.

"No charge," said Polly. "Just consider it a charitable act of good will!"

"I guess it would've been bad for business to have me leave here looking the way I did." Judith smiled again. A small smile perhaps, but at least it was sincere. "Thanks, Polly."

"My pleasure, honey, and I'm real sorry about having to give you the cold shoulder like that earlier."

"Can I take you to dinner?" asked Judith. "As a thank you for your charitable efforts?"

"Okay, but if you want to keep talking openly like this, we'll have to get out of this town to do it. There's a pretty good restaurant over in Jasper—about fifteen minutes from here."

"That's fine with me, but I must confess I don't really understand all this cloak-and-dagger stuff. Is it really necessary?"

Polly looked at her with startling intensity. "For me it is. Like I said, Judith, I *live* here. I can't afford to land on nobody's hate list."

Five

JASPER, THOUGH SLIGHTLY SMALLER than Cedar Crest,
seemed more lively and prosperous than its sister town to the south.
Numerous cars were parked along its tree-lined streets, and people
filled the sidewalks, strolling along in the warm evening air.

"This place has changed." noted Judith as she parked her MG
next to an old-fashioned lamppost with a basket of red geraniums
suspended from it.

"Yes, they seem to be thriving over here. The *Cascadia* ran
a feature about how Jasper is growing by leaps and bounds,
and they described it as being so much more cosmopolitan than
the rednecked town of Cedar Crest." Polly shut the door to the
small car with a hefty bang. "That's exactly what they actually
called us too—*rednecked.* Well, folks in town didn't take too kindly
to that kind of talk, and a number of them wrote in and canceled
their subscriptions to the paper." She pointed across the street to
a restaurant where several umbrella-covered tables crowded the
sidewalk. "That's a pretty decent place to eat if you like Italian
food."

Judith didn't dare admit that she thought the reporter might be right on the money in his comparison of the two towns. Already she could see a vast difference. "Shall we sit outside?" she asked as she lingered by an empty cloth-covered table.

"I suppose we could.. ." Polly frowned. "That is if you're not worried about having flies dive-bombing your food while you eat."

Judith shrugged. "You decide, Polly."

They ate inside.

"Don't you like your lasagna?" asked Polly as she took another bite.

"It's great." admitted Judith. "But to be honest, I haven't been eating too well the past couple weeks—since school got out. I don't have much of an appetite."

"Sounds like you've been pretty depressed."

Judith nodded as she absently pushed a piece of pasta across the plate. "Well, I think things were kind of getting to me lately. I'm not exactly sure why."

"You've been through a lot. First losing your son to cancer, then your husband in that plane wreck." Polly shook her head. "Seems like the women in our family have bad luck with men. Say, how's your mom doing? I know she remarried a few years ago. How's that going for her?"

"They seem to be happy. She and George just left for a South Pacific cruise."

"Mmm, that sounds dreamy."

They chatted on about mutual relatives, some dead and others Judith barely remembered. They covered the ups and downs of most of Polly's life during the past twenty years, including a hysterectomy and a peptic ulcer which didn't appear to affect her appetite. All the while Judith struggled to think of a way to gently redirect the conversation back to Jasmine. Finally she just jumped in.

"Polly, I can't stop wondering why Jasmine never called me during the past year." Judith ran her hand over the cool wet surface of her iced tea glass. "We were so close at one time, I wish she would've called."

Polly broke off another chunk of bread, liberally slathering it with butter. "I don't really know, honey, but my guess is that her husband kept her pretty much under his thumb, if you know what I mean."

"It's hard to imagine Jasmine being kept under *anyone's* thumb—"

"Well, how "bout her father?" Polly raised one auburn-tinted eyebrow in suspicion.

Judith nodded. "Yes, you're right about that. Her father *was* a bit of a tyrant. But Jasmine was a grown woman— had been for over twenty years. It seems she would've escaped his influence long ago."

"I don't know. I've seen women who almost seem imprinted—you know, they just go from one bad man to the next." Polly laughed. "Take me, for instance. Not that I ever let my men bully me around—well, at least not physically. Why, if they ever so much as took a hand to me, I'd give it right back to them, and then some!"

Judith smiled wryly. "I'll bet you did."

"But I've seen women so browbeaten and intimidated; they remind me of little scared mice, all hunched down and fearful of every little thing. And to be honest, when I first saw Jasmine that day, why, that's exactly what she looked like to me. Either that or, like I said earlier, the girl was on drugs of some kind."

Judith shook her head. "Poor thing. It's just so sad and confusing. Jasmine had so much potential. Her life should have gone differently."

"When you get right down to it, none of us has much control over our lives. Just look at you, Judith Anne. You're a prime example of how bad things *do* happen to good people. Far's I can tell, there's just no rhyme or reason for any of it."

"Maybe not. But I'd still like to make some sense of Jasmine's life if I can. For some reason it's becoming important to me. It's as though I *need* to know what happened to her. For instance, I still don't even know what caused her death." She looked at Polly pleadingly. "Do you know?"

Polly diverted her eyes down to her nearly empty plate, neatly rearranging her flatware with lips pressed firmly together as if determined not to say too much.

"Please, tell me what happened, Polly."

"Well, I guess you'll find out sooner or later; you might as well hear it from your own relative." She looked up at Judith. "It was a gunshot wound to the head."

Judith's glass slipped from her grip, hitting the table with a loud whack. She stared at Polly in horror. "Jasmine was *shot?*"

Polly glanced around nervously as if to see if anyone was listening, then she leaned forward and lowered her voice. *"Self-inflicted."*

For the second time that day, Judith was surprised to feel tears fill her eyes. Her words escaped in a husky whisper. "Jasmine killed herself?"

Polly nodded soberly. "That's what I heard in my shop. Of course, Hal and Jasmine's folks tried to keep everything all hush-hush. I'm sure it was a real source of humiliation to them. They being the ones who are always so caught up in appearances and all."

Judith used the heavy linen napkin to absorb the tear that had escaped, but a painful lump began to grow in her throat. She wasn't sure she could even speak, not that words could express her conflicting thoughts. The image of Jasmine Marie putting a firearm to her head, taking her own life; it was unimaginable.

"I know, honey, it was a real shock to me too. I even felt guilty for not reaching out to the poor thing. I mean, especially since you two girls were so thick and all, it was almost as if she were kin. I'd had no idea that she was so desperate—I mean, to do something like that."

Judith finally found her voice. "I just can't believe she'd do that. Not the Jasmine I knew."

"Like I said, people change. You admitted yourself that you hadn't actually seen her since you girls were teens." Then Polly's eyes lit, as if suddenly remembering something. "And now that I think about it, I had seen her once before—one summer a few years after you and your mother had already moved back over to the coast. Jasmine came out to stay with her great-aunt—"

"Aunt Lenore?"

"Yes. Jasmine had just graduated from high school. She came to stay with Lenore and was going to look for a job in town. She even asked me for work, but I didn't have a thing for her. Although I did give her a haircut. She was still wearing it fairly short back then, even though most of the girls were wearing theirs long and straight—making it awfully hard on us folks in the haircutting business. But Jasmine had me layer it into a cute little shag style— you know, the kind that was popular in the seventies. I even remember her laughing and saying how her father wouldn't like it at all, and that seemed to make her real happy. Anyway, we chatted for awhile, and I remember thinking how much she'd changed from the young Jasmine I remembered."

Judith leaned forward with interest. "How did she change?"

"Well, for one thing, she was *very* Southern. I mean, the way she talked and all sounded like straight out of *Gone with the Wind*. But what really got me was how she seemed sort of hard and toughened—like *ya'll better not mess with me*. She told me how her dad had put her and her little sister into this private, all-white school; if I remember right, it was some sort of military academy "cause she told me how the kids all marched around and shot guns at targets and everything. Sounded pretty weird to me."

"That does sound strange. Especially for someone like Jasmine. When we were little, she was always finding sick or injured animals and then nursing them back to health. And if they didn't make it, she'd give them these beautiful funerals, complete with flowers and a proper burial under the back hedge. She even made little crosses out of Popsicle sticks and rubber bands. She was always a very nonviolent person."

"Like I said, people change."

"Or can be forced to change."

"Whatever." Polly sipped her coffee, then wiped her mouth with her napkin. "I've probably already said way too much."

"That's the other thing I don't get. Why all this secrecy?"

Polly's eyes narrowed. "There's some things just better left unsaid in Cedar Crest. And for those of us who have to make our living there, you can't be too careful."

Judith frowned. "You make it sound as if the town is ruled by the Mafia."

Polly's eyes scanned the room again. "Something like that."

"What do you mean?"

Polly lowered her voice again. "Well, just look around this restaurant, for instance."

Judith looked around the nearly full restaurant. Waiters bustling about the tables. People happily chatting and laughing as they ate and drank. "So? It looks pretty normal to me."

Polly nodded. "Well, do you see that Asian family in the corner? And that black couple over there by the window?"

Judith shrugged. "So?"

"Well, next time you're in Cedar Crest, you just look around and see if you see any people like that there."

"What about the Paxtons?"

"Long gone. It's a sad story, and don't ask."

"Are you saying—"

"That's *all* I'm saying, Judith." Polly waved her hand for their bill. "I can't afford to say anything else. And if you care about me, you won't let on that I even insinuated as much as I did."

"But I don't get it—if there's some connection—"

"Look, Judith," Polly took on a stern expression that instantly added years to her face. "If you want to think there's some connection to something, then that's your business. I've said about all I dare to say on the subject—period."

"But I just want to get to the bottom of it."

"Well, that's your decision. Just don't expect to drag me along for the ride."

Judith placed her cash card on top of the bill. "I don't expect you to help me, Polly. I really do appreciate everything that you've told me, and I promise to respect your desire for anonymity. But... do you know where I might possibly find some more answers?"

Polly laughed loudly. "Answers? In Cedar Crest? You must be joking." She paused for a moment as she picked up her purse. "Although there is this one guy.. .well, he doesn't actually *have* the answers, but he does seem to have plenty of questions."

"And who's that?"

"Adam Ford." She sighed dreamily. "And what a knockout— looks just like an older version of James Dean. Anyway, he's a detective; just joined the Cedar Crest police force last week. He came by my shop asking me questions a few days ago. "Course, other than giving him a *real* warm welcome, if ya know what I mean, I knew enough to keep my big mouth shut I seriously doubt he'll have many answers from anyone else by now, but I doubt it'll be for lack of trying."

Judith shook her head. "I feel so confused about all this. Maybe I should just go home and forget about Jasmine."

"I think that would be a good idea."

The waiter returned with the bill and Judith signed the receipt and left a generous tip. Then she closed her billfold and looked across the table to see Polly now frowning at her with what appeared to be some serious concern.

"I just feel so confused, Polly."

"Sticking around Cedar Crest won't change that."

Judith nodded. Suddenly everything seemed crazy and upside down, almost as if everything were spinning. What in the world was she doing down here anyway? An emotional reaction to Jasmine's obituary had caused her to jump into her car and drive down here like a mad woman. And for what exactly? She painfully remembered their old blood sister vow again—*nothing will ever come between us.* But something had come between them—actually it was many things, uncontrollable things like time and space, life and death.

"Maybe you just need to let her go." said Polly gently. She reached over and patted her hand. "Nothing you do will ever bring her back."

"I know." Judith nodded sadly.

"You know what they say, honey: Some stones are better left unturned."

"You may be right, but it's hard to just let go of her. I keep feeling like I need to know more, like I need to understand what happened. Who knows, maybe it's for her sake."

"Well, whatever you do, and especially if you decide to continue asking these questions, just take my advice, dear: be very careful."

ON THE WAY BACK to Cedar Crest, Polly skillfully kept the conversation well away from anything to do with Jasmine. Probably her years of doing hair had enhanced her natural gift of gab. But oddly enough, Judith found the incessant chatter somewhat soothing—sort of like white noise; it distracted her from her own troubling thoughts. It was just getting dusky when she pulled up in front of Polly's little beauty shop. Thanking her for her help, Judith promised once again not to reveal anything that Polly had said to anyone.

She drove down the street a few blocks to where an old fifties-style motor inn was still situated, looking very much like it had when she was a kid, only much shabbier. The same large sign boasted in green neon tubes that there was indeed a vacancy. Actually, there appeared to be many vacancies. And for good reason, she thought, when she surveyed the tiny, dingy room with its paper-thin walls and a mattress that sagged in the middle. Her nostrils flared at the stale smell of what must be years worth of accumulated cigarette smoke as she dropped her suitcase on the floor. Who in their right mind would choose to stay in a fleabag like this? But then again, who would have thought she was in her right mind when, only this morning, she'd come perilously close to doing what it now appeared her friend Jasmine had done? She swallowed hard. She had left her little blue pills back in her apartment. And, for the moment, thoughts of suicide seemed surprisingly remote and even somewhat unrealistic. She kicked off her sandals, and without removing her clothing or peeling back the limp, threadbare chenille bedspread, she fell across the lumpy mattress and immediately tumbled into an exhausted and long-overdue sleep.

Six

A STRIP OF WARM light cut across the bed, and Judith opened her eyes to see a slit of bright white dissecting the otherwise darkness of the drapes. Where was she? She sat up and listened to the silence all around her. No hiss of semi air brakes, no honking horns, no sirens blaring. And then she remembered, Cedar Crest. Glancing at her watch, she blinked in surprise. Nearly nine—the longest uninterrupted sleep she'd had in ages. But perhaps even more remarkable was how her stomach suddenly gnawed with actual hunger. She hadn't felt hungry for days, weeks even.

Feeling a bit like Alice on the other side of the looking glass, she pulled the greasy cord of the heavy rubber-backed drapes to allow the midmorning light to flood in, painfully exposing the interior of the dreary motel room: Fake-wood paneling in a dark shade, plastic-laminate Mediterranean style furnishings, and matted avocado shag carpet that felt coated with who knew what beneath her bare feet. She stood for a moment gazing blankly at the thousands of dust particles now illuminated in the bright sunlight like miniature fireflies floating weightlessly on the air. With an awkward shove she forced open the aluminum window to allow some much-needed air into the stale and weary little room. She wondered vaguely if breathing this old, smoke-tainted air might be just as hazardous as actual secondhand smoke. It was equally disgusting.

She went into the tiny bathroom, a departure by at least two decades from the rest of the room with its pink plumbing fixtures and aqua-blue tile accents. Its odor suggested a mixture of mildew, old decaying wood, and still more stale smoke. She stood on the cold linoleum floor staring at her reflection lit by the harsh and unforgiving glare of a vibrating fluorescent light above a foggy mirror. Even with the obscuring factor of the blurry glass she looked truly frightening—even to herself. Traces of the dark eye makeup that Polly had applied yesterday were now smeared like soot under her eyes and onto her cheeks, and beneath the dark smears her skin looked pasty white as if she'd been ill for some time. It was ironic, because for most of her adult life she'd been admired for her appearance. Now it seemed that must've been somebody else all along. For the woman in the mirror looked haggard and old and, yes, *ugly!* But, in a morbid sort of way, it was almost fascinating—probably akin to the way people couldn't help but stare at a dead animal alongside the road or someone disfigured by a bad accident.

Somehow in that very instant, she knew intuitively that she'd reached a very real crossroads in her life. To continue her previous path could only guarantee things to get worse—most likely to the point of no return. Yet to make an intentional U-turn right now, and to walk towards life seemed almost frightening. Was she really up to it? She thought of Peter and Jonathan—no doubt about what they would say. She knew they would both shake a firm fist at her and say: buck up, persevere, choose life. Neither of them had ever been quitters.

And so, in a moment of crystal clarity, standing before the

clouded bathroom mirror, she decided she *must* at least attempt
that U-turn—somehow she must choose life. And though she
wasn't quite sure that it was entirely possible or even plausible,
she determined that she would remember this point in time, to
somehow etch this decision into her being. She stared hard at her
face again, imprinting the image indelibly into her brain—she
wanted to remember this look of utter wretchedness and devastation.
Her grandmother used to repeat a saying of how "the eyes were
a window to the soul." Judging by her eyes, her soul lurked like a
foreign thing, dark and forlorn and empty. She leaned forward, staring
hard into her sad eyes, searching for just the merest trace of light or
hope. And perhaps it was actually there, flickering ever so faintly,
but she couldn't quite see it yet.

She ran warm water into the sink and washed her face and
when she looked in the mirror again she noticed the usual dark
circles beneath her eyes now appeared just slightly diminished.
Or was it her imagination? Perhaps a few more solid nights' sleep
in a quiet place like Cedar Crest would erase some of the years
that had sneaked in and carved themselves into her countenance.
She reached up to touch her hair; yesterday's haircut was a definite
improvement. And as Polly had said, it really was her best asset,
thick and dark brown. How amazing that it hadn't turned gray.
Could it be she wasn't as old as she felt after all?

Following a long, hot shower, she dumped the hastily packed
contents of her suitcase onto the rumpled bed, and perused through
the pile of mismatched clothing until she found a sleeveless white
top and pair of khaki walking shorts, leftovers from the magical
summer just two years ago when Peter had signed on with the law
firm. It seemed another lifetime now, but at least they'd had
that one summer together. That was something. She pulled on the
two garments, amazed that they were fairly wrinkle free. At least

compared with the rest of the things she'd so haphazardly tossed in yesterday. Perhaps she might even locate an iron in this hapless motel, that is, if she stuck around town another day. Otherwise she might be mistaken for a transient, homeless person.

She looked in the mirror once more. This was the most interest she'd taken in her appearance since school had let out, and that wasn't saying much. She looked slightly better than the image she'd seen first thing this morning, but her face still looked ghostly and somewhat stricken. Not wanting to frighten the people of Cedar Crest—especially when she needed their help and cooperation, she decided to take Polly's advice and apply a little makeup to make her look a bit more human and approachable. She dug through her purse until she found an old tube of plum lipstick and a powder compact. Remembering an old trick her mother had taught her, she artfully combined a spot of the lipstick with a dab of moisturizer to create a makeshift blush which she cautiously applied to her cheeks. Then a little powder to add color to her complexion, and just a touch of lipstick to her mouth. She looked critically at her reflection. A bit better than the bride of Frankenstein. It would have to do for now.

The business district was only a few blocks from the motel, and she decided to walk that short distance, allowing herself more time to acclimate to the town and observe what had or, it seemed more likely, had not changed over the years. As she walked down Main Street, it felt as though she'd stepped into the Twilight Zone. Many shops and buildings were almost exactly as she remembered them. Older and shabbier perhaps, but still the same. But instead of being comforted to find Cedar Crest unchanged, it troubled her. The town seemed stagnant, as if it had been trapped in a time warp, turning into a sludgy backwater where no one cared anymore. She knew she was making snap judgments based on first impressions, but something indescribable seemed wrong here. She spotted her destination, the small café still situated next to the shoe-and-boot repair shop. Other than what certainly must be new gingham curtains in the window, it also looked exactly the same. And despite the past two decades of antilogging rhetoric bubbling in and about the Pacific Northwest, this little eatery had retained its original lumberjack name—the Timber Topper. But she knew from childhood that loggers and millworkers were a stubborn breed, proud of their rugged heritage and antagonistic toward environmentalists who seemed bent upon closing down their woods. As she walked in the door, she wondered wryly if the Timber Topper might even list spotted owls as one of its regular blue plate specials.

No surprises here, she observed quickly as she walked in the door. The same glass-eyed, taxidermy heads of antlered deer, elk, and antelope still proudly hung high on the wood-paneled wall. She suddenly recalled how she and Jasmine used to joke that the missing bodies of those animals were probably ground into the hamburgers they so often consumed at the little café (which might not have been too far from the truth). Then there was the same sparkly plastic-laminate that topped the soda counter, only now yellow and faded with age, and the same row of rotating chrome stools with peeling red vinyl seats. She and Jasmine used to sit up there to order cherry cokes, pretending to be mature. And there against the other wall, oilcloth covered tables and red padded booths with deep, comfortable seats where men, too old to work in the woods or lumber mill, had always been known to drink cup after cup of coffee and shoot the breeze for hours at a time. She'd often wondered how they had so much to talk about.

But, unlike her childhood when she'd always felt at home here, she now felt totally alien and completely out of place. Several pairs of eyes looked up to inspect her after the little bell on the door finally stopped jingling. And it seemed their gazes lingered just a bit too long, perhaps just a second or two beyond what most might consider to be a polite glance. She stood for a moment, considering sitting on a stool, but then realized she'd feel even more conspicuous all alone at the otherwise vacant counter. So she slipped into an empty booth near the front door and took out the plastic-coated menu from its nesting place next to the napkin dispenser. But as she skimmed over the breakfast selections of eggs and bacon and pancakes, she realized that these foods would most likely be swimming in grease. Even as a girl, she'd often get a stomachache after dining on the greasy burgers and fries they served here. Her mother would warn her, but being strong willed as a child, she'd always refused to admit it was the food.

"What can I get for you?" asked a plump, middle-aged woman with dark roots showing beneath her overly permed and brassy hair.

"I'd like some coffee, black—and, uh, do you have anything light?"

"Light?" The woman frowned at her curiously, then rolling her eyes, said, "Well, there's always the Tiny Topper breakfast with one egg, a strip of bacon, and toast. *That's* pretty light."

Just then, Judith spotted oatmeal listed with a few other side dishes on the bottom of the menu. "That's okay, I think I'll just have the oatmeal. And a glass of orange juice, please."

The woman didn't write down the order, but continued peering at Judith with obvious interest, then finally said, "Don't I know you from somewhere?"

Judith read the name tag pinned to the woman's stained white uniform: *Glenda.* She thought for a moment. "You're not Glenda Roberts, are you?" she asked, not believing it could even be so. She remembered the robust teenager on the cheerleading squad in high school. But this thick-waisted, middle-aged woman couldn't possibly be the same person.

The woman smiled, revealing stained teeth. "That's right. Anyway, I *used* to be Glenda Roberts. My last name's been Miller for over twenty-six years now."

Judith forced a friendly smile to her lips. "You were a couple years ahead of me in school, but my name was Judith McPhearson then—now it's Blackwell."

Glenda's brows raised slightly. "Now I remember you. Didn't you used to run around with the Morrison girl?"

She nodded sadly. "Actually, that's what brought me to town. I heard the sad news." After Polly's incessant warnings yesterday, Judith knew to watch her guard as she continued. "I guess I just needed to take a sentimental journey back to Cedar Crest."

"Well, I'm sure you'll find everything's just about the same as you left it," said Glenda flatly. Was Judith imagining it or was this woman slightly disillusioned herself?

"Say, didn't the Miller family used to own this café?" asked Judith.

Glenda nodded. "Yep. I married Jeff Miller. Remember he played football for Cedar Crest High? He was their star quarterback the year they went to state. Now his folks are mostly retired. Him and me run this place with the help of our youngest daughter, Katie. She's still in high school; the others are all gone now. But Katie is my right-hand girl."

"That must be nice."

"And how about you?" Glenda stuck the pencil stub behind her ear and adjusted her apron. "Have you got some family too?"

Judith sighed. "My husband and son have both passed on."

Glenda frowned. "Now, that's too bad." She shook her head as she turned back towards the counter to grab the coffeepot, but Judith could still hear her clicking her tongue as she muttered,

"That's just too darn bad.. ." She set a full mug of steaming coffee before Judith before returning to the kitchen, still shaking her head in pity.

Judith looked around at the other customers, now resuming their conversations or reading their papers, with a furtive glance tossed her way from time to time. Strangers must be unusual in a town like this, or was it possible that some of them recognized her? She studied them more closely, but not a single face looked familiar. Still, it'd been almost thirty years since she'd lived here. People's appearances could change a lot. Certainly, hers had. And yet, oddly enough, Glenda had seemed to recognize her.

Before long, Glenda returned with a generous bowl of oatmeal and what appeared to be hand-squeezed fresh orange juice. "Here you go, honey. I even dug up some brown sugar for your oatmeal."

Judith smiled and placed the paper napkin in her lap. "Thanks, it looks good."

Glenda lingered a moment, a look of perplexity across her face. "It's just so odd," she said without further explanation.

"What's that?" Judith peered up curiously.

"You look a bit like her."

"Who?"

"Your old friend, Jasmine Morrison, or rather Emery."

Judith caught her breath. "Did you know her?"

Glenda shook her head sharply. "No, not really. Oh sure, she came in here once in a while with Hal. But she was a real quiet little gal, kept mostly to herself."

"That's what I've heard. It seems funny though, because she was never like that as a child. I wonder what made her change."

Glenda seemed to visibly bristle at this new line of questioning. "Well, you know, I never really knew her that good. So *I* wouldn't have a clue. Enjoy your breakfast now, and your visit while you're here in Cedar Crest."

Judith finished her breakfast, paid the bill and left a tip, and then quietly made her way back outside. The town looked a little livelier now, although only slightly. The overall impression was still that of a place that had been left behind and forgotten long ago. She peered down the street toward Polly's salon and the hardware store across from it. As curious as she was to view a recent photo of Jasmine, the very thought of seeing Hal Emery again made her feel just a little queasy. Although she had never considered herself an overly judgmental person, something about that man just gave her the creeps. And the realization that Jasmine had actually been married to such a man left Judith completely bewildered. For those pallid eyes and doughy face, that slippery handshake and combed-over hairline were just the sort of things the two girls would have made fun of as teens. And yet Jasmine had married him and lived with him. But then again, she'd changed a lot, and ultimately she'd taken her own life. Certainly, all had not been well with Jasmine Morrison.

Judith, now just steps away from the hardware store, considered turning back. Yet how could she *not* go inside? She owed as much to her friend. And so she mentally braced herself, pushed open the plate glass door, and entered the dim, musty store. An elderly man leaned against the counter, inquiring about ordering a particular plumbing part, and Judith pretended to browse among the limited selection of camping supplies. Only a very desperate camper would come in here to search out a necessary item. She heard the door open and close.

"Hello again." called Hal Emery, still behind the counter.

She walked over, pasting what she hoped was a convincing smile on her face. "Hello, Mr. Emery," she said. "It's a lovely day out there." She wanted to add that he might consider opening a window or door to allow some fresh air inside, but didn't.

"Please, call me Hal." he said pressing his fingertips onto the countertop. "You were friends with Jasmine, now shouldn't that make you a friend of mine too?"

She nodded. "Of course. Thank you."

"Funny thing, I searched all over the house last night, and could only scrape up a couple of photos of Jasmine. And they're nothin' to speak of—"

"Oh, that's all right. I'd love to see them." She moved closer to the counter.

He turned around and reached into a shelf to remove an envelope, then took out a couple of color snapshots and laid them on the counter between them.

Judith leaned forward to view the two photos almost as if she were examining some ancient archives and somehow was afraid to actually touch them or pick them up.

He pointed to the one she was looking at. "That was taken when Jasmine and I got hitched."

Judith nodded, staring at the forlorn face of the woman standing between Hal and the tall man Judith knew to be Mr. Morrison/his hair no longer blond but white, yet his eyes remained the same, blue and steely. But it was the expression in Jasmine's eyes that stopped Judith cold. That empty, sad, hopelessness—as if her life was already over. "On your wedding day?" said Judith almost without expression. "When was that?"

"About a year ago, as I recollect. I'm not one to pay much mind to dates, but it was just coming on summer, as I recall." He pointed to the other photo, this one of Jasmine sitting in a camp chair, huddled in a blanket with a tin mug in her hand. This time her eyes were downcast, but the expression looked the same. "This was taken last hunting season. I got me a four-point elk last year. Got lots of pictures of that too, but didn't think you'd be interested."

He made a sound that sounded something like a chuckle.

Judith couldn't peel her eyes away from the photos. She wanted to study them and figure out what was going on. Why was Jasmine so unhappy? Why had she married this strange man? But Judith knew these were questions she couldn't ask.

"Like I said, these photos ain't much. Jasmine never was one to have her picture took. Most of the time she'd put something over her face. I'm surprised I could even find these, now that I think of it."

Judith just nodded again, her eyes still pinned to the images. Finally, she reached out with one finger and touched the edge of the camping photo, as if she might absorb some sense of what was going on. "I wish I could've seen her again," she said quietly.

He made a sniffing sound. "Well, Jasmine wasn't a real social gal, if you know what I mean. She kept mostly to herself. Never called anyone or got together with friends or anything."

She nodded again. "I see..." But it was a lie. She *didn't* see. She didn't understand any of it—not a single word he was saying. Jasmine, the girl who dreamed of being an actress, *didn't* like being photographed? And *wasn't* social? Who was this strange woman he was speaking of? And what had he done to her?

The door opened from behind Judith, and Hal quickly scooped up the photos from the counter, holding them in his hand as he nodded to the patron. Apparently, the viewing was over.

"Well, thank you for, uh, showing me these," she stammered. "It helps a little."

Then he shoved the photos toward her. "Go ahead and keep "em if you want."

"Really?" She stared at him in wonder. "Oh, thank you so much. But are you sure? I mean, you said they were all you have—"

"I can probably dig up the negatives if I ever need to look at "em again. Y'all go ahead and take "em. Makes no difference to me."

"Okay, then." She quickly backed away, the precious photos in her hands, almost as if she were afraid he'd change his mind. "And thanks so much. I really do appreciate it. You have a good day, Hal."

He smiled at her. "You too, Judith."

She walked down the street feeling slightly dazed. How kind of him to let her keep the photos. Maybe she had misjudged him. But as she continued walking toward the other end of town, toward the motel, she wondered why he didn't want to keep the only photos he had of his recently deceased wife. Sure, they weren't good shots, but didn't he want something to remember her by? And what if he couldn't find the negatives? But then, she wondered, perhaps he didn't want anything to remind him of Jasmine. Perhaps he simply wanted to forget her altogether.

Seven

WITH NO DESIRE TO return to the dingy motel room, Judith
slipped the key into the door just the same. She needed a quiet place
to sit and think and gather her frazzled thoughts—a place away
from curious onlookers. Having left the windows open, the air in the
room smelled slightly fresher than before, but the overall affect was
still dismal and depressing. Appropriate, she thought.

She went into the bathroom where the light from its window
was somewhat better and proceeded to examine the two photos
again, this time studying every small detail for some sort of hidden
clue, some signal as to what had gone so horribly wrong in
Jasmine's life. The "wedding" photo appeared to be taken in some
little commercial wedding chapel—probably Reno as Polly had
suggested. Mr. Morrison had on a pale blue western shirt tucked into
dark pants, with a cool and controlled smile playing across his thin
lips, but his eyes were like ice. Hal wore a frumpy-looking tan
sports jacket over a plaid shirt, but at least his smile appeared to be
somewhat sincere, as if he were truly glad to be marrying Jasmine.
And why shouldn't he have been? Despite her forlorn expression,
Jasmine was still a very pretty woman. She wore her dark hair long,

the natural waves cascading over her shoulders. But she had on a
dress that Judith felt certain she couldn't have picked out for herself.
For one thing it was yellow, and Jasmine had always hated yellow;
she'd said it made her skin look sallow. Besides that, the dress
had a wide round neckline, snd Jasmine had always shirked from
such styles, claiming they made her face look overly plump. Both
Mrs. Morrison and Jasmine had always been very fashion conscious
about such details. Suddenly, Judith wondered where Mrs. Morrison
had been during this wedding. Taking the photo perhaps? She
wished she'd thought to ask Hal about her.

She studied Jasmine's eyes carefully. Surprised again at the
familiarity she recognized there. Not so much in their size or
shape, but in the expression. Judith had seen that exact same
hopeless look before—in her own eyes. And if eyes truly were
a window to the soul, then Jasmine, like Judith, had been very
troubled just a year ago.

"Oh, Jasmine." moaned Judith as she tucked the photos safely
into her purse, unable to look at them any longer. "What in the
world went wrong in your life?" And then she began to pace,
running what little information she had over and over through her
mind. But mostly she came up with questions. Lots of unanswered
questions. She pulled out the envelope containing the obituary and
studied the handwriting again. Was it possible that Jasmine's
great-aunt, Lenore Barker, was still living? Why, the old woman
must be nearly a hundred by now since she had retired from
teaching when the girls were still in grade school. Could she have
possibly sent this envelope? And, if so, why anonymously? Judith
decided to try to find out.

Once again, she left her little car behind, looking foreign and
out of place, parked in front of the seedy motel. But she felt
determined to experience this town as she had during most of her

childhood. And that was at a leisurely pace, and on foot. She walked toward the old grade school, noticing that little in this neighborhood had changed. Shabbier perhaps, but mostly the same, except for the number of vacant houses. She walked past the house where her good friend Eli Paxton had once lived. It too was vacant and looked as though it had been for some time. Overgrown with weeds and brush, the paint was falling off in large chunks. How sad, she thought, remembering how Mr. Paxton had always kept everything on their property in "shipshape condition" as he would proudly say, having actually served during World War II in the navy. She glanced up to notice the old rusty basketball hoop still in place over the small separate garage. It appeared that sometime over the years, someone had replaced the old rickety wooden garage doors with a newer metal one—an improvement of sorts.

She continued on, noticing how some homes had the outward signs of children; strewn about—bikes and swing sets and the like—but at the same time the neighborhood seemed oddly quiet compared to how it had been back when she and Jasmine were young. Back then, this neighborhood teemed with kids of all ages, yelling and playing and cutting up during their summer vacation. But she knew this quietness wasn't something only found in Cedar Crest. Silent neighborhoods like this probably lurked all around the country these days, with kids parked like zombies in front of the electronic baby-sitters found in TVs and VCRs and computers. Yes, things had definitely changed since the times when she and Jasmine had roamed the town's streets like vagabonds, always on the lookout for some new adventure.

Soon she came to the little rental house where she and her mother had lived for more than ten years. Painted turquoise green now, and in need of a fresh coat, the house looked even smaller than she remembered. And the covered front porch where she used to play on rainy days, where she'd parked her bike, was unbelievably tiny. The

weed-infested lawn needed mowing, and the peony bushes no longer
grew prolifically along the footpath. She remembered how much she
had loved the cheerful peonies as a child, often cutting large bouquets
which she'd place on the tiny plastic-topped kitchen table to surprise
her mother after a hard day's work. She smiled to herself. She and her
mother had been happy in this little house—just the two of them.
And as a child, it was only when watching a family sitcom like *The
Adventures of Ozzie and Harriet* or *Father Knows Best,* or when
a thoughtless grown-up might mention "how sad that she came
from a broken home..." that she actually realized her home life was
different from most. But during those early years the absence of
her father hadn't worried her too much.

Suddenly she noticed movement behind the front room curtain,
and she felt slightly conspicuous standing motion-lessly and staring
at the house for so long. How long had she stared? Hopefully she
hadn't upset anyone in there. She quickly turned away and moved
on toward the grade school, just a few blocks north. The grade
school looked exactly the same except that all the laurel bushes
that had grown like a hedge along the brick walls had been
removed. Probably for security reasons—they had always made
such good hiding places. She walked across the blacktopped
playground, remembering how she and Jasmine loved to stop at
the swings on a warm summer day. They'd sit and swing slowly
back and forth, visiting and planning their next escapade. Even
after they entered junior high they'd still sneak back onto the old
elementary playground and reminisce about their "good ol' grade
school days." But the playground, like the neighborhood, was
vacant of children today. Too bad. It seemed so much had been lost
over the years.

She spotted the small house that Lenore Barker used to live in.
She and Jasmine had always called it the gingerbread house because

it had zigzag trim along its steeply pitched roof line. To her
pleased surprise, it was still painted a soft shade of brown, just
the color of cocoa, and the gingerbread trim was still a clean, crisp
white. And as Judith drew closer, she noticed the. flower beds were
still well tended, filled with pansies, mums, zinnias, and all those
old-fashioned flowers that dear "Aunt Lenore" had so loved.

Judith remembered the day when the older woman had invited
her to call her "Aunt Lenore." It was the summer after she had
retired from teaching high school English, and the girls had been
invited for afternoon tea. And as she passed a delicate plate of
spice cookies to Judith, she had said, "Judith dear, you're so much
like a part of Jasmine's family that I think you should also call me
Aunt Lenore, if you'd like." Of course, Judith had been honored,
and from that day on she'd always called her by that familiar
name. And for some time she'd kept a thin strand of contact,
exchanging Christmas cards, an occasional birthday card. But not
in the past several years. For all she knew, the old woman could be
dead and buried. She hoped not.

So she stood on the sidewalk out in front of the house and tried to
convince herself that Aunt Lenore might still possibly live there. Or
if not, at least someone who had known her then. A relative perhaps,
because this little cottage-style house just looked too much the
same—as if one could still feel Aunt Lenore's presence close by.
Even so, Judith hesitated before walking up the little brick path to
ring the doorbell. She felt unwilling to discover she was wrong.

After a short wait, the door slowly opened, and there stood a
tiny, fragile-looking woman wearing an old-fashioned housedress in
soft shades of lilac and blue. Her hair stood out from her head in fluffy
white wisps, giving her an almost otherworldly look.

"Lenore Barker?" asked Judith, speaking loudly just in case the
woman was hard of hearing.

The old woman nodded, a curious expression passing over her brow.

Judith felt tears unexplainably welling in her eyes. "Is that really you? Do you remember me? I'm Judith. Jasmine's old friend."

Aunt Lenore slowly smiled. "Why, Judith McPhearson," she said clearly as she reached for her hand. "Of course I remember you. Come on in, dear. What a pleasure to see you again."

Judith gently grasped the tiny, wrinkled hand and smiled. "It's so good to see you, Aunt Lenore. You look absolutely wonderful."

"Oh, pish posh," she said, waving her free hand. "I'm old and wrinkled and not good for much of anything these days."

With quick little steps, she led Judith directly into the sunlit kitchen. "Now you sit right here. Let me put the kettle on, and I'll make us some tea. Then I'll sit down and have a good, long look at you."

"Everything seems exactly the same in here," said Judith as she gazed around the cheerful room in wonder, her eyes resting for a moment on the old knickknack shelf that still held a prized collection of unique salt and pepper shakers. "It's just as I remember it."

"Yes, I am rather set in my old-fashioned ways." Aunt Lenore carefully made her way to the table with a teapot.

Judith started to rise. "Let me help you—"

"No, no, you just sit tight. I may be old, but I need to keep moving. Otherwise I won't be good for much of anything. I still grow my little vegetable garden out back, do all my own yard work, cook and clean, and do my own shopping too." With a slightly trembling hand, she placed a plate of sliced banana bread on the table, then went back to the cupboard for teacups.

Finally, she sat down across the table, and folding her hands, looked directly at Judith. "You may pour now, Judith."

Judith smiled and poured them both a cup of steaming amber tea. "This is a real treat for me."

Aunt Lenore sipped her tea, her eyes still fixed on her guest. "A treat for me too, dear. But have you been unwell, Judith?"

She set down her cup and shook her head. "No, not exactly. Not in the physical sense anyway. But—"

"Troubled in your soul?"

Judith nodded. "Yes, that would pretty much describe it."

Aunt Lenore shook her head. "You and Jasmine, both so much alike, even after all these years...to think you were both troubled in the soul."

"I'm so sorry about Jasmine, Aunt Lenore. That's why I came back to Cedar Crest. I only just heard the news yesterday—such a shock."

"Nearly broke my heart." She set the cup back in her saucer with a loud clink. "Such a horrible, horrible waste. A pitiful, pitiful waste. Why, it pains me right here in my heart to even think about it now."

"I know. I still can't quite believe it myself." Although Judith felt eager to ask more questions, she recognized pure agony etched onto the old woman's face. It seemed a clear warning to change the subject, at least for the time being.

Aunt Lenore looked back up at Judith with curiosity. "But tell me, child, why is it that *you're* troubled in your soul? What has befallen you?"

Judith quickly explained about first losing her only son and then more recently her husband. "I continued teaching after Peter died, and then I taught summer school, and went into the next year...but by the end of this school year I just couldn't go on. I declined teaching summer school, and, to tell the truth, I just sort of fell completely apart."

"Well, that's because you never allowed yourself enough time to properly grieve for your husband. The heart can't heal unless it's permitted to cry and suffer and to carry on for a little."

Judith nodded. "I'm sure you're right."

"But perhaps you're on a better path now."

"I hope so."

"And so, you became a teacher?" Aunt Lenore smiled.

"Yes, I had some very good role models as a child."

"Thank you. And how is your mother doing?"

"She's fine. Retired, of course. She married again, a few years ago, and she seems happy. They live over at the coast, in my grandmother's old house. George just had bypass surgery last winter, but he appears to be doing okay, and my mom still keeps herself busy with volunteering and whatnot. Right now they're off on a cruise."

"Good for them. Activity keeps a body young. Do you still do your art, Judith? I always thought you had the potential of greatness in you."

Judith laughed. "That's sweet of you, but I think it was only a hobby sort of interest. And I haven't done a thing in years."

"That's a shame. Gifts like that weren't meant to be wasted."

"Unfortunately, there's been a lot of waste in my life, Aunt Lenore."

She looked Judith right in the eye, then spoke with conviction. "Judith, with God, *nothing* is ever wasted."

Judith considered this for a moment, but couldn't seem to wrap her mind around the vastness of it. Perhaps it was time to change the subject. "Aunt Lenore?"

"Yes, dear?"

"Was it you who sent me the obituary clipping?"

"Why, yes, of course. Didn't you get my note along with it?"

"Note?"

The old woman frowned. "Yes, telling you about the death and all. Good grief, I was just so upset around that time, do you suppose I forgot to slip the note in?"

Judith smiled. "I'll bet that's what happened. And then there was no return address on the envelope, so it was all rather mysterious."

"Oh, goodness gracious, and to think I used to teach English. All I can say is that I was very upset at the time and not thinking clearly."

"Maybe it was a good thing." Judith considered how the curious envelope and contents had derailed her possible suicide attempt, and then how it had compelled her to return to Cedar Crest. "I was so shook up by the news that I decided to drive over and find out what had happened for myself."

Aunt Lenore's face grew cloudy. "And have you been able to do so?"

"Not really. To be honest, if anything I feel more confused than ever."

"You aren't alone." She stood and began carrying the empty dishes to the sink.

Judith rose to help. "I met Hal Emery."

"What did you think of him?"

"Well, he wasn't exactly what I'd expected."

Aunt Lenore made a "humph" sound and began running hot water into a plastic dish tub. "There was certainly no love lost in that marriage."

"Why did Jasmine marry him?"

"Why do you think?" Aunt Lenore handed her a tea towel and a plate to dry.

"I have no idea."

"Burt."

"Mr. Morrison?" Judith set the plate in the cupboard and then turned to study Aunt Lenore's expression. "That's so archaic. Are you suggesting Jasmine's father actually forced her into a marriage she didn't want? But she was a grown woman."

"I believe he somehow coerced her into marrying *that man.*"

Judith sensed by the tone that Aunt Lenore wasn't overly fond of Hal Emery either. "But why? And why in the world would Jasmine go along with it?"

"That's what I don't understand. *Why?*" Aunt Lenore handed her the last saucer. "I tried to find out from Jasmine, but she kept her lips sealed tight as a drum when it came to Hal and her father."

"Then you did get to spend some time with her?"

"Not much. When she first came to town, I would try and try to get her to come visit me, but she always had some excuse not to. At first I thought it was because I'm just a boring old lady, and why should a young woman want to spend time with me? But then when she actually came, we had such a pleasant time together, and she seemed honestly glad to be here. And yet, I could tell she was keeping something bottled inside, holding something back that was deeply troubling to her. And she never seemed eager to go, and I always felt that she was about to tell me something, but then she would stop herself. Unfortunately, her visits were far apart and few between. In fact, the last time I saw her was around Christmastime last year. And she was so unhappy." Aunt Lenore closed her eyes for a moment and swayed slightly, reaching for the edge of the counter to balance herself.

"Are you all right?" Judith asked with alarm. "Do you need to sit down?"

"Please, help me into the living room."

Judith led her into the tiny living room and eased her down onto the mohair sofa. "Can I get you anything?"

"No, no, I'll be fine. I may have overdone it a little this morning. I weeded and then I watered and then I hung out some laundry and.. ."

"Oh my, and then I show up on your doorstep for morning tea. You must be worn out. Perhaps I should go and let you get some rest."

Aunt Lenore nodded. "But please, do come back, my dear. We have so much more to talk about. Will you be in town for a while?"

"Yes, a few days at least."

"Good, good...then you must come back. Perhaps you can stay here." She leaned her head against a crocheted pillow and began to close her eyes again, but stopped. "Say, Judith, I just remembered. There's a box of her things, something she left in the spare room the last time she was here. I've been meaning to open it, but I just haven't been able to make myself do it.. .perhaps we could go through it together. Who knows, maybe we'll find some answers."

Judith gently squeezed her hand. "Yes, Aunt Lenore. We'll definitely do that. I'll try to come back later today. Or perhaps even tomorrow, when you've had a chance to rest up a little more."

Then she quietly let herself out the front door. Walking back to the motel, she wondered at the things she'd learned today. Not all that much really. But *a forced* marriage? In this day and age? It seemed crazy and far-fetched and unbelievable. And yet there was that strange wedding photo. Didn't it seem to silently confirm such a possibility? But why? *Why?*

Eight

JUDITH MADE HER WAY up the hill to where Jasmine had once lived. And although the noonday sun was beating down on her and she didn't consider herself to be in very good physical condition, she felt surprised by how easily she walked up the sloped sidewalk, as if the hill had shrunk in size. She remembered how it had seemed so steep to her as she'd huff and puff and then push her bike up that last block. She blinked up at the white two-story house, almost blinding in the bright sun. Shading her eyes with her hands, she studied it carefully. Same lap siding, same round columns on the front porch. But, despite its manicured appearance, it seemed empty. All the shades were down, no potted plants on the porch, no cars in the driveway, no sign of life anywhere. But to her surprised relief, the house no longer seemed so austere and intimidating. In fact, to her grown-up eyes, it actually looked slightly cheap and cheesy, as if some sly architect had been trying to fool someone into thinking this was some grand Southern mansion, when in reality it was just a fifties, midsized family home with very little in the way of style or personality. Scarlett O'Hara would never have wanted to live here.

"You looking for someone?"

Judith turned to see a young woman staring at her as she balanced a sticky-faced toddler over one hip. "Are you lost or something?" asked the woman with a curious frown.

"Oh no, I was just looking at this house. My best friend used to live here, back when we were little girls. I haven't seen it in ages."

The woman smiled and shifted the child to her other hip. "Oh, that's cool. Does it bring back some good memories?"

"Actually, I was just looking at that deck." Judith pointed to the sundeck on the west side. "I remember when my friend's dad built that deck and we two girls pretended like it was our stage. We gave several talent shows that summer, singing and dancing and all sorts of things. And neighbor kids actually came round and paid a dime just to see us acting like a couple of idiots." Judith laughed.

"That sounds like fun. How long ago was that?"

"Goodness, another lifetime." She glanced at the young woman who looked to be in her twenties. "Probably before you were even born." She looked back over to the house. "It looks sort of vacant. Does anyone live here?"

"Yeah, but the folks who own it only come here once in a great while, and the rest of the time it just sits empty. They're sure not much in the way of neighbors either. I just wish they'd sell it to a real family." She playfully poked her son's tummy. "Then Ryan here might get some neighbor kids to play with. But those mean old Morrisons don't seem to care about that."

"Morrisons?" Judith stared at the woman. "You don't mean Burt and Ellen Morrison?"

Now the young woman's face grew dark. "You know them?"

Judith nodded.

"That's your friend's family?"

"Her parents."

"You mean your friend—she was that woman who— uh—you

know, died just recently?"

"Jasmine Emery."

The woman took a step back, almost as if in fear. "Well, I'm sorry. But I gotta go now. Ryan gets real cranky if he doesn't get his nap."

Judith eyed the smiling boy who didn't look a bit cranky. "Yeah, sure. Thanks for talking." But without saying another word the woman and child hurried back into the house next door. Despite the heat of the sun, Judith felt chilled inside. What did that look mean? Why did the once friendly woman suddenly turn cold like that? Just when Judith had hoped to find someone who might be able to shed a little light on what was going on in this town. She turned and began to walk down the hill. Unsure of where she was going or what she was doing, a plan seemed to unfold with each step. She would return to the motel, look through the phone directory for Hal Emery's address, then stop by the hardware store under the guise of buying something—what? A flashlight perhaps. Then if Hal was there and working, she'd drive on over to his house just to get a little glimpse of the last place where Jasmine had actually lived. Sure, it was probably a silly plan—and for what purpose? And, yet, somehow it comforted her to think she'd come up with it.

"Hello again." said Hal in a friendly tone as Judith walked back into his store.

"Hi, Hal." She tried to look and sound normal, but felt as if she were on some sort of spy mission. "I forgot when I was in this morning that I'd meant to pick up a flashlight. I just hate staying in a strange motel without having one. I mean, you never know when the electricity might go. And I remember how this town could lose energy in a thunderstorm."

"Smart thinking. And you're right too, we still get hit with an outage from time to time. Best to be prepared." He led her to a rack of flashlights. "And I "spect you'll need batteries too."

"Yes, of course, thank you."

Back at the counter, he smiled at her. "I hope you'll stop back in here again, Judith." Then he looked back down at the till. "It's nice seeing you around."

She wasn't quite sure what to think of his comment. Was he actually flirting with her? Or did she just remind him of his deceased wife? "Thanks. I do plan to stick around for a few more days."

"Well, don't be a stranger."

She forced a laugh. "Oh, I suppose one can always think of something they need from a hardware store."

"That's what keeps me in business."

She nodded, glancing around and wondering how he actually managed to stay in business. His stock looked old and dusty, and there wasn't another single customer in the store. "Are you the only one who works here?" she asked.

"Yep, pretty much. I thought about hiring me a high school boy at the beginning of summer, but then so much happened and all..." his voice trailed off.

"Well, don't work too hard." She smiled then made her way to the door and waved. "Bye now."

His face brightened. "See ya around, Judith."

Something about him saying her name like that made her uncomfortable. Silly perhaps, but it seemed disloyal to Jasmine. What *would* Jasmine think? Perhaps she wouldn't give a rip, as they used to say. After all, Aunt Lenore had said there was no love lost in that marriage. And Judith, for the life of her, could not imagine Jasmine loving someone like Hal Emery—no matter how nice he might try to act.

Knowing that Hal was safely tucked away at the store, Judith drove her car over to Arrowroot Road to search for his house. She came to a rural area with mailboxes along the road. Finally she spied a rusty mailbox with the name "Emery" on it. She started to pull into the long gravel driveway, but was stopped by a locked gate with a large No Trespassing sign wired to it. Judith got out of the car to take a closer look. Suddenly a pair of wildly barking dogs ran up. Normally, she loved dogs of all kinds, but these vicious beasts appeared to be trained as guard dogs. And their snarling, barred teeth were enough to cause her to quickly back up. But she paused a moment, squinting her eyes to see the house that was barely visible from the road. Shrouded in overgrown brush and trees, she spied what looked like an old mobile home—the kind made of metal with wheels hiding beneath and a hideous aqua and white. How could it possibly be that Jasmine had spent her last days here? No wonder she'd taken her own life! Or had she? This was another piece of the puzzle that Judith could not accept. Jasmine had always been so spunky—a fighter, a dreamer, a doer. But that had been years ago, and as Polly had said, people change. The dogs continued to bark, and Judith finally decided to leave rather than draw some neighbor's curiosity. But before she could go, she attempted to speak to her friend. She knew it seemed *crazy,* but she couldn't stop herself.

"Jasmine?" she whispered intently. "Can you hear me? Why did you come'here to live in this horrible place?" She stared at the house again. "And why did you marry that man? Did you love him? What happened to you, Jasmine? Can't you somehow show me?" Just then the larger of the two dogs lunged at the gate, shaking it so hard she felt sure he'd break through. She turned and quickly climbed into her car and drove away. Tears instantly blurred her eyes.

After a few moments, she pulled to the side of the road and continued to mourn her friend's sad life. As Aunt Lenore had explained, Judith's heart needed to grieve if it was ever going to heal. And then, instead of trying to talk to Jasmine, she attempted a feeble prayer—her first attempt in years. It was only a few words, a desperate plea for help, but perhaps it was a beginning of sorts. Then she wiped her eyes and reached for the ignition key. But in the same moment, she heard a knock on her door. Startled and frightened, she turned to see that it was only a boy, and so she rolled down the window.

"You okay, ma'am?" he asked with a raised brow. "Is your car broken down or something?"

"No, I just pulled over for a minute to think. But thanks for asking."

His face looked clearly perplexed. "But was that you I just saw over at Emerys' old place?"

"Well, yes, I just stopped for a moment..."

"Why were you stopping over there?"

She was quickly feeling trapped by this overly curious youth. "Do you live around here?" she asked, hoping to change the subject.

"Yeah, I live in that red house next door to Emerys'." He peered curiously at her. "You remind me of her."

"You mean Jasmine?" she asked hopefully.

He nodded. "Yeah."

"Did you know her?"

"Yeah. I liked her. And she and me talked sometimes." He glanced nervously over his shoulder as if to see if anyone was watching.

Judith smiled. "Jasmine and I were best friends when we were about your age."

"Yeah. You kinda look like her."

She smiled again. "Do you think you could tell me a little about her?"

He glanced over his shoulder again. "I dunno. Maybe some

other time. But I don't think so. My pa won't like it if he catches me talking to you."

"Why?"

"He don't like me talking to strangers."

"Well, I'm Judith. Judith Blackwell. I'm a schoolteacher. And I was Jasmine's friend. Tell him I was Jasmine's best friend."

"'That won't help none. He never liked me talking to her neither."

"Oh."

"Well, I gotta go. Maybe some other time."

"Like when?"

But it was too late, he took off running back toward his house. Judith punched her steering wheel. What was it with these people? What was going on in this town? And why did so much seem to surround someone like Jasmine? It just made no sense. Other than her conversation with Aunt Lenore, nothing made much sense. What was everyone so afraid of? She remembered the cop that Polly had told her about, some special detective who had been asking questions about Jasmine. Maybe it was time to ask him some questions. What was his name?

She wanted to stop by Polly's and ask, but feared she'd get the cold treatment again if Polly had customers. And it appeared that she did, so Judith just continued on to her motel room where she called, the hair salon, and as if by miracle, she got a straight answer from her cousin.

"His name is Adam something-or-other, can't recall his last name right now. Guess I'm having another one of my senior moments. But don't worry, there's only a handful of men on the force anyway, so it's no problem to just ask for him by his first name."

"Thanks, Polly, I appreciate it. Don't you have any customers right now?"

"Nah, just sent Gertie Sanders outta here looking like Shelley Winters—the old version." She laughed.

"Well, I've had an interesting day, and I think I'm ready to talk to this detective. Maybe he'll know something by now."

"I'm curious to hear what you find out. Hey, if you want to stop by here for supper, I could fix us some grilled cheese sandwiches or something easy like that. Nothing fancy, though. I'm not much good at entertaining anymore."

"Thanks, Polly. That sounds really good."

"Sixish then?"

"Looking forward to it."

Next, Judith dialed the police department and asked to speak to a Detective Adam.

"And this is regarding?"

"Oh, nothing important, really. I just wanted to talk with him for a moment."

"Hmm. Well, he's not here right now. You want to leave a message?"

She gave him her first name and motel phone number and then hung up. Something about the tone of the man's voice aggravated her. Maybe it was just small-town cops with too much time on their hands, acting a little too nosy, but it felt wrong.

Tired from her unusually energetic day, she decided to lie down and rest a bit. But sometime later, she awoke to the phone jangling in her ear. Disoriented, she knocked it to the floor first, before finally grappling for the receiver and saying, "Hello!"

"Are you okay?" asked a strange masculine voice.

"Yeah, I'm fine. Who is this?" she asked irately.

"This is Detective Ford."

"Who?"

"Look, I have a message to call a Judith, no last name, at this number. Is that you or not?"

"Oh." Realization hit and she sat up straight. "Detective Adam Ford?"

"Yes, that's me. Now, what can I do for you?"

"I'm not sure, really..." She wondered how to put this.

"Well, do you want to call me back when you're feeling a little more sure?" He sounded irritated now.

"No, no, I'm sorry. You just caught me off guard. You see, someone gave me your name, and I wanted to find out about my friend Jasmine Emery."

"Your friend?" He sounded skeptical.

"Well, actually, we were childhood friends. And I only just heard about her—death, you know. And I came to town and, well, I only seem to come up with more questions, and I'd really like to know what happened—"

"Look, lady I'm a detective. I'm the one who usually asks the questions—not the one giving out the information."

"I know. But she was my best friend—" She felt her voice catch. "We were blood sisters, and we lost touch, and then I hear about this. And, well, nothing makes any sense."

"And you think I'll have all the answers?" His voice was sarcastic.

"I hoped you might."

"Look, lady, I'm sorry about your friend. But unless you've got something to help me, I don't see any reason why I should help you."

Judith considered hanging up on this incredibly rude policeman. But then she imagined Jasmine living in that ugly single-wide mobile home, and controlled herself. "Well, how can you be so sure I might not have some helpful information?"

"Do you?"

She could just imagine this man, leaning smugly back in his chair, feet propped on the desk with a pot belly and a disinterested expression across his dull face. He was probably thinking about donuts. Then suddenly she remembered Aunt Lenore's box. "Yes. I do have information."

"Hmm… well, how about if we meet tomorrow morning then. Say, ten. Does that work for you?"

"Ten is fine."

She hung up and glanced at her watch. It was almost five. She had slept for nearly two hours! It was probably too late to pay another visit to Aunt Lenore's and still make it to Polly's. But she suspected the old woman to be an early riser. She'd stop by first thing in the morning before her appointment with the rude Detective Ford and see if she couldn't take a peek into that box.

Nine

POLLY'S APARTMENT HADN'T CHANGED a lot since the last time Judith had been there. And, like the foam curlers now rolled into Polly's red hair, pink still ruled. But not that dusty-rose shade that had become popular in more recent decades. No, Polly still clung to that Pepto-Bismol shade straight out of the fifties, making Judith unexpectedly long for a spoonful of the chalky, wintergreen-flavored medicine. Or perhaps it was simply the effect of the overpoweringly sweet and musky smell that permeated the entire room. She walked gingerly across the matted pale pink carpet, trying not to stare at the numerous telltale stains, most likely the result of the fluffy creature Polly was just now confining to the tiny bathroom. "Sorry about that." she called over her shoulder. "Go ahead and sit down. Make yourself at home."

The moment Judith had entered Polly's pink haven, the tiny white dog had yipped nonstop while it simultaneously nipped at her loafers, acting like some deranged, shoe-eating, mechanical windup toy. Her second negative encounter with canines today. And here she thought she liked dogs and they liked her. Well, people do change. Maybe there was something about her that animals could sniff out. Or maybe she was just imagining things.

She sat down on the worn velvet sofa which was, no big surprise, pink as well. And like everything else in Polly's life, the sofa sagged in the middle. She studied the chipped vase on the wood laminate coffee table across from her; it was filled with a stiff bouquet of faded pink roses, their rigid petals coated with a greasy layer of old dust. Plastic, of course, and yet she couldn't recall seeing real plastic flowers since back in the seventies. Like a life frozen in time. With only mild interest, she wondered if the strange plastic blooms might actually be collectable in some circles nowadays.

"Sorry about that, honey." huffed Polly as she treaded back into the tiny living room, her slippers flipping at her red callused heels. "My little Muffy is my best friend, but he can get awfully riled with visitors sometimes. Just jealous, I think. A lot like some of the men I've known, but, oh, so much easier to live with." She flopped down into the rose-colored recliner situated directly across from a small portable TV and sighed deeply. "I've got the soup all ready to heat up, and was just getting the sandwiches going, but I think I need to sit down here for a moment and catch my breath. I swear the years are catching up with me, Judith Anne, that and being on my feet all day.. .well, it's no way for a woman my age to live."

"How about if I finish up in the kitchen?" suggested Judith.

"Oh, would you do that for me, doll?"

Judith smiled. "Sure, no problem. Put your feet up and have a little rest."

"Just holler if you need anything."

Judith easily found her way around the compact kitchen, marveling again how she seemed to have stepped into a time warp as she discovered dishes and utensils that she felt sure were collectible. And yet somehow all this strange but familiar milieu brought a very real comfort with it—it reminded her of childhood. "Dinner's about ready, Polly. Shall I set it up in here?"

"Nah, let's just use TV trays and eat in here where it's more comfortable."

Judith brought their dishes in from the kitchen and then laughed. "This reminds me so much of when I was little, Polly. Mom and I always ate off TV trays in the living room. It got so that we only used the dining table for special occasions, and even that was rare."

"Yeah, I don't know what I'd do without them. That's one of the first things I look for in a man."

"You mean that he'd be willing to eat from a TV tray?"

"Well, it's a start, at least. Not that I'm really looking for a man these days. But I'm not completely opposed to the idea either. Can't abide the thought of living out the rest of my days all alone."

Judith dipped her spoon into the soup. "Just make sure he's really the right one, Polly. Don't waste your time on the losers."

Polly laughed sarcastically. "Well, I don't think I'll need to worry about it one way or another. There's not a whole lot to choose from in this town."

"Speaking of eligible bachelors, I've become better acquainted with Hal Emery."

Polly groaned. "Now, *there's* a man that'd encourage any girl to remain single."

"Oh, maybe he's not so bad. I mean, he's trying to be friendly."

Polly blinked. "Not so bad? Just yesterday you thought he was lower than slug slime."

Judith chuckled. "I didn't say that. I just couldn't understand why someone like Jasmine would marry him."

"You and me both, honey. So, have you turned anything up?"

Judith told her about her visit with Aunt Lenore and the mysterious box.

"You just be careful though, Judith. Don't you go digging yourself into something that's over your head."

"Over my head? What do you mean?"

"Like I already told you. There's folks in this town a body's got to be careful of. If you don't say the wrong things or ask the wrong questions, you'll be fine." She set her empty bowl down. "And that's all I want to say about that."

"Well, I made an appointment with that detective you told me about. Although, he seemed pretty rude on the phone."

Polly smiled. "I think that's just because of what he does for a living. You know how those detective types on TV are always kind of bossy and abrupt. But just wait until you see him in person, you'll forgive all his personality flaws in a heartbeat."

Judith rolled her eyes. "I seriously doubt it. I just hope he can answer some questions. He seems to know something. Or at least he acts like it. But he made it sound as if we were going to do some sort of information exchange. I tell him something about Jasmine, and he'll tell me something. Pretty strange, if you ask me."

"Well, like I said, you just be careful. And don't go around trusting everyone. Especially where the police are concerned." Then she pretended to zip her lips. "Now, honestly, that's all I'm going to say about that."

Judith had considered asking her about Hal's neighbor boy, but thought better of it. In the first place, Polly obviously didn't want to get overly involved here, and secondly, if Judith were to have a follow-up conversation with the boy, perhaps she shouldn't mention his name to anyone. Even as both these thoughts went through her head with lightning speed, she wondered at how she was so quickly falling into all this mysterious cloak-and-dagger stuff. With some effort, she managed to steer their conversation into safer channels, and after they finished eating she picked up their dirty dishes and went back into the kitchen.

"Thanks, honey." called Polly as her chair creaked back into its reclining position again. "Just leave those things in the sink."

The outdated kitchen had no conveniences such as dishwashers or garbage disposals, and so Judith quietly filled the sink with hot sudsy water. She hadn't washed dishes by hand since she was a girl. And once again, something about the old-fashioned chore brought a comfort of sorts. By the time she was done, she could hear Polly peacefully snoring from her chair. Judith wrote a little thank-you note, then quietly let herself out the door, smiling as she went down the steps. Some people would consider Polly to be a horribly inept hostess, and yet it had been just the sort of evening Judith had needed.

She walked slowly through the quiet town. Almost nine and it was just getting dusky. She remembered how she and Jasmine used to love these long summer nights—more time to play and be together. She remembered the times when they would use Jasmine's father's camping gear and make camp in Jasmine's backyard. This was one activity Mr. Morrison wholeheartedly supported. He was glad his daughter liked the outdoors. He taught her to build a campfire, to cook outside, and to take care of herself in the woods. He wanted her to hunt and fish with him, but this was where she drew the line. Judith, on the other hand, had no problem with these things. Well, she'd never actually hunted, but she had enjoyed the few fishing trips she'd taken with Jasmine and her father. Those were the earlier days of their friendship, the days when Mr. Morrison could do no wrong in her eyes. And Judith, unafraid to push a squirming worm onto a sharp hook, and hungry for a father figure, had relished Mr. Morrison's open admiration at her skill. Yet Jasmine would complain and even act squeamish about such things—claiming it cruel to torture a worm in such a way. In fact, there were times in those early days when Judith would vie for Mr. Morrison's attention by acting the brave tomboy he had always wanted Jasmine to be. And oddly enough, Jasmine never seemed to mind—or at least she never showed it. That was one of the rare and wonderful qualities of their friendship. It never seemed to be affected by jealousy of any kind.

The little town looked rather quaint and sweet in the dusky evening light. Harsh shapes were softened in the yellow light of the street lamps. Judith could see how a town like this could have real charm. And in this day and age, with so many people becoming disenchanted with city life, it was surprising that a town like this wasn't filling up with families eager to flee the urban areas and live a quieter, simpler existence. It's exactly what she would want to do if she still had a family. *If.*

It was fairly dark by the time she reached the motel. How long could she stand to stay in this awful place? At first, she'd been so distraught and depressed she hadn't minded the squalor, but as she began to think and function more normally—at least more normally than she had for some time—it became more disgusting than ever. She would check out of her room the next morning. Maybe she'd take Aunt Lenore up on that offer. Or if she couldn't find accommodations in Cedar Crest, she'd just look to the nearby towns. Yet even as she thought these things, she wondered why in the world she should continue staying here at all. But the town and the mystery surrounding Jasmine's life and death seemed to have some sort of magnetic hold on her. She felt certain she wouldn't be able to leave until some things were resolved. Perhaps that would all happen tomorrow when she met with the unfriendly detective.

◌‹◖ ◗›◌

IT TOOK LONGER THAN she anticipated to check out the

following morning. No one was in the office, and she had to traipse all over the grounds until she finally found a woman to help her.

"Did you enjoy your stay?" asked the woman.

"Sure." lied Judith. But what was she supposed to say— no, this place is a nasty fleabag, hole-in-the-wall motel that would best be torched? Instead, she paid her bill, thanked the woman, and left, promising herself to never stay in such a place again.

By the time she reached Aunt Lenore's it was after nine. Not much time to visit and go through the mysterious box that Aunt Lenore had told her about. Judith knocked on the door, taking a moment to enjoy the pretty blooms around the porch. She waited for what seemed enough time for the old woman to make it to the front door, then knocked again, louder this time. Again, she waited. Finally, she walked around back, suspecting that Aunt Lenore might be outside, weeding her garden or hanging her wash or whatever else her unusually energetic old friend might be doing in the morning. But there was no sign of her back there either, and it didn't appear that she'd watered or done anything yet today. Judith tried knocking on the back door. Still no answer. Now she was concerned. Aunt Lenore hadn't felt all that well when she'd left her yesterday. What if something had happened? She knocked loudly on the door now, calling out her name.

"Excuse me," called a voice from behind her.

Judith turned to see a woman of retirement age coming slowly up the walkway toward her. She used an ornately carved cane to help her walk.

"Are you looking for Miss Barker?" she asked, peering at Judith curiously.

"Yes, actually I am. I told her I'd come by today."

"Well, I don't know for certain, but I think she must've become ill or something yesterday, because last night there was a car here, and I saw some people helping Miss Barker into the backseat. She didn't look too well."

"How odd. Did you recognize anyone?"

"Well, it was dark, and the car wasn't familiar to me. But I noticed a man carrying a suitcase, probably Miss Barker's. My guess is that she was taken to some sort of elderly care facility. You know, she was in her nineties. It's amazing she's lasted so long on her own all this time."

Judith swallowed. "Yes, I suppose so. But she seemed so—so well yesterday. I mean, she said she'd been out working in her garden and hanging her wash—"

"You saw her yesterday?"

"Yes, we had a lovely visit. Of course, she was a little worn out when I left her. But I didn't think it was anything serious."

"You just never know with older people."

"I suppose not. I wonder how I could find out where she is."

The woman's brow creased. "Are you family?"

"Not exactly." Not wanting to alienate another possible source of information, Judith decided to conceal her hand this time. "But I've known Miss Barker since childhood. She's been a dear friend to me, and I've always called her Aunt Lenore."

The woman frowned. "Well, you might try checking with her family then. I don't know them personally, but I suspect you do if you've been close friends with Miss Barker all these years." Somehow, she seemed to turn slightly cool and skeptical.

"Yes, I'll have to see what I can find out. Thanks for your help."

"Well, Miss Barker's been a good neighbor to me. I'll be sad to lose her."

"Hopefully, you're not going to lose her." Judith couldn't bear to think of dear Aunt Lenore passing away just now— not after they'd only just begun to renew their friendship.

The woman shook her head. "Well, these old folks don't last forever, you know."

"I know. I just hope..."

The woman looked at her more carefully. "You really care about her."

"Yes." Judith sighed as she looked over the flower beds. "Maybe I should come by and see that her garden and flowers are watered while she's away."

The woman smiled. "That'd be good of you. I'd do it myself, but my arthritis is becoming somewhat burdensome to me."

"That's too bad." Then Judith realized she didn't even know the woman's name. "I'm sorry, I should've introduced myself. I'm Judith Blackwell. I grew up here in Cedar Crest, but I haven't been back for over twenty years."

The woman extended her hand. "I'm Martha Anderson. My husband moved us here back in the seventies. He was a teacher."

"Mr. Anderson? The art teacher at the high school?"

"Yes, that was him. He passed away a couple years ago."

"Oh, Mrs. Anderson, it's such a pleasure to meet you. I only had him for a year, but Mr. Anderson was one of my all-time favorite teachers."

She smiled. "I'm happy to hear that. Now please, just call me Martha."

"I'm so sorry to hear that he passed away. He was a wonderful man! Why, he's the first one to inspire me to take art seriously."

"And so, do you?"

"Well, I used to. I haven't done it in years."

"That's too bad. Warren used to always say that art was good for the soul. He never gave it up—painted right up until the day he died."

"Well, I've been toying with the idea of getting a sketch pad and taking it up again. I think it might be good therapy for me."

Martha reached over and squeezed her hand. "Then do it, Judith."

"I think I will." Judith glanced at her watch. "I hate to go, but I have an appointment at ten. I'll try to find out what's happened with Aunt Lenore, and I'll let you know if you like."

"Yes, I'd appreciate that."

The blow of Judith's concern for Aunt Lenore's health was somewhat softened by meeting Mr. Anderson's wife. She felt an instant kinship with the woman, and hoped that when she came back to water and tend Aunt Lenore's garden, she might spend more time chatting with her.

Ten

JUDITH WALKED INTO THE tiny cinder-block police department at ten o'clock sharp and inquired after Detective Ford. The man at the front desk raised his thick brows and eyed her with what seemed open suspicion. "This business or personal, ma'am?"

Trying not show her irritation at what seemed a rude insinuation, she forced a smile to her lips and crisply said, "Business, of course."

"Have a seat over there, and I'll buzz him."

She went over to where several burnt orange vinyl chairs sat arranged in a straight line, but feeling somewhat affronted, she stubbornly decided not to sit down. Instead, she picked up a dated news magazine and absently flipped through it, all the while surveying the layout of this old building. She'd been here a couple of times before. Once when her bike had been stolen, and then the time she and Jasmine had found a lost dog. Despite her mother's animal allergies, Judith had desperately wanted to keep that dog, a sweet collie mix with big soulful, golden eyes. But to her dismay, the owners showed up, and her mother had said it was just as well.

"Ms. Blackwell?"

She looked up to see a dark-haired man of medium height and build nodding her way. "Yes?" she answered.

"I'm Detective Ford," he approached her and extended his hand, giving hers a formal shake and quickly releasing it. She noticed the fanned-out creases at the outside of his dark eyes, as if he might actually smile upon occasion. But not now. Right now, his face looked grim.

"Thank you for seeing me." she replied, glancing back to the man at the front desk who was now drumming a pencil and staring directly at them. "I'm sure you must be busy." *Busy?* she thought, instantly feeling stupid for saying it. Who was busy in a town this size? But then what did it matter anyway, it was only small talk.

"Come on back to my office." said the detective, "such as it is."

"This place hasn't changed much," she commented as she followed him down a narrow hallway.

"You've been here before?" he asked as he pointed to another burnt orange vinyl chair across from his cluttered desk. He moved toward the other side and sank down into a well-worn avocado green desk chair that squeaked loudly as he leaned back. "Been in trouble with the law here in Cedar Crest in the past?"

She forced a laugh. "No. But I was in here a couple times as a kid. Just routine things involving bikes and dogs, you know."

"Yeah, you don't much look like the kind of woman who's had a lot of run-ins with the police."

She wasn't sure what he meant by that, but decided to ignore it and move on. "Detective Ford, I know you have other things to do, so let me get right to the point."

He leaned forward and pushed a pile of papers aside. "Suits me."

"Well, as I told you on the phone, Jasmine Morrison—uh, Emery—was a dear friend of mine. And her death has really shaken me up. I came to town hoping to get some answers, and all I've come up with are more questions."

"Well, join the crowd."

She looked at him curiously. Was he teasing her? "So, have you been investigating her death then?"

"I'm a detective, lady. It's my job to investigate."

She bristled. "So, then I assume it's still a—what do you call it—an open case?"

He leaned back in his chair. "Yeah, I guess you could say it's still an open case."

"So.. .can you tell me anything about it?"

He rolled his eyes and sat forward again, then picked up a pen and clicked it over and over, studying her closely as he did. "Look, lady, unless you're immediate family or some other arm of the law, I don't need to be telling you anything."

She felt her eyes flash in anger. But it was too late, she knew he'd noticed. Still, she was determined to remain cool and calm—at least outwardly. "First of all, I'd appreciate it if you'd quit calling me "lady.' Judith is fine. Secondly, I was as close as a sister to Jasmine. And I'm only inquiring because I care."

"Look, la—" he stopped himself. *"Judith,* I don't know a thing about you. You walk into town and expect me to disclose private information about an investigation. This isn't Mayberry, you know. Besides that, if you were such a good friend to Jasmine Emery, then where have you been all these years?"

"I lost touch with her. I didn't know how to locate her—"

"You said you grew up with her here in Cedar Crest. Ever think of looking in the phone book?"

"I didn't know she'd come back. Years ago, I tried over and

over to contact her in Mississippi. I had no idea she was here—" her voice broke "—only a few hours from where I live." She felt tears in her eyes, but didn't care. If this was to be her last ditch effort for Jasmine, she might as well get it over with. "If I'd known she was here, I would've dropped everything and come. I would've done anything to help her—to have prevented—this—this—" She couldn't go on. Digging, in her purse she finally found a rumpled tissue and wiped her eyes. She knew she was making a complete fool of herself, but somehow she just didn't care.

After a brief and uncomfortable silence, the detective spoke up. "I'm sorry. I didn't mean to sound so harsh, but this is an odd case."

She looked up at him, and saw he was glancing toward the open door. "An odd case?"

"You know, small-town stuff. I'm trying to do a thorough investigation, is all." He set down his pen and looked evenly into her eyes. "If there's anything you can share to help me out, I'd appreciate it."

"Well, I'd expected to have something more by now..." She considered her next words. She was about to tell him about Aunt Lenore's box, but suddenly felt cautious. Only moments ago, this Detective Ford had felt like her enemy. Just because he seemed to be softening didn't necessarily mean she could trust him. Perhaps it was best not to divulge too much information. He'd certainly told her nothing she didn't know.

"Something more?" he led.

"I'd hoped that by meeting Jasmine's husband and whatnot—*well*, that I'd find some answers..."

"So, you've met Hal Emery then?" He studied her carefully. She nodded.

"And what did you think of Jasmine's husband?"

"I was a little surprised."

"Surprised?"

"Well, he wasn't exactly the sort of man that I would've imagined someone like Jasmine marrying."

"Why's that?"

"Did you know Jasmine at all?"

He shook his head. "Not in person. Although I feel like I'm getting to know her now."

Her eyes lit up. "Really?"

He nodded. "Yep, and let me tell you, it was one sad little life."

She pointed her finger in the air. "See! That's what makes absolutely no sense. The Jasmine Morrison I knew was beautiful and funny and creative and kind and—" She felt her voice choke again, but determined not to give in to tears. "She was strong and clever and smart—and I just *know* she never would've married someone like Hal Emery of her own free will." Before she had finished that sentence, the detective quickly rose and closed the door. "I'm sorry," she said. "I didn't mean to get so loud."

"That's okay. But you should know that there are certain things that are better left unsaid in this town." He sat down on the edge of his desk and studied her closely.

"So I've heard."

"From whom?"

She pressed her lips together and firmly shook her head.

He nodded knowingly. "I guess you have been asking around."

She felt another part of her guard come down. "But I don't get it. What's going on here? I feel like there's some deep, dark oppression hovering over this place, and I just can't—"

He glanced toward the door again, and then pressed his forefinger to his lips and shook his head. "You grew up in a small town, Judith. I'm sure you know how a small town can be—a little ingrown, you know."

She wanted to say it was more than that—much, much more than that! But she knew he was clueing her into something. And then she remembered what Polly had said about watching who she trusted at the police department. She looked at him carefully, and despite herself, felt he had an honest face. Yet who could tell? She sighed in frustration. "I just don't know what to do."

"Go home."

She bit her lip.

"Go home to your husband, your family, your dog, cat, or whatever. I'm sure you have a happy little life somewhere far, far away from here."

"Don't be so sure."

He stared at her for a long moment, then continued. "Go home, Judith. There's nothing you can do for your friend now. So, why don't you just save yourself a lot of unnecessary heartache and go on back home."

"Look, Detective," she said firmly. "Heartache is something I'm pretty familiar with. And for some reason I can't let go of Jasmine just yet. And if it's all the same to you— and even if it's not—I intend to stick around as long as it takes to find out what in the world happened to her!" She stood up now, her hand poised on the doorknob.

"Suit yourself, then. But don't say I didn't warn you."

"Thanks for nothing!"

And with that, she stormed out of his office, out of the police station, and back into the bright June sunlight. A lot of good that little meeting did! She got into her car and started the engine and prepared to tear right out of the parking lot. But where was she to go? Last night, she'd planned to see Aunt Lenore again and perhaps even stay with her for a few days. But now that seemed highly unlikely. She had no idea where Aunt Lenore had been taken. And by whom? She remembered her promise to Martha that she'd water over there. Perhaps that was the best thing to do. Go and care for Aunt Lenore's beloved garden, and perhaps she might even get to talk with Martha again. Somehow their brief chat had given Judith a faint glimmer of hope. Next to Aunt Lenore, Martha seemed like the most normal person she'd met since returning to Cedar Crest.

After her unsuccessful and somewhat tumultuous meeting with Detective Ford, it felt soothing to be in Aunt Lenore's little backyard, watering her vegetable garden and puttering about pulling weeds. Judith had kept an old-fashioned garden very similar to this in their Victorian house in Vancouver, back before Jonathan had become sick. She'd forgotten how much pleasure tending green, living things had once given her.

"Hello there." called Martha from the other side of the fence. "Is that you, Judith? I thought I saw your little green car out front."

"Yes," answered Judith, coming over to peer beyond the gate where Martha sat comfortably in a chaise lounge on her patio. "I'm watering and whatnot over here. This is such a lovely place, I could stay here all day."

"Any news on Miss Barker yet?"

Judith shook her head. "No, but I plan to do some checking when I finish up here. I just can't imagine anything bad happening to her."

"Well, she's awfully old, dear. Best to prepare yourself for the inevitable."

"I suppose, but I've had so many losses...I just hate to think of another."

"Want to come over and have a glass of iced tea?"

"Oh, that sounds divine." Judith opened the gate and walked over. "But you look comfortable there, and I know your arthritis is bothering you, so why don't you just give me directions and let me get it?"

"Thank you, dear, that would be lovely." Then she told Judith to go right through the dining room and turn left to find the kitchen.

Judith took a moment to examine a beautiful oil painting in the dining room, a landscape of a mountain lake, obviously the work of the late Mr. Anderson. She examined several other nice pieces here and there as she gathered the iced tea and glasses and returned to the patio. "I couldn't help but notice Mr. Anderson's artwork in there. I had no idea he was so talented."

Martha laughed. "He never liked the kids at school to see his work because he was afraid they'd either criticize his amateur efforts, or else feel discouraged that they weren't at that level yet. But in my opinion, he really was a fine painter."

"I agree." Judith took a sip of the tea. "In fact, it might even be inspiring me to pick up a brush again."

"Great, you've gone from considering sketching on to painting in just one day." Martha took a long sip. "Now, tell me, how did you happen to meet Miss Barker? I'm sure you're much too young to have had her as a high school teacher before she retired."

"Yes, you're right. Actually she was my friend's great-aunt."

"Your friend?" Martha's brow raised.

"Yes, uh—Jasmine Morrison—well, Emery. Did you know her?"

Martha set down her glass and cleared her throat. "So, you met Miss Barker through the Morrison family?"

Oh no, thought Judith, realizing she'd let her guard down again. And she could tell by the edge in Martha's voice that it was too late to backtrack. But perhaps she could explain. "Yes, you see, as children, Jasmine and I were best friends, and—"

"Then you must be friends with the Morrisons as well?"

"No, not exactly. We lost touch and—"

"Do you have any idea how Miss Barker felt about the

Morrisons?"

"Well, not exactly. We'd been out of touch since yesterday—"

"And what did you say to her yesterday?"

"Well, not much really, we just talked about my life and what had happened with Jasmine and—"

"Do you think it's possible you may have upset her? Perhaps your visit is what has brought on her sudden illness or whatever it is."

"Oh, but we had a—"

"I can appreciate that my husband was your teacher, Judith, and I am sorry for the loss of your friend. But you should be aware that there are some of us in this town who don't cater to the Morrison family or their ways. And although we may be the minority, we do keep to ourselves and our own opinions."

"But I—"

"And now I'm afraid that I've had a little too much sun and I must be going inside. Just leave your glass on the table out here." Martha pushed herself up from the lounge, the effort causing her glass on the table to fall and splatter into a mess of broken shards across the patio.

Judith jumped up and began to pick up the pieces. "I'm so sorry—"

"Just leave it!" snapped Martha as she went into the house, closing the sliding glass door behind her with a bang.

But Judith continued gathering the broken glass, her hands shaking as she set each piece on the table next to her half-full glass. Then just as she picked up a large, wet, shard, it slid between her fingers and sliced right between her thumb and forefinger, instantly bleeding. Hardly feeling the pain, she pressed her free hand against the wound to stop the blood flow. How had she managed to do such a stupid thing? Somehow she opened the gate and make her way back to the garden, finding the hose. As she washed the blood from her hand, she thought about Martha and how embittered she sounded toward the Morrisons. How could Judith make her understand that she was not friends with them—that she had her own concerns and suspicions about them? She wanted Martha to know that she only wanted to find out what the Morrisons were up to and what sort of influence they'd wielded over Jasmine. She knew that Mr. Morrison had always been extremely racist and bigoted, but she wanted to find out how all this was connected. Because for some reason, Judith felt that it was connected. She just wasn't quite sure how or why.

By now she could tell that her cut was deep enough to require stitches. While applying more pressure, she grabbed a clean tea towel still hanging on the back porch line and firmly wrapped it around her now-throbbing hand. She hoped she could find her way to the hospital before she lost much blood.

Eleven

IT'S TOO DARK IN here. And I think I hear spiders crawling down that wall, or maybe it's them other bugs—them big, brown, shiny ones that rattle across the floor so fast when you walk into the room. Maybe if I wrap myself up real tight and make myself into a little ball, then maybe they'll all forget about me and just leave me alone. Alone. Alone. Always alone. But I don't wanna be alone.

Well, then maybe I'll just make friends with them bugs, maybe they can help me get out of this bad place. This bad dark place I hate so much. I'm scared. Miss Molly downstairs says that when I'm scared I should talk to God. She says he's always listening to his children. But I'm not so sure he can hear me.

Oh, God, why do I have to stay here with these people that hate me so bad? Can you hear me, God? Can you see me here all by myself? Hiding in all this dark? I'm hiding in the closet, God, just until their voices stop yelling. Can you see your little Pearl? My mama used to call me that. And I don't care what Carmen and Larry say, I do so have a mama. I know it. And I remember how much my mama loved me. And if I think real hard, I can still see her pretty face inside my head, "cepting it's all kinda blurry and fuzzy like. But where is she,

God? Where'd my mama go? And when's she coming back to get me and take me back home with her? And why'd she leave me here? And does she know that Carmen is mean to me? I want my mama back, God. Do you think that if I'm very, very, very good, and if I don't make Carmen mad no more, do you think that I could have my mama back? Old Miss Molly downstairs says that if I be good enough, I won't get them whuppings no more. And I try and I try to be good, but I just can't never seem to get it right.

I wish Carmen would quit screaming at Larry. Not 'cause I like him much, 'cause I don't. I don't even care if he does act all nice sometimes, or even that he gives me candy, 'cause the rest of the time he makes me feel real scared. Carmen says he's only bad when he needs his fix, but I think he's bad all the time. And sometimes I think Carmen might not be so mean to me if harry just went away and never came back. But Carmen says that without Larry we wouldn't have no roof over our head or nothing to eat. Most of the time we don't got much to eat anyway, and that white stuff always falls off the ceiling every time them people upstairs start to clomp around. So if you ask me, Larry ain't doing such a great job there neither. And besides, I heard him and Carmen talking once about some kind of money Carmen gets to take care of me. So I'm thinking I just might be the one who's doing most of the helping out here. I don't know nothing for sure. But I'm thinking maybe my mama is sending money to Carmen for me—not that I ever seen any of it myself

Even when I put my hands over my ears, I can still hear their voices screaming and yelling at each other—using those words that Miss Molly says are nasty bad. Hearing them going on and on like this makes me feel all sick inside of my stomach. Just like getting your innards all squashed flatter than a balloon that won't hold air no more. And sometimes I worry that Larry is going to get so mad at Carmen that he'll just take out his gun (and he's got himself a big gun) and just shoot Carmen dead— kabam! And then what'll I do? A boy named Lemuel, 'cross the street, got shot dead. But I heard Sharista say her brother Sam's gonna, shoot that kid who killed Lemuel. Sharista lives right next door to Miss Molly, and she's the only real kid I ever get to play with 'cause Carmen don't never let me go outside on the street, not without getting a really bad whupping, that is. Sharista is nine years old and goes to real school. Her eyes are crossed, and Carmen says she's retarded, but I think she's real nice, and aside from Miss Molly, she's my only friend.

Miss Molly says the reason Carmen and Larry fight all the time is "cause they be living in sin. I asked her what sin is ('cause I figure I must be living there too since we live in the same place). And she told me sin is real bad. So, I guess I was right, "cause it's real bad here. But I don't like living in sin none. And I sure wanna go live someplace else. Most of all I wanna go live with my mama, "cause I know she still loves me. And I miss her.

Miss Molly downstairs says that when I feel lonely I should pray to you. And that's why I started all this praying business in the first place. But I'm just not sure you're listening, God, "cause nothing never seems to change "round here—except for maybe getting worse is all, like tonight. And I'm also getting real worried that I won't even get to go to school in the fall. Carmen keeps telling me that I'm too stupid and they don't let stupid girls like me go to school (although that don't make sense, "cause she says that Sharista is stupid too, and she goes to school). But Miss Molly says Carmen's wrong and that I'm real smart. I think that maybe Carmen just don't want to let me out of this stinking apartment—ever! I don't know why she hates me so much. I try and be nice to her, but I know she hates me. And sometimes when she look at me, I think maybe she'd like to kill me. But then she wouldn't get no more of that money that my mama sends her for me. God, can't you please, please, pretty please with sugar on top, help me?

Twelve

THE HOSPITAL WAS JUST where it had always been; south of town, just on the outskirts. Other than a new wing that really didn't look all that new, nothing appeared to have changed since the last time she'd been there nearly thirty years before. She parked in the nearly empty parking lot and walked calmly into the emergency room. It did seem slightly modernized and updated since the time she'd broken her arm in eighth grade. That had been just before Jasmine's family moved back to Mississippi. The two girls had been swimming down at the quarry and playing on the big rope swing, and somehow Judith had tangled her arm in the rope just as she was trying to drop off, which resulted in a loud snap and more pain than she cared to remember. But Jasmine had jumped into the water and rescued her, then run up to the road sopping wet, yelling and screaming until she finally flagged down an old pickup truck full of teenage boys who took them both to the hospital.

"Can I help you?"

Judith held up her throbbing hand still wrapped in the tea towel with blood just beginning to seep through. "I think I need stitches," she explained somewhat sheepishly.

"Can you fill out these forms?" asked the woman, pushing a clipboard her way.

"Not very well. I have an insurance card in my purse. Maybe you could reach in there and get it for me."

The woman fumbled through her purse until she found the wallet, then dug through the wallet until she located the card. Just then, Judith began to feel slightly woozy. "I.. .uh...better sit down." she said as the woman took the card back to the copy machine.

"Yeah, sure. Over there."

Judith sat down and managed to fill out the form with a shaky hand. She could think of no one when she reached the spot for an emergency number, and so she left it blank. She stared for a long moment at that white, empty space. Who would she want contacted in the event of a real emergency? Her mother was out of the country, and she could think of no one else who would care very much. Finally, her pen still held in midair, she was interrupted by a nurse and then led to an examining room.

Perched on the paper-covered examining table, she felt just like that long ago six-year-old who'd stepped on a nail—in pain, but ashamed of her foolishness. Perhaps she had overreacted. Perhaps she didn't even need stitches. But just as she opened the towel to take a peek, an elderly man came in. "How's it look?" he asked in a cheerful voice.

"Not so good." She looked up and made a face. "I think I might need some stitches."

He examined the cut more closely. "Yep, I'll have to concur with you there."

She peered at him curiously. "Dr. Warner?"

He grinned over his bifocals. "Yes, that's me. Do I know you?"

She smiled. "I used to be Judith McPhearson. Now I'm Judith

Blackwell. You used to take care of me and my mom."

"Of course, I remember you, Judith. How's that arm?"

"Fine, thanks. I'm surprised you're still practicing."

He grinned. "I keep thinking I'm about to retire, but then I don't know what I'll do with myself if I do." As he spoke, he cleaned the cut.

"So, you work at the hospital now?"

"Just one day a week. They're a little shorthanded over here."

"Do you still have your office in Cedar Crest?"

"Nooo, no, not for years. Now, hang on there, this'll hurt a little." He gave her a shot to numb her hand. "I live and practice in Jasper now."

"Oh, that seems like a nice little town."

He nodded, then began to stitch up her cut. "It's a good place to live."

Looking the other way, so she wouldn't feel faint again, she breathed deeply and focused her eyes on a colorful poster of a tropical bird on the wall. "I just can't believe I did this."

"What's that?"

"I mean cutting my hand on a stupid piece of glass. Pretty dumb."

He laughed. "We all have accidents, Judith. Now, tell me what brings you into our neck of the woods anyway?"

She briefly explained about Jasmine, preparing herself in case he suddenly turned cold and harsh, as others had done. But to her pleased surprise he didn't even blink. "Yes, I heard all about that. So sad." He took another slow stitch. "So very sad."

"And so shocking," added Judith. "At least to me. I never would've thought she'd do something like that. But then I hadn't seen her in years."

"Hatred has such devastating results."

"Hatred? But I never knew Jasmine to hate anyone or

anything."

"I don't mean Jasmine personally. But those around her, you know."
He finished tying off the last stitch. "There, that ought to do you. But
let's have the nurse come and give you a tetanus booster and then wrap
this up."

"By those around her, do you mean her dad?" she asked, hoping
to extract as much information as possible from the kind doctor.

He nodded sadly. "Yes, her father and others like him." Then
he lowered his voice. "There's bad blood in this town, Judith. That's
why the wife and I finally had to move on. As much as we loved
Cedar Crest and wanted to see things change, we could no longer
sit by and watch what was happening all around us."

"You mean the racist influence?" she whispered back.

He nodded grimly. "It's like an incurable disease."

"But couldn't you and others like you do anything about it?"

"We really tried for a while. But we were outnumbered, and
it turned into an uphill battle, often against forces we couldn't
even put our finger on. And then too many good people just started
giving up and moving away—a number of them to Jasper. Finally,
for the sake of our own loved ones, we decided to cut our losses
and move on too. We figured perhaps in time things would
either return to normal or the town would just dry up and blow
away."

"Well, it's pretty dried up, but it hasn't blown away yet."

He shook his head, then glanced at his watch. "Too bad. And
too bad about your friend Jasmine too. Well, I've got to get upstairs
and check on a gallbladder patient now. But you take care, you hear,
and stay away from sharp objects."

She smiled. "Thanks, Doc. Good to see you again."

After the nurse finished, Judith decided to go to the main
entrance and see if Aunt Lenore might possibly be in the hospital

somewhere.

"No," said the woman at the front desk, "I show no record of a Lenore Barker having been admitted."

"Are there any nursing homes or elderly care centers in town?" asked Judith.

"Well, there's Green Hill." said the woman. "It's over by the high school. It's a home for elderly people who are still fairly mobile. And then there's Crest View—that's more of a full-care facility. It's just down the road a ways." She pointed south. "About two miles down the highway."

Judith decided to stop by Crest View to look for Aunt Lenore. And if she had no luck there, she'd go on to check at Green Hill. She remembered when they'd first built that nursing home. It had been the talk of the town, and her mother had even considered moving Judith's grandmother there at one time. When Judith reached Crest View, she wondered if it might not have been better to phone ahead first because the area was fenced and gated and didn't look very welcoming. But the electronic gates opened automatically, so she just drove in. She inquired at the desk and a friendly girl searched on her computer and confirmed that a Miss Lenore Barker had indeed been admitted just last night.

"Oh, I'm so relieved to have found her," exclaimed Judith. "We were having the best visit just yesterday, and I had no idea she was unwell. Do you think I could see her now?"

"I don't know why not."

"Do you know why she was admitted?"

"It says here that it was respiratory problems, but her condition is listed as good now. So she must be feeling better. She's in room 34. Right down that hallway, then take a left."

"Thank you." Judith followed the directions, pleased at her good luck, and eager to see Aunt Lenore again. She could tell her that she had watered her garden for her. "Hello?" she called quietly as she entered the room. "Aunt Lenore?" She saw someone in a bed by the window, but other than the wisps of white hair, the lifeless, shrunken form didn't seem anything like the lively woman she'd seen just yesterday. Her eyes were closed, and she was so still that, at first, Judith thought she might actually have died. But finally she noticed the fragile chest moving up and down, but just barely. Obviously, she was in a deep sleep. Judith hated to wake her, but at the same time felt worried for Aunt Lenore's welfare. Perhaps she was sicker than the girl at the front desk knew. Although a respirator was next to the bed, it was not hooked up.

Judith sat down in the chair next to the bed and wondered what to do. Finally, she simply took the old woman's hand in her own and began to pray a silent, wordless prayer. She felt slightly strange doing so, but at the same time oddly compelled—as if someone other than herself were leading her. After a few minutes, she felt the frail, old hand give hers a slight squeeze, and she looked down to see Aunt Lenore's eyes fluttering open. But she still looked groggy.

"Jasmine?" her speech sounded slightly slurred.

"No, Aunt Lenore, it's Judith. Remember me?"

She nodded slightly. "Judith, yes, Judith."

"Are you all right?"

"All right," she repeated groggily.

"I was worried about you."

Her eyes clouded. "Worried."

"What happened? How did you get here?"

She frowned now and shook her head slightly, as if she were trying to keep herself awake. "Burt and..."

"Burt Morrison brought you here?"

"I want.. .to go home."

"I know you do. But are you sick, Aunt Lenore?"

"Not sick..." She closed her eyes again and sighed. "Home."

"I watered your garden and your flowers for you."

Aunt Lenore's grip tightened on Judith's hand. "Good. Good girl."

"How can I help you, Aunt Lenore?"

"Help me..." She repeated the words slowly, her eyes still closed.

"Yes, I want to help you. What can I do?"

"Help me." This time it sounded like a real plea, but Judith couldn't be sure.

"What can I do to help you?"

"Home...."

"I don't think they will let me take you home, Aunt Lenore. But I can take care of your garden for you until you're well enough to come home. And I can come visit you. Would that make you happy?"

She opened her eyes and this time looked a little less groggy. "Yes. Take care of my garden, Judith."

"I will. And you must take care to get well."

"Yes. Well." She sighed deeply, then frowned as if she were struggling to think of something. "Judith?"

"Yes?"

"Birdhouse." She closed her eyes again.

"Birdhouse?" Judith wondered if Aunt Lenore had possibly suffered a stroke or something that had diminished her mental abilities, and yet her facial features looked even and normal. Perhaps she was just heavily sedated. But why?

"Home." Aunt Lenore pointed a wrinkled finger at Judith.

"You want me to go home?"

Her eyes lit up. "My home."

"You want me to *stay* in your home?" Judith hoped she wasn't reading too much into this conversation, but it was difficult to understand.

"Yes, stay—"

"What's going on here?" demanded a sharp voice.

Judith turned to see a uniformed nurse walk in. "Hello, I'm—"

"Who let you in here?" demanded the nurse.

"I thought it was okay—"

"Well, it's not. Miss Barker is to have no visitors. She's in serious condition. We may have to move her to the hospital if she doesn't improve soon."

"Oh, I'm so sorry. She's a good friend and—"

"Makes no difference. You'll have to go."

Judith gave Aunt Lenore's hand a last gentle squeeze. "Take care, Aunt Lenore. I'll do what you say. And remember I love you." Then feeling like a reprimanded child, she quickly made her way out of the room without looking back at the formidable nurse.

She drove slowly back toward town, thinking once again how she felt like Alice on the other side of the looking glass. Nothing made sense. And she was starting to feel like an emotional basket case again. Tired, confused, hungry, she didn't even know where she would be sleeping tonight. She hardly knew what she was doing or even why. She felt as if she'd come on a fool's errand and was only making matters worse by sticking around. It seemed that whatever emotional energy had originally propelled her along had long since run out, because she was running on empty now. At this moment, she felt so weary and exhausted, she didn't even care if she slept in her car for the night. She considered just pulling off the road and napping—escaping the crazi-ness of everything for a while, and then perhaps figuring it all out later, if that were even possible.

With her bandaged hand throbbing, she parked on a wide shoulder next to the road, and for the third time that day, she prayed. But now all she could say was, "Help me, God. Please, help me." And then she leaned her head back, and closing her eyes, tried to relax. She breathed in and out deeply and slowly, willing herself to think of nothing for the next few minutes.

When she finally opened her eyes she felt slightly better. She placed both hands on the steering wheel and suddenly remembered what Dr. Warner had said about Jasper—how it was a good place to be. The sign ahead said it was only twenty miles away. She knew she could get a decent meal there, and if she were lucky, perhaps even find a clean motel for the night, giving herself a chance to relax and regroup and figure some things out.

And as it turned out, she did better than that. She found the Pine Lodge Resort, located just outside of Jasper, complete with quiet riverside rooms, a lovely restaurant, swimming pool, and a hot tub. A little expensive, perhaps, but she could easily afford it. And she felt fairly certain she couldn't afford not to. After a delicious meal, she fell into the comfortable queen-sized bed, utterly spent. For the following day, she did little but relax, swim in the pool, eat good food, and sleep. But when she called Cedar View to check on Aunt Lenore, she was informed that Miss Barker was to have no visitors. The following day, Judith decided to return to Cedar Crest again. And her first stop was at Polly's.

"Hey there, Judith." said Polly. "I thought you'd gone home without even telling me goodbye."

"No, I just moved over to the Pine Lodge Resort for a bit."

"Wow, lifestyles of the rich and famous, eh?"

"I just needed a little rest." Judith glanced around the shop to see only one woman, and she was under the dryer reading a magazine. "Got time for an appointment?"

"Appointment for what?" Polly frowned suspiciously, then lowered her voice. "You know I can't really talk now."

Judith smiled. "I just want a haircut."

"A haircut? But you just had one."

"I know. But now I want it all cut off. Short."

"Short? But your hair is so pretty long."

Judith shrugged. "I don't care. I decided it's just a bother like this. I want it cut like Jas—" she stopped herself before she said the name. "Like I used to wear it as a kid. It was so easy to take care of then."

Polly shook her head, then pointed to the chair. "Go ahead if you want, it's your hair. Now, you're sure?"

"I'm sure." Judith leaned back and closed her eyes, relaxing a little more with each snip-snip of the scissors. And before she knew it Polly announced that the deed was done.

"And, you know, it doesn't look half bad either," commented Polly as she spun the chair around for Judith to see the mirror.

Judith reached up to touch her short dark locks. "Wow, that really looks different."

Polly smiled. "It looks fantastic, Judith. I swear, you look at least ten years younger. And I just love how all that wave frames your face. Very pretty. I don't know why you didn't think of this a long time ago."

Judith tossed her a sideways glance. "Hey, and you were the one trying to talk me out of it."

Polly laughed. "Well, I guess I was wrong. You look great."

Judith glanced over to the woman still under the dryer then spoke quietly. "And do you think I look a little less like Jasmine now?"

Polly nodded. "Definitely."

"Good." This time, she paid and even left a nice tip. "Thanks, Polly. You did a great job."

"It's just like I used to cut it when you were a kid."

After her one day of rest and the new haircut, Judith felt surprisingly invigorated. And now she even had a plan. Or at least the beginnings of a plan. At this point, she'd just have to take it a day at a time and see what unfolded. But to start with she intended to pay a visit to Aunt Lenore's. And there she would search for a birdhouse.

Thirteen

AUNT LENORE HAD A number of wooden birdhouses and bird feeders spotted throughout her backyard, but Judith decided to ignore them for the moment and proceed with the watering. The vegetable garden was looking somewhat wilted from its previous hot day of neglect, but a good soaking perked it up. It was only after the plants were all cared for that Judith went from birdhouse to birdhouse until she finally came to the faded red one not far from the back porch. And there she found exactly what she'd been looking for. A key! And, just as she'd imagined, it unlocked the back door. She tried to suppress her feeling of being a trespasser as she entered the quaint little kitchen. For she felt certain this was what Aunt Lenore had been trying to communicate to her from her hospital bed. Still, she wasn't sure why. Did Aunt Lenore want Judith to actually stay in her home and take care of things until she could return? Or was she worried that Judith had no place to stay? Or perhaps, and this was what brought Judith here today, she wanted her to find that box that Jasmine had left behind. And so Judith began to search the spare bedroom.

She looked in all the expected places, the closet, the bureau, beneath the bed. The small, tidy room had only a few places to hide a box. Of course, she had no idea how big or small this particular box might be or even what it looked like. Still, after half an hour of going through everything, she had found no box. She sat down on the bed to think. If it was true that Burt Morrison had taken Aunt Lenore to the nursing home—and Judith wasn't even sure about this as Aunt Lenore seemed somewhat confused— but if he'd actually been in Aunt Lenore's house, was it possible that he might also have taken the box? But then *why?* And why would he take his wife's aunt to a nursing home? Had she really been sick? Or was something else going on? And just where was Mrs. Morrison in all this? Were they both now staying in their house, the one that had been vacant just days ago? Or was Judith simply imagining things now, and becoming unrealistically suspicious?

Finally, she decided to lock up Aunt Lenore's house and drive over by the Morrisons' to look around and see if Jasmine's parents were really back in town. After that, she'd head back over to Crest View and see if that nice receptionist might possibly allow her to see Aunt Lenore again. Or perhaps, if she were feeling really brave, she'd just sneak in. What could they do to her anyway? Arrest her? And if they did, she could show that know-it-all Detective Ford that perhaps she was the sort of woman who could get herself into police trouble after all.

✦✦✦

BUT AFTER WHAT SEEMED a completely wasted afternoon (the Morrison house still looked vacant and the nice receptionist was not at the front desk and Judith could not sneak past the hawkeyed man who'd replaced her), she returned, in defeat, to the Pine Lodge Resort and bought a glossy magazine to take out and read by the pool. But even so, she couldn't simply let go and relax. Finally, after running everything she'd seen and heard during the past few days over and over through her mind, she decided her only course of action would be to have another conversation with Detective Ford. Only this time she wouldn't let him get to her. She felt certain he had information about Jasmine that she wanted, but for some reason he'd tried to discourage her that day. Perhaps it was because the police station wasn't the best place to talk. Like Polly had suggested, too many watchful eyes and eavesdropping ears around there. Just the same, Judith wasn't entirely sure she could trust that detective. She'd need to play it safe with him, keeping her cards close to her chest as Peter used to say when he first began practicing law. Right now she longed for Peter's analytical mind. She remembered how he used to get out his yellow legal pad and start making a great long list, then he'd cross some things off, and put other things on. Perhaps that's what she needed to do herself.

She found a small stationary shop in Jasper, and there she bought a legal pad as well as some sketching materials, then returned to her room where she began to make lists. Lists of people, lists of all her unanswered questions, lists of her suspicions, lists of all information she had that was relevant to Jasmine. On and on she went until it felt as if her brain had been drained. And then she got out the phone book and looked to see if Adam Ford's home phone number was listed. But of course it was not. She knew he was new in town. She then tried information, and to her surprise was given a number and was immediately connected.

"Hello?" answered a deep voice.

"Uh, yes, is this Adam Ford?"

"Who's this?"

"I'm sorry to bother you at home—this is Judith Blackwell, we met the other day in Cedar—"

"Yeah, sure, I remember you, Judith. But where are you?"

She grew suspicious. "Uh, what do you mean?"

"I mean, you left town, right? But you didn't go home, did you."

Now she felt nervous. "How did you know that?"

"Well, if you're at home, you're not answering your phone. And besides, I have Caller ID, which I am just now looking at." He paused. "And it says you're calling from the Pine Lodge Resort. You staying there?"

"No," she lied, her heart starting to pound. "I just stopped for dinner. It's a nice enough place to stay, but a little too rich for my blood."

"Oh, well, where've you been then?"

"Around."

"Well, I thought you'd taken my advice and gone home like a good little girl."

She felt her chest tighten in anger. "Look, Detective, as far as I know it's still a free country, and I will come and go as I please."

"Yeah, yeah. But you ought to be careful. Now, you want to tell me why you're calling me?"

"Yes," she took a breath. "I'm sorry to bother you at home, but I wondered if we could get together and talk."

"Talk?"

"Yes, but I was thinking not at the police station."

He chuckled. "You asking me out, Judith?"

She bristled. "No, no, nothing like that. I just thought we could talk, you know, maybe exchange some information."

"You have information?"

"I might."

"When do you suggest we have this little talk?"

"I was hoping soon."

"How about now?" He paused. "Did you say you've already

had your dinner?"

"Well, not yet. I was just going in."

"Why don't I meet you there? I could be there by six-thirty. That is, unless you don't want to wait or unless you have a problem sharing a meal with a cop."

"No, that's okay." She looked down at her shorts and T-shirt, knowing she needed to change first anyway. "I don't mind waiting."

"Good. I'll be there as quickly as I can."

Judith hung up and looked through her sparse closet for something that looked presentable to wear to dinner. Not that she wanted to impress this surly detective, but at the same time she didn't like the idea of him looking down on her either. And, although she hated to admit it, he was awfully good looking, even if his manners were somewhat lacking. Finally she settled on a khaki skirt that needed a good pressing. She got out the iron and set to work with a vengeance. This, she paired with a black T-shirt and some sandals. She knew the outfit needed a bit of jewelry, but in her haste of packing, she had naturally neglected to bring anything. Then she remembered the resort's gift shop where she'd purchased her bathing suit. They had an interesting rack of earrings down there. Perhaps she'd give them a quick look while she waited.

After purchasing a pair of handsome silver hoops, Judith proceeded to the restaurant to wait. But to her surprise, he was already there waiting for her. "I thought maybe you'd run out on me," he said when he spotted her coming his way.

"Sorry, I was just killing time at the gift shop." She glanced at her watch. "You must've driven fast."

"I'm a cop," he said with a sly smile. "If I get stopped for speeding, I just flash 'em my ID."

"How convenient." She didn't like the sarcastic edge in her voice, but this man just seemed to bring out the ire in her.

"What happened to your hand?" He pointed to the bandage.

"Oh, I cut it. Had to get a few stitches. No big deal."

"Well, you ready to eat now?"

She nodded, determined to be nicer. "Sure. The food is pretty good here."

"You've eaten here before?"

She caught herself, remembering that he didn't know she was staying at the resort. "Yes, when I first came to Cedar Crest, my cousin and I came over to Jasper to eat." Not exactly a lie.

"You have a cousin around here?"

She grimaced. This guy didn't miss a thing. "Yes, actually it's my mom's cousin."

"It?"

"Table for two?" asked the hostess.

"Yes, please," said Judith, forcing a laugh as they were led to a table. Once seated, she turned to Adam. "You sure ask a lot of questions."

He shrugged. "I'm a detective, it's what I do."

"Well, how about if we take turns. Question for a question."

"What about the answers?"

"Answer for an answer."

He stuck out his hand. "Deal."

She shook his hand then smiled. "My turn now."

"Fine, shoot away."

She thought for a minute, unsure of the best place to begin. But worried that she might not get far, she decided to ask the most troublesome question first. "After investigating Jasmine's death, are you absolutely certain that it was really suicide?"

His brows shot up. "Well, you don't beat around the bush, do you?"

"Answer for an answer."

"Am I certain that Jasmine killed herself? No, I'm not certain."

Judith nodded. "I knew it."

"But," he continued, "do I think someone else did it? No, not necessarily. You see, Judith, as an investigator, I have to keep an open mind. Maybe she did. Maybe she didn't."

Judith frowned. "That's not very much help."

"Just being honest. Okay, now it's my turn. How long are you planning on sticking around?"

"I don't know."

"That's not a very good answer."

She smiled. "Just being honest."

The waiter came to take their orders. Judith ordered the grilled salmon, and to her surprise, Adam ordered the same. She took a sip of water, then studied him for a moment. "Okay, it's my turn again. Where was Jasmine living before she came back to Cedar Crest and married Hal Emery?"

"Hmm, you're good," said Adam. "She was living in Seattle."

"Seattle?" repeated Judith. "What was she doing up there?"

He shook his finger at her. "No, you don't; it's my turn now." Then, after pausing a moment, as if to think: "Do you consider yourself a strong person, Judith?"

She blinked. "Is that your question?"

He nodded.

"Strong? What do you mean exactly?"

"Well, I don't mean as in lifting weights. I mean as in character, will, determination?" He eyed her carefully. "Do you consider yourself very strong in those ways?"

She didn't know how to answer him. *Strong?* Was she strong? "I'm not totally sure. To be honest, if you'd asked me this question a couple weeks ago, I'd have said, "Definitely not.' But just lately I've begun to feel a little stronger, or more driven. But why are you asking me that?"

"Is that your next question?"

She wondered if she wanted to waste a question on that, but then knew she would be troubled by this if she didn't. "Yes, I suppose that's my next question."

He nodded. "Good one."

Just then the waitress came and set their salads on the table. Then after she left, Adam bowed his head as if to pray. Judith stared at him in wonder. This hardened and tough-talking cop actually prayed over his food? Embarrassed, she too bowed her head, unsure of what she was supposed to do, but when she peeked up, she saw that he had apparently finished and was already picking up his salad fork. She did likewise, unable to speak.

"Now, in answer to your question." he began. "Why do I want to know if you're a strong person?"

She nodded, then took a bite of salad, glad to have the conversation continue, but still perplexed at the picture in her mind of this guy bowing his head over his food.

"Because I happen to know that you've been through a lot in recent years. Lost a son to cancer." He looked directly into her eyes. "I'm sorry. Then you lost your husband in a plane wreck. Then you discover your best friend has died under what seems, to you, mysterious circumstances. And then you come back to Cedar Crest, and the first time I meet you, you literally fall apart in my office."

She had tried to forget that little episode at the police station and didn't appreciate him bringing it up now. "I'm sorry about that. I guess I was a little stressed."

He nodded. "Yeah, you looked it." Then he smiled. "By the way, nice haircut."

Once again caught off guard, she thanked him. "But you still haven't answered my question. Why do you care about whether I'm strong, as you put it, or not?"

He slowly buttered a piece of bread, then finally continued. "Because I want to know if you're able to handle what's going on around here. Are you able to make it through the long haul, or are you going to fall apart and mess things up worse than they already are?"

"Mess things up?"

"Yeah, Judith, you're swimming in some pretty deep waters right now, whether you realize it or not. I just want to know if you're really made of the right stuff to make it.

And if you're not, I'd suggest you go back to your safe little apartment and forget all about Cedar Crest."

"My safe little apartment?" She studied his face. "You seem to know an awful lot about me, Detective. I'd like to know why and maybe even how."

He shook his head. "You're breaking the rules, Judith. It's my turn to ask you a question."

"Fine." She frowned. "Ask away."

"Then I'll go back to my earlier question. But this time I won't accept "I don't know' as an answer. So, tell me, just how strong are you, Judith?"

She felt relieved to see the waitress returning with their entrées now, buying her some time. How strong was she? She'd like to know the answer to this herself. Finally the waitress finished up by refilling their water glasses and then departed.

"This looks good," said Judith as she forked her tender piece of salmon.

"Delicious," he answered after finishing a bite.

After a brief spell of quietly eating, Judith knew she needed to answer his question. "I'm not sure how to measure how strong I am," she began slowly. "I feel stronger than I've felt since losing my husband. Yet in many ways I still feel pretty weak. To be perfectly honest, I'm just not sure. Can you accept that as an answer?"

He swallowed a bite and nodded. "Guess it'll have to do for now. Your turn."

"Okay, what was Jasmine doing in Seattle?"

"Well, it hasn't been easy tracking down her whereabouts up there. Seems she was trying to keep a pretty low profile."

"Why?"

"Uh-uh," he pointed his fork at her playfully. "Not your turn."

She smiled. "Sorry. Go ahead."

"How committed are you to finding out the truth about Jasmine? Say on a scale of one to ten. One being mildly curious and ten being you're willing to die to know."

"Good question." She carefully considered this. "I'd say around nine."

"Nine? That's pretty committed."

"I almost said ten, but I was trying to be realistic. But to be completely honest, I feel a strange compulsion to get to the bottom of this whole thing. Whatever it takes. It's as if Jasmine herself is compelling me to find out the truth about her. I think I told you about our childhood friendship, about being blood sisters and all that."

"Yeah, I had some good childhood friends too, but I'm not sure I'd be willing to go to the mat to find out what happened to them the way you seem to be."

"Well, Jasmine was very special to me. Besides that, my curiosity about her is probably what saved me from—" Judith stopped, surprised at what she had nearly disclosed.

"Saved you from what?"

"Is that really your next question?"

"Yeah, if you don't mind."

Judith set down her fork, caught off guard by his apparent, and unexpected, sensitivity about all this. But perhaps he already knew the truth anyway. He seemed to know so much about her. "Well, in a way, she sort of saved me from myself. Saved me from giving up completely."

He nodded. "You were feeling pretty low then?"

"Just about at the end of my rope."

"That can be tough. I'm sorry."

"Thanks. It's a place I'd rather not go to again." She forced a small smile. "So, looks like it's my turn to ask. Why do you think Jasmine was trying to keep a low profile, as you say, before she moved back to Cedar Crest?"

"My guess is to avoid contact with her family."

"Even her sister, Constance?"

"That's two questions in a row, Judith, but I'll give that one to you. Constance is dead."

Judith frowned. "Dead?"

He held up three fingers as if keeping score. "Natural causes. About a year ago."

"The poor Morrisons. Losing both daughters. How sad."

"Okay, my turn. How is your relationship with Jasmine's parents?"

"I haven't seen them since we were kids."

"How was it then?"

"Okay, I guess. Of course, I didn't agree with Mr. Morrison's views. But in order to remain friends with Jasmine, I kept my mouth shut around him." She felt her cheeks redden in shame.

He held up one finger. "I think I still have one question left," he began, then looked her directly in the eyes. "Would you consider yourself to be racist, Judith?"

She felt herself draw back. "No! Of course not. Not at all. That was probably the hardest part about my friendship with Jasmine. And I suspect if the Morrisons hadn't moved during junior high school, it might have eventually ruined our friendship altogether. I suppose it was a blessing in a way that they left when they did. It allowed us both to remember our friendship in the sweet frame of childhood and young adolescence."

He nodded. "I guess that makes sense. And I happen to know that you've taught in a mostly black inner-city school for the past several years. So I really didn't think you were racist, but I just wanted to hear it from you."

"I see. Okay, here's my next question. What can you tell me about Jasmine's parents, these days—are they still in Mississippi?"

"Nice move, asking several questions in the form of one." He smiled. "Okay, the Morrisons...they own homes in both Cedar Crest and Jackson, Mississippi. During the early seventies, they lived in Mississippi, renting their Cedar Crest home. Then in 1976 they moved back over to Cedar Crest. Just the parents and Constance. Jasmine had gone off on her own by then."

"College?"

He shook his head. "Not that I've found any record of."

"Too bad. She was really smart."

The waitress began clearing their table now, and to Judith's dismay she realized the meal was over. Adam glanced at his watch. "I suppose I should let you be getting on your way. May I ask where you're staying these days? Or perhaps you're heading home?"

For some reason, she no longer distrusted him as much. But at the same time questioned whether that was wise or not. She also realized how many questions she'd not had time to ask. "You may as well know that I'm staying here," she admitted.

He smiled. "I thought so."

"Okay, let me ask you one more question. What brings a sharp detective like you to a little hole-in-the-wall town like Cedar Crest?"

He grinned. "You're good. Well, you see the government has implemented a new program to help disperse more experienced law officers to smaller towns. I was becoming a little jaded about big-city life, and so I decided to take a break and try small-town living for a while."

"And how do you like it?"

His mouth twisted up on one side. "Actually, there are some things I really like. And unfortunately there are lots of others I don't."

"Yeah, I know what you mean."

"Look, Judith, I really want to continue this conversation, but I have some things I need to take care of tonight. Do you think we could meet again?"

"Sure. I have lots more questions."

"So do I. Maybe we should make a list."

"I already have."

"Good for you," He picked up the check.

"Let me pay for mine." insisted Judith.

"Nah, this one's on me."

"But—"

"You should know better than to argue with a cop."

She held up her hands. "Fine, go ahead then. I don't want to wind up in jail."

He grinned. "Smart."

They agreed to meet at the same time, same place tomorrow, then said good night. As Judith walked back to her room, she wondered if perhaps she'd been all wrong about him in the first place. Or could it be that he was just trying to win her over so that he could extract more information? She wasn't sure, but somehow it didn't worry her too much. What did worry her was spending too many more nights at this expensive resort. Perhaps she could get in to see Aunt Lenore tomorrow, and find out if the old woman had really intended for her to stay in her home or not. That option was looking better all the time.

Fourteen

"LENORE BARKER IS NO longer here." said the woman at the front desk.

"Has she gone home then?" asked Judith hopefully.

She looked down at her computer screen then spoke. "I'm not allowed to give out any personal information regarding our patients."

Judith frowned. "But she's a very dear friend and—"

"I'm sorry." The woman turned away, obviously finished with their brief conversation.

Judith went back to her car and decided to head over to Aunt Lenore's house and see for herself. Maybe she'd find the old woman back at home, happily tending her garden. Judith had checked out of her room at the resort this morning, unsure of where she would stay next, but Aunt Lenore's house was an option she still considered. And the more she'd thought about it, the more certain she felt that this was what the old woman had been trying to say. Still, she wondered, what if Aunt Lenore had taken a turn for the worse? What if she had died even? "Oh, please, God, not that." She prayed as she turned down Aunt Lenore's street. "Please, let her be okay."

She pulled into the narrow driveway. The house still had an abandoned look to it, and she strongly suspected that Aunt Lenore was not here. Just the same, she knocked loudly on the door and waited, glancing over her shoulder in case Martha might be around. She longed for a second chance to speak to her, to explain that although Judith had been friends with Jasmine, other than sweet Aunt Lenore she had no real connections to the Morrison family. But Martha was nowhere in sight. So Judith proceeded to the back door, taking a moment to glance once again over the gate into Martha's yard, but all was quiet and still over there. She knocked on the back door now, then unlocked it and let herself into the house. She called, "Aunt Lenore, are you here?" but only heard silence against the exterior sound of a feisty blue jay screeching in the backyard.

"Well, Aunt Lenore." she said aloud to no one in particular. "I shall take you up on your gracious invitation and stay here for a while." She smiled at herself, pleased at her decision. She felt fairly certain that Aunt Lenore would be pleased as well. She looked through the refrigerator and cupboards, threw out several spoiled things, washed a few dishes and cleaned up, then made a quick list of some provisions she might need to keep her for a few days. Then she locked everything up and started to drive over to the grocery store. On her way, she decided to go through her old neighborhood once more, wanting another glimpse of her childhood home. As she drove down her old street, she noticed a U-Haul truck parked right in front of the old Paxton place. She slowed down for a better look, wondering what kind of people might be moving into Eli's old house, when she observed a tall man in the driveway, carrying a large cardboard box. But what really caught her attention was the color of his skin—a rich hue of burnished bronze. She pulled her car to a stop and studied this man more carefully. To her stunned amazement, he looked so much like Mr. Paxton that she thought she must be hallucinating. Yet surely, Mr. Paxton would be in his seventies by now. Then it occurred to her— *Eli!* She jumped out of her car, and quickly made her way to him, yet even in the same moment, questioned herself as to whether she was simply imagining the resemblance or not.

"Eli?" she called out with uncertainty.

He turned and looked, a smile of recognition slowly breaking onto his face. "Judith? Judith McPhearson?"

She nodded, rushing over to him as he set down his box and threw open his arms. In the same instant, they both fell into a big hug. "Oh, Eli!" she cried. "I can't believe it's really you. What in the world are you doing here?"

"I'm wondering the same about you." Then he held her back at arm's length and studied her face. "You've gotten older, girl."

She gently punched him in the arm. "Same back at you. In fact, I think I see some gray hair on your temples. And whatever happened to that old "fro I used to love?"

He threw back his head and laughed. Same rich, hearty, throaty laugh, only deeper. "I lost that a long time ago. Man, Judith, it's sure good to see you again."

"But tell me, Eli, what *are* you doing here? It looks like you're moving in."

He grinned. "I am. Coming back to my roots."

She shook her head. "Amazing. That's sort of how I've been feeling lately too."

"So, how about you? Are you moving back to the old stomping ground too?"

She sighed. "No, not really. I've been here about a week. But I plan to stick around awhile longer."

"Just a vacation then?"

"Sort of. Do you remember Jasmine Morrison, Eli?"

He frowned. "Yeah. Mostly I remember her folks. Why?"

"Well, she died—they say she shot herself. Several weeks ago. I came out here to figure it out."

"Shoot, Judith, I'm sorry. I remember how close you two were. But why did you come *here* to figure it out? Jasmine wasn't living here, was she?"

"Actually, she moved back about a year ago and married a guy in town, which is a long story in itself. But there are many unanswered questions surrounding her death and her family."

He nodded his head knowingly. "Well, it's been my experience that anything to do with the Morrison family comes with all sorts of unanswered questions."

She looked into his dark eyes, laced, it seemed, with sadness. "I still don't get why you're moving back here, Eli. Are you on your own or do you have a family?"

"I think what you're really wanting to say is "Have you lost your mind?""

She smiled. "Well, sort of. From what I've been hearing lately, this town isn't really accepting of...cultural differences."

"Believe me, I'm fully aware of the racism that runs rampant in Cedar Crest. It's what drove me and eventually my entire family out of here. Another long story, Judith—a bad one, at that."

"Well, Eli, I hate to take up too much of your time. I know you're busy and..." She glanced over to the moving truck. "Hey, maybe I could help you unload things."

He grinned. "You sure you know what you're getting yourself into?"

"Eli, I'd love to help you. That way we can talk and catch up."

While carrying in boxes, Judith learned that Eli had moved

from the Seattle area.

"That's so weird," she said. "Jasmine had been living up there too."

"Small world." Then he went on to tell her that he had two college-aged sons, but had lost his wife to cancer just a year ago.

"Oh, I'm so sorry, Eli," she said as she carefully set a box marked "fragile" on the kitchen counter. Without trying to make too much of it, she quickly told him of her own losses. "I know where you're coming from."

"Sounds like we have a lot in common." he said as he opened the box and removed a dinner plate.

"Those are beautiful." said Judith, admiring the pattern.

"My wife, Kate, picked these out a couple years ago. She decided with the boys grown and off to college, it was time for some new dishes. Unfortunately she didn't get to use them for very long."

"Too bad. Would you like me to put the kitchen things away for you while you continue unloading the truck?"

"Thanks, Judith. I'm still pretty hopeless in the kitchen." He grinned. "In fact, I wasn't looking forward to that part at all. You must be my angel in disguise."

She listened to him whistling as he went in and out of the little house. She wiped down cupboards before carefully placing Eli's beautiful dishes into their small spaces. She was impressed by the quality of Eli's things. Apparently money, or the lack of it, wasn't an issue for him. But why in the world was he moving back here of all places? Finished with the kitchen, she found him hanging his shirts in the bedroom closet.

"Eli, I was about to head to the store to get some food for myself. Would you like me to pick up a few things for you while I'm out? I see you've got staples, but I thought you might like some fresh produce and dairy products."

"Thanks, Judith, I'd appreciate it. Here, let me make a quick list." He jotted down a number of things, then fished in his wallet to hand her a hundred dollar bill. "I think that'll cover it."

"Sure." she said, thinking once again how he seemed to be doing pretty well financially. "Eli, you still haven't told me why you're moving back here—"

"How about if we sit down to some lunch when you come back. I promise to explain everything then."

At the grocery store, Judith replayed the last time she and Eli had gone together in high school. She remembered how they had broken up shortly before she and her mom had moved. But what was it that had broken them up that time? She picked up a head of romaine lettuce when it hit her—marijuana! Eli and some of his buddies had begun experimenting with marijuana, and for some reason that whole scene had put her off. But then she had moved, and naturally the two had lost touch. Until today. Now, she felt relieved that Eli had moved on from his drug experimentation and toward a more successful life. Or, she frowned as she picked out some tomatoes, how was she to know whether or not he'd continued along those same lines? What if he'd actually made his money by selling drugs? She shook her head. No, that was totally ridiculous. Eli seemed like a good man, a responsible citizen. She was simply imagining things.

Suddenly, she remembered what Adam had asked her last night about being racist. Was it possible that because Eli was black and had money she had made the racist assumption that he'd become wealthy illicitly? The thought sickened her. No, she told herself, race had nothing to do with it. In fact, she would wonder the same thing about Tommy Reynolds. He'd been Eli's best friend and the one who'd introduced Eli to pot in the first place. If she would make assumptions about anyone, it would be Tommy. So race had nothing to do with it. Still, it bothered her that she had paused to even consider such a possibility.

"Hey, there." she called as she walked through the opened door. "Anyone home?"

"In here," said Eli from the kitchen.

She unloaded two bags onto the oak table while noticing that Eli looked somewhat grim. "Something wrong?" she asked as she put a carton of milk into the refrigerator.

"Got met by the neighborhood welcoming committee." he said as he stood looking out the kitchen window toward the street.

Judith felt her insides twist. "Your neighbors aren't being too neighborly?"

He laughed, but it sounded hollow. "Well, I didn't expect them to be. But I guess I was hoping they'd hold themselves back on the first day." He turned and faced Judith. "Sorry to sound so glum. Believe me, this is no surprise, and I do know what I'm getting myself into."

"Do you really?" She began to set the ingredients for sandwiches on the counter; then carefully layered slices of roast beef and lettuce and tomato onto whole wheat bread.

"Yes, probably better than you do."

"Care to explain?" She poured them each a tall glass of lemonade.

"Well, I promised I'd explain everything over lunch. By the way, thanks for fixing that. I don't know what's become of my manners."

"No problem." She arranged their sandwiches onto plates, then opened a bag of chips and placed their lunch on the space he had just cleared on the table.

"You see, when my wife died, I began to look at my life very closely. And suddenly I became aware that all I'd been living for was to make money—and lots of it. I think I had something to prove, you know, to show the world that I was just as good as the rest of you white folks."

"Ouch."

"I don't mean you personally, Judith. You've always treated me right." He paused then added. "Well, almost always."

She grimaced. "But I've already apologized for my stupid years, Eli. After Jasmine moved back to Mississippi I came running back to you and practically fell on my hands and knees to beg your forgiveness. And we were okay after that, weren't we?"

He nodded. "But the pain of those years still hits me sometimes. That and a lot of other things. But, hey, I'm getting sidetracked here."

"Yes, tell me about what happened to you when you lost your wife."

"I began to take this sort of inventory of my entire life. And despite a beautiful home overlooking the Sound, a great job, more stocks than I'd ever imagined owning, two intelligent sons in a couple of the finest colleges in the country, I still came up bankrupt. Spiritually bankrupt, as it turns out."

"Spiritually?" Judith took another bite of her sandwich and listened with interest.

"Yes. My wife and I had attended church for most of our. married lives. Both boys grew up going to Sunday school and church camp. I was even on the church board. But I suddenly came to the realization that I really didn't know God at all. My wife, during her last months, had graciously tried to point this out to me. I swear, she was more worried about my eternal well-being than she was her own. Of course, now I know why. So, I began to read—I mean really read—my Bible. And then I rededicated my life to God. And I told him that I would do whatever it was that he wanted me to do with the rest of my life." He paused to take a bite.

"Wow, that was brave."

He nodded. "You're telling me. But you know what, Judith? I've never felt more fulfilled and alive in my entire life. I took early retirement, which I'd been considering anyway—you can only last so long in the computer software business, and since I'd gotten in on the ground floor, I was pretty well set. Then I took a couple semesters of Bible college, all the while asking God what it was he wanted me to do with the rest of my life. And for some reason I kept thinking about Cedar Crest. It's like I couldn't get it out of my mind."

"But why?"

"I kept feeling this pull on me to come back here—I know it sounds crazy—but I wanted to see if I could help change things."

"How?"

"I don't know. I guess this is sort of a faith journey for me." He smiled. "And what a confirmation it was to see you here today! I'm not exactly sure how it'll all happen, but I really believe that God is up to something."

Then Judith told Eli about her own personal faith struggles and how for the first time since losing Peter she'd actually been able to pray.

"That's the first step, Judith. Just keep walking that direction. I know God will lead you. I really believe it."

She stood and rinsed off their dishes in the old chipped enamel sink. "But Eli, I'm sure you could've afforded any place in town. What made you decide to move back into your family's old house?"

He sighed. "Good memories, I guess. And when I called a local Realtor, I asked him about something in this neighborhood, never dreaming this place would be for sale. And when it was, it just seemed another confirmation that God was leading. My plan is to work on this place until everything in it is "shipshape,' as Dad used to say."

"How are your parents, Eli?"

"Dad passed on a few years ago. Mom's at a good retirement home in Seattle. I hated to leave her up there, but she knows all about what I'm doing, and she's probably my best prayer partner right now."

"So she's not worried?"

"Not worried?" He laughed. "Why do you think she's praying so hard?"

Judith dried her hands on a towel. "Eli, my cousin suggested that all had not gone well for your family here in Cedar Crest."

"Come into the living room and help me with these books while I get my computer set up, and I'll try to tell you the story—or at least the shortened version."

While Judith placed books onto the bookshelf that filled half a wall, she listened to Eli's story.

"I left Cedar Crest right after graduation. Got an athletic scholarship at the university. Andrew had already moved on by then too. But James was still in high school. He should've graduated in "78.""

"Should've?"

"Yeah. In "76 the Morrisons moved back to town, bringing a lot of others with them."

"Others?"

"Southerners. Folks who were getting more than a little put out at all the equal rights that blacks were starting to get down in the South by then. Folks who thought a sleepy, little town like Cedar Crest—a town with only one black family in it—would be the perfect place to raise their lily-white children in. Apparently, Burt Morrison had bragged about how white the Northwest was and these fellas got it in their heads that this was the place to be."

"Oh, Eli, I had no idea it was that bad."

"Yeah, well, you were long gone by then. Anyway, Jasmine

wasn't with her folks when they moved back. Just their other daughter, the younger girl, Constance."

"You know, I just found out that Constance died a year ago."

He shook his head. "That's too bad. Although, I must confess I have to remind myself to forgive that girl and keep forgiving her. I think this is one of those places where that "seven times seventy' rule comes to play."

"What's that?"

"In the Bible Jesus says how we need to be willing to forgive someone seven times seventy, and I've come to believe that sometimes that means we have to forgive someone for the same thing, over and over again—until it's no longer an issue in our lives."

Judith placed a thick theology book on an upper shelf. "I've never heard it put exactly that way, but I think it makes sense."

"So, the Morrisons were back in town, along with their good ol' boy buddies. And you can just guess where they had their sites aimed."

Judith groaned. "Your family."

"Yep. First off, they tried to make my dad lose his job at the school by starting some mean and completely unfounded rumors about him. But the good people in this town fought for him, and for a while he stayed on. But that's when the constant heckling and badgering started. A rock through a window here. A punctured tire there. And my poor parents could hardly go to town without running into some of these new Southerners. And it got ugly."

Judith stopped putting books away. "Oh, I feel so bad for them, Eli. Your parents were such good people. That was so wrong! But didn't it help that other people in town stood up for them?"

"A little. But it didn't take long before Burt and his buddies started setting their sites on the others too. Jewish, Latino,

Asian—anyone who was different was picked out, as well as anyone who tried to oppose them. Mr. Anderson, the high school art teacher, used to write letters to the editor on a regular basis—and he actually got a burning cross planted in his front yard."

"You're kidding?"

"No, stuff like that was becoming commonplace around here. And slowly but surely the good folks of Cedar Crest began moving on."

"Folks like Dr. Warner."

"Yeah, and those like him. Only a few brave ones remained."

"Like the Andersons."

"Yeah. But here's the hardest part of this story, Judith." He turned away from his computer and looked at her. "You see, James was a junior in high school, the same age as Constance Morrison..."

"Oh no," breathed Judith, suddenly knowing where this was headed.

"Oh yes. It seemed Constance was going through a little rebellious period with her folks. You know, like most of us did at one time or another. But, unfortunately for my little brother, Constance knew the best way to get her father really riled."

Judith felt her clenched fist pressing into her lips. "You mean Constance went after James?"

He nodded, his eyes filled with sadness. "And she was a pretty girl. Had that same sparkle as Jasmine, except she was a blonde. Anyway, despite my father's warnings, James fell right into her trap. I'm sure, being sixteen, he thought he was invincible, or in love, or something. But he and Constance would sneak out together in the evening. And one night he borrowed my folks' car to take some friends to the movies, but he never came home. The car was found smashed into a tree out by the rock quarry, and James was in the driver's seat, dead. Naturally, the police say they found

an empty bottle of Jack Daniels and the
word around town was that the no good n   boy got
himself killed by drinking and driving."

Tears were trailing down her cheeks now. "Oh, I'm so, so
sorry," she sobbed. "That's so horrible! I never heard anything
about that before. I feel so bad for you and your family. And—
poor James—" Her voice choked. "I can still remember when he
used to come outside and try to shoot baskets with us. He was so
little and cute—" She went into the bathroom for a tissue for her
nose, then returned. "Wasn't there something people could do?
Some sort of investigation? Anything?"

"My dad tried, but it was useless. My folks left town right after
that happened."

"It's so...so wrong! So evil! How can you stand it?"

"It's been a real hard story to remember, Judith, and even a harder
one to tell," Eli spoke in a somewhat apologetic tone. "And over
the years, I've tried not to tell it too often."

She nodded. "But, Eli, it's a story that really needs to be heard.
Maybe it could even make a difference."

"That's why I'm here."

"To tell James's story?"

He shook his head. "To make a difference."

Fifteen

AS JUDITH CARRIED HER bags down the nasturtium-lined path towards Aunt Lenore's back porch, she intuitively felt a pair of eyes watching her. She turned to find Martha's gray head peering over the top of the gate.

"Hello." called Judith in her friendliest tone. "I saw Aunt Lenore." She hoped this tidbit of information might arouse Martha's curiosity enough to allow Judith the chance to speak with her.

"Is she all right?" asked Martha in a stiff, formal voice.

"Well, to tell you the truth, I'm not completely sure." Judith set down her bags and walked slowly toward the fence, as if making a quick move right now might frighten the older woman away. "Martha, if you'd just let me, I'd really like to explain some things to you."

Martha's eyes focused tightly on Judith, but her lips remained in a firm line. "Well, then go ahead."

"You see, the other day when I told you about Jasmine, I'm afraid you assumed that I was still involved with Jasmine's family. And now that I know more about what has gone on here in Cedar

Crest, I can totally understand how that might have alarmed or concerned you."

"Yes." said Martha crisply. "You're right about that."

"But you need to know I have been completely out of touch with the Morrisons for nearly thirty years, and I certainly don't hold any of Mr. Morrison's views on things like—like—" She struggled for the right words. "Well, things like racism or bigotry. I'm just not like that. Really, not at all."

Martha's eyebrows raised, possibly with disbelief. "When you've been through and seen the sorts of things that I have seen, you know when to be careful. I've never met you before, Judith, and, quite frankly, I have no reason to believe your story."

At least she had called her by her first name. That was something. "Well," began Judith hesitantly, "what if I were to tell you that I was also friends with the Paxtons—a family who has suffered greatly, I've only just learned, at the hands of people like the Morrisons."

"You're friends with the Paxtons?" Martha scowled in disbelief. "Why, they don't even live around here anymore."

"Eli does."

Martha let out a sarcastic laugh. "Now I know you're lying." She started to turn away, leaning into her cane and shaking her head with disgust.

"I swear to you, Martha, as we speak, Eli Paxton is moving into his parents' old house."

Martha turned around and glared at her. "That's ridiculous! You can't possibly know what you're talking about."

"It's true. I just spent the better half of the day with Eli," claimed Judith. "His wife died last year. He has two boys in college. And he took early retirement and has moved down from Seattle. He plans to restore his parents' old home and live right here in Cedar

Crest."

Now Martha seemed at a loss for words. Afraid that the poor woman might think her to be completely nuts, Judith continued quickly, "I was as shocked as you are, Martha. I just ran into him this morning, and then I stayed and helped him unpack. That's when I learned the story of what happened here in Cedar Crest during the late seventies. I'm so sorry. I had no idea. And furthermore, Eli used to be one of my very best friends. We even dated in high school."

Martha's eyes narrowed in skepticism. "You dated Eli in high school?"

"Yes, and the only reason I broke up with him was because he started smoking pot. .. " In the same instant, her throat constricted with emotions that threatened to get out of hand. Why was she trying so hard? Maybe it was just useless. "Oh, just forget it." She grabbed her bags and hurried into the house, certain she'd made a complete fool of herself in front of one of the few people left in Cedar Crest whom she respected. She threw her bags down on the kitchen floor and headed over to the sink for a glass of water. Why was she crying and carrying on like this? Perhaps what Adam had suggested last night was true. Perhaps she wasn't a strong person. Perhaps all that had happened—and was still happening—in Cedar Crest was too much for her. Perhaps she would be better off, as Dr. Warner had described, to just cut her losses and move on. The problems here were too dark and too deep for a weakling like her. How could she ever hope to rise above them if she were to break into tears all the time?

"Judith?" called a voice from the back porch. "Judith, can I come in?"

She turned to see Martha sticking her head through the opened back door, her face a mixture of pity and curiosity. Judith grabbed up one of Aunt Lenore's pretty tea towels to wipe her eyes, then said, "Sure, come on in. You can stand here and watch me having a total breakdown."

Martha came across the kitchen and extended her arms. "Come here, dear."

Unbelieving, Judith walked toward the open arms and continued to sob uncontrollably. "I don't know..." she choked on her words. "I don't know what to do. I probably *should* go...go home. I'm probably *not* strong enough to face all these horrible things. Everything that Eli told me today...it's just too awful, too ghastly...how could all this have really happened? I loved James like a little brother..."

"There, there." soothed Martha. "Go ahead and cry. It's something we all need to do more of. I know how many times I've kept my own tears from flowing when I should've sobbed like a baby. Just go ahead and cry, Judith."

After a bit, Judith stepped back, embarrassed for her open display of confused emotion. She held up her hands helplessly. "I just don't know what to do, Martha. I came here only to find out what happened to Jasmine, and now I'm finding out about all this... all this...ugliness. I had no idea. It's overwhelming."

Martha sunk into a kitchen chair and shook her head. "Believe me, I know."

Judith sat down across from her. "Eli even told me how Mr. Anderson was one of the few who really hung in there, one of the only ones to stand up to Mr. Morrison and his gang. Eli told me about them burning a cross in your yard. I thought that was something that only happened in the deep South."

Martha made a mocking laugh. "Unfortunately, racism is alive and well here in the Northwest. And I'm not just talking about Idaho and Montana. Oregon and Washington both have a lot of their own dirty little secrets. Why, not until the fifties, I believe it was, a college-educated African American schoolteacher couldn't legally teach in our state. And they couldn't buy homes until around then too. Sure, they could go off to war and fight for their country, but when they got home, at least in Oregon, they could secure neither jobs nor housing. I'll bet that Mr. Paxton was one of the first African Americans to legally purchase a home in this area. That place might just be a historical site." She shook her head. "'And don't kid yourself. That little cross-burning episode was just one of the many things we've been through here in Cedar Crest. Warren kept a scrapbook full of the things that happened here in the last thirty years. He'd always planned to write a book."

"But he never got the chance."

"No, but I'm still toying with the idea. I even bought a computer last year, thinking I'd start getting some of this down."

"Well, I admire what you and Mr. Anderson have done in this fight."

"To be honest, I used to shy away from all this controversy. But dear Warren, bless his soul, was a principled man. He refused to back down on these issues, and he refused to let them run him out of town."

"Good for him!" Judith hit her fist on the table, then shook her head. "I just wish I could be that strong."

"Maybe you will be. But now tell me more about this news that Eli Paxton has moved back to town. It's rather unbelievable. Even now, I find myself wondering why I should believe such a tale."

Judith looked her straight in the eye. "I swear, it's true. I'm still shocked. Especially in light of what he and his family went through. I can hardly believe what Eli told me about poor James." She felt fresh tears fill her eyes and reached for the tea towel again.

"One of Cedar Crest's darkest days, as far as I'm concerned."

Martha looked out the window. "I still remember that funeral. A small group of Burt Morrison's buddies showed up at the graveside with a great, big, flashy wreath. No one said anything, but we all knew. They'd only come to rub our noses in it. To show us who was in charge of this town—and who could get away with murder."

"How could this happen? Where were the police? The FBI?'

"The police? Ha! The police were all in on it too. Even when some of us tried to get outside help from the FBI, it just fell apart. Of course, we had no proof—just theory. And before we knew it, the police had the FBI eating out of their hands. It was so discouraging that many folks moved away that year. I wanted to, but Warren just wouldn't give up. Even when the Paxtons moved, right after losing James, Warren simply refused to budge. He used to say he'd rather die than give in to them. And that's what he did. And so here I am," she held up her hands, "unable to make myself leave now, even though I know it would be the sensible thing to do."

"You must be a strong person."

Martha smiled. "Strong or stupid. I'm not always sure which. Now, you mentioned something about Miss Barker. How is she? Where is she?"

"I saw her a couple days back at Crest View. We talked a little, but she seemed very groggy, almost as if she were heavily sedated. Then a nurse came in and shooed me away, saying she was in serious condition and was to have no visitors. The next time I went in they wouldn't even let me see her. And then today, they told me she'd been released. So I called Green Hill and the hospital, but no one seems to have her anywhere. And frankly, this has got me pretty worried."

"But what was wrong with her? Why did they take her in? And who do you think came and got her? I know it wasn't an ambulance."

Judith pressed her lips together and thought. "Well, she mentioned Burt, and I thought maybe she meant he'd taken her in. But I've checked at the old Morrison place and it looks like no one's around."

"Oh, they don't stay there very much, dear."

"I know, but I thought if they were in town—"

Martha nodded knowingly. "You don't know about the lake yet, do you?"

"The lake?"

"It's their private club. It has some secret name—something about the brotherhood. We've always just called it the KKK Club, although they are two separate, albeit very similar, organizations. It's where all the bad boys reside, and where others like them go to socialize and plan their next dirty deed. Only the racist elite are allowed to live there. It's completely gated with dogs and electronic security and who knows what else. You can't see it from the road at all."

"Are you talking about the lake off of Rattlesnake Road? Wasn't it called Parker Lake?"

"That's the one. Just as the timber industry started falling apart, Burt Morrison came in here with money from who knows where and bought up the whole darned thing, part and parcel, and immediately turned it into a private lake. No more public access. This made a lot of locals pretty mad. Then Morrison began selling off lots along the water. Well, some of us thought we'd get a piece of that beautiful lakefront property, but our money wasn't good enough for Burt Morrison. Only racists need apply. We figured it all out pretty quick."

"So, are there really a lot of them?"

"Not as many as there were in the eighties, but we still have the diehards."

"And is Hal Emery among those?"

Martha rolled her eyes. "One of Burt's best buddies."

"It's all starting to make more sense. But I still have so many questions."

"Join the club." She smiled. "Well, not the KKK Club."

Judith glanced around the old-fashioned kitchen. "What do you think has become of Aunt Lenore?"

"I have no idea. I just hope she's all right." Martha glanced at Judith's bags still lying on the floor. "Are you going to be staying here?"

"For now. Aunt Lenore wasn't communicating very clearly, but she told me where the key was hidden and told me to go home and stay. I asked if she meant for me to stay at her house, and she said yes. So here I am. At least this way I can keep an eye on things for her and water her garden. I just wish I knew where she is and if she's okay."

"Do you suppose she might still be at Crest View, but they've been told to say she's not?"

"You mean by the Morrisons?"

"Who else?"

"I suppose that's possible. After all I've heard today, it sounds likely. I actually considered sneaking in there to see if I could find her."

Martha shook her finger at her. "You be careful, Judith. This might all sound like a fascinating suspense story to you, but these dangers are real. Morrison and his buddies honestly believe they rule this town. And I suppose in many ways they do." Her voice grew sad. "Although it's sure not much to rule anymore. Things have gone steadily downhill."

"That's reassuring in itself."

"How's that?"

"Well, what if things had improved? What if the town was thriving amid all this hatred and bigotry? Wouldn't that be awful?"

Martha nodded. "Yes, you're right." Then she reached for her cane and began to stand. "I'm sorry I misjudged you earlier, my dear. I can see I had you pegged all wrong."

"Under the circumstances it was easy to do."

"Now, I think I'll go put together a little welcome basket for Eli Paxton."

"Oh, that would be so nice. Unfortunately, he's already been greeted by another kind of welcoming committee."

"Was it pretty bad?"

"He didn't say much, but I could tell he was hurt by it."

Martha reached over and grabbed Judith's hand. "I feel so frightened for Eli."

"I know what you mean, but he knows what he's stepped into."

"He will be in very real danger."

Judith didn't want to think about that. "He says he wants to see things change around here. It's as if he's on a mission or something."   '

"Mission impossible, I'm afraid." Martha made her way to the door. "Let me know if you learn anything about Miss Barker. I'd like to visit her if it's at all possible."

"Yes, I'll keep trying." Judith glanced at her watch, realizing that it was already close to six and she had agreed to meet Adam back at the Pine Lodge Resort. She told Martha goodbye and then quickly dialed his number, hoping she might catch him before he left.

"Hello?"

"Adam? I'm so glad you haven't left yet."

"Is this Judith?"

"Yes."

"Have you got a cell phone I can call you on?"

"Yeah, sure, but why?"

"Never mind, just give me the number."

She gave him the number, hung up Aunt Lenore's phone, then turned on her cell phone and waited, hoping the battery wasn't dead.

"Hi," he said. "Sorry about that, I'll explain later. Looks like you were calling from Lenore Barker's place. Is she back home yet?"

Once again he caught her off guard. "Caller ID, right? But how did you know Miss Barker is gone?" Still unsure if she could trust him, she was careful not to call her Aunt Lenore.

"As I said before, it's my job to know stuff. But if Miss Barker's still gone, then what are you doing at her place?"

"She invited me to stay here."

"When did you see her?"

"A few days ago. Hey, are we playing the question for a question game? Because I think you owe me about five by now."

He laughed. "Sorry about that. And you can ask me as many as you like."

"Really?"

"Sure, why not. I didn't say I'd answer them."

"Well, I was calling to suggest that perhaps we could meet in town instead of over in Jasper since—"

"Nah, we can't meet in town, Judith."

"Well, I suppose you want me to drive back over to Jasper then..." The idea of getting in her car and going didn't sound appealing.

"No, I have another idea. Why don't you just come over to my place."

"Your place?" What was this all about? "I don't even know where you live."

"Go out onto the back porch."

"What?"

"Come on, just do it."

So she went out on the back porch and stood there. feeling a little silly. "Okay, I'm out here."

"Now look out toward the back fence."

She looked out over Aunt Lenore's garden to see hands waving over the back fence. "Is that *you?*" she asked.

"Yep."

"You mean you live on the other side of the fence?"

"That's right. Now if you walk back to where that big lilac bush is, over in the corner, you'll see the secret pass-through."

Smiling, she walked around the garden and over to the lilac bush, and there she noticed a couple loose boards pushed aside to reveal an opening of about a foot, just wide enough for a child or small adult to slip through.

"Come on over." he called from the other side of the fence.

She pushed back some lilac branches and eased herself through the opening, her cell phone still next to her ear.

"You can hang up now," he said with a big grin as she emerged on the other side.

She looked around his yard. "This is pretty back here," she commented as she turned off her phone and admired the cool shady place. "This cedar tree is gigantic."

He looked up at the green canopy overhead. "Yeah, I kinda like it. It's what sold me on this place."

"Do you own it?"

"Nah, just renting." He nodded over to where a picnic table was situated next to a barbecue. "Want to join me for dinner? I could throw some steaks on."

Suddenly she felt uncomfortable, as if this relationship could be heading to places she had no intentions of going. "Oh, I don't know..."

"Hey, Dad!" A teenage boy stuck his head out the back door and saw them. "Oh, sorry, I didn't know you had company."

"Come on out here, Josh." Adam motioned him over.

"What's up?" The tall, gangly youth walked across the yard.

"Someone I'd like you to meet. Judith, this is my son Josh." He pointed over the back fence. "Judith lives over there."

She stuck out her hand. "Nice to meet you, Josh."

"Yeah, you too. But I thought an old lady lived over there." said Josh.

Judith smiled. "Miss Barker does live there. I'm just her houseguest right now. Taking care of things until she can come home."

"Is she sick?"

"Something like that." Judith peered over to Adam, wondering if she'd get a chance to ask him some questions about Aunt Lenore.

"I invited Judith to join us for dinner," said Adam.

"I thought you were going out tonight."

"I decided to stay home. You up for a grilled steak?"

Josh smacked his lips. "Sounds good to me."

Adam looked back to Judith now. "So, will you join us?"

She smiled. "Sure, why not? How about if I bring a salad? I noticed some things are ready to be picked out in Aunt Lenore's garden."

"Aunt Lenore?" Adam repeated.

"Is that old lady your aunt?" asked Josh.

"Sort of," said Judith. "What time shall I come over then?"

"Give us about thirty minutes," said Adam. "If we don't have it together by then, we'll just put you to work."

"Sounds fine."

Sixteen

DEAR GOD, ARE YOU even listening to me? Do you know that I'm thinking about running away today, or someday real soon? I seen this show on Miss Molly's TV about a girl not much bigger than me that runned away to find her dad. She even had to pretend like she was a boy and hop a train and everything. But I think I could act like a boy and do all that stuff if it would help me find my mama. I think I look like a boy anyway since Carmen cut my hair all off short and nappy. But if I runned away, I'm just not sure which way I would go to find my mama. I did find this cool backpack "neath the stairs that I can use to put my stuff in. I showed it to Miss Molly just in case it was stealing for me to take it.. But she wrinkled up her nose and said, "Someone just left that there for trash, Pearl. Now if you be a smart girl you won't even touch it, "cause God only knows where it's been." But I don't care. I scrubbed and cleaned it all up in the bathtub and, excepting for one strap that's broke, I think it's cool. I hid it "neath my bed, and when I'm ready to run away from here I'll put all my stuff in it and I'll put that one strap over my shoulder and I'll just go.

Dear God, I'm trying real hard to remember my mama "cause

it's been such a long, long time since I seen her. But maybe you could help me out a little. Do you know where she is? Can you tell me? Sometimes just when I'm waking up after a good dream I can remember playing with my mama in this place where there was lots of green grass, just like a great, big tickly rug "neath my bare feet. And there was lots of pretty things a growing there—bushes and flowers and trees and such—not like nothing around here, "cepting the park, and I only been there once when I sneaked off with Sharista, then got beat real bad when I come home. But I think that pretty place is where I lived with my mama one time. Unless it's just heaven, and I'm just a dreaming about heaven. "Cause Miss Molly says heaven's real pretty like that. But I think I'm just remembering what used to be my home. I just don't know why it ain't my home no more. What went wrong? Did my mama quit wanting me around? I can't remember my daddy at all, God. Did I have me a daddy? I heard Carmen telling Larry I ain't got no daddy when he said they should go give me back to my daddy since they ain't heard nothing from my mama in ages. And then Larry said if they don't hear nothing from my mama by next week, he's gonna throw me and Carmen both outta his apartment for good. So Carmen's been real mad at me all week. I'm just trying to stay outta her way. But I don't know how to make my mama come back. You know I would, God, if I could. Couldn't you just help me out a little bit here?

Miss Molly keeps telling me to keep saying my prayers. And sometimes it feels like all I do is pray and pray all day long. But nothing's getting any better. I told Miss Molly I'm pretty sure that Carmen and Larry both hate me, and she says if them two don't start treating me better, she's gonna call the authorities. I don't know what the authorities is, but the way she says them words scares me inside. I don't want no authorities coming in here and making more trouble. Seems to me I've got trouble enough as it is.

So now I don't tell Miss Molly no more about what Carmen and Larry do. I just keep it to myself. And I just keep trying to tiptoe around here, pretending I'm invisible and hoping I don't make no one too mad at me. And I'm afraid to go visit Miss Molly these days 'cause I'm worried she might call them authorities to come make trouble.

Dear God, I'm trying real hard to believe in you the way Miss Molly say I should. But I don't never hear you talking to me none. I talk and talk and talk to you. And I guess the truth be it does make me feel better, some. But, even if you be listening, God, and I'm not entirely sure you is, it just don't seem like you'll ever answer my -prayers. Won't you please do something, God? Won't you please help me find my mama and get me outta here? Won't you, please, remember me, your little Pearl? Amen!

Seventeen

FOR SOME REASON JUDITH had assumed that Adam Ford, like her, was single and alone in the world. She had no idea why. Perhaps it was his abrupt mannerisms or his independent spirit, but seeing him just now with a teenage son was a sharp contrast to her prior image of him. And since there was indeed a son, it now seemed quite likely there might also be a wife. But why she even wasted time thinking about these insignificant things bothered her a bit. She just shook her head and continued to tear pieces from the fresh, leafy heads of red and green lettuces, then carefully, still mindful of her stitched up hand, she sliced tomatoes and cucumber and green onions—all just picked from Aunt Lenore's garden. Then, after mixing some oil and vinegar dressing, she went to freshen up.

Feeling like an intruder in Aunt Lenore's little bathroom, she was careful not to move anything out of place. But even as she used the little rose-shaped soap and dried her hands on the tiny linen finger towel, she found her eyes searching the quaint old bathroom, looking for that missing box. Of course, she suspected the box would be too large to be in this compact space, but just the same she opened the cupboard door and discreetly poked around the old linens and ancient boxes of soaps and toiletries—the kinds of things appreciative students give their teachers over the years. Judith, herself, had a few of these tokens at home. She smiled. Although her students could never afford much, when they gave a gift, it always seemed to come from the heart.

Her half hour passed, she picked up her salad and dressing and crossed back over to the lilac bush, glancing over her shoulder just in case Martha might be looking and wondering what her new neighbor was up to. With no sign of anyone looking her way, Judith pushed back the loose boards and slipped through the fence to the other side.

"Hello there." she called out to Josh so as not to take him by surprise. "I hope it's okay if I use the secret passageway again. It's so much handier."

"Yeah, that's fine. Dad just made a quick run to the store. I'm supposed to be watching the steaks, but I'm not real good at this. You wanna come take a look?"

She went over to the barbecue and peered over his shoulder. "Actually, I'm kind of a novice myself. My late husband used to be pretty territorial about this sort of thing, but those look just fine to me. Maybe you could turn the gas down a little though, just to keep them from getting charred."

"Okay, thanks. So did your husband die?"

"Yes, a couple of years ago." She glanced over to the partially set picnic table. "Can I lend a hand here?"

"Yeah, sure."

She set down her salad and began to arrange the plates and silverware, noticing that there were place settings for four. But who was the fourth person? Of course, she remembered, there must be a *Mrs.* Ford. She glanced back toward the house. Perhaps she was in there, right now, preparing something for their dinner. She wondered what Adam's wife would be like. Maybe like Josh, fair and blue-eyed, tall and thin. Probably pretty. She studied Josh from a side angle as he focused his attention on the grill. Although different than Adam, she could see traits of his father in him. And he was a good-looking young man. She wondered how old he might be. Looked to be late teens perhaps, but it was hard to say at this age.

Then, without warning, thoughts of her own dear Jonathan assailed her. Perhaps the two boys would've been about the same age. Jonathan would've turned eighteen last January, and he would've graduated from high school this spring. It was something she hadn't even allowed herself to think about at the end of the school year—had, in truth, almost totally blocked it out. In fact, the pain was so real that she'd completely ignored a graduation announcement from one good friend's daughter. She found herself staring at Josh with wonder. "How old are you, Josh?" she asked, hoping her voice sounded normal, nonchalant, just making idle conversation to pass the time.

"I'll be eighteen next month." He turned and grinned. "Just graduated, and now I get to do whatever I want."

She swallowed hard. He was the same age as Jonathan. She managed to force a smile. "And what would that be?"

"I don't really know. I just know I'm not ready to go on to college yet. And that's really ticking my dad off. I mean, he just doesn't get it." He flipped a steak over.

She nodded, hoping her eyes didn't appear overly bright. "So what do *you* want to do then?"

"Mostly, I'd just like to take a break and figure stuff out. You know, work and save up some money, then maybe travel a little, go surfing in Hawaii. I'm not real sure yet."

"I think that sounds like a good plan."

"You do?"

"Yeah, I think too many kids just automatically head off to college without knowing exactly what they're going for. What's wrong with taking some time to think about what you want out of life? I mean, really, what's the big hurry?"

He nodded earnestly. "That's *exactly* how I see it." Then he grinned slyly. "Hey, you think maybe you could explain that to my old man?"

She glanced back at the table and the four place settings, then shrugged. "Sure, but I don't know why he'd listen to me."

"Hello out there," called Adam from inside the house. "I'm back, and we'll be out in a couple minutes, Judith. Had to make an ice cream run for dessert."

"No problem," she called back. "Josh is taking good care of me."

"You think these are done now?" he asked her again.

She took another look and nodded, "Looks like it." She felt a familiar lump stick in her throat as she considered how her son might've been about this same height, might've been asking her these same kinds of questions, having these same youthful doubts and struggles as he searched to find his own place in the world. What would it have been like to be the parent of a grown child? She turned away, tightly shutting her eyes against these haunting thoughts, determining she *would* be strong. She must prove to herself, if not to Adam, that she could be strong even under these most trying of circumstances. *Oh, God, help me,* she thought.

"Well, here we go," called out Adam as he placed a plate of corn on the cob on the table. "Nothing fancy, but it should be good." He turned to Josh. "How're those steaks doing?"

Josh proudly held the platter before his dad. "Judith thought they looked okay."

Adam rubbed his hands together. "They look better than okay." Then he turned back to the house and yelled, "You coming?"

Judith, distracted from thoughts of Jonathan, turned her focus to the open doorway in time to see a white-haired man slowly make his way down the steps. He was wearing two bright-colored oven mitts and carrying a cast iron pot between them.

"Gotta wait for my baked beans." he said with a wide grin. "And believe you me, they're worth waiting for."

"This is my father." said Adam. "Jack Ford."

The old man glanced sharply at Adam and then back to Judith. "And I've heard that you're Judith, our new neighbor. Welcome to the neighborhood."

She smiled at him. "Do you welcome all the new neighbors like this?"

He chuckled. "Don't know as we've had any new neighbors before this."

"Pops and Josh are just visiting me," Adam quickly explained as they all sat down. "They've been here a week and will stay another, then head on back home."

"Depends," said Jack.

"Yeah, yeah," said Adam, waving his hands in dismissal. "Pops, you want to pray before the food gets cold?"

Jack bowed his head, then simply said, "Lord, bless this here food and all who are about to partake. And keep us safe in your care. Amen."

Judith felt a strange sense of relief as she forked a steak onto her plate, but wasn't quite sure why. "These look delicious, Josh. I think they turned out perfectly."

"Wait'll you taste my beans," said Jack as he eased the black pot toward her, one red oven mitt still on his hand. "It's my own secret recipe."

"So where is home for you, Jack?" she asked as she spooned out some beans.

Jack glanced over to Adam then back at her. "California. But not for long, I'm hoping."

"Why's that?" She sprinkled some dressing onto her salad.

"Well, it's just getting too durned crowded down there. Traffic is a nightmare. And since coming up here with Josh to visit Adam, I'm thinking this is a pretty nice place for a feller to land. I wouldn't mind living out the rest of my days in a spot like this." He looked up at the cedar canopy overhead. "Nice quiet little town."

Adam made a grunting sound. "Pops is something of an idealist. I've told him about some of the problems in Cedar Crest, and he thinks if he sticks around he might be able to make a difference."

Judith's fork paused in midair. "That's odd."

"Odd?" Jack looked at her curiously.

"Well, I ran into an old friend today who's just moved back to town. And he said the same thing—that he wants to make a difference."

"See!" exclaimed Jack, sticking his steak knife straight into the air as if to further drive his point home. "I'm not the only idealist in town."

"Problem is," she continued, not quite sure how to put it. "I'm afraid this man has some even tougher obstacles ahead of him."

"Like what?" asked Josh.

She glanced over to Adam. "I assume these guys are aware of this town's racist history?"

Adam nodded. "Warned "em right off the bat."

"Well, my friend is black."

Adam looked at her with furrowed brows. "Are you kidding?"

She shook her head. "No. I almost wish I were. I'm worried for him."

"You should be. What's his name and where does he live?"

"I don't know the exact address, but it's over on Aspen Street between Third and Fourth. His name is Eli Paxton."

"Paxton?" Adam's brows shot up. "Related to the late James Paxton?"

"His brother. James was younger. Eli is my age."

Adam shook his head. "This is serious, Judith."

"What is it, son?" asked Jack, his brow furrowed with concern.

Adam just shook his head and sighed. Then suddenly Judith felt guilty. "I'm sorry." she began quickly. "I didn't mean to bring up something so negative at dinner. Where are my manners? Besides, Eli assured me he'll be okay and that he knows what he's doing. So, please, don't worry about him right now."

"No, no, it's okay," reassured Adam. "I need to know about this. And believe me, these guys can handle it."

"Yeah," laughed Josh. "We're used to this kind of stuff with Dad. But I want to know more. What's with this James guy? How'd he die?"

"He was in a car wreck about twenty-five years ago."

"So, what's the big deal about that?"

"Shall I?" offered Judith, unsure of how much Adam really knew.

"Go ahead," urged Jack as he reached for another ear of corn. "You got my curiosity running."

"Well, to put it in a nutshell, James was seeing the daughter of the worst racist family in town, a Morrison girl. And on a night he'd taken her to the movies, he was in what some people think was a mysterious car wreck. Of course, he was alone by then."

Josh whistled slowly. "Sounds like something outta a Grisham novel."

"Yeah," agreed Judith, "but now perhaps we should change the subject to more cheerful things. Say, do you guys know Martha Anderson, your other neighbor over there?" She pointed diagonally across the fence.

"Know of her," said Adam between bites. "But haven't met her yet."

"Well, she's a good person," said Judith. "Worth knowing. Her husband, who happened to be one of my favorite teachers, strongly opposed the racist activities in this town."

"Not many of those left around." said Adam.

"Actually, her husband passed on a few years back. But I suspect she's just as strong in her convictions as he ever was."

"Good for her," said Jack. "Care for some more beans, Judith?"

"No, thanks. But you're right, they were delicious."

He nodded. "Yep, I thought you'd like "em."

"So, where will you be heading off to after next week, Josh?" she asked as she forked a piece of steak.

"Well, Dad thinks he's sending me back to California to live with Pops," said Josh. "But I've been telling him he'd better think again. I kind of like it up here too."

"Up here, as in Cedar Crest?" asked Judith. "Or do you just mean Oregon in general?"

"Both. It's a nice change from California. And I thought maybe I could get a job at the grocery store in town, just to earn some money this summer. They've got a "help wanted' sign on the window. And when I asked about it, the manager gave me an application and invited me back for an interview tomorrow."

"An interview you don't need to schedule," said Adam with a sour expression.

"Dad," began Josh, "I'm not a kid anymore. I can do what I want now."

Hoping to soothe the conversation, Judith jumped in. "Then you're from California too, Josh?" She glanced at Adam. "Didn't you say you moved down here from the Portland area?"

"Yeah, I lived in Laguna with my mom and stepdad," offered Josh. "Talk about a crazy place with a bunch of totally warped-out people."

Adam laughed. "Can't disagree with you there, son. But if you stay in California, think how much well save on your college tuition—"

"See." Josh nodded to Judith. "There he goes again about college."

Adam looked at Judith. "Josh has been talking to you about college?"

"Well, a little..."

"And she agrees with me, Dad." Josh looked at her. "Tell him, Judith."

She held up her hands. "Wait a minute, I don't know if I want to get in the middle here."

"Go ahead," said Adam. "I'd like to hear this."

"Well," she began slowly, "I only said I think too many kids graduate high school and just automatically assume they should go to college without even knowing what they really want out of life. What's the harm in taking some time off until you know for sure what it is you'd like to do? It's a good age to travel and explore some things. I mean, take my own life. I went straight from high school to college, obtained my teaching degree just like my mom, got married, started teaching, had a baby, yada-yada, and suddenly I'm middle-aged, stuck on a treadmill, and asking myself if I ever really wanted to be a teacher at all."

Josh looked at her curiously. "What do you think you'd have rather done?"

"Maybe pursue art."

"As in an artist?" asked Josh.

"Yes; I used to love doing art. But life got so busy that I gave it up." She smiled. "Although lately, I've started to sketch again. I'm not very good, but I find it rather soothing and fun."

"You mentioned a husband and children," said Jack.

Adam glanced at Judith and then back to his father, but remained quiet. Perhaps he was testing Judith's strength again.

"Yes. Unfortunately, they're no longer with me. My son, who would've been almost the same age as Josh here, died as a boy from leukemia. And my husband was killed in a plane wreck just a couple of years ago." She forced a smile. "So, here I am, all on my own and having somewhat of a midlife crisis."

"I'm sorry," said Jack, sadly shaking his head. "I lost my wife about five years back, and I still roll over in the morning and reach out for her."

Judith nodded. "Yeah, I know what you mean."

"I hear we're supposed to get a thunderstorm tonight," said Adam looking over to the dark clouds gathering on the horizon.

Grateful for this shift in conversation, Judith joined in and slowly they moved to less emotional subjects, finally just chatting idly while they leisurely finished up their meal. Then the three men began to clear the table.

"Can I help?" offered Judith.

"Nah," said Jack. "Adam, why not let me and Josh take care of this? I know you and Judith have some business to talk about."

"Thanks, you guys," said Adam. "Why don't you give us about an hour or so to go over some things, and then we'll all reconvene for some of those fresh berries and ice cream."

"Sounds good to me," said Josh as he carried off a stack of dirty plates.

Adam looked around the yard. "But maybe we should go inside to talk."

Judith felt her brows raise. "Why's that? Do you think someone would listen out here?"

"It's possible."

He led her through the house, which, although generally neat in appearance, seemed rather stark and void of any personal touches, not to mention much furniture. "I've set up an office in here." he said as he showed her into what must've originally been a bedroom. He pointed to a leather chair across from his desk. "Have a seat."

She looked around. A few more personal touches had landed in here. Several trophies, she wasn't sure for what, and some nicely framed photos of landscapes and wildlife of the Pacific Northwest warmed up the room. She was drawn to a particularly nice one of a misty waterfall with autumn foliage all around. "That's pretty," she commented before she sat down.

"Thanks. Photography used to be a hobby of mine."

"You took these?"

He nodded. "Strictly amateur, but, like you said about your sketching, it was relaxing and fun." He picked up a pencil and began drumming it on his desk as if he was considering how to begin. "Okay, Judith, there's something I want to discuss with you."

"No more question-and-answer games?" she said teas-ingly.

The edges of his eyes wrinkled in a half smile. "Actually, you can ask me all the questions you like later. But I think I know most of what I need to know about you, at least for the time being."

"You've been doing more investigating?"

"Not really." He stopped drumming his pencil and turned serious. "Mind if I get right to the point?"

"No, please do. The suspense is killing me."

"Okay, then. I've come up with what could either be a really brilliant plan or a totally stupid idea." He studied her carefully.

"And?"

He sighed deeply and looked down at his desk. I'm just not sure..."

"Come on, Adam, don't leave me hanging like this. What's your idea?"

He took a deep breath. "Okay. I've been looking for a way to infiltrate into the brotherhood, if you know what I mean. But no one in this town seems to trust me very much. The fact is, no one's even willing to give me the time of day. Especially the boys down on the force." He shook his head. "They're constantly watching every move I make."

"Not surprising, I suppose."

"No, it's what I expected to start with. Although I hoped I might be able to get further than this by now." He moved his hand across his desk. "That's why I try to do most of my work here at home."

Judith decided to cut to the chase herself. "Did the state send you out here to investigate the integrity of the police department?"

"Something like that." He waved his hand. "But that's not so important. What I'd really like to do is to uncover exactly what's going on out at Parker Lake—at "the club' I'd like to know exactly who's involved and what they're up to. But that place is locked up tighter than Fort Knox. The only way to get in is to be "in with the in crowd,' if you know what I mean."

"Sort of. But you're thinking you're never going to be "in with the in crowd' right?"

He shook his head. "The boys don't seem to like me."

Suddenly, her heart began to pound with realization. "You're not...you don't think...I mean, you couldn't possibly mean... " She pointed to her own chest with a frightened and questioning look.

He nodded. "I know, I know, it's probably certifiably crazy.

And I have no right to even ask. But I was thinking, here you are and you already have this great inside track with Jasmine's family, and you said yourself that Hal seemed to like you, and you used to live in this town, and—"

He stopped himself and sighed deeply. "It's totally ridiculous, isn't it?"

He looked so dismayed that she felt a small wave of pity for him. "No, I can see how it might seem. I suppose if people didn't really know me, they might even assume I was an insider." She laughed lightly. "I mean, poor Martha next door wanted nothing to do with me once she heard about my relationship with the Morrisons."

"See. That's what I was thinking too."

"So, that's why you asked me if I was strong?"

"Partly. To be honest, the plan was just evolving in my brain last night. It seemed too crazy to seriously consider. And, yet, all day I've been thinking about it, playing it through my mind. How you could get in and then get out, pass your information on to me, and then just be on your way. And you told me you were determined to find out what happened with Jasmine. This might be the only way to the truth."

She nodded. "I *am* committed to finding out the truth about Jasmine."

"Committed enough to stick around here and keep asking questions?"

"Yes."

"If you do that on your own, as an outsider, you could be putting yourself into some real serious danger."

"Yes, I suppose you're right."

"But if you pretended to be one of them while you're asking questions, you wouldn't be in so much danger. Plus, you'd have me looking out for your welfare."

"You?"

"Yes, we'd have to coordinate your activities so I could keep close surveillance, maybe even wire you or use a tracking device. You know, all that fun cops-and-robbers stuff."

"You sound like the FBI."

He grinned. "Well, a cop's gotta be prepared for anything."

"I suppose what you're saying does make `sense. If I really plan to get to the bottom of all this, I can't very well walk up to Hal Emery and say, "Hey, did you kill your wife?""

"Not without putting yourself at serious risk, although, I believe you thought you had nothing to lose when you first came down here..." He looked straight into her eyes with open curiosity. "But somehow I sense that life's becoming more precious to you all the time."

"Yes, that's true, but then it's all due to Jasmine. It's as if she's called out to me and drawn me down here. I don't think I could leave town with all these unanswered questions just hanging on me." She shook her head with conviction. "In fact, I know I can't. I must find out what really happened. And not just for Jasmine now, but for James and for Eli too. And who knows how many others?"

He smiled. "Now you're starting to sound like you want to be a hero, Judith. We don't want you going into this thinking you're going to save the world. You've got to be practical, okay? I mean, at best, I'd like you to find out who's involved and what kind of agenda they've got going. But to think you can do much more is pretty unrealistic. Do you understand what I'm saying?"

"I suppose so. But if I'm going to actually agree to this crazy scheme, isn't it okay if I hope or dream of something more?"

"I guess that's only natural. I just don't want to see your expectations get too high. And I don't want you pulling any superwoman stunts or anything like that. I just need you to connect with the family, win their trust, and see if you can get in and look around and retrieve some evidence, no matter how small and insignificant it might seem. Does that sound doable to you?"

"Yes, I think so. By the way, if I agree to do this for you, can you help me find out a few things too?"

"Sure, I can try. Like what?"

"Well, I already told you about Lenore Barker. But I'm hitting a dead end at the nursing home. They say she's released, but I can't find her anywhere. A little old woman can't just disappear into thin air. You're so good at snooping, can't you find out where she is and if she's okay?"

"I'll try." He made a note. "And what else?"

"Eli. Can you watch over—" She stopped as a new realization hit. "Oh, Adam, wait a minute—how can I do this? I can't do this to Eli. I'll have to tell him what I'm doing or he'll think—"

"No!" Adam stood and firmly shook his head. "If you agree to this, Judith, it must be done in absolute secrecy. No one, and I mean *no one,* must know."

"What about Martha? We've just become friends. This will break her heart—"

"Judith!" His voice was hard now. "You've got to understand that if you commit to this, you commit to telling no one. Is that clear?"

"No one?"

"No one. You and I are the only ones who know."

"But...but why?"

He sank back down into his chair. "To keep you safe."

"But I'm not worried about me—"

"Judith, let me finish. First off, it's to keep you safe. But next it's to keep *them* safe. Can't you see that if you involve people like Eli or Martha in this, they are immediately in danger too? In order to carry this whole thing off, you need to appear completely removed and separate from anyone who opposes, or is opposed by, the brotherhood."

She nodded sadly, understanding slowly seeping into her as to what she was about to agree to do. "Adam," she began hesitantly, "this is much, much bigger than I'd imagined at first. I really need to think about this."

"I understand completely. I sure don't want you jumping into this and then regretting it later. It's a big decision."

"Do you mind if I don't stick around for dessert?" she asked quietly. "I'm not really hungry right now, and I want to go think about this some more."

"Sure, I understand completely."

"It's a lot to ask, you know." She stood and reached for the door.

"I know, and to be honest I'm sorry I have to ask."

"I know."

"And it might even be a mistake."

"I know."

"So, really give it some good hard thought."

She nodded.

"In fact, it wouldn't hurt to pray about it too, Judith."

She pressed her lips together, wondering if she could even pray about it. What would she say? "Sure," she said slowly as she turned the doorknob. "I'll let you know."

Eighteen

THUNDER RUMBLED IN THE nearby hills as Judith made her way back across Adam's backyard and through the fence. Jack and Josh had both appeared disappointed when she didn't stay for dessert, but her stomach felt as if it'd been twisted into dozens of tight knots, and she knew she couldn't trust herself not to cry—a real sign of weakness, she felt certain. And in the same moment that heavy drops of rain pelted down on her, it occurred to her that even those two sweet guys would have to remain in the dark in regard to an allegiance with the enemy. What would Jack and Josh think if they saw her conspiring with people from the club? She wondered if she could possibly do this thing. It felt impossible.

Inside the house, she locked and bolted the door, leaning her weight against it, as if she might somehow keep all that darkness and evil and innuendo that threatened to overcome her at bay. The whole idea of infiltrating into the racist world of people like the Morrisons now horrified her. And besides, how could she do this to Eli? To Martha? To herself? She suspected even Polly, who tried to maintain such a low profile, would find Judith's actions confusing, not to mention repulsive. But Eli, dear, wonderful Eli—she had hurt him like this once before during the summer going into sixth grade when the only way she could hope to maintain a friendship with Jasmine was to completely swear off socializing with him. Just the memory of it sickened her. Of course, she'd explained the entire thing to him later, apologizing over and over. How could she put him through that again? How could she put herself through it?

"Oh, God, this is too difficult!" she cried out, as if God himself had personally asked her to accept this overwhelming challenge. "I'm sure I'm not strong enough to do this thing." She shook her head in confusion, then sank down into a squatting position, her back still pressed against the kitchen door. "Oh, God, please help me," she sobbed. "I don't know what to do. Can you hear me, God? Do you even care? Can you possibly show me what to do?"

For a long time she waited there, squatted down on the old, cracked linoleum of Aunt Lenore's kitchen floor. There she stayed frozen in time, waiting for God to answer. Her legs became numbed from their cramped position, but still no answer came. All she could hear was the rumble of thunder growing louder as the storm drew closer. Then she bowed her head onto her knees and prayed again, this time with a sense of resolution. "God, if you really want me to move forward into this crazy charade that Adam has suggested, then I ask that you would fill me with a sense of real peace." Now, to be perfectly honest, even as she prayed this specific prayer, she felt a wave of doubt wash over her. For when had she ever, in nearly two years, felt a sense of peace? Did she actually think she could trick God? Or even fool herself? Nonetheless, it was what she had prayed, and now she felt determined to stick by it as she stiffly rose to her feet.

Just then a bright flash of lightning illuminated all of Aunt Lenore's previously darkened kitchen—bright as the noonday—

followed by a huge crash of thunder that rattled the glass pane windows as well as all the little glass trinkets throughout the kitchen. Startled by the noise, Judith jumped then relaxed as she realized it was only the thunderstorm finally here. She walked across the kitchen to turn on the light only to find that the electricity was out, probably with that last close strike. Nothing new in Cedar Crest, she thought as she recalled how power outages and lightning storms used to frighten her as a child. She fumbled around in the darkness, going through drawers until she finally fingered what felt like wax candles. And, yes, a box of wooden matches! Obviously, Aunt Lenore was used to this sort of thing.

After lighting and carefully placing half a dozen candles about the kitchen, Judith discovered that Aunt Lenore's stove was gas. She lit a burner and filled the teakettle, searching again until she found a tin of tea. Then she stood by the window and watched with interested amusement as streaks of jagged lightning played across the darkened sky and thunder continued to crash and boom around her. The kitchen looked cozy and sweet in the golden candlelight and before long the teakettle was whistling happily. She filled the porcelain teapot and waited as the brew steeped, the fragrant lavenderlike smell of Earl Grey wafting up to her. Then she filled one of Aunt Lenore's pretty teacups and sat down at the table to continue watching the magnificent storm as she sipped her tea. Just as a bright bolt flashed, she heard someone knock upon the back door, followed by another loud boom of thunder. "Hello?" called Adam's voice through the din. "Judith?" She went over and opened the door. "You're soaking wet," she said, stepping aside as he walked in.

"We were worried about you, Judith, over here by yourself—" he stopped and glanced around the candlelit kitchen. "We thought you might be lonely or frightened in the dark." Then he laughed.

"But it looks as if I got soaked for nothing. Looks like you can take care of yourself after all."

She smiled. "I guess so. Do you want a cup of hot tea?"

"Sounds great." He slipped off his jacket and set it out on the back porch. "Judith," he began as he sat down before his cup of steaming tea, "maybe you should forget all about what I suggested tonight. I could see by your face that it was really upsetting to you. I swear, you went completely white when I told you that you could tell no one. I can see that your friendship with Eli and Martha—and well, whomever, is more precious to you than my crazy scheme."

She closed her eyes and signed. "I don't know..."

"Besides that," he continued. "I may have played down the risks. The fact is, it *is* dangerous. And the more I thought about it, the more I knew I can't ask you to do it."

Then suddenly it occurred to her. "You know what, Adam?" she began. "You're right, I was pretty upset when I came home tonight. Horribly upset, in fact. And it prompted me to do something I haven't done too much of during the past couple of years—although I seem to have been doing more of it lately."

"What's that?"

"It forced me to my knees and it made me pray."

"Like I said, praying is good."

She nodded. "Yes, I've noticed that you pray—at least before meals."

"I pray more than you know."

"I suspected that. But anyway, it forced me to *really* pray. And I just realized as I was sitting here that God answered my prayer."

"He did?"

She pressed her fingers to her lips, almost afraid to admit what she felt certain was true. "He did."

"Dare I ask what you prayed for?"

"I think you'd better. I think I should tell someone before I convince myself that it never happened or that I imagined it. Although, I doubt that I could do that. Even now I'm starting to feel sort of tingly with excitement."

"You mean about the answer?"

"Yes, but maybe even more about the fact that it seems God *actually* answered me."

"You mean, you didn't believe he'd answer you?"

"Maybe not. Maybe if I'd really believed I wouldn't have asked in the first place."

His smile was warm and encouraging. "Can you tell me what you asked for, Judith?"

"I told God that what you'd asked me to do was too hard, too overwhelming, too impossible. But then I told God that if he wanted me to do it he'd have to show me." She took a sip of tea, still pondering these things. "I asked God to show me I should do this by giving me a sense of real peace." She considered it for a moment. "Yes, I'm pretty sure those were my *exact* words. But here's where it's getting my attention right now. No sooner were the words out of my mouth than I realized I hadn't had a real sense of peace since Peter—my husband—died. And maybe not even before that. But then what really makes this interesting—" she paused and looked out the window as another bolt of lightning flashed, although the storm was now passing over. "What makes this interesting is that I've never liked thunderstorms. And ever since I prayed, this one hasn't bothered me in the least. The truth is, I *do* have a feeling of peace. And I'm thinking God must've done that. Don't you think so?"

"I...uh...I don't know, Judith. I'm not sure I still have a sense of peace about what I asked you to do, myself. Honestly, I'm beginning to think it's too dangerous and foolhardy and—"

She held up her hand to stop him. "Are you going to argue with God about this?"

"Judith, you might've just imagined—"

"No," she said firmly. "I didn't imagine anything. I was shaken and upset and crying when I got back here. And in just a moment," she snapped her fingers, "I was calm and peaceful and in control. I couldn't imagine that. And I couldn't fake it either. I know myself too well."

He rubbed his hands over his eyes, shaking his head. "I sure don't want to argue with God. Believe me, I know better. And I don't want to argue with you either. But I really am having serious second thoughts about all this, and I think you should be having them too."

She took another long sip of tea. "Adam, I appreciate that you're trying to be careful, but for some reason I believe I'm *supposed* to do this. And while it still breaks my heart to hurt Eli, and Martha too, I think in the long run, it will all work out for the best."

"But it's going to be lonely, Judith."

"I realize that."

"There are no guarantees."

"I know."

"It could be dangerous."

She nodded. "So you've said."

"And you're still absolutely certain?"

"Certain." She set her cup into the saucer and looked evenly across the table at him, his face a worried mixture of shadows and lines in the candlelight. "But can you promise me one thing, Adam?"

"I'll try."

"Please watch after my friends—Eli and Martha and Polly and

Aunt Lenore and...anyone else who might not understand what I'm doing, anyone who might be hurt. But mostly watch out for Eli."

He nodded. "I will. And for you."

"Another thing?"

"Name it."

"Do you think Josh and Jack will hate me?"

He sighed deeply. "I don't know. I wish they'd just go back to California, and soon. I don't want them around if things get messy."

"Messy?"

"It could, Judith. It could get real messy. We're poking our heads into what might turn out to be a real hornets' nest. It could get messy. And if Pops and Josh are still around then, by connection to me they become at risk too, you know what I mean?"

"I think so. And there's no way you can tell them about all this?"

"Not without making them want to stay even more. They already know enough to suspect things, and they're both awfully stubborn." He grinned. "Seems to run in my family."

Suddenly, and for no explainable reason, she wanted to ask him about his ex-wife and what had gone wrong with them, but she didn't. She knew it was personal, and their relationship should remain professional. Strictly professional. Still, she couldn't help but notice the warm, golden flecks in his eyes—perhaps just a trick of the candlelight, but handsome just the same. "Well, hopefully it won't get messy, Adam, and maybe Jack and Josh will get bored with this hole-in-the-wall town and just move on by next week."

"Let's hope." He finished up his tea. "Well, I better get back before they get suspicious. From now on we'll have to meet in secret. Pops and Josh can't even know. I'll start working out a plan tonight and then touch base with you in the morning. I'll give you a special phone to use just for our conversations. Feel free to use Lenore Barker's for anything in connection with the Morrisons. I'll make you a list of dos and don'ts and you'll have to memorize it and then destroy it. And as you've figured out, the hardest part of all this will be the harsh looks and judgments from the people who don't understand what you're trying to do. But each time you get one of those looks, just consider it a victory. It means you're making them believe that you're really one of the bad guys, and that's good."

She nodded. "That's good."

"Did you ever want to be an actress, Judith?"

She smiled. "It was Jasmine who had all the dramatic flare. She was a natural. But I did take drama in high school, and I liked it pretty well."

"It'll take a lot of good acting to pull this off. You've got to become a good liar. You've got to play along with them, and hide your emotions—" His hands flew to his face and he groaned loudly. "Oh, good night, what am I thinking, Judith? You'll never be able to carry this off. You wear your heart on your sleeve, and your face is an open book for all the world to read. They'll figure you out the first time they use the n-word and you flinch."

"I'll practice," she promised. "I'll be tough. I'll make myself believable. I'll do it for Jasmine, and if I feel weak, I'll just remind myself of what they did to her."

"What you *think* they did to her. We still don't know for sure."

"Okay. But what about James?"

"Again, we don't know for sure. But if we could get just one hard shred of evidence, we could have his body exhumed and autopsied—this time for real."

"Okay, I'll just focus myself on finding evidence, on getting justice. And—" she looked him sharply in the eye, "I will pray.

Because just look at what God did in me tonight. And it seems completely obvious, to me anyway, that he is telling me to go through with this. If he really is sending me down this difficult road, don't you think he might help me along the way?"

Adam smiled and stood. "That's the most sensible thing you've said all night."

She walked him to the door. "And thank you."

"For what?"

"For giving me a chance to prove I'm strong."

He shook his head. "You would be wiser to start realizing that you, Judith Blackwell, are very, very weak. We all are, underneath everything else. But I believe if we bring our weakness to God, *he* can reconstruct it into strength."

"You know this from experience?"

"I do, as a matter of fact. And, if it's any comfort, there was a time in my life when you wouldn't have recognized me for who I am today."

"I'd like to hear about that."

"Yeah, sure. Sometime, when we have more time, I'll be happy to tell the whole story to you."

"By the way, is that your real name?" she looked at him curiously.

"Well, now, little lady," he began in what sounded like a pretty good James Cagney imitation, "I could give you the answer to that question, but then I'd have to kill you." .

She laughed and held the door open for him against the blustery wind. "Well, you just might have to get in line to do it, Mr. Ford."

He frowned. "I certainly hope not."

Nineteen

AFTER A SOUND NIGHT'S sleep, Judith awoke early. It took
her a moment to remember where she was, but the old-fashioned
pink-and-yellow crocheted bedspread in the guest room reminded
her. She showered and dressed, then took her breakfast outside to
enjoy in the cool morning air. After thoroughly watering the garden
and flower beds, she kept herself busy by dusting and cleaning Aunt
Lenore's house. For although everything was neatly in its place,
it was obvious that a good, thorough cleaning hadn't been done in
some time. No doubt that Aunt Lenore, in her elderly state, might
have found deep cleaning to be too strenuous. But Judith didn't
mind a bit.

As she cleaned, she continued to role-play in her mind, setting
up every possible scenario where she would have to respond, or
perhaps control her reactions, according to this new character she
was steadily creating. She paused before the cloudy antique mirror
above the guest room bureau, a bottle of glass cleaner still in
her hand and stared at her reflection. "Hello, my name is Judith
Blackwell. And I am a racist bigot." *No,* she thought in dismay,
it's simply not believable. Not the dialogue, which she knew was

absolutely ridiculous, but something about her appearance seemed seriously amiss as well.

She studied herself carefully. What exactly was the image she normally projected anyway? Middle-class, middle-aged, middle-of-the-road? She looked sensible, careful, maybe even tasteful. In her neat jeans and loafers and white shirt, she looked like someone who didn't really wish to stick out in a crowd, someone who kept to herself, someone's mom. But it was definitely all wrong. She tried to remember how Jasmine's mother used to dress. Although, in Judith's opinion, she never had the best taste, Ellen Morrison had always taken great care in her appearance. She enjoyed color and jewelry—the flashier, the better, it seemed. Judith studied herself again. Surely Mrs. Morrison would find her drab and plain, dreary and dull. And perhaps, *if* Mrs. Morrison were around, and Judith wasn't even sure that she was, then perhaps it would be important to win this woman over. Not that Mrs. Morrison ever exerted much influence over her hardheaded husband. There'd never been any doubt in Judith's mind over who ruled the Morrison household. And furthermore, Mr. Morrison firmly believed a woman's place was in the home. Not that Judith necessarily disagreed with that—well, at least not in theory. She thought again how much she missed her husband. She and Peter had always treated each other as equals, and he'd never been intimidated by her life or teaching career. In fact, he had often encouraged her to pursue her interests.

Judith dragged her thoughts from Peter back to Mrs. Morrison—how might she change her appearance to win this woman over? She knew Mrs. Morrison would approve of the haircut. She'd always liked it when Jasmine and Judith wore their hair short and neat. But Judith needed clothes with more color, more vitality, and perhaps some accessories too. And maybe if she looked the role, it would help her to play it and carry it off. So she began to make a short list of the wardrobe and props that she might need. Right off, she knew that her car was all wrong. An import. She could just hear Mr. Morrison scolding her for not "buying American." She could apologetically tell him that it had been her late husband's car. Yes, that would work and perhaps even evoke a little sympathy at the same time. But how was she to establish contact with the Morrisons in the first place? That was assuming they were even in town. Perhaps she'd start with Hal. Though she hadn't been back to his hardware store in days, he had been somewhat friendly during her last visit there. It suddenly occurred to her that if Hal could help her to make contact with the Morrisons, she might even discover where Aunt Lenore was staying. In fact, the more she considered everything, it seemed only natural that she should be looking for the Morrisons now. She had a right to find out about Aunt Lenore's welfare. She found herself smiling at her reflection in the mirror. It felt good to have a real plan to follow.

"Hello?" called Adam from the back of the house.

"I'm coming," she called.

"Sorry to just walk in like that," he apologized, "but I knocked several times and no one answered. I was a little concerned."

"I was back in the spare room."

He handed her a spiral notebook. "I want you to study these notes I made, and then return it to me or destroy it. We don't want to take a chance of anyone else seeing it."

"Thanks." She scanned the first page. It was her list of dos and don'ts. "There's a lot to take in here, Adam."

"I know. I hope you have a good memory."

She smiled faintly. "Well, in the past I've been accused of having too good of a memory."

"That'll help." Adam frowned. "Judith, are you absolutely

certain you still want to go through with this?"

She nodded. "Positive. In fact, I've already been practicing. And I think I'll go shopping for my costume this morning."

"Costume?"

"Yeah. I just realized that the way I look is all wrong."

He studied her appearance then nodded. "I think you're right. Totally wrong." A crooked smile played across his mouth. "I mean, don't misunderstand me, I think you look perfectly fine and everything—"

She laughed. "But it's not right for the person I'm trying to portray."

"Exactly. You look too, well, how would I describe it, sort of collegiate and classy, I suppose."

"Well, thank you."

"Not that racists all have a certain look." he added. "Of course, there's the traditional redneck image, and believe me, they do exist. But that's not how I'd describe these people. Well, not all of them anyway, and not the leaders. I think you're smart to change your image, and hopefully it'll help remind you that you're playing a part, you know, sort of keep you in character."

"That's exactly what I was thinking."

He smiled at her enthusiasm for a moment before saying, "Judith, there's something else. I wrote it in the notebook, but I wanted to remind you in person too."

"What's that?"

"Well, just because you're trying to fit in with them, be careful not to go overboard. Keep in mind that you really don't need to act like you're just like them. In fact, I think it would make them suspicious. I think you need to act more like you're sort of ambivalent, you know what I mean? As though you've never really given racism that much thought, but perhaps you don't like what's happening in our country politically. And also, it'll help if you seem very traditional and conservative."

"Well, I am fairly conservative."

He laughed. "Not by these people's definition. Believe me, your version of conservative is quite different than theirs."

She nodded. "Yes, I suppose you're right."

"What I'm trying to say is that I think you should play it like you're sort of undecided about these things, you know? Like you mostly just loved Jasmine and you care about them. That way you can allow them the chance to try to recruit you into their circle. They really like doing that."

"Recruiting?"

"Yes. I think it gives them a sense of power and accomplishment. Playing the lost lamb is very appealing."

"To the wolves."

He nodded grimly. "You get the picture."

"Thanks, that's helpful." She closed the notebook. "I'll study this today."

"Well, I'd better get to work now." He glanced at his watch. "I figured you should probably just spend today going over all this and getting yourself prepared for your role."

She frowned. "Really? I was hoping for something more. I thought I might at least drop by the hardware store later today to say hello to Hal."

"Are you sure you're ready?"

"I think so. I just realized that it's perfectly natural for me to go to him and inquire about Aunt Lenore's whereabouts. I'll tell him how she invited me to stay but then disappeared, and ask him if he can put me in contact with Jasmine's parents."

He nodded. "Good thinking. Makes sense. But I want you to get back to me before you try to contact the Morrisons, okay?"

"Okay."

He looked into her eyes. "You're really sure about this, Judith?"
"Positive."

"All right then. I'll be in touch."

She began studying the notebook as soon as he left. She immediately noticed that Adam was very good at this sort of thing. It seemed he'd thought of everything. He even gave her the name of another school that she had supposedly been teaching at, just in case they asked, as well as a fictitious law firm that Peter had supposedly worked for. However, everything else about her history was to remain exactly as it was. Well, that was easy enough. Actually, the more she studied the notebook, the simpler it all seemed to her. All she needed to pull this off was to put on a convincing act. And to *not* react to the sorts of things she might be exposed to. Adam listed derogatory words and sayings that were common to people like the Morrisons, but again he noted that she didn't have to use these words herself. She simply needed to familiarize herself with them and appear comfortable when hearing them. She knew that would be her greatest challenge.

In the notebook, he suggested standing before the mirror and repeating these horrible words out loud until her face appeared natural and at ease. She took the notebook into the spare room and tried to do this exercise, but she was surprised at how difficult it was. She saw her eyes flinch as she tried to pronounce words that were disgusting and insulting. Words she had never allowed her students to use. She couldn't bear to think what those children would think or feel if they witnessed her using such foul terminology. Well, like Adam had said, she didn't need to speak like this herself. But she needed to keep her eyes from flinching, her lips from compressing, her brows from lifting, be it ever so slightly. So over and over she practiced saying these detestable words, reminding herself that she was doing this for the sake of people like James, who'd possibly been victimized by hatred, and also for Jasmine.

Finally, she thought she was able to say the words with a blank face, without thinking about the meaning or emotions behind them. And she felt nearly convinced that she might be able to overhear those words without reacting or revealing her true feelings. After studying the notebook carefully, she felt confident that she had digested all she could from Adam's notes. She felt ready. She hid the notebook under her mattress for now; she planned on returning it to Adam later. Then she drove over to Jasper to shop for her costume.

She wasn't exactly sure what sort of clothing store she was looking for. She knew she needed something traditional and conservative, but also with the kind of color and flare that would appeal to Mrs. Morrison. She drove slowly through the business district of Jasper, glancing at shops and wondering where to stop when she saw the sign—Dusty Periwinkle's Western Wear for Women. Perfect. She pulled into a parking place and got out. *Yes!* she thought triumphantly. Mr. Morrison had even worn a western shirt in Jasmine's wedding photo. And, now that she thought about it, that awful yellow dress of Jasmine's had been western too. Not that Judith thought that everyone who wore western clothing was racist—not by any means. In fact, she could think of a number of friends who enjoyed western wear and were the farthest thing from being racists. But at the same time, she knew this style would appeal to the Morrisons.

Once the young sales girl recognized that Judith was a serious shopper, she gave her full attention to helping her. Judith suspected the girl worked on commission and would be rewarded for her efforts.

"That turquoise outfit will look fantastic on you," gushed the girl as she handed her another item. "And I've got the perfect earrings to go with it."

In no time Judith had picked out enough pieces to make a number of interesting and varied ensembles. And to her surprise, some that didn't look half bad either. Then, with the help of the girl, she chose complementary belts, shoes, accessories, and even a white straw cowboy hat.

"Nothing will beat this for keeping off the sun." assured the girl. She nodded at the current outfit that Judith had on, a multicolored western shirt and an aqua denim skirt. "And that shirt looks so great tucked in like that. You're lucky you've got the tiny waist for it. And look how great this belt looks."

Judith smiled. "Thanks for all your help. Maybe I'll wear this outfit right out of here."

"Sure, I'll cut the tags off for you."

Judith practiced her nonflinching techniques as the girl totaled her bill. Stoically, she reminded herself that this expense was also for Jasmine. And besides, it wasn't as if she couldn't afford it. It was just that she'd lived so frugally since losing Peter—almost as if she were afraid her money would soon run out. She remembered the days when both she and Peter used to say they'd do their best and then trust God to take care of them in their old age. Somehow, it had seemed easier when Peter was alive. But perhaps if she were really trusting God with her life now—embarking on this slightly crazy, not to mention dangerous, venture; well, maybe it was time to trust him with things like her savings account too. At least, she could try.

The girl helped her load the packages into her car. "Thanks," said Judith again. "You were a great help."

"Thank *you.*" said the girl with a bright smile. "That was the best fun I've had since I first started working here. Come back again any ol' time."

Judith waved and drove off. So far, so good. She turned on
the radio, tuning into a country station as she drove back to Cedar
Crest. Suddenly she remembered the old good-natured argument
she and Jasmine used to enjoy at regular intervals. It was about
the only thing they could never agree on. Although the day did
come when Jasmine was almost swayed.

"Beatles!" Judith would declare with all the conviction of a
twelve-year-old.

"Elvis!" Jasmine would counter.

"No way." Judith would firmly shake her head. "No one is, or
ever has been, greater than the Beatles. Just admit it. Even Dick
Clark says so."

"No way," Jasmine would stomp her foot and shout. "Elvis
is, and always will be, king. Just ask my mom."

Well, maybe Jasmine had been right about that king business.
But just the same, Judith felt certain that the Beatles still ruled!

She smiled as she pulled into town. So many good memories
from when she and Jasmine had grown up together. She'd have to
take some time before meeting with the Morrisons to ensure some
of the best ones were fresh in her mind. And somehow she would
block out the bad ones. Thankfully, there weren't many. She parked
directly in front of the hardware store, no longer concerned about
who might notice her going in or out of there. After all, this was the
new Judith now. But just as she closed her car door, she noticed Eli
Paxton on the other side of the street. She diverted her eyes, and
yet felt certain that he saw her. Suddenly her heart began to race as
she realized what she had to do. *Oh, God,* she prayed silently, *how
can I possibly do this ? How can this possibly be right?* She felt
torn in two as she quickly turned away.

Ignoring Eli, she hurried into the hardware store, praying in
desperation that he would not follow her in. Thankfully, Hal was

waiting on someone at the counter, and she went into the back
of the store where it was dark and cool and where she hoped
any flush that had crept up into her cheeks might fade. She
must regain her composure if she was to carry this thing off. To
think that something as simple as seeing her friend Eli could so
completely unnerve her was unsettling. This thing was going to be
much harder than she'd expected. She pressed her hands against
her cheeks and prayed once again. *God, if you really want me to do this
thing, I desperately need your help. Please, help me.* Then she took a
slow, deep breath and began walking toward the front of the store.
She watched as the man exited. No other customers were in the
store, and thankfully, Eli had not followed her inside. She pushed his
image from her mind. She must not think about him now or at all.

"Hi, Hal." she said as she approached the counter.

"Hey there, Judith," replied Hal. "I didn't see you come in."
Then he looked at her for a long moment. "You look different.
What'd you do? New hairstyle or something?"

She smiled. "I cut my hair. It's lots cooler like this."

He nodded. "Well, normally I like long hair on a lady, but I
think that cut looks real good on you."

"Thanks. Say, Hal, I came in to see if you know what's up with
Aunt Lenore."

"You mean Lenore Barker?"

"Yes. I came by to visit her last week, and she invited me to stay
with her. She gave me a key and everything. Then the next thing I
know, she's gone. I'm staying at her house, but—"

"You're staying at Lenore Barker's house?" He scratched his
head.

"Well, yes. Like I said, she invited me. But I can't figure out
where she's gone. Do you know how I could get in touch with
Jasmine's parents?"

He rubbed his chin and studied her curiously. "Well, yes. I could give 'em a call for you, if you'd like."

"Thank you. Unless you'd rather just give me their number, and then I can call them myself."

He shook his head. "Nah, I couldn't do that."

She nodded, acting as if there was nothing suspicious about his overly careful response. "Well, sure, then whatever you can do. I just can't figure out why she would take off like that after inviting me to stay."

"Yeah, that's odd." He was still looking at her in a curious way.

"So, are the Morrisons still in Mississippi?"

"Well, now, I'm not real sure. They went out there for Jasmine's burial and all, but they may be coming back this way. You never know."

Judith thought, *I'll bet you know,* but simply said, "That's right, I'd forgotten that Jasmine was buried in Mississippi. Was there a reason for that? I don't mean to be nosy, but I'm just curious. Maybe it was what she would've wanted."

He nodded. "Yes, that's what we all thought. You know, she was born in the South, and it seemed fitting that she be buried in the South."

"Well, that makes sense." She started to head for the door, then paused. "I really appreciate your help with this, Hal. I know I've only just met you, but because of your relationship to Jasmine, um, I guess you sort of feel like family to me. And I really don't know hardly anyone in town anymore. And, well, with Aunt Lenore taking off like that, it just was feeling sort of lonely around here."

He smiled. "Now, that's too bad. We should be making you feel more at home, Judith. I'll tell you what. I'll see if I can reach Burt and find out what's going on with Miss Barker, and then I'll give you a call over at her house. Would that be okay with you?"

She nodded, smiling in what she hoped was a shy and helpless sort of way. "Oh, thank you so much, Hal. I really do appreciate it. And, please, if you reach the Morrisons, tell them hello for me, and give them my love, and—" she paused for effect, holding her hand over her lips for a moment, "please, tell them how devastated I was to hear about Jasmine. I'm sure they'll remember how we were like sisters growing up. I just feel so sorry for their loss."

"I'll do that, Judith." He nodded soberly. "I know it'll mean a lot to them."

"Thank you, Hal. You're a true friend." She hoped that wasn't laying it on too thick, but he seemed to appreciate it. "Bye now."

She stepped out into the bright noonday sun, and without looking up or down the street, got directly in her car, and quickly drove away. She wanted to take no chance of seeing Eli or anyone else for that matter. Not even Polly. She knew it would be impossible to avoid people in a town this size, but she would certainly try.

She went back to Aunt Lenore's and unloaded her packages. Feeling less like an intruder, she hung up her new clothes and opened some windows to let in some fresh air. Then she fixed herself a late lunch and started to take it outside to eat in the sunshine. She paused as she remembered Martha. What if she ran into her out there? What would she say? How would she act? Perhaps it was better to simply stay inside and avoid the chance of meeting her at all. Hopefully, this uncomfortable little charade wouldn't need to last for too long. Oh, how she looked forward to the day when she could explain everything to innocent people like Martha and Eli. But until then, she'd just have to push them into the safest recesses of her mind.

Twenty

THE PHONE RANG JUST as she filled the small washing machine out on the back porch with her laundry. She ran inside to get it, thinking it might be Adam, but then remembered how he'd said he wouldn't use Lenore's phone line.

"Hello?" she answered breathlessly.

"Hello?" said a woman's voice, followed by a long pause.

Judith's heart began to pound. Something in her knew, whether from the Southern accent or just old familiarity, that this had to be Jasmine's mother. Just the same she decided to play it safe. "Hello?" she said again. "If you're calling for Miss Barker, she's not here. But this is her house-guest speaking."

"Judith McPhearson?" said the woman at last. "Is that really you?"

"Yes, it is." *Watch out, Judith,* she warned herself. Mrs. Morrison had always been a stickler for good manners. "And may I ask who is calling, please?"

"This is Ellen Morrison."

"Mrs. Morrison!" exclaimed Judith, trying to insert great pleasure into her voice. "Oh, is it really you? I can hardly believe it after all these years."

"Well, now how are you, Judith?"

"I'm doing all right, I guess. Of course, I'm still very sad about Jasmine's death. It's such a tragic loss, Mrs. Morrison." She felt authentic emotion coming on now. "I was really devastated by the news. And I feel so sorry for you, and for Mr. Morrison too. Please, accept my most sincere sympathy."

"Why, thank you, Judith. I recollect how close you two girls used to be—I swear, you were just like two peas in a pod."

"She was my dearest friend." said Judith honestly. "Really, I never had a friend as close as Jasmine. And it's just so sad how we lost touch over the years. I tried and tried to reach her for a while, but my letters always came back."

"That's too bad, dear. You know, it's awful hard these days with people moving around so much."

"It's good to hear your voice again, Mrs. Morrison. You sound just the same. Are you and Mr. Morrison still in Mississippi?"

"No, dear. We came back last week. And let me tell you, it was awfully hard to leave my firstborn baby behind like that—" Her voice grew thick. "Parents should never outlive their children."

"I understand how you feel," offered Judith. "You see, I lost a child too. My only son. I don't think you ever get over it completely."

"Oh, Judith, I'm so sorry for y'all. How old was your little boy?"

Judith briefly told the story of Jonathan's struggle against cancer, and even about her husband's accident, but then tried to steer the conversation in another direction. "Of course, I know you didn't call to hear about my troubles, Mrs. Morrison."

"Please, Judith, honey, I don't go in for all that Mr. and Mrs. formality much anymore. Just call me Ellen."

"Well, thank you, um, Ellen. Did Hal tell you that I was

concerned about Aunt Lenore and was hoping you might know something?"

"Why, yes, as a matter of fact, and I must admit I was a little curious about how you came to be staying at her house, Judith."

This caught Judith slightly off balance, as if she were suddenly on the defensive, but she determined to keep her wits. "Yes, it is rather odd, Ellen. You see, I'd come to town wanting to find out more about what had happened to Jasmine. Naturally, Aunt Lenore had sent me a clipping of her obituary, but somehow she'd forgotten to include a note of explanation—you know how she's becoming a little absentminded in her old age. Anyway, I was so shocked by the news that I just hopped in my car and drove down here. I came to see Aunt Lenore, and we had a very nice visit. But when she found out that I was staying in that horrible fleabag motel downtown, she insisted that I come stay here with her. She even gave me my own key. So the next day I left the motel, but when I got to her house she was gone. I thought maybe she'd gone to the store or something, so I just let myself in and unpacked. But then she never came home. I called around to a number of places like the hospital and nursing home and whatnot, but I couldn't find her anywhere. A neighbor thought she'd seen a car come over the evening before, and thought maybe someone took her out for dinner or something. But that was all she knew. And to tell you the truth, the neighbor wasn't too friendly." Judith felt surprised, yet pleased, at how easily these lies were coming to her.

"Oh, that must be Martha Anderson. She's not a very nice woman, Judith. You'd best stay out of her way."

"Yes, that's what I thought too." Judith mentally scored herself a point. "But what in the world has become of Aunt Lenore? I wondered if she might not have absentmindedly forgotten that she'd had previous plans for a trip or something. Do you know anything?"

Ellen cleared her throat. "As a matter of fact, we stopped by to see her when we got back into town last week. You know, I feel it's my responsibility to check on her when I can. And she, um, well, she seemed to be having some little health problems. But she hadn't said a word to anyone about your impending visit, or I surely would've called to let you know. Anyway, we thought it best to take her in and put her under some supervised care until we felt assured that she was all right and ready to be back home on her own again."

"Oh, dear. Is she okay?"

"Well, she's doing a little better. But they want to keep her there for observation for a bit yet."

"Is she nearby?" asked Judith. "Maybe it would cheer her up if I went to visit."

"No, no, dear. I don't think that's a good idea right now. She was a little run down, and the doctor says she needs her rest to fully recover."

"Oh. Well, I feel rather foolish staying at her house now, although I've been watering her garden for her and doing some cleaning and whatnot. I thought she might appreciate it. But now I suppose I should go back to that motel—"

"Oh, I don't think there's any reason to do that, dear. After all, Aunt Lenore invited you to stay, and you're right, she'd be grateful to know you're taking care of things for her. Why, you know how much she adores that garden out back."

"I know. Well, then I think I'll just stick around. I sure wish I could visit her and reassure her that I'm keeping everything alive."

"Don't you worry. I'll see that she hears all about it."

"And perhaps when she's better, I could help take care of her at home for a while. You know, I've always loved her like a real aunt. I never had too many relatives, and Aunt Lenore was always so good to me. In fact, do you know that she helped inspire me to become a teacher too?"

"Well, isn't that nice, Judith. I'm sure that made Aunt Lenore proud." She cleared her throat. "So how long do you intend to stay in town, dear?"

"Actually, I'm not sure. But I've found that I really love being here. It brings back so many good memories of when Jasmine and I were kids." She sighed. "Who knows, I might just stay the whole summer."

"Well, that settles it then. We're going to have to get together with you. Let me talk to Burt and see what we can do. I'd love to see you again, Judith. It would be almost like having—" she stopped herself, and Judith felt certain she was about to mention Jasmine's name.

"I'd like to see you too, Ellen. And Mr. Morrison too. I was just remembering that time he took Jasmine and me fishing." She laughed. "Jasmine absolutely hated it, but I loved it. And I so admired Mr. Morrison." She took a breath and controlled her facial features. "He was such a wonderful father figure to me at a time when it wasn't all that easy being a child of divorce."

"Oh, I know, dear. I remember how we used to fret for you not having a daddy of your own to look out for you."

"Well, Mr. Morrison was a good substitute." She bit her lip, reminding herself how she'd have to do better if she actually got to see them in person.

"It's been such a pleasure talking to you, Judith," said Ellen. "And I suspect you've grown up to be a fine woman. I'll call you back and see what we can do to get together for a nice long chat. Hopefully, real soon."

"Great. I'll look forward to it."

Judith's heart continued to race for several minutes after she hung up the phone. To pretend that she liked Mr. Morrison when lately she'd begun to hate him more than ever was completely repugnant to her. She felt she could tolerate Ellen Morrison for a bit, although she didn't know for how long. But the whole thing made her feel like such a liar. She hated it! She knew this was exactly what she was supposed to be doing and how she was supposed to feel, but she found herself wondering if she could really do this. She pressed her fists against her eyelids and silently prayed, once again, begging for tangible guidance. Then finally she prayed aloud, "And, God, if what I'm doing is wrong, please, I beg you, please, just show me. Or just make this whole thing fall apart before it even gets started." She said amen, and then realized that it was quite probable the whole thing would fall apart. Everything, including herself, seemed opposed to this scheme succeeding. Simply talking on the phone with Ellen had been a horrible challenge. How much harder would it be face-to-face? Plus she would have to deal with Mr. Morrison too!

To distract herself and relieve stress, Judith pulled out her sketch pad and began to furiously sketch a vase of flowers that she had just picked and arranged that morning. And to her pleased surprise, it wasn't turning out too badly. Caught up in creating a realistic looking shadow, she jumped at the loud jangle of the phone's ring. She glanced at the clock as she picked up the phone, amazed to see that it was nearly four in the afternoon.

"Hello?"

"Hello, Judith, this is Ellen again. I just spoke with Burt, and we'd like it if you could join us for dinner tonight, that is if you don't have any other plans."

"Oh, that would be great. I'd love to see you both."

"Good. Now, Burt still likes to eat at six-thirty sharp. So, do you think you might possibly meet us at the Timber Topper then?"

"The Timber Topper?" Judith felt her heart begin to pound again as she realized she'd be meeting them in a very public place. Somehow, she had expected they could meet privately, hopefully at their home.

"Sure, honey, is that okay with you?"

"Of course, that's fine. Actually, I've only been there once since I got back in town."

"Well, then, I'd say you're long overdue for another visit. I know it's not the fanciest place to eat, but Burt really enjoys their chicken-fried steak and gravy. The truth is, we don't have a whole lot to choose from here in Cedar Crest, and Burt absolutely refuses to eat in Jasper, even though I hear they've got themselves some good eateries over that way."

"Well, the Timber Topper sounds great. I'll see you both there at six-thirty, then."

"I can hardly wait." said Ellen. She sounded genuinely excited.

Judith hung up the phone. This time she forced her face to remain placid, void of all the emotion that raged through her right now. It was good practice. Besides, she reminded herself, she had never disliked Ellen when she and Jasmine were kids. Sure, Ellen could be cranky sometimes, and she was often stressed out trying to keep a perfectly clean house for Mr. Morrison. Judith remembered how Ellen used to shoo the two older girls outside to play, worried that they might muss something up before "Daddy" got home. But Judith also remembered how, when "Daddy" was off on one of his numerous trips and Ellen would loosen up, she'd allow the housework to go undone and actually be rather fun. During those times she'd allow the girls to play dress-up in her old clothes. And she'd had a trunk filled with the most beautiful gowns, covered in ruffles and bows, all in sweet pastels and just perfect for playing a Southern belle or princess. And she'd had the best selection of high-heeled shoes. She gave Judith and Jasmine each a pair of high stiletto heels to wear when they were about eleven.

Judith remembered the hot summer day when the two girls wore their fancy heels, along with their summer shorts, and clip-clopped all over town. Judith could still remember her pair, pink satin with sparkling rhinestone clasps at the toes. And because Ellen's feet were so tiny, the shoes had actually fit the little girls. Of course, Ellen had no idea they were traipsing all over town in her old shoes, and most likely would have been chagrined if she had. But she had been fun as long as Mr. Morrison wasn't around or the baby wasn't fussing. Suddenly, Judith realized she hadn't even inquired about Constance. She must do so this evening, although it wouldn't be easy to discuss another death. Perhaps she would save that question in case things got too sticky. She couldn't even guess how it might go with Mr. Morrison. Talking to Ellen was fairly challenging, but she'd have to be especially on her guard with Mr. Morrison. Once again, she prayed for help. How many times had she prayed today? And the day wasn't even over with yet.

After a cool shower, she carefully dressed in the turquoise outfit. She paused to look at herself in the mirror, then remembered the silver-and-turquoise earrings the salesgirl had talked her into buying. She slipped them on and studied her image. The fitted western-cut shirt tucked neatly into the long skirt and was accented with a large leather belt and silver buckle. Not anything she would've normally selected, but it wasn't so bad either. She glanced at her watch and wondered if Adam might be home by now. She had promised to talk to him before actually meeting with the Morrisons, but she knew she couldn't call him at work, and it was nearly six now. She reached for her cell phone but, just as she began to dial, heard someone knocking on the back door. She turned off her phone and hurried to the door, certain Adam was checking up on her.

Without looking to see, she threw open the door and to her surprise was met by Martha Anderson and a sunny smile as she held out a bowl of purple plums.

"Hello, Judith." she said warmly. "I wondered how you were getting on, and I thought I'd share some of these plums with you. Thanks to all this sunshine, they've come on extra early this year."

Despite her pleasure of seeing Martha, Judith controlled her facial features to appear somewhat uninterested, and she kept her voice even and crisp. "Thank you. Those look lovely."

"I noticed your car was gone for part of the day, and I wondered if everything was going okay."

"Oh, yes, everything's just fine." She made an obvious effort to look at her watch. "And to tell you the truth, I was just on my way out."

"Oh, I'm sorry. I better not delay you." Martha handed her the bowl. "But I hoped we could talk sometime soon. Perhaps tomorrow?"

"Uh...sure," said Judith, wishing for some excuse to avoid any future conversations. Anything not to lead this good woman on. "I think I'll be around tomorrow."

"Well, just give a holler over the fence," said Martha as she gripped her cane and eased herself down the back porch steps.

Judith felt a sharp twinge of guilt.. .or was it regret? How she longed to become better acquainted with Martha, to explain everything to this dear woman. But she couldn't put Martha or her mission at risk like that. "Take care now," called Judith.

"You can just give me a phone call, if that's easier," said Martha over her shoulder. Then she stopped and turned. "I mostly wanted to talk to you about Eli. I saw him today."

"Eli..." Judith's voice trailed off. "Is...is he all right?"

"Oh, sure, he's as right as rain. I'm the one who's getting worried."

"Oh..." Judith bit her lip, then instantly made herself stop. She must stay in character, even if no one was looking. "'Well, I'm sure he'll be fine."

Martha frowned. "I don't know how you can be so sure of that."

Judith shrugged. "Well, it was his choice to move here. He knew what he was getting into."

Martha stood on the walkway, her head cocked curiously to one side as she studied Judith. Judith knew that her flippant response had probably offended the older woman, but just the same she kept her expression nonchalant, void of emotion, refusing to show how much this whole situation was upsetting her. Perhaps it was simply best to just get it over with as quickly as possible.

"I thought you said Eli was your friend."

Judith looked down at her watch again. "I'm sorry, but I really need to go now."

"Sure." Martha turned and walked slowly away, shaking her head as she went.

Judith went back inside, closing and locking the door, then she leaned against it and took a deep breath. Her stomach twisted as she slowly exhaled and told herself to maintain her focus. *You are trying to expose the truth,* she reminded herself sharply. *If Martha understood what was up, she would support you wholeheartedly right now.* But there was no way to share this with her. Better to hurt her like this, Judith told herself sternly, than to risk everything. She took another calming breath, and then dialed Adam's number.

"Hello?" A man answered the phone in a gruff but warm tone.

"Hi, is this Jack?" guessed Judith. She quickly identified herself and inquired after Adam.

"Sorry, Judith. He's not home from work yet. Usually gets home before this, but every now and again you just never know when he'll be in."

"Hmm..." She considered leaving a message, but wasn't sure how much she should say. "I'd hoped to catch him. Well, maybe you could just let him know I'm meeting some old friends for dinner this evening."

"Oh, did you and Adam have plans?"

"Well, not actually. But he'd asked me to call him about something tonight." She looked at her watch nervously, for now it really was getting close to six-thirty. "So, just give him that message. I have to go now. My friends are expecting me at the Timber Topper in just a few minutes."

"Okay, Judith, I'll be sure to let him know. If I see him, that is."

"Thanks, Jack." She hung up the phone and sighed. Hopefully Adam would figure out what she meant by meeting friends. *God, help me,* she thought as she ran out to the car, mentally bracing herself for the evening ahead.

Twenty-One

TO JUDITH'S DISMAY IT appeared that nearly all the tables at the Timber Topper were filled. The place was buzzing with what seemed to be locals eating, talking, and a number of them smoking. Well, so much for being inconspicuous. Despite it being Friday, she'd hoped to find the diner quiet and deserted. But it seemed her first meeting with the Morrisons was destined to be a public affair, with plenty of curious onlookers who would probably wonder and gossip.

"Sorry, we don't have any tables available," said a blonde teenage girl from behind the cash register. "But you can go ahead and take a seat at the counter if you like."

Judith read *Katie* on her name tag. "Say, is Glenda Miller your mom?" she asked, knowing full well this was just an avoidance tactic to announcing exactly who it was she was planning to meet here tonight.

The girl nodded glumly. "Yeah, she's the slave driver who made me work on a Friday night when I could've been out having fun instead."

Judith smiled. "I knew your mom in high school. You remind

me a little of her."

"Oh, great!" Katie groaned. "Now you've really made my night."

"Sorry," Judith laughed. "I meant when she was younger, back in high school, you know. Your mom was really pretty and quite popular back then."

Katie rolled her eyes dramatically. "Yeah, I can just imagine." Then she smiled slightly. "Sorry about that, guess I'm just a little fed up with Mom tonight. Now, would you like to sit here at the counter or—"

"Actually, I'm meeting some people." said Judith, glancing across the filled tables. "Do you know the Morrisons, by any chance?"

Katie's gaze narrowed as she studied Judith carefully. "You're meeting the Morrisons?"

Judith nodded, keeping her face blank. "Yes, have you seen them here tonight?"

"They're back around that corner." Her voice went flat as she turned around and walked into the kitchen.

Interesting, thought Judith as she made her way back through the dining room, past the bathrooms and around the corner, to a more secluded area. Katie didn't seem to approve of the Morrisons. And for some reason that gave Judith a small glimmer of hope for this town. Perhaps not everyone was under Mr. Morrison's thumb. She felt eyes upon her as she walked past the tables. Some people actually paused in conversation as she passed by. Obviously, this town wasn't used to strangers. Or perhaps word had already gotten around about who she was or that she'd once been friends with Jasmine Morrison. Perhaps she was just being paranoid.

Just as she turned the corner, she saw them. Older, of course, but still very much the same. Mr. Morrison was sitting up straight with his back to the wall, sipping a cup of coffee as he conversed with a foursome at an adjacent table. But as Judith approached them, he turned and looked up at her, watching with a cool, calm, almost nonchalant expression. Then Mrs. Morrison (Judith wondered if she should really call her Ellen in front of Mr. Morrison) waved and smiled her way, nervously glancing at her husband almost to check whether such actions were permissible or not. He excused himself from the two couples at the other table, then slowly stood and stretched out his hand to her. "Evening, Judith." he said in a relaxed Southern drawl as he gave her hand a firm shake, his cold, blue eyes never leaving hers.

"Hello, Mr. Morrison." she said with her warmest smile. "It's so good to see you again after all these years." She turned and smiled at Ellen. "And you too, Mrs. Morrison. You've hardly changed at all."

"Oh, don't be silly," she scolded with a smile. "And don't you go forgetting how I told you to call me Ellen when we spoke on the phone. We're both grown women now, Judith, no sense in acting all prim and proper like."

"Have a seat, Judith," said Mr. Morrison.

"Thank you." She sat down and looked at both of them and nodded. "Yes, I'm sure I would've known you both anywhere. You really haven't changed that much."

"Well, goodness, Judith, you certainly have," gushed Ellen. "Why, you're all grown up now. And a fine-looking young woman too."

Judith laughed. "Not really young though."

"Well, you look young enough to my way of thinking. Better than me—" Ellen patted her carefully styled hair. "Why, just look at all this silver hair the good Lord has blessed me with."

"And I think it looks lovely on you." Then Judith turned

her attention to Mr. Morrison and grew more serious. "I hope that Ellen conveyed to you how terribly sorry I was to hear about Jasmine." She paused and shook her head. "I was so shocked and saddened by it. I mean, even though we'd lost touch over the years, I will always remember Jasmine as one of my all-time dearest friends."

He nodded with a pained expression. "Yes, it was a shocking tragedy for all of us."

"And I just felt so bad for you and Ellen. It seems there's no greater loss than losing a child."

"Yes." said Ellen. "And I hope you don't mind, but I told Burt about your son and husband too."

"May I express my sympathy to you as well." said Mr. Morrison, a very formal expression over his stern features.

"Thank you. It's not easy to get over these things, but it seems to be getting better with time."

"They say that time heals all wounds, dear," said Ellen as she patted her hand. "We just have to learn to move on and get back to our normal lives, put the past behind us."

Judith understood Ellen's desire to change the course of their conversation, but she felt she needed to bring up Constance first. Besides it would appear as if she were trying to talk about something else since she would have no way of knowing that Constance was no longer living. "And how is your other daughter, Constance, doing?" asked Judith brightly. "She must be in her mid thirties by now. Although I still think of her as that little girl with all those blonde curls."

Mr. Morrison cleared his throat. "We lost Constance about a year ago. She was in an accident."

"Oh, I'm so terribly sorry." Judith saw Ellen's chin tremble, and she felt truly awful for bringing up another painful subject. She reached for the older woman's hand and looked directly into her eyes. "How hard this all must've been for you."

Ellen wrapped her fingers tightly around Judith's. "Yes, both girls gone, barely a year apart. I could hardly bear it." Her voice broke and she reached for her purse, then pulled out a handkerchief.

Judith took a deep breath then looked evenly at both of them. "Well, at least you still have each other. How long have you been married anyway?"

A weak smile crept onto Ellen's lips. "We just celebrated our fiftieth last winter."

"Congratulations. That's quite a milestone these days when so many marriages end in divorce. You should be proud."

"And how is your mother, Judith?" asked Ellen. "Did she ever marry again?"

Judith told them about her mother's life, about George and their cruise. Then Katie came to their table and asked to take their order. The teen wrote down their order in a cool and impersonal manner, with perhaps just a trace of hostility mixed in.

"Teenagers can be so rude these days," said Ellen as soon as Katie was out of earshot. "Back in my day, it was "yes, ma'am, yes, sir.' Nowadays, you're lucky if you can get the time of day from one."

"Well, at least our Cedar Crest teens aren't as out of control as the ones you see in other parts of the country," said Mr. Morrison in a voice that demanded their attention and respect. "We don't see all those tattoos and pierced body parts and wild-colored hairstyles the way you do in some of the bigger cities."

"Not so much in Southern cities, mind you," said Ellen defensively. "But you wouldn't believe the kinds of things Burt says he saw up in Seattle." She pronounced the name of the city as though it was Sodom or Gomorrah.

"What were you doing in Seattle?" asked Judith innocently.

Mr. Morrison studied her carefully, as if trying to figure her out. But she simply smiled back at him without even blinking. "Business," he said.

"Well, I know that I, for one, have gotten sick and tired of city dwelling," said Judith, turning to Ellen now. "And since I've been here in Cedar Crest I've found myself considering the benefits of living in a quiet and controlled community like this."

Ellen nodded. "Yes, I feel so much safer here."

"Even safer than in the South?" asked Judith.

"Oh, yes, most definitely..." Ellen glanced over to her husband as if to secure permission to speak further.

But instead, he continued. "The South has changed a lot in the last fifty years, Judith." He spoke as if she should be familiar with such things, and to play along she nodded, a concerned look upon her brow as he continued, "Yes, when I was a boy, we knew what to expect from folks. And people knew their place in this world and, believe me, they kept it. As a result, life was peaceful and quiet back then."

"Yes," Judith agreed. "That's as I've always imagined the South to be—peaceful and quiet. Folks pleasantly sitting out on their front porches, sipping their mint juleps, and visiting with their neighbors. All nice and slow and friendly." She hoped she wasn't laying it on too thick.

Ellen smiled with a faraway expression in her eyes. "Yes, it used to be like that. Oh, of course, my daddy would never let us kids drink a mint julep, but the rest of what you said was fairly accurate. I sure do miss those days."

"But what happened to change things?" asked Judith.

Again, those icy blue eyes studied her as if he knew exactly what she was up to, as if he could see right through her. "Well, I know you were just a child, Judith, but do you remember the sixties at all?"

"Well, it's not my most brilliant period of history," she admitted honestly. "But I do remember Kennedy getting shot, and the miniskirt and, of course, the Beatles." She laughed. "I guess I was too busy just being a kid back then." She glanced back at Ellen. "I suppose the thing I remember most of all from the sixties was being best friends with your daughter. We had so much fun as children." She looked back over to Mr. Morrison, hoping to catch him off guard now. "And I remember you too, Mr. Morrison, and how you took us fishing and the times we cut down Christmas trees and drove over those old, narrow logging roads. Mostly I remember things like that from the sixties. Happy things."

He nodded and almost smiled. "Yes, I suppose that's the best way for you to remember the sixties. But those of us who are older remember the sixties with great sadness. For us it was the end of a good era and the beginning of something dark and ugly. And that's a big part of the reason that we find ourselves more at home in Cedar Crest than we do in Jackson, Mississippi."

Judith pretended to take this all in. "I see."

"Do you?" Again, those penetrating eyes.

She smiled and shrugged innocently. "Well, probably not everything. But I think I understand some of it. And I think I've been longing for a quieter, calmer sort of life too. A place where a person can feel safe and secure from danger."

"Yes, dear," said Ellen again eagerly. "That's exactly how we feel when we come home to Cedar Crest." Just then Katie began to place their orders on the table.

Before Katie stepped away, Mr. Morrison bowed his head and began to say a blessing. Judith felt Katie's eyes burning down upon them as they all sat quietly with bowed heads waiting for him to finish. Judith wondered if she'd ever felt such humiliation and hypocrisy as she did in that flash of a moment with Katie Miller watching them. She longed to stand up and say that this was all wrong, that she was just playing a stupid role, that her intentions were really good. *Dear God,* she prayed silently with clenched teeth, *please, if it's your will, please, help me keep this charade up.*

"Amen," said Mr. Morrison. He smiled as he looked at his plate, the first full smile she'd seen on him all evening, then he picked up his knife. "Mm-mmm. I just love their chicken-fried steak." The threesome grew quieter as they began to eat. Judith now observed that Ellen's hands shook just slightly as she cut her meat, and how her eyes darted back and forth across the room like a frightened bird. But all the while she kept a pleasant, albeit frozen, expression on her face, and like clockwork she would toss out some insignificant comment about the food or the weather just to keep an amicable feeling at their table.

"It just occurred to me that the Fourth of July is only a couple of days away." said Judith, trying to do her part to keep the conversation going too. "I don't know where the time has flown."

"Do you have any plans to celebrate?" asked Ellen.

"Oh no. I don't really know anyone—"

"Oh, then you must join us out at the lake!" Ellen's eyes lit up, then she glanced uncertainly to her husband, and in her little-girl voice spoke, "Is that okay with you, Daddy? Wouldn't it be fun to have Judith over that day?"

He scowled, then scratched his head. "Ellen, you might've jumped the gun. But I suppose I can see what I can do. You do remember that we're having a special weekend at the club for the Fourth."

"Oh, I know, Daddy, but you could go to your silly old meetings and Judith could stay up at the house with me." Ellen turned and smiled warmly at Judith. "She'd be such good company for me—almost like, well, you know..." Her voice drifted away and her eyes grew misty.

"I'll see what I can do."

"I don't want to be any trouble," said Judith.

"Oh, honey, you're no trouble at all," Ellen reassured her. "It's just those silly rules, you know. You see, the lake's a private club and we have our members-only rules." She winked at her husband. "But then, Burt's the president of the club, so I think he might be able to wheedle his way around things a little, just this once anyway."

"I hate to be a bother."

"Don't you worry about it, Judith." Ellen patted her arm. "It'll be just fine, you'll see. Daddy'll work everything all out." She patted the napkin to her lips. "And now if that snippy little waitress would ever show her face back here again, I've got me a hankering for a big piece of that coconut cream pie."

"I remember how you used to make the most wonderful lemon meringue pie, Ellen," said Judith. "Do you still love to cook?"

"Of course. And lemon is Burt's favorite too. In fact, I guess I'd better make sure to whip one up before the Fourth for you two." She smiled at Mr. Morrison. "You know, Burt, having Judith with us feels almost like family."

This seemed to soften him a bit. "Well, we did help raise her, didn't we?" He smiled at Judith now. And to her surprise there actually seemed to be some warmth attached to it.

"You sure did," said Judith. "I told Ellen earlier today how you were such an important father figure to me as a child. It was good of Jasmine to share you with me. I don't ever recall her being jealous or anything."

"You two used to have such fun," said Ellen. "I still remember that time you and Jasmine dressed up in those old kimonos that Burt brought me from Okinawa, from back when he was in the navy. And I remember how he came down so hard on you two." She smiled as she shook her finger at her husband.

Mr. Morrison's jaw tightened. "Well, as I've told Ellen before, I may have overreacted about that silly thing."

Judith's memory raced back to the volatile night of their elementary school talent show when Jasmine's dad had thrown a fit and called them by what she later learned was a Japanese racial slur. She knew it was time to think fast. "Well, I can just imagine now how we must've caught you off guard that night, Mr. Morrison. Being so young and naive, I'm sure we thought you'd love our little Japanese getups and song-and-dance routine, but I guess we didn't take into account how much the war against Japan had affected servicemen like you who'd risked your lives for your country." She paused. "And for that I'm sorry."

He nodded. "I'm sure you girls never meant any harm in it. But when I saw you up there looking like a couple of geishas, it was just too much."

"Oh, I thought they looked adorable." said Ellen soothingly. "And you girls must've worked so hard on that act, and to think that you memorized all those Japanese words and everything."

"Actually, Jasmine wrote them all out for us and pasted them to the backs of our fans just in case we forgot."

"You two were such clever little things. You were always up to something. Do you remember those talent shows you used to put on in our backyard after Daddy built that sun-deck?"

Judith laughed. "Actually, Jasmine was the mastermind behind those little productions. In fact, I'm surprised she didn't end up on Broadway or the silver screen. She always had such a dramatic flare about her."

"Well, actually she did attempt some—" Ellen stopped herself as she caught her husband's sharp look.

"Oh, there's our waitress now," said Judith. Relieved for an interruption, she waved to Katie. "Excuse me, we'd like to order some dessert over here."

Katie came back and woodenly took their dessert order, refilled their water glasses, and strutted away.

"Looks like Jeff Miller needs to give his daughter a little lesson on manners."

"Is that the same Jeff Miller who used to be the star quarterback?" asked Judith feigning mild interest, although she already knew the answer.

"Yes, and he's a good man, but he doesn't seem to have much control over that daughter of his."

"Oh, Burt," said Ellen. "'You know that it can be hard raising teenagers."

His brows came together. "That's why fathers need to be firm—to keep those kids in line before it's too late."

Ellen looked away, and Judith struggled to think of something to say to change the subject again. But before she had a chance, a middle-aged man stepped up to the table.

"Evening, Burt." he said in a familiar tone. "Evening, Ellen."

"Evening, Gary." Mr. Morrison nodded over to Judith. "This is a good friend of the family, Judith McPhearson."

"Actually, it's Blackwell now." She smiled up at the potbellied and slightly balding man.

"Nice to meet you, ma'am." He turned his attention back to Mr. Morrison. "Hate to disturb your dinner like this, but I wanted to talk to you about something—something pretty important."

"We're about done here, Gary. What's going on?"

Gary glanced at Judith with a questioning look, then continued. "Well, don't know that you're aware of it or not, but we got our selves a little infestation problem."

One of Mr. Morrison's brows shot up. "Where 'bouts?"

"Right here in town."

"In Cedar Crest?"

Gary nodded with a sly smile. "Yep. We got us a real live varmint right here in town—yep, right here in river city."

Judith felt her pulse begin to quicken, but she took a calming breath and looked evenly at the two men. Were they talking about what she *thought* they were talking about? She glanced over to see Ellen neatly folding and refolding her paper napkin, creasing it each time with her spoon, hands trembling just slightly.

"Well, there's nothing we can do about this right now, Gary. But why don't you give me a call later tonight and fill me in on all the details?"

"Just thought you'd like to know," said Gary as he nodded politely to the women and then moved away.

Ellen, still absorbed in her napkin folding, didn't even seem to notice as Katie set their desserts down before them.

"This looks delicious," said Judith, hoping her voice sounded more calm and undisturbed than she felt. She looked over to Mr. Morrison as he forked into his chocolate cream pie, and then she continued talking. "So, was Gary talking about some sort of wild animal that's gotten loose in town? When I stayed at that fleabag motel downtown, I saw a huge rat in the parking lot. But then that's probably not so unusual around there."

Mr. Morrison laughed, but there was no mirth in the sound. "Nope, Gary's not talking about a rat. He's referring to a different sort of varmint. You see, Judith, living out near the wilderness like we do, varmints sometimes wander into town. And, of course, they don't realize they've gone beyond their natural habitat. Sometimes we've got to give them a hand and help them to remember to stay where they belong."

"Like the time that cougar walked through the middle of town when Jasmine and I were kids?" asked Judith. "I remember how we got so scared we climbed up into a tree." She laughed. "Of course, it didn't occur to us, back then, that a cougar could easily climb a tree too."

"Yes, something like that. And do you recall how we men got together a hunting party and how we stayed out all night until we finally found that cat and put her down?"

"Yes, I remember thinking you were really brave."

"Well, we needed to protect our wives and children. It was our duty."

Judith concealed her abhorrence at the gruesome image that had just assaulted her memory—the way the men had proudly displayed the lifeless and bloodied body of the old, female cougar right out on the sidewalk in front of the police station. Of course, it was the girls' own fault, since Judith and Jasmine had both insisted upon going down to see the cougar the following morning. But Jasmine had broken into tears as she knelt down and petted the furry coat, saying, "Poor old cat, you couldn't help it that you were old and lost and hungry and had no place else to go."

"And if memory serves me," said Judith, determined to be strong, "you were the one to finally shoot the cougar."

He nodded proudly. "Took her out with one clean shot too."

Ellen looked up now, and as if just noticing her coconut pie, she picked up her fork and smiled. "Well, now doesn't this look good."

"So, do you still do any hunting, Mr. Morrison?"

"Now, Judith," he smiled at her again. "I'm thinking that if you're going to be like part of the family, you should start calling me Burt."

Ellen nodded. "Yes, of course, she should." She turned to Judith. "No more of that Mr. Morrison silliness. From now on, you just call Daddy 'Burt.'" She giggled. "Or, you can even call him 'Daddy,' if you like."

"Thank you," murmured Judith, pretending that her chagrin

was really only embarrassment.

"And, to answer your question, yes, Judith, I do still hunt. Hal Emery has been a good hunting buddy of mine. We even got Jasmine to go out with us last year." He shook his head. "I was looking forward to more years of hunting with my girl, but it seems the good Lord had other plans for her." He eyed Judith. "How about you? You used to be pretty comfortable in the great outdoors. Do you hunt or fish?"

"I'd like to. Actually, I've fished a bit. Not nearly as much as I'd like. You see, my late husband, although he was a wonderful person, wasn't much of an outdoorsman. But I think I'd like to do more. I think I'm ready for some changes in my lifestyle."

He grinned and forked up the last bite of his pie. "Well then, Judith, it seems you've come to the right place."

She smiled brightly. "It sure seems that way."

Burt picked up the bill, then reached into his pocket to find a penny which he set in the center of the table. "That's all that little snit of a waitress is getting from me tonight."

"Oh, Burt," murmured Ellen with a slight scowl.

As they made their way through the still busy restaurant, Judith noticed how many people smiled, nodded, or greeted the Morrisons. It was clear Burt and Ellen were in their element here, completely at home with their fellow citizens of Cedar Crest. Respected even. And in the same moment a wave of hopelessness swept over Judith. Was it even possible that things could ever change for this unfortunate town?

Twenty-Two

SHE DIDN'T KNOW IF it was a result of the greasy, fried food or simply the stress of spending an evening with the Morrisons, but Judith barely made it home and to the bathroom before she lost her dinner. Not that Ellen was so horrible, she thought, as she splashed cool water on her face. In fact, she felt somewhat sorry for the woman—it seemed as if she were trapped. Now Burt was another story. He was the man in control, he called all the shots, he held all the power. To be honest, perhaps the most disturbing thing about Burt was the way he'd finally warmed up to Judith; but even worse than that was the way she'd almost enjoyed playing the game with him and finally winning him over like that. Maybe that's what sickened her in the end.

She went into the kitchen and put the teakettle on, watching as the blue flame steadily glowed beneath the copper kettle and listening to the reassuring hum of metal warming. How could she possibly keep this up? Meeting with the Morrisons was only the beginning, and yet she felt emotionally drained and totally exhausted. She was wearily mulling over the evening when she heard a quiet tapping at the backdoor. She flicked on the porch light and peered through the curtains to see Adam standing out there, his hands in his pockets while he waited.

She opened the door. "Come in," she said, her voice flat. Just then the teakettle began to whistle, and she returned to the stove. "I'm just making tea, would you like some?"

"Sure. That sounds good. Tonight turned a little chilly on us." He sat down at the kitchen table. "So, Judith, don't keep me in suspense. How did it go with the Morrisons tonight?"

She set the tea tray down and then stared at him in wonder. "How did you know who I was with? I only told Jack I was meeting some friends."

He smiled. "I have my ways."

She shook her head, sighing deeply as she sat down. "Oh, I suppose it went fine, but I was feeling a little overwhelmed just now."

He nodded then began to fill the two cups. "Is it going to be too much for you? Too hard? You know, Judith, it's not too late to quit."

She took a sip of tea. "I know. But at the same time I feel overwhelmed I also feel this strange compulsion to continue. I mean, even as I'm completely repulsed by this whole situation, I'm also intrigued to find out what's really going on, what's gone on. I want to see those people exposed for who they really are."

"Good." He took a sip. "That's good."

"But it's disturbing too."

"Why's that?"

"Well, on one hand, I've been telling myself that Jasmine's parents are the evil enemy here, and that I'm spying on them in order to expose them, but at the same time I feel sort of sorry for Ellen. She seems so unhappy and, well, sort of trapped."

"That's understandable. But you need to remember that she's a grown woman and responsible for her own choices in this situation. Even if her own choices have been to bury her head in the sand and pretend that everything is just peachy."

"I know, I know..." Judith set down her cup. "Can I be totally honest with you, Adam?"

"I was hoping you would be."

"Okay, the thing is, I'm feeling really disturbed about *Mr. Morrison*—actually he's even invited me to call him *Burt*—and you see—" she pointed her finger into the air as if to drive home her point, "—that's just it! I think he's starting to trust me and to even like me—"

"That's great."

"Yes, and I know that's my goal, but it's really upsetting me, because to be honest, it's almost as if...as if I like it!" She gritted her teeth and tightened her features into a repulsed expression. "And *that* seriously frightens me. I mean, why on earth would I *like* it?"

He smiled in a knowing, yet slightly aggravating way. "Well, it seems pretty natural to me, Judith."

"What do you mean, natural?"

"Well, you told me how you and Jasmine grew up together. And I know that you didn't have a father in your home—"

"How did you know—" She stopped herself and waved her hand. "Oh yeah, I forgot, you have your ways."

"Yes. And anyway, Burt Morrison was something of a father figure for you."

"Some father figure!"

"But you were just a kid, and I'm sure you admired him— at least a little. And, no doubt, you were looking for his approval. And even though you're all grown up now, there's probably this little girl deep down inside you that still wants his approval."

"Did you study psychology?"

He laughed. "Sort of. It comes with the territory."

She nodded and took a sip of tea. "I guess that makes sense. But just the same, it's pretty disturbing."

"So, tell me, Judith, how did it really go? Did you learn anything significant, or just mostly establish a relationship where they're beginning to trust you?"

"Actually, I think I've pretty much won them over. They even invited me out to the lake on the Fourth."

"Wow, that's something."

"And a couple of other things too. I'd meant to write them down when I got home, but I was.. .um.. .distracted." She sighed and looked him right in the eye. "To tell you the truth, I became sick to my stomach as soon as I walked in the door."

He chuckled. "Not surprising." Then he pulled out a small notebook. "Go ahead and talk, and I'll take notes. And, just for the record, it might be better if you don't write these things down. I don't want you leaving anything lying around that someone could find—you know, and use to blow your cover."

"Yeah, that makes sense. Okay, the biggest thing that's got me worried tonight is that this guy, Gary, I don't think I heard a last name, but he's middle height, balding, and has a pretty good beer belly on him—"

"Gary Rider." He jotted it down. "A member of the club."

"I figured. Anyway, he came up to our table and said there was an 'infestation problem' in town. At first I actually thought he was talking about rats, but then he said it was a 'varmint,' and Burt immediately got it. And that's when I remembered some of the names you'd written in your notes for me. And it made me feel sick, but I think I knew who they meant."

Adam nodded. "Yeah, when they're in public they like to use names that sound subhuman for any non-WASP people.

Varmints, animals, savages, whatever it takes to help them to believe in their own superiority. Of course, what they call them in private is something altogether different."

"Yeah, I can imagine. But now I'm really worried about Eli. I'm afraid they might to do something to hurt him."

"That's a legitimate concern."

She set down her cup and frowned. "But can't you do something to protect him?"

He smiled. "Don't worry, I've got someone already on it. Don't kid yourself, Eli knows what he's gotten himself into. He has a good head on his shoulders. You just keep yourself focused on your own mission here, Judith."

"Okay, I'm trying. Just as long as I know Eli's not in any real danger."

"I didn't say he's *not* in any danger, Judith. I can't make that kind of promise. Not for Eli, not for you, not for me, not even for my family." He grimaced.

"What's wrong?"

"It's Josh." He exhaled loudly between his clenched teeth. "That stubborn kid took the job at the grocery store even after I told him not to."

"Oh."

"And now Pops thinks he'd better stick around too."

"That complicates things."

"Well, it gives me two more people to worry about."

"Sorry."

"Thanks, but it's my problem, not yours. Okay, what else did you learn?"

"Well, here's something interesting.. .when I asked them about Constance, they said she was in an accident, but I thought you said she died from a natural cause. I assumed that meant an illness. Do you know how she died?"

"Records say a natural cause, but I do know that she was heavily involved in drugs before her death."

"Drugs? Constance?"

He nodded. "Probably her own personal escape from Mommy and Daddy."

"Do you think Constance and Jasmine remained in contact?"

"I think it's possible. They both lived in the Seattle area."

"Yes, Burt also mentioned being in Seattle."

"He did?" Adam made a note. "He probably didn't say when, did he?"

She shook her head. "No, but it didn't seem like it was a long time ago."

"Hmm..."

"I didn't learn anything more about Aunt Lenore tonight. But Ellen said she'd had some health problems, and that they'd been concerned and taken her in and she would remain there until she was stabilized, or something to that effect. But she wouldn't say where she was at. Have you had any luck locating her?"

"No. But I'm fairly certain that she's not at any of the local care facilities."

"Doesn't that seem weird?"

"Depends. Actually, I wonder if she's not out at the club."

"At the club? You mean at the lake?"

"Yeah. I wonder if she doesn't know something and that maybe they're trying to keep her quiet."

"That could be. She was certainly full of questions. And she had some suspicions of her own. I wish we could've talked longer that day."

"What were her suspicions?"

"Well, like she thought perhaps Jasmine had been forced into marrying Hal. And she didn't have anything good to say about Burt. And then she mentioned this box that Jasmine had left in her spare room, and she wanted me to go through it with her. But I've searched that room completely and have found nothing."

"Have you searched the whole house? It's possible she may have moved it to another room."

"I haven't searched her bedroom yet. I feel so intrusive as it is."

"Just ask yourself, 'What would Aunt Lenore want me to do under these circumstances?'"

"Yes. You're right. She'd want me to get to the bottom of this. I'll search her room tonight, but it had occurred to me that if Burt and Ellen took Aunt Lenore away, well, perhaps they may have taken Jasmine's box with them."

"I suppose that's possible. But do a thorough search, just in case. I suspect that box could contain something important. Why else would Jasmine leave it in her aunt's house and not her own?"

"Have you seen her own house?" Judith sadly shook her head. "I got a glimpse of that horrible trailer from the road."

"Yeah, the trailer was pretty bad, but it's my understanding that was just supposed to have been a temporary thing—that trailer had belonged to Hal's brother. Apparently, Hal had just finished building her a nice place up at the lake, but according to local gossip, Jasmine didn't want to live up there and had been known to stay down at the trailer on occasion."

"That's weird." Judith held up her hands in a helpless gesture. "But then what about this whole thing makes much sense anyway?"

"Hopefully, the more we learn, the more sense it will make. And right now, you're our best inside source for getting the answers. Are you sure you can keep this up?"

"I think so. You know, I've been praying quite a bit in the past few days. It's kind of strange, but I really believe it's making a difference. And it probably doesn't make much sense, but it makes me feel more connected to my son Jonathan. He was a firm believer in God and prayer and spiritual things."

"It makes sense to me." His voice softened. "It sounds like he was a fine boy, Judith."

She looked down into her now empty cup. "He was."

"Well, you look wiped out. I think I'll let you get to bed. Pops thinks I'm out taking a walk, so I'd better get back."

"Thanks for coming by." She smiled. "Your encouragement is helpful."

He stood. "Well, your help on this is invaluable to me. Keep up the good work."

"I'll try." She opened the door for him. "And I'll keep looking for that box too."

"Good. Now, do you plan to see the Morrisons before the Fourth?"

"Not that I know of, but Ellen seemed so needy tonight, I almost wouldn't be surprised if I hear from her before Monday."

"That's great, Judith. Just keep me informed. And we'll have to get you wired before you go out to the lake on the Fourth. Maybe I can stop by tomorrow evening and explain how that all works."

"Wired?"

"You know, a listening device."

"You really think that's necessary? Won't it be enough that I hear what they say?"

His countenance grew sober. "It's not just for evidence, Judith. It's a safety measure as well."

"Oh." She didn't want to think about that.

"Well, let me know if you hear from them. And if I'm not around, feel free to leave a message with Pops, just like you did today without giving anything specific away." He scratched his head. "In fact, if it's okay with you, I might allude to Pops and Josh that you and I are interested in one another—you know, just so they won't wonder if they should see me coming over here sometime, or why it is you're calling me so much. It'll be a good cover."

"Sure, that's okay." As her cheeks grew warm, she felt thankful for the dimly lit porch. "But won't they get suspicious if they see me fraternizing with the Morrisons? Surely they know you wouldn't be interested in someone like that."

"We'll just have to do the best we can, sort of play this thing by ear."

"Yeah, I kind of figure that's what I'll have to do."

"But if you see me around town, just ignore me. You never know who might be watching. And just so you'll know, I drive a Ford pickup, dark blue, not so different from half the other trucks in town. But the first letters on my plates are *DBS,* and I remember them by thinking *don't be stupid.* It's a reminder I have to give myself from time to time in this business."

"Okay, I think I can remember that—don't be stupid."

"That advice goes for you too." He grinned.

She said good night, then closed and locked the door while smiling to herself. So Josh and Jack were going to think that she was Adam's new girlfriend. But what would they think the first time they saw her mixing in with the wrong crowd? Oh, well, like Adam had said, they'd just have to deal with it when the time came.

She hesitantly approached Aunt Lenore's closed bedroom door, almost feeling she should be tiptoeing. She opened the door, and for a moment felt reluctant to turn on the overhead light, but then realized this room faced toward the backyard and the only ones who might notice the light would be from Adam's house anyway, and that wasn't a problem.

She flipped on the light switch to see a neat, orderly room. The small bed, covered in an old patchwork quilt with a basket design, dominated the center of the room, with a rocking chair on one side and a bedside table on the other. On the bedside table was an old Bible, a tissue box, and a water glass. A large bureau with a mirror stood against one wall. Nothing unusual here. Nothing out of place. She knelt down and looked under the bed to discover several dust-covered boxes, but upon closer examination found these only contained old clothing and linens and things. Surely nothing of Jasmine's. She looked inside the bureau to find neatly folded articles of clothing and everything you'd expect to find in an old lady's dresser. But no boxes. She went through the closet, discovering several old hatboxes, shoe boxes, and even a trunk. But all of these contained old items that were clearly not Jasmine's. Interesting, but of no help.

She stood and looked all around the room, studied the pictures and photos on the wall, the old lace curtains, a small bookshelf filled with old children's books—a nice collection. She surveyed the top of the bureau: a silver tray filled with old bottles of various perfumes and creams, a tortoiseshell mirror and comb set, some framed photos, a basket full of hairpins, a small jewelry box inlaid with mother-of-pearl, and a neatly pressed handkerchief all ready for use. Nothing unusual. She turned off the light and closed the door, certain that Jasmine's box had been confiscated by her parents. Perhaps on the Fourth she'd get a chance to snoop around their home a little.

Twenty-Three

THE NEXT MORNING, JUDITH spent a couple of hours weeding and watering and puttering about in Aunt Lenore's garden. She found the sunshine soothing on her back and the sounds of the birds peaceful to her ears. She understood why Aunt Lenore loved her little garden so dearly. Around ten, she was interrupted by a phone call.

"Hello, dear, this is Ellen again. I hope I'm not disturbing you."

"Not at all. I was just outside doing a little weeding."

"How good of you. You're such an angel. You know, I had the most lovely time with you last night, Judith. Why, you were just like a breath of fresh air to me. And, well, I wondered if you were terribly busy today."

"No, Ellen. I'm not. In fact, I was just wondering what I was going to do."

"Well, I know I'm just an old lady and all, but I thought I'd love to spend some more time with you—that is, if you're interested."

"Of course I'm interested. I'd love to see you, Ellen."

"Well, then, if it's all right with Burt, I thought perhaps I could come on over there. And that way, I could pick up some things for Aunt Lenore too. She mentioned wanting her Bible. And maybe I could bring her some produce from her garden. It might cheer her up a little."

"Oh, that's a wonderful idea. I'll get some things all ready for you. Maybe you'd like to come for lunch."

"Now, I don't want to be any trouble—"

"It's no trouble at all. I'd love to have you come."

"Well, thank you, dear." Her voice sounded like a happy bird.

"Shall I expect you around noon?"

"That sounds just perfect."

Judith went right to work cleaning and straightening the little kitchen. Not that it was so messy, but she wanted it to look absolutely perfect for Ellen. She remembered Ellen's high standards (or were they only Burt's high expectations?) as she scoured and scrubbed and polished. Finally, after everything looked shiny and clean, she began to plan for their lunch. She decided to keep it simple so that less could go wrong. She mixed up some tuna for sandwiches, a pitcher of lemonade; then she tore up some lettuce greens for a garden salad. And then she went to quickly freshen up herself, changing into a western style shirt with a denim skirt. She even put in a new pair of silver earrings and a little touch of makeup. Ellen should like that.

Suddenly, she realized that she needed to inform Adam. She called over to his house, but got an answering machine. "Hi, Adam," she said to the recorder. "I just wanted to let you know that my friend's mom is coming over for lunch today, so I'll have to see you some other time. Maybe this evening."

Satisfied with her coded message, she picked up the garden basket and went outside to select a few pieces of produce, some to use with their lunch, and some to send back to Aunt Lenore by way of Ellen. The tomatoes were coming on nicely these days. She knew

Aunt Lenore would be pleased. Perhaps she might even find out where the old woman was staying. She picked a green pepper and gently dropped it in the basket. Suddenly, she felt hopeful about the idea of conversing with Ellen without Burf's dominating interference. Who knew what she might be able to uncover with a couple hours of friendly, undisturbed chatting. Perhaps she might even find out more about Jasmine's past life or why she married or—

"Hello, there." A woman's voice interrupted her thoughts.

"Hello." Judith set down her basket and reluctantly walked over to the gate. She knew it was Martha, and remembered how her neighbor had wanted to talk to her about Eli today. Judith glanced at her watch. It was nearly twelve.

"I thought I heard you out here," said Martha. She opened the gate and stepped out, leaning onto her cane as she studied Judith closely. "I was hoping I'd catch you. You look nice, Judith. Are you on your way out again?"

"No, I was just picking some produce from the garden."

"Oh, good. Well, as I said yesterday, I'm a little concerned about Eli Paxton. And I realize he knows what he's getting into, but I think it's imperative that his friends—what few there are of us—well, that we rally 'round and show our support for him. The worst thing that could happen right now is for him to appear isolated and alone— and as if no one in this town wants him here. Because, even though we're few in number, we still count for something. And, who knows, Eli could be right—it might not be too late to turn this town around."

Judith felt torn as she saw the glimmer of hope in Martha's eyes. She could tell this woman was excited about what seemed a chance for real change. And Judith hated to spoil her enthusiasm with her own charade of indifference, or worse. After a brief struggle with her conscience, she forced herself to say coldly, "What is it you want from me?"

Martha blinked, but continued. "Actually, this is Eli's idea, not mine. You see, I've never considered myself to be a particularly religious woman. I mean, when I consider the wickedness some people have done in the name of Christianity, it just sickens me. So, I made it perfectly clear to Eli that I have absolutely no interest in religion whatsoever—and he said that was just fine with him." She stopped and shook her head as if this idea actually confused her. "So, anyway, Eli wants to start having a Sunday morning meeting. I think he called it a Bible study or something like that, but he also said that we would pray for our town. And like I said, Fm not a religious person, but I'm willing to do this to show my support for Eli. And he said he'd like you to come too, but he didn't know your phone number, so I said, no problem, I'll just go over and invite her myself. Anyway, the first meeting will be tomorrow at ten o'clock, and I offered to have it at my house. Can you join us?" She paused to smile. "By the way, Eli said some very nice things about you, Judith."

Twist the knife, thought Judith. She frowned as she searched for some excuse—any excuse—or just a good lie. "Actually, I already have plans for tomorrow morning..." Just then she heard the car engine, and glanced down the side of the house to see a big, white Cadillac pull up into the driveway.

"Are you expecting someone?" asked Martha as she moved into full view of the driveway.

"Yes, as a matter of fact. Jasmine's mother is coming over to have lunch with me today." Judith stepped out and waved as Burt climbed from the car. "Hello, there." she called out in a friendly voice. She turned and glanced back at Martha, who now wore a suspicious scowl. "Excuse me, Martha," she said in a crisp voice. "I have to go now."

"So I see."

Judith smiled brightly as she walked toward the driveway. "Hello, Burt," she said as he closed his car door. "Are you joining us for lunch too?"

"No." He looked past her shoulder to where Martha was now returning to her own yard. "What does *she* want?"

Judith rolled her eyes for the sake of drama. "Oh, I was playing the radio out in the backyard this morning, and I think I may have disturbed her."

He walked around to the passenger door, then grunted. "Doesn't the old bat know it's a free country?"

Judith shrugged. "Apparently not."

"Hello there, dear," called Ellen as she climbed from the car.

Judith opened up her arms to embrace the older woman. "It's good to see you again, Ellen. I'm so glad you called."

Ellen was beaming now. "Oh, so am I." She turned to Burt. "You can go ahead and leave now, Daddy. I'll be just fine here with Judith."

"Yes, I promise to take good care of her."

Ellen laughed. "You see, I don't drive anymore, Judith. So if I want to do anything or go anywhere, I have to beg Daddy to take me."

"Well, thank you for bringing her, Burt. And if it would help, I'd be happy to drive her back."

"In that little tin can?" Burt was eyeing her MG.

Judith smiled. "I suppose it is rather small. You see, it was my late husband's car, and I just haven't had the heart to get rid of it yet."

"Well, when you do, you make sure you buy American." He tipped his head slightly, as if giving her an order.

She mock saluted him. "Yes, sir."

Fortunately this made him laugh. "I'll be back around two.

Will that give you girls plenty of time to finish up your chitchat session?"

"I don't know," said Ellen. "We'll probably just be getting warmed up by then."

"We'll do the best we can," Judith assured him. "And if we don't finish, we'll have plenty of times to get together in the future."

Ellen reached for Judith's hand as they walked toward the house. "Oh, I certainly hope so, dear."

After a quick tour of Aunt Lenore's garden and flower beds, Judith invited Ellen to sit in the kitchen while she put the finishing touches on their lunch.

"It feels so good to be here again." said Ellen as she sipped her lemonade. "It's been ages since I've been in Aunt Lenore's kitchen, and yet everything looks exactly the same."

"That's just how I felt when I first came back," said Judith as she set a plate of neat triangular sandwiches on the table. "But I would've imagined that you'd been here a lot over the years."

"No, not really. Aunt Lenore and I had grown apart over time."

"Oh, I'm sorry." Judith sat down across from her. "Did you have a disagreement or something?"

"Something. I think Aunt Lenore has become a little persnickety in her old age," she winked at Judith, "if you know what I mean." She looked at the table all set for lunch before them. "Shall I say grace?"

"Thank you." Judith bowed her head as Ellen said a blessing over their food. But in her mind, Judith still heard Martha's words about false religion and the wicked things people had done in the name of Christianity.

"There now," said Ellen. "This looks very nice, Judith."

"Did you notice I even remembered to cut the crusts off the

bread, Ellen? I learned that from you."

"You are a smart girl. You'd have made a good Southern belle, Judith."

Judith laughed. "I don't know about that, but I do remember how much I used to love dressing up in your old party dresses with Jasmine. I always imagined that you'd come from a very rich family—just like Scarlett O'Hara."

Ellen giggled. "Well, not quite like Scarlett O'Hara. My daddy was a businessman though, and we lived comfortably enough. My family did own a fairly large plantation once, long before my time, of course, but all that was lost after the war. My great-granddaddy used to tell me stories about being a boy on the plantation and all the fun they used to have. But then the war came, and they lost it all. My granddaddy said his daddy never got over it. He came home from the war all bitter and angry and nothing was ever the same again. Terribly sad."

"That's so amazing that you actually had conversations with someone who'd been alive during the Civil War."

Ellen chuckled. "Yes, it must make me seem ancient. But I was just a little girl back then, and it was during the Depression, and I suspect Great-Granddaddy was trying to impart some sort of his age-old wisdom onto me. He died not much after that."

"And did Burt's family own a plantation too?"

"Oh, heavens, no. The Morrisons were sharecroppers who lived in a tumbledown shanty on the wrong side of the tracks. Goodness knows, there were colored folks doing better than the Morrison family back in those days. Why, my daddy threw an absolute fit when I started dating Burt in high school."

"I had no idea. Was it because he was poor?"

"Well, partially."

"But you saw him anyway?"

Ellen took a bite and nodded. "Oh yes, and it was something scandalous. But there was just something about Burt. Why, he was so tall and handsome, and with that curly blond hair and those beautiful blue eyes. And despite his impoverished upbringing, he was the smartest boy in the class, and athletic too. And I knew how his daddy was a mean ol' cuss; why, everyone in town knew that, but then I suppose that endeared me to Burt all the more. Despite what my daddy said, I just knew that Burt Morrison was going to make something of himself someday."

"So what did your parents do when you wanted to marry Burt?"

"Well, fortunately for us the war came on, and all the boys went off to fight for Uncle Sam. But I promised Burt that if he made it back safe and sound, I would marry him. He still says that's the only thing that kept him alive over in the Pacific."

"And so you were married after the war?"

"Well, not quite. You see, despite Burt's handsome uniform and earning some mighty pretty medals, my daddy was still not convinced anything good could come from the Morrison clan. So he and Burt had themselves a nice, long chat, and Burt agreed that if we could get engaged, he'd go off to college on the GI bill."

"So you were married after he finished college?"

"Not exactly. It's not that Burt wasn't smart enough, because he was. But he just didn't agree with a lot of things they were teaching him up at that college. And so, after a couple years he quit and got himself a job at the lumber mill. He worked real hard there, starting with the lowliest job of sweeping up—I still remember how much he hated it. Why, there were coloreds with better paying jobs than him. It was real hard on him, especially after the way he'd grown up with nothing, and being looked down upon by everybody. I felt terribly sorry for him, and that's when I stood up to my daddy and told him I was going to marry Burt no matter what my family thought."

"And did your father agree?"

She shook her head with a puckered mouth. "Not at all! Mother and Daddy never did come around to accepting my marriage. I think from the beginning they were just poisoned against the Morrisons altogether. Why, even when Burt worked his way up to a really good supervisory position at the mill, it still wasn't good enough for my daddy. I hate to admit it, but I think my family were just a bunch of social snobs. My brother was a doctor, and my sister married a lawyer who later became a congressman. And I guess in their eyes, Burt and me were just a couple of ne'er-do-well hicks."

"That's too bad. I remember Jasmine saying that she didn't have any grandparents, and I always thought that was kind of strange, because even though I didn't have a dad, I did have grandparents."

"Yes, I suppose that was another reason it was easy to leave our home in Mississippi."

"But then you went back?" Judith refilled Ellen's glass.

"Yes, things hadn't worked out here quite the way Burt had intended. He needed to go back down South to get some things together. He thought it was just going to be for a year or two, but it was about six years before we could return."

"Was that when he began organizing the club at the lake?"

She nodded. "Yes, he needed more members to buy into his plan. He had to do some campaigning and whatnot. And as it turned out, the late sixties and early seventies were a good time to introduce people to his ideas. A lot of people were getting fed up with the way things were going in Mississippi around then."

"So a lot of people moved out here then?"

"Oh my, yes. We had about a hundred families back then. But our numbers have dwindled a little over the years." She pushed her empty plate aside. "I'm not sure why that is. Burt says it's because we need young blood. Too many people got old. Their children moved on. Oh, I don't know..."

Judith sensed it was time to change the subject. "Well, I think the story of how you and Burt got together is pretty romantic, Ellen. Thanks for sharing it with me." She rose and began to clear the table. "I have some orange sherbet, if you'd like, for dessert. And I could make us a pot of tea, if that doesn't sound too warm."

"No, that sounds heavenly, dear."

Judith put on the teakettle. "All this talk about romance makes me curious about Jasmine's marriage to Hal. I think he said they'd been married just about a year."

"That's right."

Judith dished some sherbet into a pair of delicate dishes and set them on the tray just as the kettle began to whistle. "Had Jasmine ever been married before?"

Judith watched from the corner of her eye as Ellen pressed her lips tightly together as if considering whether or not to answer. "You may as well know, Judith, that Jasmine did not lead a very happy life."

Judith set the tray containing tea and dessert on the table. "I had suspected as much." She poured their tea. "But I just don't understand why, Ellen. I mean, Jasmine was always such a happy girl. She was so creative and motivated, and—well, it just made no sense to me that she would take her own life."

Ellen nodded. "I know how you feel, but Jasmine had changed. She wasn't the girl you or I remembered." She looked up with misty eyes. "Not like you, Judith. You've grown up to be a fine woman. Why, I'm sure your mother must be very proud of you."

Judith reached across the table and squeezed Ellen's hand. "I'm sure you were proud of Jasmine too, in your own way."

She took a sip of tea. "Perhaps, in my own way, maybe.. .."

"So, Jasmine never married before? Never had children? What had she been doing all those years?"

"I don't really know, dear. She ran off just as soon as she got out of high school. She had gotten terribly rebellious and disrespectful to both her daddy and me. Of course, a lot of the kids were acting like that in the seventies. We were just getting ready to move back here to Oregon when we lost touch with her completely. Oh, believe me, Burt tried and tried to track her down. But she clearly didn't want to be found. Burt said it was probably because she was making such a mess of her life and because she was too embarrassed to show her face to us."

"How sad. But at least you still had Constance."

"Not for long, it turned out. Of course, Constance had moved out here with us since she was still in school back then. But just as soon as she graduated, she did the exact same thing as her sister. Just took off, following right in Jasmine's footsteps."

"Oh, I'm sorry. That must've been so hard on you."

"Yes, in many ways, it seemed both my daughters had already been dead and buried for a long time before this."

"And they never got in touch with you? Not during all those years?"

"Well, every once in a great long while, I'd hear word from Constance. Naturally, it was always for money. And I'd usually give in without admitting as much to Burt, and then for a short while I'd hear from her off and on. And then, after that, nothing at all.

"Then the last time she called, Burt put his foot down and told her no. Well, she just begged and begged, but Burt wouldn't budge. Then she told him she knew where Jasmine was, and she offered to give us information about her sister if Burt would just send her money—a lot of money, as it turned out. Well, Burt was torn about it, but I wanted to know how Jasmine was doing, so I begged him to send Constance the money. By then we suspected that Constance had a drug problem, and to be honest we didn't have much hope for her. But to think I had the chance to find out where Jasmine was—to know that she was alive and doing okay—well, that was worth a lot to me. I suppose, to be perfectly honest, and no mother likes to admit such things, I suppose I always did favor Jasmine just a little. Anyway, I pleaded with Burt and finally he decided to make a deal with Constance."

"And that's when you were reunited with Jasmine?"

"Yes. Burt went up to meet Constance somewhere in the Seattle area. He wanted to arrange a meeting with Jasmine. He wound up staying up there for a whole month. And then when he came home, he had Jasmine with him! Why, I was so excited, I could hardly stand it. But, oh my, how she had changed. I suspect she may have been using drugs too, although she swore up and down that she never had. But she was so hard and cold and bitter and upset. And she was all jittery and nervous all the time. Why, she'd jump at the slightest little thing. And she and her daddy, well, they just didn't get along at all! I finally just tried to keep them away from each other altogether. Jasmine only stayed with us for about a month. Burt had introduced her to Hal Emery, and well, the next thing I knew, she had actually agreed to marry Hal. Now, I know this doesn't sound very nice, but I was just totally taken back that she actually wanted to marry him. I mean, Hal of all people. Not that he's not a good person, mind you; Burt thinks the world of Hal. But it just made no sense to me. Just the same she married him. Burt went by himself with the two of them down to Reno. I couldn't go because I was having some health problems at the time, but I felt hopeful that maybe, after all those lost years, just maybe we'd actually be a family again. And despite Jasmine's age, I even had hopes of becoming a grandmother." She shook her head. "Silly of me, I know."

"Not so silly. These days lots of women start their families after forty."

"Yes, I suppose. But I should've known by that pitiful look in Jasmine's eyes, by the way she acted so unhappy all the time, I should've known that something was wrong. Terribly wrong. And I guess I blame myself for what happened to her. I should've been a better mother to her. I should've known she was troubled in her heart. A mother ought to know these things—" And then she began to sob.

Judith went for a box of tissues. She then sat right next to Ellen and put her arm around her shoulders. "You can't blame yourself, Ellen. It's not your fault. Jasmine was a grown woman. She made her own choices."

Ellen blew her nose. "But I should've known something was wrong."

She patted her back. "Even if you had known, what could you have done differently?"

"I don't know..." She blotted her eyes. "I just don't know."

Judith cleared the table. "I'm sorry for bringing up such a hard subject, Ellen. I didn't realize that so much had gone on."

"Of course you didn't, dear. And you have every right to know. You were Jasmine's best friend. I remember how she cried and cried for you when we went back to Mississippi, saying she'd never have a friend half as good as you. And, as it turned out, she didn't. In fact, there were a number of times when I encouraged her to go see your Aunt Polly."

"Actually, she's my cousin."

"That's right. But I told Jasmine to go in and see her and see if she could put her in touch with you. I thought it would cheer her up. But to my knowledge, she never did. It's as if she were already dead, Judith. Dead and in her grave. I just don't understand it at all. Why would a beautiful young woman like that just give up on her life? Why would she go off and kill herself?"

"I don't know." A large lump filled her throat and tears gathered in her eyes. Well, maybe she *did* know something about giving up, but then again her own situation was completely different from Jasmine's. She had lost everything— whereas Jasmine had simply thrown it all away. Jolted back to the present by the ringing doorbell, Judith looked up to the clock. "Oh, dear." she said as she stood. "It's already two. And now Burt is going to find us in here all weepy and red-eyed, after I promised to take good care of you." Ellen rose quickly to her feet. "Nonsense, Judith, you *did* take good care of me." She linked her arm with Judith's as they walked toward the front door. "And the truth is, dear, I feel much, much better now. I think I just needed to say all those things out loud. Thank you so much. You were a good listener to a mother's broken heart."

Twenty-Four

"OH, DADDY." SAID ELLEN in a babyish voice as Judith opened the door. "You're just too prompt. Why, Judith and I were having the best little talk just now, and I hate to go so soon."

Judith smiled, her arm still entwined with Ellen's. "That's right. We were hoping you'd be late."

He looked at his watch and frowned. "Sorry, ladies. But I have to be back at the lake before three."

"Oh, I forgot all about that silly registration today." said Ellen as she hurried over to get her purse.

"Registration?" asked Judith, hoping not to sound overly curious.

"Oh, it's nothing," said Burt. "Just some visitors for the holiday weekend. But I need to be on hand to help out."

"Yes, Burt's got all kinds of meetings going on this weekend and into the Fourth, and I'll be off by myself, all alone by my little lonesome." Ellen looked longingly at Judith. "Oh, I just wish I could take you home with me, dear." Then suddenly she turned to Burt. "And why not, Daddy? Why can't I just take her home with me?"

Judith held up her hands. "Oh no, Ellen, I wouldn't want to impose—"

"Nonsense, it would be wonderful!" Ellen's eyes lit up as she grabbed Burt's hand. "Oh, Daddy, couldn't Judith come home and spend the weekend with me—"

"I'm sure she has other plans," said Burt coolly, tossing a sharp warning glance towards his wife.

"You don't have plans, do you, Judith?" asked Ellen with the eagerness of a small child. "Wouldn't you like to come out to the lake and stay with me for a few days? Oh, it's real pretty out there right now. I'll bet you haven't seen it since you were a kid."

Judith smiled. "You're right. But I really don't want to intrude. And it sounds like Burt's got a lot going on right now. I'd hate to get in the way."

Burt pressed his lips together and looked back and forth between the two women. "Well, I know that Ellen would appreciate the company. She never likes going to the meetings anyway." He studied Judith carefully, his blue eyes piercing and calculating, as if trying to determine her motives. "Are you certain that you really want to come out there, Judith?"

She shrugged slightly. "Well, I guess so. I mean, it's been so great getting reacquainted with both of you. And to be perfectly honest, I have been a little lonely lately, not really knowing anyone in town. You two are the closest thing to family for me right now." She smiled with lifted brows.

"Oh, that just settles it!" exclaimed Ellen as she looked at her watch. "Now you run and pack your bags, dear. Burt can wait a few minutes. It only takes ten minutes to get to the lake, and it's just barely after two now."

Judith looked at Burt, hoping to appear sincere and caring. "Are you sure this is okay with you, Burt?"

He nodded, but his brow remained furrowed. "Yeah, sure. Just go and get your things. And hurry it up."

"And don't forget to bring your swimsuit," called Ellen. "I'm sure you'll want to take a dip if it gets as hot as the weatherman's predicting."

She quickly filled her suitcase, remembering to put in the little extras that Ellen might appreciate. But just as she zipped it closed, she remembered Adam and how he'd insisted she must be wired before going out to the lake. But to put the brakes on at this stage might stir suspicion, especially with Burt. And it was such a victory to win him over like this. Besides, she was curious about these meetings that would be going on out there during the next few days. This could be her best chance to learn something important. She tucked her cell phone into her purse. She'd just give Adam a call once she was out there and let him know what was up.

"Ready to go," she announced.

"My, you really are fast," said Ellen.

Burt reached for her bag. "Yes, it would take Ellen at least half a day to pack, spur of the moment, like this."

"Oh, not that long, Daddy." Ellen laughed as she linked her arm into Judith's again. "We're going to have such fun!"

"I'll have to explain a few things as we drive, Judith," said Burt as he waited for her to lock the front door. "I'm sure you may have guessed that there are reasons that we keep the lake a private club. And, naturally, we have a few rules you'll need to be aware of."

"Of course," said Judith. "That seems only right."

She watched as he placed her suitcase into the immaculate trunk of his car. She noticed a well-packed box in one corner containing what appeared to be some emergency supplies, and then a long padded case that she guessed contained a firearm of some sort. "Have you been hunting lately?" she asked with what she hoped seemed innocent interest.

"Nah, I just like to be prepared for any emergencies. You never know what you might run into when you're out in the wild."

"You drive this pretty car around in the wild?"

"Oh no," said Ellen. "Daddy has a nice four-wheel-drive pickup that he uses to go hunting and out into the woods. But sometimes we have to drive places where it feels a little unsafe. And Daddy just likes to keep us nice and secure."

"That sounds sensible." Judith climbed into the leather upholstered backseat. "This is a beautiful car, Burt. I think you must be right about buying American."

"You better believe it." He turned on the ignition. "We gotta stay loyal to our country even if it is being run by a bunch of idiots."

She laughed, remembering some of the rhetoric she'd read in Adam's notes about fierce patriotism mixed with an almost paranoid distrust of government. If she were smart, she could play right into his hand. "I know just what you mean, Burt. Sometimes I consider how our country was founded, and I shudder to think what our forefathers would say if they were alive to see what's going on these days."

"That's exactly right." Burt nodded his head vigorously. "Throughout our history, men have given up everything, including their very own lives, to secure our independence, and nowadays we're losing our freedoms and rights in almost every imaginable way. It's enough to make a body sick."

Ellen made a laughing sound. "Oh, don't you get him going, Judith. He can talk for hours about this stuff."

"I think it's interesting," said Judith, thankful that they weren't looking at her. "It's refreshing to hear someone who really believes in what our country was built upon. I teach American history to fifth graders, and I really try to impart an appreciation for all that it's taken to make our country what it is today."

"Hmph. Problem is, we're only a shadow of what we could've been, what we *should've* been by now," said Burt. "If we could only get rid of all those left-wing radicals who keep making more useless laws, just increasing the size of our government while they strip the average citizen of all his inalienable rights." He thumped his hand on the steering wheel. "Then we'd all be a lot better off."

"Oh, dear." said Ellen with a nervous laugh. "Now we've really got him going. Uh, Burt, maybe we should talk about something else."

"It's okay." said Judith. "I'd love to hear more of his thoughts."

"Really?" said Burt, eyeing her from the rearview mirror.

"Yes. What you're saying makes sense to me."

"Hmm..." He tapped his fingers on the steering wheel thoughtfully. "You may want to consider coming to hear a certain speaker who's flying in tomorrow."

"Shame on you, Daddy!" exclaimed Ellen. "There you go, trying to steal my houseguest away from me already."

"Well, you can't keep her all to yourself," said Burt as he waited at the stoplight in town. Just then Judith saw Eli Paxton waiting at the crosswalk with a bag in his hand. Trying to register no visible emotion, Judith glanced over to see if Burt had noticed him as well.

"Oh, my!" exclaimed Ellen in a high-pitched voice, her head turned directly toward Eli. "What in the name of—"

"There goes our little infestation problem right now," said Burt in a quiet but bitter tone, his lips barely moving as he spoke. "Just a little something else that's wrong with this country."

Her heart pounding, Judith said nothing. Despite her role, she simply could not force herself to join in this part of the conversation. "Say, Burt," she began after a moment, pretending not to have noticed what had just transpired. "You said you'd tell me about your rules at the lake—"

"That's right," he gunned his engine as the light turned green, speeding across the intersection. Judith wondered if it was an attempt to get Eli's attention. Perhaps to send some sort of power message, or threat, or something equally ugly. But in that same moment, Eli had looked directly into the car and straight into Judith's eyes. She had felt horrified, but was unable to turn her head, and she feared her face had given her completely away. She glanced into the rearview mirror long enough to assure herself that Burt hadn't noticed. His attention was still fixed on Eli.

And as they continued down Main Street, it seemed that one of her worst fears about this whole little charade had suddenly been realized. She had betrayed Eli right to his face. But it was odd how his expression had remained unchanged in that painful instant. And he had looked right at her, clearly seeing her. But then he'd simply turned away and continued walking, almost as if he hadn't even recognized her. And yet she felt certain he had, and the pain from that moment cut her like a knife.

Burt cleared his throat as they continued out of town. "Now, we were about to go over a few rules and things. To start out with, we have a very tight security system, for the protection of the good citizens who live there. And we don't allow guests to bring cameras, cell phones, computers, and well," he chuckled, "a few other things that I don't think we need to worry about with you. Unless I'm mistaken." He caught her eye in the rearview mirror, and she forced herself to laugh.

"Well, I'm not carrying anything dangerous, if that's what you mean." She remembered Adam's notes about being as honest as possible about anything that she could possibly get caught on. If

Burt found out she'd lied about something that would really bring on the suspicion. "But I do have my cell phone with me. I didn't realize it was a problem. What should I do with it?"

Ellen turned and smiled. "Oh, that's okay, honey—"

"Sorry," interrupted Burt. "You'll have to hand it over."

She opened her purse and dug for her phone, then handed it to him. "Since Peter died, I've always carried it with me—I guess it makes me feel safer somehow."

Burt nodded. "Well, you won't need to worry about your safety when you're with us, Judith. Especially out at the lake."

"That's right, honey," reassured Ellen. "I think it must be the safest place in the entire world. Just wait and see."

"Also, after you fill out some forms in the office, you'll be issued a guest security card. It will get you into certain facilities like the health club and pool and tennis courts, but not every place. Some things are strictly off limits."

"That makes sense." She wondered what questions might be on the forms and silently sent up a prayer for help. "How many people live at the lake?"

"We're down to just over a hundred now," said Burt as he turned on the road that led to the lake. "But we expect that to change soon."

"Yes," said Ellen. "The Freedom Celebration this weekend will surely bring in some new members."

Burt tossed a look her way, and Judith expected him to hush her up again, but instead he seemed to change his mind. "Yes, we're trying to get more young people involved in our cause."

It was the first time she'd heard him call it a "cause." "So, do you have some special ways to recruit them?"

He nodded, slowing down as he came to a tall set of iron gates barricading the road. "We have a fine Web site and lots of connections to affiliate groups. It's just a matter of getting the word out."

"Yes, they've just hired a brilliant young man who's an expert at these things," said Ellen with pride. "Maybe you'll get to meet him. I'm sure you'd like him. And he's a single man, about your age, I'd guess."

Judith's eyes moved from the gates to the tall, sturdy chain-link fences, topped with coils of razor wire. Next to the gates was an unmanned outpost. The place looked just like a prison, as able to keep someone in as to keep someone out. She felt a shudder go through her, but forced a smile to her lips and into her voice. "Now, don't you go playing matchmaker with me, Ellen. I'm not ready for such things yet."

"Oh, you never know, dear. Sometimes the right man comes along, and well, it can just change everything."

Burt inserted a card and angrily punched a set of numbers, then waited for the gates to slowly open. "Don't know why we don't have a man out here today," he grumbled as he drove through. "Hand me my phone, Ellen. Better yet, dial up Bob for me." She opened the glove box, removed a phone, and quickly dialed, handing it over to her husband.

"What's going on?" barked Burt. "There's no one down here at the gates. And we've got guests coming any minute now." He paused a moment to listen, then continued. "I don't care what Jerry did to his hand. You get someone else down here—and fast!" Then he hung up. "Morons! Leaving the gate unattended on a day like today!"

"Now, now, Daddy. No use getting your blood pressure up." She turned and looked back at Judith. "The doctor in Mississippi told Burt to start taking it easier. He's on blood pressure medicine as it is, but he's not supposed to get himself all riled up."

"Well, you tell that to Bob Garret!" snapped Burt.

"Now this road takes us directly to the main complex," said Ellen soothingly, obviously trying to ignore her husband's angry display. "That big building straight ahead is the clubhouse with the pool to the right. There's a sports facility next to the pool. And then to your left is the Café. They mostly just serve hot dogs and burgers and such, and then there's the general store and post office after that." Judith quickly surveyed the buildings, large but unimpressive. They appeared to have been quickly and perhaps shoddily built, and definitely lacked any sense of style, creativity, or charm.

Burt pulled up in front of the stark clubhouse and parked in a reserved spot with his name in white uppercase letters. "Ellen, you get Judith registered." he ordered, "and I'll go see if those idiots have got someone out at the gate yet."

Ellen patted Judith's arm as they walked toward the front door. "Don't you let Burt scare you, honey. His bark's much worse than his bite."

Judith pasted a bright smile across her face. "Oh, it's okay. I can understand his concern." She looked up at the big wooden building, almost military-like with its tall flagpole in front. "This looks like a great place, Ellen; I'm sure it's worth keeping the best possible security."

Ellen nodded. "Yes, dear, you're right about that. No telling what might happen to us without our security system. Burt says crime rates get worse every blessed minute, and God knows there are all sorts of horrible and undesirable people in this world we live in. I certainly wouldn't want any of *them* getting in here."

Judith wondered if she wasn't one of *them* herself. But she just smiled and pushed open the heavy wooden door for Ellen. "What a nice building."

"Hello, Ellen," called a short man from behind the front desk.

"Hello, Henry. This is my dear friend, Judith. I've known her since she was a little girl—almost like one of my own. So I want you to treat her with special care, just like part of the family." She glanced over her shoulder. "And if you don't mind, Judith, I'll make a quick run to the powder room."

"Pleasure to make your acquaintance, ma'am," said Henry with a distinctly Southern accent. "Now, I'll just need you to fill out these forms here. Shouldn't take but a few minutes." He smiled and slid a clipboard over to her.

She looked down at the papers. "Goodness, it looks like a job application."

"That's what everyone says. But it's for security reasons." He nodded to an area furnished with a couple of club chairs and a chunky coffee table. "Just make yourself comfortable."

She sat down and began to fill in the forms, remembering what Adam had said about honesty in most things. But she also remembered how he'd invented different places of employment for her and Peter. Thankfully, he'd made her memorize them, including the phone numbers. But she wondered now if her hand didn't shake just slightly as she wrote them down. Would a lie detector test follow? She swallowed hard and prayed that God would calm her and give her strength. It had occurred to her, just as Burt had driven through the formidable gates, that coming here without first consulting with Adam could've been a big mistake. But she had no choice now but to continue, praying as she went. Just as she finished up by signing a legal disclaimer that guaranteed she wouldn't sue their organization, Ellen walked over and sat down.

"Poor dear," said Ellen. "I hate that my guests have to go through all this nonsense. But at least you seem to understand."

"Oh, it's okay." She laid down the pen. "Do you have many

guests come to visit?"

"No, not really. Burt's the one who has people coming and going all the time. Of course, they don't stay at the house. Goodness knows, the last time I had a houseguest must've been back when Jasmine came out, and that was a year ago." She shook her head sadly. "But I felt so bad having to make my very own daughter fill out these silly forms." Then she lowered her voice. "And to tell you the truth, Jasmine left most of the blanks empty. But then her daddy took care of that for her."

"Okay, Henry." said Judith as she set the clipboard back on the counter. "I think this should take care of it." She turned to go.

"Not quite yet." said Henry in an apologetic tone. "Got to take you through the metal detector first."

"You have a metal detector?" She tried to make her voice sound as if she was full of admiration.

He beamed. "You bet. We're keeping right up with the latest technology. Burt already dropped your suitcase 'round back to be scanned. But I'll need to take your handbag as well. And then we'll have you step back into this room so I can scan you too. And don't you worry none, it's just like them ones at the airport. Don't hurt a bit."

She obediently handed over her purse and waited for him to go around the back, and then come out and lead her to a side room with a table and chairs and a large black scanning wand. He waved the wand down all four sides of her body, a few beeps went off here and there as he passed over what were obviously metal snaps on her shirt and jewelry pieces and even the back closure on her bra, which he explained with some embarrassment.

Finally, he turned it off and smiled. "All right, then, you pass."

"I'm just curious, Henry. What is it you're actually looking for? Weapons?"

He nodded seriously. "Yeah, that and other things too.

You know, things like listening devices and hidden cameras and surveillance stuff like that. You'd be surprised at how many lowlifes would like to sneak in here and snoop around if they could. We just gotta be real careful, is all."

She nodded. "Well, that makes perfect sense. And it looks like you're doing an excellent job of it too, Henry."

"Why, thank you, ma'am. I'll just go and fetch your handbag and your suitcase, and y'all can be on your way now."

"Yes, I'm sure you must be busy today. Will you have to go through this with all your visitors this weekend?"

"Yeah, but we got us a whole crew lined up to help with all the scanning. And the guests have already filled out their application forms in advance, so that part's all done. But you're right, it's going to be one busy weekend. And they're due to start arriving any minute now."

"Well, I hope it goes smoothly for you."

Burt was in the waiting area with Ellen now. "Everything all right?" This he directed to Henry.

"You bet, sir. Right as rain." He smiled at Judith. "I hope you folks have yourselves a real nice little visit."

Ellen reached for Judith's hand. "Oh, believe me, we plan on it!"

Twenty-Five

"ELLEN, YOUR VIEW IS beautiful." Judith felt relieved to finally say something honest as she gazed across the room where a full window view looked out over the pristine mountain lake. "And your home is lovely too." Now, this was slightly honest. She did like the open-beamed ceilings, but in Judith's opinion, Ellen's taste in decor was a mix of tacky and gloomy. Of course, that dark blue velvet sectional may not have been Ellen's choice, thought Judith as she examined a large wolverine snarling from his post atop a bulky oak gun cabinet, filled with all sorts of rifles and handguns. She noticed a secure lock on the glass door, but what would keep someone from breaking the glass? She turned and looked around the room. From the numerous trophy heads to the framed print of a wolf pack running through the snow, the general feeling here was masculine, aggressive, and cold. Not unlike Burt.

"Why, thank you, dear." Ellen beamed with pride. "We built our home a few years ago. Burt felt it was important to upgrade for our image, you know. After all, he's an important man around here, and we'd lived in the same little cabin since the late seventies. And then our friends from down South came up here and started building these big, fancy houses, and let me tell you, it didn't take long until we began to look like poor white trash." She laughed. "Now we got ourselves the biggest and fanciest house on the lake. Burt saw to that. After we got finished, they made a building ordinance saying that homes couldn't be any bigger than three thousand square feet. They say it's to save building space, but I think it's just to make sure no one outbuilds Burt. Although, when he helped Hal on his house last year, he suspected it might be just a hair over three thousand, but he hasn't told a soul."

Judith glanced absently over the magazines and periodicals on the coffee table. A *Ladies' Home Journal* sat right next to a couple of gun and sportsman magazines and what appeared to be an ultra-conservative political newsletter. "I'm curious, where is Hal's house located?"

"Just on up the road a bit from us. It's the most recently built home and sits right next to the undeveloped area. We could probably walk down there sometime and have a little look-see if you'd like. I'm sure Hal wouldn't mind a bit."

"Oh, I would like that. Maybe I'd feel more connected to Jasmine to see where she'd spent some of her time, before— well, you know."

"Then you really ought to go down to that awful little trailer." Ellen made a tsk-tsk sound, then visibly shuddered. "Not that I actually recommend it. Why, it's simply disgusting and detestable down there."

Judith nodded thoughtfully. "I understand. But truthfully, I really wouldn't mind seeing it—if it somehow made her seem closer. You know what I mean?"

"Maybe. I've considered going down there myself a time or two, but I just haven't got up the nerve. Hal won't even step foot in there anymore. You know, he plans to burn the place to the ground just as soon as burning season begins. Of course, you can't burn this time of year due to fire danger."

"Yes, I've heard reports on how dry the forests are right now. Do you worry at all about forest fires, being so isolated out here next to the wilderness area?"

"Well, you know we've got the water right there. And Burt's got himself a little fishing boat. I s'pect if worse came to worst, we could just hop in and row ourselves out to the middle of the lake." She laughed nervously. "But besides that, we've got us a volunteer fire crew who swear they can put out anything. The boys out here try to be prepared for all sorts of emergencies. Burt says we can survive anything, maybe even a nuclear holocaust. And we have all sorts of plans all written up in a notebook somewhere, and there's even one that tells everyone exactly what to do in case of a forest fire. Living where we do over in this newer part of the development, we're supposed to use the new fire exit road over on the west side of the lake. But to tell you the truth, I don't really concern myself too greatly over fire danger. I think there's no use in worrying about something you can't control anyway."

"Yes, that makes sense." In more ways than one, she thought.

"Well, let's go upstairs now and I'll show you your room. You can get yourself all settled in and comfortable." She reached for the handrail then paused. "I don't hardly ever come up here anymore; I guess these stairs just leave me a little breathless."

"Why don't you just point me in the right direction and wait down here?"

"No, no, that's all right. I can make it. I'm just sorry I didn't get a chance to fix up your room for you. Why, I'd have brought you in some fresh flowers and whatnot." She huffed her way slowly up the stairs.

"Oh, I'm glad you didn't have to go to any trouble for me."

"There's just the one bedroom up here," she opened the door and looked around the large room with a sad expression. "But it has its own bath. This was Jasmine's room when she stayed here with us that month. Fact is, she's the only one who's ever stayed up here." She pressed her hand to her lips and Judith could see the tears forming in her eyes again. "Then she married Hal and that was the end of that."

Judith put her arm around Ellen's shoulder. "It's hard, isn't it? I remember how I couldn't bear to go into Jonathan's room after he died. And that was after a lingering illness where we knew we were eventually going to lose him. But, just the same, it was weeks before I could go in there without falling apart. Finally, we sold the house and moved away. It was just too painful to stay."

Ellen nodded, blotting her eyes with a handkerchief. "That was wise, Judith. Best to simply move on and forget these unpleasantries altogether."

Judith peered at Ellen. "You look pretty tired to me, Ellen. And I know you've had a busy day. Would you like to take a rest? I'll be fine. I can unpack and make myself at home for now."

"Oh, thank you, dear. I usually do take a little catnap in the afternoon. You know, I can't hardly get over what a kind and caring person you've grown up to be, Judith. Your mother must be awfully proud of you."

Judith sighed. "Maybe she is. I couldn't really say. Sometimes mothers and daughters forget to tell each other such things."

Ellen nodded. "Yes, that's true enough. But if I was your mother, I'd surely tell you what a fine woman you've grown up to be."

She squeezed Ellen's hand. "Thanks. Now you go have your rest. And don't worry about me. I'll just relax too. I even brought a novel along that I've been wanting to start. And I also have my sketch pad to keep me busy."

"Good for you." She paused at the door. "And don't forget that Daddy likes his dinner at six-thirty sharp. So if by some chance I'm still asleep by five-thirty, please, dear, would you come in and wake me up?"

"I will."

She stood before the west window, listening to the sound of each heavy step as Ellen slowly made her way back down the stairs. Without really seeing, Judith stared out through the trees. She stayed there for several minutes, quiet and still, almost afraid to move, as if she expected to hear something or feel something or know something that would somehow connect her to Jasmine. But nothing came. Nothing.

She looked around the room. Unlike the downstairs, this room had a pleasant simplicity to it. The antique metal bed frame was topped with what appeared to be an old quilt made of faded pastel calicos. And it looked familiar. She went closer to examine it more carefully. Of course! It was Jasmine's old sunbonnet baby quilt that her grandmother had made for her. Judith fingered the quilt, now mellowed and softened by the years. She had slept under this very quilt as a child on some of those rare occasions when she'd spent the night at the Morrisons'. Usually, the girls preferred to sleep over at Judith's home where the atmosphere was more fun and relaxed and they could stay up as long as they liked, talking and giggling until the early morning hours. But at Jasmine's house they always had to be very quiet because of the baby or because Mr. Morrison wanted them to act like ladies, and then, of course, they always had to be in bed by ten. But there had also been those times when they'd risen while it was still dark out to go on some sort of outdoor adventure with Jasmine's dad. So perhaps those early bedtimes had been for a reason.

Judith opened her suitcase and began to hang clothes in the empty closet. It was strange to think that Jasmine had done the same thing just last year. What had she hung in here? Did she leave anything behind? Judith quietly began to go through drawers, searching the highboy dresser and bedside table, hunting for something—anything that might connect her to her friend. She removed each drawer, looking carefully beneath and behind for something hidden. But other than a few old sachets and a handkerchief that had slipped behind a drawer, she found nothing.

Then she went into the bathroom to continue her strange search, but instead she just stood there looking around the small tidy room, feeling somewhat foolish. What in the world was she looking for anyway? And why did she think there would be anything here to find? Still, as if compelled by another force, she continued her search, thoroughly examining the linen closet, removing the small stacks of neatly folded towels and sheets and feeling all around the darkened corners. And then she went through the drawers on the vanity, quietly taking each one out and examining the ordinary contents of soaps and tissue and bath products.

Now, feeling slightly ridiculous, she even got down on her hands and knees and opened the door beneath the vanity, looking all around, past the wastebasket and cleansers and sponges. As she searched the dark cavity beneath the sink, she questioned her sanity. But that's when she found it! Her hand bumped something dangling from the backside of the sink. It was a small bundle wrapped in bathroom tissue and attached with several Band-Aids to the back of the sink. She pulled it off and unwrapped the strange package to discover an attractive wedding ring set. She held the two shiny rings in her palm—an engagement ring with a large solitaire set in platinum and a matching wedding band with numerous smaller diamonds surrounding it. Probably worth quite a bit too.

She stared at the beautiful rings in wonder. Had *these* belonged to Jasmine? Perhaps given to her by Hal? But then why on earth would they be hidden here? Judith tried them on her ring finger. Too small. Jasmine had always had delicate hands. A lump grew in her throat as she imagined her friend wearing these precious rings, and then the desperation that might drive her to wrap them up and hide them behind the bathroom sink like this. Why would she do this strange thing? What did it all mean? Suddenly, she remembered the two photos that Hal had given her, still securely tucked in her purse. Would they be clear enough to show a ring?

She examined the wedding photo, but Jasmine's left hand was hidden in a fold of that hideous yellow dress. But there in the camping photo, both hands were clearly visible. And there on her wedding ring finger was a small plain band of yellow gold. Not anything like this lovely platinum wedding set.

Judith's heart began to race. For some reason these rings seemed an important piece of evidence. They meant something! She longed to call Adam right now and tell him of her amazing find, but knew better than to use the Morrisons' phone—Adam had warned her that the lines could be tapped. But somehow, she had to get this ring set out of here where he could examine it, perhaps even determine its origins. A horrible thought hit her—what if they searched people who were leaving the lake as carefully as they searched them arriving. She looked down at her left hand where she still wore her own wedding rings, not nearly as nice as these. There would be no way for her to explain having two sets of wedding rings. Well, she'd just have to deal with this later. In the meantime, she carefully wrapped the rings back in tissue and placed them in a metal pill box, then she made a small hole in the seam of her cosmetic bag and slid the box between the lining. That was the best she could do for the moment.

Feeling emotionally spent, she sank into the armchair by the window and looked around the room again. "What happened to you, Jasmine?" she whispered, almost inaudibly, once again wary to the possibility of surveillance in this house. Adam had warned of the general paranoia of most survivalist groups, how they derived great pleasure in employing the latest devices and how she was never to let her guard down while out there.

Now more than ever, she couldn't dismiss the feeling that something had happened to her friend. How she longed to snoop around and unravel this perplexing story. Just holding those rings had filled her with the certainty that Jasmine had been previously married after all. And apparently to someone with money, or at the minimum, very expensive and good taste. But what had happened to him? Divorce? And if there'd been a marriage, wasn't it possible there had been children? But if so, where might they be? Judith resisted the strong temptation to begin pacing. She didn't want to bother Ellen. And yet this new bit of information disturbed her deeply. Something about these hidden rings felt insidious and wrong. To suppress her frustration, she picked up her sketch pad and began to furiously sketch the metal bed frame and quilt. At first her artwork was only a means of distraction, a way to soothe her perplexed mind. But as the drawing took shape, she realized it would be a sweet keepsake to remember her childhood days with her dear friend.

Just as she was putting the last finishing touch on her drawing, she heard someone stir downstairs. It was already five-thirty. She set aside her sketch pad and went down to find Ellen puttering about the kitchen. This room felt slightly friendlier than the rest of the downstairs, and yet the dated shades of blue and mauve seemed somewhat chilly, and the barren, white laminate countertops looked clinical and sterile.

"Can I help?"

"Oh, there you are, Judith. Well, I'm just fixing to fry up this chicken. But you could grate that cabbage for slaw if you like. Does fried chicken sound okay to you, dear?"

"Sounds delicious. I always loved your Southern fried chicken."

Ellen smiled. "See, you really are like a part of this family, Judith."

"Thanks." She washed her hands then proceeded to grate cabbage. "I noticed Jasmine's old sunbonnet quilt on the bed upstairs. It brought back some happy memories for me."

"Yes, I dug that old thing out when she first came to stay with us. I thought it might help make her feel more at home somehow."

"Didn't her grandmother in Mississippi make it?"

"That's right."

"Was that your mother?"

Ellen laughed. "Oh, heavens, no. My mother never would've dreamed of making a patchwork quilt, not to mention for one of *my* girls."

"I know you said your parents didn't approve of you marrying Burt, but didn't they ever get over it?"

"Unfortunately, things only got worse between them and us. That's one of the main reasons we moved out here in the first place—to start up a new life apart from them. I think I mentioned how my sister Susan got married in the early sixties, just about the time when the South started to go to pieces. And, as fate would have it, her husband had just graduated from some big, fancy law school up North, and anyway, when Don brought his law practice down to Jackson, he brought his liberal views right along with it. Before we knew it, he started brainwashing Daddy with all his wild political views." She made a sour face as she cut off a drumstick. "Why, Burt even told me that Don was affiliated with the ACLU!" She pointed her knife at Judith as if to make a point.

"So Burt and Don didn't exactly see eye to eye then?"

"You can say that again! Well, it was right around that time my daddy really started picking on Burt and belittling his opinions right and left. And we just finally had to cut ourselves off from my family altogether. Burt was absolutely certain that my family was trying to poison little Jasmine with their misinformed views. And even though she was just small, she did like to listen in as the grown-ups talked—you know what they say about little pitchers having big ears. So it was about that time Burt got the opportunity to come out here and take the job at the Cedar Crest mill."

"And did he start developing this place at the lake then?"

"Not exactly. He had some funding to start things up with, but not really enough to accomplish all that he wanted." She removed the lid from a big can of lard. "You see, Burt's what some folks call a visionary-type person. He had this big idea of creating a place where like-minded people could gather and live and, well, you know, be safe from the outside influences and dangers. Sort of a Utopia, you might say."

"So are most of the people who live out here from the South?"

"Well, a lot are from the South—you know, friends we had back in Mississippi and all—people, like us, who were fed up with all the new laws they were bringing in down there. But a fair amount are from the Northwest too." She turned and looked squarely at Judith. "You know, a lot of people think folks like us are just Southerners, but what we believe in reaches a whole lot further than just the South, let me tell you."

"I don't mean to be nosy, Ellen, but I'm curious about what it is, exactly, that you and Burt do believe in." Judith tried to appear sincerely interested.

"Well, you know, honey, it's just simple things like loving our country, and menfolk wanting to protect their women and young'uns, and preserving our rights to bear arms, and, well, wanting to keep our race pure. Just all that basic kind of stuff—you know, like what's written in the Constitution and all." She placed a large cast iron skillet on the stove with a thud. "But Burt's better at explaining these things than I am."

"Oh, I think you're doing just fine, Ellen." She smiled and set aside the bowl of shredded cabbage. "So, if you don't mind me asking, is your group related to the KKK at all? I really don't know much about these things, but I've heard the name of that organization before."

Ellen turned and looked at her with one brow slightly raised. "Well, now, that's a real tricky question, Judith. You see, we're our own independent organization, but we do have some affiliate groups, and yes, I do believe the Klan is one of them. And of course, Burt's dad was a Klan man— that's one of the reasons my daddy was so against that family in the first place. But you need to understand how a lot of people really misunderstand the Klan. I mean, take that Michael Marks fellow: Why, he's a well-respected man and he's been, and probably still is, a Klan member. But that doesn't seem to bother most folks. And like Burt says, the Klan takes a pretty bad beating from the press."

Judith swallowed hard then nodded. "Yes, I've heard the Klan gets a bad rap. But then I've also heard that most of the news sources are pretty liberal and don't always report fairly."

A smile of relief swept across Ellen's face. "Yes, that's just what Burt says too."

Judith turned away, her stomach in tight knots. "Uh, shall I put this dressing on the slaw now?"

"Yes, then go ahead and stick it in the fridge for a while."

Judith took several slow, deep breaths as she stirred the dressing into the cabbage, silently praying for help, and fearing she wouldn't be able to keep this up much longer. Finally, she placed the bowl in the refrigerator and turned toward the stove, watching as Ellen placed floured chicken pieces into the hot fat.

"You know, I was a little worried at first," said Ellen as she shook loose flour from a wing. "I was afraid you might not understand our views, Judith, or that you might judge us the way so many of the younger people do, but you seem real open-minded to me, dear. And I appreciate that. "

Judith jumped as a large splatter of fat came her way. "Yes, I try to keep an open mind. Although, to be honest, I don't understand everything."

"Goodness, who in the world does?"

Judith forced a laugh. "I guess you're right. But I suppose this thing about keeping the race pure is the most confusing part to me."

Ellen started turning the pieces over to brown on the other sides. "Well, that's not so unusual, dear. Let me tell you, it's not real easy to understand. Long ago, Burt had me read a booklet that has a whole bunch of Bible Scriptures in it that prove how white people really are the superior race, but I must admit that I found the whole thing somewhat confusing at first. But whenever I hear Burt or one of the other leaders explaining these things, it always seems to make perfect sense."

"Maybe I'll get to hear that speaker that Burt was telling me about."

She put the lid over the pan, then turned down the heat. "You know, Judith, I think that's a real smart idea. I don't explain these things very well. To tell you the truth, I don't even waste much time thinking about those racial problems much. I leave that to Daddy and the other men. Although, I must admit that when we went back to Mississippi to bury Jasmine last month, I was real alarmed at the horrible wickedness I saw in all those dark faces there. Why, I felt certain that they were going to murder me in my bed right there in the Holiday Inn!"

Judith turned away to conceal her disgust, pretending to wash her hands at the sink once again. "It does sound frightening."

"Oh my, was it ever! Made me honestly thankful we don't live down there anymore. Goodness knows what might happen to us with coloreds running rampant all over the place like that. Why, they act just like they own the whole country, lock, stock, and barrel! And let me tell you, it wasn't always like that, Judith. When I was growing up, coloreds knew their place and, by golly, they stayed put. But nowadays everything's all out of control. And Burt says the crime rate goes up every single day. So let me tell you, I was right glad to get out of there, even though I felt real sorry that I had to leave my baby behind amid all that vile darkness and evil."

"Yes, I didn't quite understand that. Why was it that you decided to bury Jasmine's body in Mississippi?"

"Well, it was Burt's idea, and at first I couldn't understand it, but then he explained that it was a show of loyalty to our Southern roots, and that since she'd been born in Mississippi, she should be buried down there too. He also told me about this time when she was just a little girl and we went to his mother's graveside—Grandma Morrison—just shortly after she died, and I don't recollect this myself, but Burt clearly recalls how Jasmine said she wanted to be buried right next to her grandma. Now isn't that just dear?"

Judith nodded, all the while thinking it didn't sound a bit like what a child, especially Jasmine, might say. First off, Jasmine had always had a horrific fear of death and mortality. And she had absolutely hated graveyards and would never go anywhere near them. Not even on the Halloween when they were twelve and Judith had begged her and finally dared her. And even though Jasmine rarely gave up a dare, she had flatly refused. But Judith kept this memory to herself. "So is that where she was buried then? Next to Grandma Morrison?"

"Well, no.. .the family plot was already full. We had to go to another cemetery. But at least it was in the same town that she was born in. That was something, after all."

Judith sighed. "Yes, I suppose so. But it's still so hard for me to let her go."

Ellen slipped her arm around Judith and gave a little squeeze. "We miss her, don't we, honey?"

"Yes. It was too soon for her to go."

Ellen nodded, then wiped her hands on a towel. "Now, I'll just get out the potato salad that I made yesterday and open a can of peaches, and I think we'll be all set."

Judith glanced over to the breakfast nook. "Can I set the table for you?"

"Sure. But Burt likes to eat dinner in the dining room and on the good china. He thinks it's more civilized. To tell you the truth, I find the kitchen more comfortable. Cozy, you know. But the dishes and silver are in the china hutch out there. The same one we got back when you and Jasmine were just kids. A little outdated I s'pect, but I like it just the same."

Judith recognized the Danish modern hutch and matching dining room set. She had admired them as a child, but wasn't so sure anymore. They seemed rather cold and formal now. She set three place settings, one at each end in the way that she remembered Jasmine's parents sitting from years ago, and one for herself in the middle. She heard the phone ring, but continued to arrange the table.

"Looks like you'll need to set another place," called Ellen. "Burt's bringing home another mouth to feed. I hope I made enough chicken. I wonder if I should make some more dessert."

Judith set another place setting across the table from hers, then returned to the kitchen. "Anything I can do?"

Ellen was holding what was more than half of a two-layer chocolate cake. "Just tell me, do you think this cake's big enough for four people, Judith?"

"Goodness, yes. Unless everyone is absolutely ravenous."

Ellen laughed. ""Well, Burt's been trying to cut down on sweets, and Hal could certainly afford to. I think we'll be just fine."

So that's who was joining them for dinner tonight. The idea of sitting across from Hal Emery put another knot in her stomach, and she began to feel, once again, that she had gotten into something way over her head. How she longed to call Adam, to simply hear his calm, soothing voice. But now she wouldn't be in touch with him for at least two, maybe three, days. And what would he think when she wasn't at home tonight? Would he get her phone message? Would he be worried? Would he call out the guard and blow her whole cover? And what *would* happen if they found out that she was really working for him? Once again, she sent up a silent and desperate prayer for help. This scheme was fast becoming too complicated for her.

Twenty-Six

JUDITH WAS JUST PLACING the bread and butter on the table when the two men walked in. "Hello," she called in her friendliest voice, yet at the same time she longed to flee this place, to get away from everyone and everything even remotely connected with the Morrisons and the community at the lake.

"Hi, Judith," said Burt. "Did Ellen tell you I was bringing this stray along home with me?"

"Yeah," Hal laughed, "I happen to know just how good Ellen's cooking is, and believe me, I never pass up a chance to sit at her table."

"Oh, there you are," called Ellen happily. "Right on time too. Y'all go ahead and sit down now, and I'll bring in the chicken."

"Fried chicken?" Hal rubbed his rotund midsection. "I guess I really got lucky tonight."

"Yes," said Ellen as she proudly set the steaming platter in the center of the table. "I just hope there's enough to go 'round."

Judith laughed. "Good grief, it looks like you've enough here to feed ten people."

Ellen grinned. "Well, I always like a little fried chicken for leftovers the next day. I think it tastes real good cold."

Then Burt bowed his head and said a brief and formal blessing. Although Judith didn't find it as surprising as she had the first night at the restaurant, it still disturbed her. She wondered if it were possible that she and Burt actually prayed to the same God, and if so, would God listen and respond to both of them in the same way?

Ellen handed the platter of chicken to Judith first. "Hal, I told Judith you might be willing to give her a little tour of your new house, if you're not too busy with the conference that is."

"Sure, it's fine with me." said Hal as he took a piece of bread. "Although we will be pretty busy during the next couple days."

"Well, you could probably take them on over there tonight before the meeting starts," suggested Burt as he dished out some potato salad. "They're having a big spaghetti feed over at the lodge tonight, and then the first meeting will start at eight-thirty."

"Yeah, I s'pose we could run on over there after we finish up here," offered Hal.

"I'm surprised you didn't go to the spaghetti feed too, Burt," said Judith. "I certainly hope you didn't feel like you needed to eat at home on my account."

Ellen laughed. "I don't mean to hurt your feelings, Judith, but Burt came home on account of just one thing."

"Burt can't stand spaghetti," whispered Hal as if he were telling a deep, dark secret.

Burt nodded as he bit into a juicy thigh. "That's right. And besides, I'll be spending plenty of time with these fel-lars before the weekend's over."

"Well, that makes me feel better." Judith focused her eyes on her plate, willing herself to at least appear to be eating, although she felt certain she could not.

Burt and Hal dominated the conversation during the meal,

and Judith tried to memorize the names that were mentioned, but before long all the Jims and Bobs and Bills seemed to mix together. And suddenly she wished that she had been wired like Adam had wanted. But then, on the other hand, maybe not—especially considering the scanning system they had going over at the clubhouse.

"Did you get your gate security all straightened out?" asked Judith.

"You better believe it." Burt pushed his chair back. "And we got the guard dogs out and everything."

"Our official welcoming committee." Hal chuckled.

"I've got German chocolate cake for dessert," offered Ellen.

"How about if we take that little walk over to Hal's place first," suggested Burt. "Let our supper settle a bit."

"Sounds good to me," said Hal, following Burt's lead.

"But you're not finished, dear," said Ellen, eyeing Judith's nearly full plate.

"I guess my eyes were bigger than my stomach," said Judith as she began to stand too. "But, really, I've had plenty. That was delicious, Ellen."

"Are you sure, honey?"

"Yes, shall I clear the table?"

"No, you go along with the boys now, and I'll take care of this. I've seen Hal's house plenty of times."

"Oh, let me help—"

"Come on, Judith," said Burt in a commanding voice. "You let Ellen take care of this."

They went outside and began to walk down the graveled road. "It cools off nicely out here by the lake," commented Judith as they went past a newer home.

"That's where the Smiths live," pointed out Hal. "They've got a couple of grade-school-age boys."

"Where do they go to school?" asked Judith, as she studied the square, plain house. One thing she'd noticed out here was that although everything was neat and tidy, there seemed to be no architectural interest in any of the homes and minimal landscaping.

"We have a small private school over by the lodge," said Burt. "About thirty kids altogether, kindergarten through high school."

"How many teachers?" she asked.

"Just one."

"Oh my, that must be quite a load."

Burt looked at her with a slightly raised brow. "That's right, you're a teacher too. Maybe we should try to talk you into sticking around."

Judith laughed, hoping that it sounded more light-hearted to their ears than it did to hers. "Oh, you just never know, Burt. What sort of curriculum do they use anyway? Similar to what homeschool kids use?"

"Similar, I suppose, but we have our own curriculum with a focus on religion and national pride. Our goal is biblically based—we believe if we bring up our children in the way they should go, when they become older they don't depart from it."

"I see." Judith wondered how Burt managed to explain his own two daughters to his followers.

"That's my house there," said Hal, proudly pointing to a two-story boxlike house straight ahead.

"It looks big," said Judith.

"Yes, I had hoped we might've filled it with children." He sadly shook his head.

"Ellen said that there's a three thousand-square-foot limit on homes," said Judith, hoping to change the subject. "Do you have to comply to any other building codes out here?"

"Just our own." Burt laughed in a cynical way. "'Course, the county might not be too pleased with that—if they knew, that is. But their stupid permits are just another way the government tries to get its hand into our pockets."

"Welcome to my castle," said Hal as he unlocked the door. "Give me a minute to disengage this." He began to punch buttons into a security system that looked exactly like the one in the Morrisons' house.

"Does everyone have the same security system?" she asked.

"You bet." said Hal as the green light came on. "And all are connected to the main security back at the lodge."

"I'm surprised you'd need all that when you live in such a remote and gated community." She walked past the entryway and looked around to furnishings that appeared startling similar to those in the Morrison home.

"We have reasons to be careful." said Burt. "We leave nothing to chance."

"This reminds me of your house, Burt." said Judith.

Burt grinned. "They say imitation is the highest form of flattery."

Hal nodded. "Burt's been like a dad to me. I guess I don't even realize how much his life has influenced mine."

"How did you guys meet in the first place?" she asked as they walked through the living area.

"Hal's daddy, Clarence Emery, was a good friend of mine back in Mississippi. Our families were real close. Clarence was a little older than me, and I greatly admired him. We both worked at the lumber mill after the war. And it was Clarence who first began dreaming of starting a place like this. He thought we'd build it in Mississippi, but when I was transferred out here, we started dreaming up bigger and better things. He was the one who kept things going back home, recruiting and gathering funds."

"Yep," added Hal, "my daddy ran all sorts of meetings and things to raise money and get people fired up about this place."

"What happened to him?"

"Heart attack." Burt shook his head. "Right in the prime of life too."

"Yep, it was a sad day." Hal leaned against a counter in the sparsely furnished kitchen. "He never even got to see this place."

"So I've tried to make it up to him." said Burt, "by taking Hal under my wing, so to speak."

"That's good of you." Judith turned from the men and studied the kitchen. *And you gave him your daughter too,* she thought. "Did Jasmine spend much time in this house?" she asked, hoping her voice sounded innocent, maybe even wistful.

"Not as much as I'd have liked," said Hal. "For some reason she just couldn't seem to get comfortable here."

Judith turned and studied his face. "That's too bad."

"Yeah, she just didn't seem to be comfortable much of anywhere." He shook his head. "Not even in her own skin."

A shiver ran down her neck. "May I see the rest of the house?"

"Excuse me," said Burt. "I need to make a phone call."

"Why don't you use my office," said Hal as he opened the door to a room with an intricate looking computer system that filled the top of a large desk.

"Wow," said Judith. "That looks impressive. You must be a real computer whiz."

"Nah, I just use it to order stuff for the hardware store, and I like to surf the Net and see what's going on in the outside world."

"Anything interesting?"

"Just things that make me glad I live where I do." Hal closed

the door to give Burt privacy for his phone call. "Do you want to see
the upstairs?"

Judith shrugged. "Sure, if we have time."

He showed her several identical bedrooms upstairs. "These
were going to be rooms for the kids." Then he opened the door
to a larger bedroom. "And this was supposed to be for me and
Jasmine."

"Supposed to be?"

He forced a laugh. "Yeah, Jasmine never slept a single night in
this room." Then he closed the door.

"Where did she sleep?"

He nodded toward a closed door. "In there. That is unless
she was down at the trailer. She stayed there sometimes too."

"Can I see this room?"

He shrugged. "I guess it don't matter, being that you were
a good friend of hers and all. But I haven't moved a thing—since
she—uh, left us."

Judith felt her breath catch as he opened the door and then
stepped back to allow her in. She started to enter the room, not
quite knowing what to expect, then paused. Meanwhile, Hal
remained in the hallway.

"I don't like to go in there," he quickly explained. "Not that I
believe in ghosts or anything.. .but..."

She turned and studied him. Did he look slightly frightened?
"No, of course not. I can understand that." She stepped into the
room, surprised at how it felt cooler, but then it was on the shady
side of the house. She quickly took in the small room. Nothing
unusual or out of the ordinary. Just a single bed, or perhaps it
was only a cot, against the far wall, pushed up into the corner
with a heap of blankets piled up, almost like a nest of sorts. She
walked over and touched the top blanket. Jasmine had slept here.

Next to the cot was a small low table, empty except for a small, familiar-looking worn Bible. A large lump grew in her throat as she reached for the Bible, then almost reverently opened it. She knew it was Jasmine's. It had been presented to her by Aunt Lenore on her twelfth birthday. Judith remembered that day which, of course, had also been her twelfth birthday. They had both been invited to Aunt Lenore's for tea. And Aunt Lenore had given both girls identical Bibles, explaining to them that twelve was the "age of accountability" and a time when they needed to take their own spiritual well-being more seriously. Both girls had listened politely, but perhaps not too intently because they were more consumed with the slumber party they were jointly having at Judith's house later that day. Judith ran her hands over the Bible. Jasmine still had this, after all these years. Judith wondered if she could even find hers. Probably buried deep in one of the many boxes stored back in her lonely apartment.

"Are you okay?"

She started at his voice, jerked back into the here and now. "Yes. I...I'm just so surprised to see Jasmine's Bible here. I mean, I had one just like it, and I haven't seen it in years. It just brings back so many memories for me."

"Yeah, Ellen had saved it for her. I think Jasmine had actually been reading it quite a bit. I had hoped it might even help to straighten her out some."

"Straighten her out?" Judith moved to where she could see his face more clearly.

"Well, she was pretty mixed up, you know."

"Oh." Judith turned and stared at the room. "Do you mind if I look a bit more?"

"Go ahead. I'm sure there's not much to see."

And there really wasn't much to see in the barren room. A small painted dresser with only a few clothing items in it. Plain and practical looking underpants and bras and socks and a few pastel colored T-shirts. But what really caught Judith's eye amid the white under things was a coral-colored pair of silky panties and a matching bra—both trimmed in lace, but tucked discreetly beneath the other more sensible looking items. And although the coral pieces didn't appear new or unused, they were definitely quite nice. Judith peeked at a tag. A French label! How strange. She quickly closed the drawer and looked away. "You're right." she said as she walked casually toward the closet. "There's really not much to see. But somehow it's a comfort to me just knowing that Jasmine was really here. And that these were her things."

He made a grunting noise and moved farther away from the doorway. She went to the closet and peered inside. Again, more ordinary clothing, not much, but neatly organized and hung evenly apart. Even the jeans were on hangers. But one pair of jeans caught her eye. An older looking pair, or perhaps just because they were faded and frayed slightly at the hems. She pulled them out and studied them, then peeked at the inside label. Ralph Lauren, size eight. She looked at the other two pairs of jeans. Both were Wranglers. Both size six. Jasmine must've lost weight. She looked at the few dresses hanging there, one with a small blue printed fabric, one was hot pink, and then she noticed the awful yellow dress, the same as in the wedding photo. But next to that dress, nearly hidden in the bulk of the hideous yellow fabric, hung another item. Just a shirt, and nothing unusual at that. But Judith recognized it. For she had purchased an identical shirt the summer before she'd lost Peter. Just a simple white shirt, but made by a popular designer. And to Judith it had cost a fortune! And even though she'd been on a splurge at the time, it had been difficult to plunk down the price for that shirt. Apparently, Jasmine had purchased the same shirt herself. Judith held the shirt close to her face and breathed a prayer.

Please, God, help me get to the bottom of this.

"Are you about ready?"

She hung the shirt back up and turned toward the door. Pausing again by the Bible on the table. "Do you think—" She stopped herself, hand poised in the air over the small black book.

"Go ahead, take anything you like." Hal shuffled his feet. "Makes no difference to me. Fact is, it'd be a big favor if someone came in here and took all this stuff out of here and gave it to Goodwill or something. I already asked Ellen, but she can't bear to do it"

"Maybe I could help out."

"Sure, that'd be great."

"You two done up there?" called Burt from below. "We need to be getting on our way, Hal. It's getting close to eight already."

"Yeah, we're coming," said Hal. Then he closed the door and followed her down the stairs.

"Judith has offered to clear out that room for me," said Hal when they reached the foot of the stairs.

"You sure that's a good idea?" Burt looked slightly suspicious.

"Hal just mentioned that he doesn't like to go in there. And I just thought if it would help him, I could box up those things and get them out of there. Then someone could drop them at Goodwill." Judith paused and looked absently at a large cabinet near the front door. But except for one rifle behind the glass doors, it was empty. "Is this your gun cabinet, Hal?"

"Yeah."

"After seeing Burt's well-stocked cabinet, I'm surprised you aren't more of a gun collector yourself."

"Actually, I am." He pulled a ring of keys from his pocket and went toward a closed door. "Do we have a minute, Burt?"

"One minute," he grumbled.

Hal opened the door to a room that looked like a small arsenal. Shelves and shelves of guns.

"Oh my!" She hoped she had feigned admiration when what she really felt was an appalled sense of shock. "Are all those yours?"

He grinned. "Actually, most of this is stock for the hardware store. But I moved my private collection in here as well." He proudly picked up a big rifle with a highly polished stock. "This used to be my granddad's."

"Very nice."

"Hurry it up." growled Burt.

"We're coming." Hal waited until she came out, then carefully locked the door. "Yeah, I guess I might as well move my guns back into my gun case now."

They waited outside while he engaged his security system again.

"Why did you take your guns out of the case in the first place?" asked Judith as they walked back toward the Morrisons'. "I would think they'd be quite safe with all your security systems."

Hal glanced over to Burt before he continued. "Actually, we were worried about Jasmine. Burt was the one who suggested I put them safely away. As it turned out, he was right."

"Oh..."

They walked along in silence now, Burt keeping a pretty brisk pace considering his age. Then finally Judith spoke. "So where did she get a gun?"

"Well, unfortunately, I'd completely forgotten about a little revolver that I used to keep out at the trailer. Jasmine found it."

"And is that where she did it?"

Burt began to walk faster.

Hal nodded. "Yeah. Not inside. She did it outside by the pond out back."

"Oh..."

They continued walking in silence.

"I'm sorry to bring this all up again," said Judith. "But it helps me to understand everything better. And I think it helps me to accept that she's really gone."

"She's gone." said Burt firmly, as they neared his house. "And there's not a thing we can do about it. Please don't speak of this anymore."

Before Judith had a chance to respond, Ellen was opening the back door and smiling. "Oh, you're back. I'd just about given up on y'all having time for dessert before you had to go back to your meeting. Come on in here."

Just after Burt and Hal quickly shoveled down their cake and gulped their coffee, Ellen spoke up. "I think you were right, Daddy," she said in her little-girl voice. "Judith should go hear John Wagner speak tomorrow night. We had a nice little chat this afternoon, and she's quite interested in learning more about what we believe."

"Good for her." Burt smiled as he stood, leaving his dirty dishes at the table. "We'll plan on it then. Let's go, Hal, that meeting won't start if we don't get there."

"Nice seeing you again, Judith," said Hal with a friendly nod.

"Yes, and thanks for showing me your home." She forced a smile to her mouth.

"Tell Ellen about your idea to box that stuff up," called Hal as he followed Burt to the door.

"What stuff?" asked Ellen after the two men were gone.

"Jasmine's things." Judith began to pick up the dishes. "Hal wants them taken out, but he can't bear to go in that room himself. So I offered to help."

"That's kind of you, dear. Do you mind?"

"Not at all. Like I said, it makes me feel more connected to her." She set the stack of dishes next to the sink, then returned to where she had discreetly placed Jasmine's Bible on a shelf by the back door. "By the way, Hal said it was okay for me to keep her Bible. It's the one Aunt Lenore gave her. Actually, she gave us both one, but I think I may have lost mine."

"Oh yes, I found that with the old sunbonnet baby quilt."

"But I got to thinking that you might want to keep this for yourself, Ellen." She held out the Bible for her.

Ellen stared at the small Bible for a long moment, but without touching it. "No. You go ahead and keep it, dear. I think it would only make me sad to have it. Better to just forget these things and move on."

"Okay, if you're sure."

Ellen turned away. "Yes, dear. I think it's better for you to keep it. Jasmine would've liked that."

Judith clutched the Bible to her chest with relief. "I hope so."

Twenty-Seven

"WHEN DO YOU THINK it would be the best time for me to box up Jasmine's things?" Judith tentatively asked as she placed the last coffee cup into the dishwasher. She didn't want to lose what might be a promising opportunity to find some other sort of clue about Jasmine. "Maybe I should try for tomorrow, since Monday is the Fourth and it sounds like we've got a full day planned."

"Actually, we'll have a pretty full day tomorrow too," said Ellen. "What with church in the morning. And then there's the ladies' luncheon and—"

"Ladies' luncheon?"

Ellen smiled sheepishly. "Yes, I forgot to mention that I'm supposed to attend a ladies' luncheon for our guests. You'll come along, won't you?"

"Well, sure. Why not?"

"I don't have an official role, exactly. But it's important for Burt's image that I attend. One of those things, you know..."

"It sounds like fun."

Ellen grabbed Judith's hand. "Oh, Judith, I'm so glad you're here with us! It's almost like having Jasmine back. I don't ever want you to leave!"

Judith forced another smile, but in the same moment she felt torn. It was as if Ellen were steadily drawing her into a tight circle of intimacy, or was it a web? And yet, despite herself, Judith sincerely cared for her—she really did. And she felt true compassion for Ellen's circumstances, her losses, her suffering. In many ways, Ellen seemed like a victim herself. And yet, Judith knew her own mission here would be to ultimately betray this woman. But she mustn't think about that now. She must remain strong. She must continue to garner their trust and hopefully more information. "Burt was just telling me that they may need another teacher at the school—"

"Oh, Judith, you would consider staying here?"

"You never know. To be honest." and this *was* the truth, "I haven't been that happy at my old job or living in the city for that matter. I think I'm just tired of the rat race."

Ellen's eyes grew bright as she squeezed her hand. "Oh, it just seems like fate—like God has brought you to us. We'll be like a family again."

Judith nodded. "Now, not to change the subject, but it sounds like we have a full day ahead of us tomorrow and the next day. Perhaps it won't work out for me to help Hal with boxing those things up after all."

"But can't you stay longer? Why don't you just move out here and stay with us indefinitely?"

Judith scrambled for a good excuse. "Actually, I'm a bit worried that I may need to go back to my apartment in Portland to take care of a few things. I left so fast that I'm concerned I've left some things undone. You know, I was pretty upset before I came out here."

"Yes, I understand. And perhaps you'll want to just pack

everything up and move out here for good. You know our little cabin is vacant now; you could even stay there if you feel the need for more privacy or space."

"Thanks, that's very generous. I just wish there was enough time to pack those things up for Hal. To be honest, I'd looked forward to doing it for Jasmine's sake too. It seems only right that a friend should take care of these things."

"I think you're absolutely right about that. And if I weren't so worn out from making dinner and all, I'd just march right over to Hal's with you and the two of us would take care of this thing once and for all." Ellen looked at the clock and sighed. "I know it's not that late, Judith, but I'm getting old. I think my get up and go must've just got up and went."

Judith laughed. "Well, we couldn't very well do it tonight anyway, what with Hal's place being all locked up."

"Oh, that's not the problem. I know how to get into his place." Ellen paused for a moment. "In fact, I could let you in, Judith, if you really want to do this tonight. I suppose I could just rest downstairs while you pack. I know Jasmine didn't have hardly a thing anyway. I'm sure it couldn't take you more than an hour to box it all up."

"Oh, not even that long, I'm sure."

"Well, I've got some bags and boxes out back," said Ellen. "Not that we'll need much. Say, I think you're about the same size as she was, perhaps there's something in there that you could use. It's a shame to let perfectly good clothes go to waste."

"Maybe so. I'll keep that in mind."

ംരⅇ ⑨ൟം

IN LESS THAN AN hour, Judith had everything bagged and boxed. She'd even removed the sheets and neatly folded and stacked the blankets on the narrow cot. And although she had carefully searched through pockets and every place possible, she found no new clues. Well, other than a nice pair of Cole Haan loafers that she knew had been costly. These, along with the coral under things and the designer shirt and jeans, which she placed at the bottom of a bag, setting the two pairs of Wrangler jeans and a couple of almost new T-shirts on top. This bag, she planned to keep. She put the other bags and boxes in a corner of Hal's garage, placed the sheets in the laundry room, then gently nudged Ellen, who had fallen asleep in an oversized recliner. "I'm done," she whispered. "We can go home now."

Ellen blinked sleepily and smiled. "Good girl. Hal will be pleased."

The moon lit their way as they walked slowly back toward Ellen's house. Judith linked one arm with Ellen, worried that she might stumble in the darkness, and in the other hand she carried the bag of Jasmine's things.

"Looks like you found a few things to keep," said Ellen.

"Yes, some jeans and T-shirts that were hardly worn."

"Those must be the things I got for her at Sears." Ellen shook her head. "It was just a shame when Burt brought her home. All she had were the clothes on her back, and her jeans looked like rags. Poor thing. Burt said that she'd been living in squalor. I was so glad to be able to help her out. But she just never seemed to appreciate it—or anything." Ellen made a sniffing sound.

"She must've been terribly unhappy."

"Yes, Burt says it's because she'd made so many bad choices in her life. I suspect he means the drugs and things—things I just can't bear to think about. Oh, my poor baby!"

They'd reached the house now. "Well, don't worry about it anymore tonight, Ellen. Nothing good ever comes from worrying."

Ellen dabbed her nose with a handkerchief. "Yes, you're right, dear. Best not to think about such things."

"I'm sure you must be ready for bed now. I know I am."

"Yes. But I'm glad we got that business taken care of, Judith. Thank you."

"You're welcome. It's the least I could do."

They said good night in the kitchen, then Judith went upstairs to her room. She considered hiding her bag of treasures, but then decided against it. After all, both Hal and Ellen had told her to take what she wanted. She picked up her sketch of the bed and quilt and stared at it, then at the bottom quickly wrote, "For Jasmine."

For a long time, she lay in bed unable to sleep. More questions about Jasmine flitted through her mind. The expensive wedding ring set and designer clothing—what did they really prove? That Jasmine had been married? That she had been well off? But then why did she leave her rich husband? Perhaps he'd been a bad person. A Mafia man? Perhaps he was a thug who sold drugs on the street. But that didn't seem like Jasmine. Of course, none of this seemed like Jasmine. At least not the Jasmine she'd known.

Then Judith began to consider her own life. What she'd said to Ellen about needing to return to her apartment in Portland was true. Fortunately her mail would've been delivered through the mail slot in her door, but surely it was piling up by now. And she knew she still had unpaid bills to attend to. Plus she wondered if it was time to give notice on that apartment. She knew she couldn't go back and live there for another year. She wasn't even sure she could go back and teach at the same school for another year. She remembered Ellen's delight at the thought of her teaching at the school here. Judith shuddered. The sooner she got away from this twisted place, the better. But if only she could find some hard piece of evidence first. But what was she looking for exactly? Oh, if only she'd been able to go over all this with Adam before she'd come out here. Hopefully, this didn't mean she'd have to come out again. She didn't know if she could do it. She didn't even know if she'd be able to make it through another day. Suddenly she felt weak and frightened and on the verge of panic.

Once again, she prayed. This time she not only prayed for strength, but she also prayed for some real evidence, as well as for a way of escape. She just didn't think she could do this thing for two more days without help. Remembering Jasmine's Bible, she was tempted to turn on the light and read from it for comfort. But she was also worried that Burt might come home and notice her light on upstairs and become suspicious that she was up to something. And so she just lay quietly in the dark, trying to calm herself and longing for peace in a place that felt fraught with a spirit of confusion and hatred. And not for the first time that day, she felt as if she were a very real prisoner. Yes, it had been her choice to come, but she knew she couldn't simply leave on her own free will. No, she was a captive, trapped inside a house with an elaborate security system, in an area surrounded by barbed wire fencing and trained guard dogs. She felt powerless—nearly hopeless. Right now, her very existence was at the mercy of a man who was ruled by bigotry and hatred and fear. Was this how Jasmine had felt?

Finally, desperate for relief and at the brink of exhaustion, she somehow imagined herself nestled into the palm of God's hand. And then, almost as if angels were guarding, she fell asleep.

She awoke early the next morning. But because it was completely quiet downstairs, she decided not to make any noise. Instead, she sat up in bed and reached for Jasmine's Bible. She let it fall open in her lap, then looked down to see it was opened to the book of Matthew. At the top of the page began a section about not judging others, and about not taking the speck out of someone's eye when you had a log in your own. But what really caught her attention was the following verse—for it was softly underlined in pencil. *"Do not give what is holy to the dogs;*

nor cast your pearls before swine, lest they trample them under their feet, and turn and tear you in pieces."

She read the verse several times, searching for the meaning—for she knew there must be some special meaning hidden there. Or else why would Jasmine have underlined it in the first place? What could those metaphorical words possibly mean? She knew it was a warning about not squandering something valuable to those who wouldn't appreciate it. Perhaps Jasmine had seen herself in this verse! Perhaps it was Jasmine's protest about having been "given to the dogs" or "cast before swine." Was that how she'd felt when her father had somehow forced her into marriage with Hal? Or *had* he forced her? She still had nothing to back this up with. And suddenly, she remembered how Aunt Lenore had been the first one to really plant this thought in her head. Aunt Lenore had seemed convinced that Jasmine had been coerced into marriage. Judith wondered again— what had become of Aunt Lenore? Where was she now? It was obvious that Ellen knew her aunt's whereabouts, but so far each query had gotten Judith nowhere.

Judith closed the Bible and thought. She remembered the basket of fresh produce she had picked in Aunt Lenore's garden just yesterday—produce she had meant to give to Ellen to share with Aunt Lenore, hoping to extract some information. All this had fallen to the wayside with the unexpected invitation to come out to the lake. But who would water the garden while Judith was away? Perhaps this was just the excuse she needed to return to town and somehow let Adam know what was up and what she had learned about Jasmine. A trip to town to water the garden seemed a flimsy excuse for an escape, but it was all she had and it was worth a try.

Finally, she heard someone moving about in the kitchen downstairs, and she rose, quickly dressed, and went down.

"Good morning, dear," said Ellen brightly. "I'm just making

some coffee."

"Sounds good," said Judith.

"Did you sleep okay?"

"Well, mostly. But I am a little worried about something."

Ellen turned and looked at her. "Oh, dear, what's got you worried?"

"It's kind of silly, but I just remembered Aunt Lenore's garden and how I've been watering it every day. And it's supposed to be quite hot today, and now it will have no water for three days. And I'm terribly worried it will all dry up and die."

"Oh, I hadn't thought about that."

"And then I got to thinking how disappointed Aunt Lenore will be to come home and find all her pretty vegetables dead. I feel just horrible."

"Oh my."

"And Burt is so busy with his meetings and you have your women's group."

"Well, that's not until noon."

"But the church service?"

"That's not until ten."

Judith looked at her watch. "But Burt probably doesn't have time to run me to town this morning."

Ellen frowned. "Burt's already gone off to the morning meeting. They started at seven with breakfast and everything."

"Oh."

"Well, now, there must be something we can do. It's not even eight o'clock now. Of course, Hal and everyone else is busy with their silly old meetings. It's too bad I don't drive anymore." Ellen's eyes lit up. "I know! How about if I let you drive me into town. I don't think Daddy will mind if I use the car this time since I'm not really doing the driving myself."

Judith let out a relieved sigh. "Oh, that would make me feel so much better. You really don't mind, Ellen?"

"Not at all. I certainly don't want Aunt Lenore's pretty garden getting ruined either."

"And then I can get that basket of produce that I picked to share with you and Aunt Lenore. Do you think you'll be able to get some of it to her?"

Ellen grew thoughtful. "I don't know, but I think maybe so."

"Do you think I might be able to see her too?"

"Now, I'm not too sure about that, dear. We'll have to check with Daddy. He's the one taking care of all this right now. He knows how stressful these things are to me. But I'll ask him."

They ate a quick breakfast and then started their trip to town. Judith was a little worried about getting through the tight security system, but just the same she had brought along her bag of Jasmine's things, including the wedding rings now tucked into one of the loafers. She had set this bag on the floor of the back seat, explaining to Ellen that it would be one less thing to take home later, and Ellen had said that sounded "real smart." Then to Judith's relieved amazement, Ellen just directed her straight to the gates where a man wearing what looked like a khaki uniform just smiled and waved them through. Judith tried not to reveal how deliriously happy she felt to be on the free side of those awful gates once again, but she literally felt her heart lighten as they drove further and further away.

"I'll just wait here for you," said Ellen when Judith pulled into the driveway.

"Are you sure? It sometimes takes me awhile to get everything nicely soaked."

"No, I'm fine. Just put the windows down and I'll lean back and enjoy the fresh morning air."

"Okay. I'll try to hurry then."

Judith couldn't believe her luck as she climbed from the car. She went straight to the backyard, taking the bag of Jasmine's things with her. First she turned on the sprinkler and giving one quick glance behind her, she streaked through the yard and toward the lilac bush in the corner. She let herself through the hole in the fence and went and knocked on Adam's back door, the bag still in her hand.

"What are you doing back here?" asked Jack as he came around the corner.

She jumped and dropped the bag, spilling some items to the ground. "Oh, Jack, you scared me." She scrambled to pick up the bag and its contents. "Is Adam home right now? I only have a minute and I've—"

Just then the door opened. "Judith!" Adam stepped out and looked at her. "Where in the world have you been?"

"It's a long story, and I only have a couple of minutes."

He pulled her into the house and back toward his office, speaking in quiet tones. "I've been worried sick about you. I suspect you've been out at the lake."

After he closed the door she set the bag on his desk. "Yes. Ellen begged me to come out with them, and I could tell I was really winning their trust—"

"Judith, it's too dangerous. I wanted you wired."

"I know. But you should see the security check they put me through. I'll bet they would've found a wire, and then where would I be? I mean, they use body scanners and everything."

"I know."

"You know?"

"Yes, we have a wire that's undetectable."

"But I don't know if I even have time. I'm supposed to be watering the garden right now. We've got to be back for church at ten."

"Church?"

"Well, you know, whatever it is they do. But first let me tell you what I've found. It's all in this bag."

"They let you walk out with a bag of evidence?" He looked clearly puzzled.

"Not exactly. Sort of. Anyway, it's Jasmine's things. But I mean, *really* her things. Not like the stuff her mom bought. I think these are the only things Jasmine brought with her from her other life. And I think she came from some sort of money and that she was married and who knows what else. But I thought if you had them, you might be able to figure something out—track something down. And I know she'd been living in the Seattle area. And I'm trying to find out where Aunt Lenore is and, oh, dear, I better go finish my watering."

"Slow down." He made her sit down in a chair. "I'll water for you. Now, first off, I'm not so sure that we can let you go back in there."

"But I thought you wanted—"

"My first priority is to keep you safe. And I have reason to believe that situation could get dangerous."

"You mean like Waco or Ruby Ridge?" She laughed. "I'll admit these guys are stupid, but they're not crazy. I don't think they'd pull something like—"

"You don't know what they might pull, Judith." He looked into her eyes. "I mean, once they get pushed."

"Pushed?"

He nodded. "I've just learned there are a couple of BATF guys who've infiltrated with the others."

"BATF?"

"Bureau of Alcohol, Tobacco, and Firearms. These guys have reason to believe there are a lot of illegal firearms out there, as well as other things."

"Yeah? Well, they should see Hal's armory then."

"Hal's not stupid. He almost always buys and sells his guns according to the laws. In fact, he's something of a cover for them. But there's another couple guys out there who aren't so smart. And it's possible they could get caught with the goods this weekend. And you never know, the whole thing could just blow up. I don't want you out there, Judith."

"But what if I wore a wire? What if I could get some hard evidence that has to do with Jasmine or maybe even James Paxton—"

"It's too risky right now."

"But how will I explain it to Ellen? I mean, I've worked so hard to establish trust. Good grief, she thinks I'm like part of her family now. Burt practically offered me a job. I could probably get Hal to propose!"

He ran his hands through his hair and groaned. "I can't let you do it, Judith."

She stood up now. "But you don't understand. I mean, last night I was scared witless. I just wanted to come home and never go back again. But suddenly, now that I'm safely here, I realize how far I've gotten—how close I might actually be. And then I get this opportunity to come back here and talk to you. And you could wire me up, and we might catch them, Adam. Doesn't that mean anything to you?"

He stared at her. "Of course. I'm just as eager as you are to break this thing wide open. But it's getting too risky. And I don't know if you noticed or not, but I kind of like you."

Her mouth still open, all ready with her next plea of resistance, she paused for a moment as she considered the meaning behind his words. Or was she just imagining things? "Well, I like you too," she continued. "But what does that have to do with anything?"

He smiled. "I just don't want to see you get hurt. It's not worth it."

"But I'm so close, Adam. I can just feel it. It's like Jasmine is there leading me along. I mean, first with the ring that was stuck to the back of the underside of the bathroom sink."

He blinked. "Man, you have been busy. I sure hope there's not surveillance in that house."

"Yeah, I've been wondering the same thing. But so far I don't see any sign of it."

A knock on the door interrupted them. "Sorry," said Jack as he stuck his head in the doorway. "But do you want me to keep an eye on the Morrison broad out in the car?"

"Huh?" they both said in unison.

"Well, do you want her traipsing over here to look for Judith?"

"No," said Adam, standing up. "Pops, just how much do you know?"

"Enough," grumped Jack. "I'll go keep a watch on her."

"Want to move the sprinkler while you're at it?" asked Judith hopefully.

"Sure."

Adam shook his head as he closed the door behind his dad. "See, that's just what I was afraid of with him."

Judith couldn't help but laugh. "He's a sweet guy."

"Yeah, and I don't want him getting hurt either."

"Well, Ellen's harmless. And speaking of Ellen, how would I explain to her and everyone else why I've suddenly decided not to come back to the lake. And how will she get home? She doesn't drive, you know. Did you want to drive her? I'm sure no one would get suspicious about that."

"Yeah, yeah. Let me think a minute. If I could just think of some way to safely get you out if trouble develops."

"There's the fire exit," said Judith. "It's on the west side of the lake, not far from the Morrisons' house. Couldn't I get out through there?"

"Maybe." He made a note. "Although I'm sure it's heavily gated too. But maybe not guarded."

She looked at her watch. Already twenty minutes had gone by. "Adam, you've got to let me go back."

"I suppose I can't really stop you, can I?" He looked hopefully into her eyes.

"No, you can't. But I'd sure appreciate it if you'd back me in this."

"And wire you?"

She nodded. "Do you mind?"

He sighed. "It goes against the grain, Judith."

"I'm sorry. But it goes against the grain for me to give up right now."

"I didn't realize you were such a fighter."

"Usually I'm not. It's just all this crazy praying I've been doing lately."

"Yeah, that'll do it to you, all right."

"So, you'll let me go back."

"Yeah. Now, I'm going to tell you something that I hadn't planned on. It's usually dangerous to give away somebody's identity like this. But I've got a guy on the inside."

"A BATF guy?"

He shook his head. "No, this guy's with me."

"A policeman?"

He shook his head again. "FBI."

"You're with the FBI?"

"Undercover. I don't usually tell because it puts me and others in danger. But right now I'm more worried about you than us. So, I'm letting you in on it. And I trust you won't blow our cover."

"Wow, FBI. I had no idea."

"It's no big deal. Anyway, my guy's about 6' 8" with red curly hair. Kinda hard to miss, if you know what I mean. He talks real rough and looks like a redneck, but he's okay. He goes by Hank. Don't do anything to give him away, but if you're in trouble and Hank's around, you can trust him to take care of you."

"He knows who I am."

"Of course. You think I'd let you go in there all by yourself?" He smiled as he reached into a drawer and pulled out a packet, then emptied the contents onto his desk. A tiny plastic transistor, thin wires, and some medical tape.

"Anything else I should be aware of?"

"Just that my hands are cold."

Twenty-Eight

*GOD, IT'S ME AGAIN, your little Pearl. And I ain't run away yet.
And that's just 'cause Miss Molly downstairs made me promise and
cross my heart that I wouldn't. She say before I run away, I better
just run to her. She say she'll take care of me. But I don't know what
Carmen would think about that. Not that she be thinking much of
anything these days, not since Larry runned off. Now, what I wanna
know is why she be so sad about losing Larry? I mean, he used to
beat her and yell at her and take her money and make ugly messes
and eat what little food we got. But now that he's gone, she just
mopes around and cries all the time. But me, I'm glad he's gone.
Miss Molly say the Bible say we ain't s'posed to hate no one, but I
think I hate Larry. Every time I see his big white face in our door,
I know it means trouble's coming. Now, Miss Molly say the Bible
say we s'posed to love everybody no matter what color they be. And
so I gotta say, God, that I don't hate Larry because he be white,
I just hate him because he be mean. The truth of things is when I
remember my mama, she got a white face just like Larry. Well, not
just like Larry, 'cause my mama's face is pretty and she's got long
dark hair that tickles my face. I remember that.*

And I remembered something else last night, God, at least I think I did. When I was just a laying in my bed, almost asleep, I think I remembered my daddy! I think I saw him laughing and playing with me, and he asked if I wanted a horsey ride. And he looked like Carmen and Miss Molly and Sharista and me. He be a black man! At least that's what Miss Molly call folk· like us. But I don't get that, God, 'cause when I look at Carmen, I think she look just like chocolate—you know, that yummy kind that isn't so dark. But then Miss Molly, she look more like that chocolate that's real dark, like the one I found behind the couch one time, it was real dark but kinda dusty gray 'round the edges. Funny thing is I like that light-color chocolate lots better, but I like Miss Molly way better than Carmen. But back to that thing Miss Molly say about how we be black and all. Now, I know all my colors, God, well most of them. And I know black is like the color of my shoes and the color of Carmen's CD player (before Larry stole it) and the color of the inside of the oven. And I look in the mirror, and I don't see no black like that. Fact is, my face is even lighter than Carmen's, it's more like the color of that mocha-nut ice cream that Carmen loves so much. So what's up with this black thing, God? What color do you say I am? What color are you? And while we be on the subject of colors, God, what's up with this white thing anyway? I know what color white be, not that I see much of it in Carmen's dirty apartment, but now Miss Molly she keep her things nice and white. She got a nice, shiny white bathtub and sink. But that ain't the color of my mama's face or Larry's face—so why we call them white? Now, Carmen's bathtub is s'posed to be white but it looks more kinda grayish yellow and if you ask me, that look more like Carmen's face. Now my mama's face? Well, I think that be more pinkish, but her eyes are dark brown like mine. I can't remember what color my daddy's eyes be.

But am I right about my daddy? Was that him I remembered last night? And is he dark brown too? And by the way, God, where did he go to? At first I got real happy when I remembered him, and then I got real sad. I asked Carmen if she remembered my daddy and she just rolled them big, gold eyes of hers and say, "No way, Jose." Then I asked her if she remembered my mama, and she got real mad. She even said a bad word. Then she say, "All I 'member 'bout your mama is she broke her promise. And if it weren't for your Aunt Constance, I'd just throw you out the front door right this minute!"

Now, I'm thinking that's pretty weird. I don't remember no Aunt Constance at all. Not ever. Who she? And fact is, I don't much care if Carmen does throw me out the front door. Maybe then I could go live with Miss Molly and play with Sharista anytime I want to, and maybe then I can go to real school and learn how to read and stuff. But I don't think that's gonna happen, 'cause Carmen be acting like she brewing up some kind of plan right now. Like she think she gonna get lucky somehow. I mean, every time she look at me lately she be a rubbin' her hands and saying stuff like, "You gonna make me rich, little girl. Cause o' you I gonna be sitting pretty before too long! There's people out there that'd pay good money for a nice little girl like you."

Now, I gotta ask you, God, what's up with that? Miss Molly say you got your eye on me. But I ain't so sure 'bout that. You got your eye on me right now, God? Right this minute? You know what Carmen be up to right now? 'Cause I ain't so smart, and I'm only five years old, but I think she gonna sell me to someone who got some money but ain't no better than her. Maybe someone a lot worse. And I be saying, hey, God, can you hear me?

Twenty-Nine

"JUDITH, YOU BETTER GET out there quick." said Jack as he came huffing into Adam's office with a small grocery bag in hand.

"What's going on?" asked Adam.

"If s that Morrison broad, all upset just 'cause she saw Eli Paxton pull up next door. I waylaid her, telling her that I was your neighbor and that you were in the backyard picking some tomatoes but that I'd go fetch you. So come on now."

"Are we all set, Adam?" Judith gently patted the transmitter now securely taped to her abdomen, a slightly embarrassing procedure, but necessary.

"Yes, now just take care not to get wet. I mean, like soaking wet. A little sprinkle from a shower won't hurt."

"Is she wearing a wire?" asked Jack.

"Pops!" Adam scowled at his dad. "You've been reading too many spy novels lately."

Jack chuckled, then handed the grocery bag to Judith. "Here take this."

She peered into the bag nearly full of garden produce. "You've been busy, Jack. Thanks."

"No problem. You just take care, little lady."

She looked curiously at Adam. Had he told his dad everything? But he just shrugged then shook his head. "You better hurry, Judith."

"See you tomorrow," she called as she ran across the yard and passed through the fence. Everything was nicely watered and the hose was neatly wound up and turned off. *Bless you, Jack,* she thought as she hurried out to the car.

"Oh, there you are." gasped Ellen. "That nice man told me he'd run get you."

"Sorry, I was just finishing up when I noticed lots of new tomatoes that needed picking." She placed the bag in the car. "I need to go lock up. Will you be okay for a minute?" Judith watched as Ellen glanced nervously toward the Land Rover parked in front of Martha's house. Probably Eli's.

"I suppose so, dear. Just hurry it up, please."

Judith went to get the other produce basket. She had forgotten about Eli's Bible study this morning. She felt relieved that she hadn't come face to face with him herself, and yet at the same time she longed to send him a signal— although she knew she couldn't. But what had he thought to see Ellen Morrison sitting in her Cadillac out in front of the house looking like a scared rabbit? He knew Judith was staying at Aunt Lenore's, and now he'd seen her twice in connection to the Morrisons. She sighed as she locked the door. Hopefully, she'd get to explain this whole thing to him, and Martha too, before long.

"Now, tell me, Ellen," she said as she slid into the driver's seat. "What's wrong? You look very upset."

"It's that man," said Ellen. "He drove up and parked right there."

"But what's wrong with that?" asked Judith innocently as she eased the car back down the short driveway. "What kind of man was it?"

"He's a colored!"

"Oh..." Judith nodded. "And that frightens you?"

"Why, yes, of course. Doesn't it frighten you? Good grief, he stopped right by your house—or rather, Aunt Lenore's house. Don't you wonder what business he has stopping there like that?"

"I guess that's just part of this thing that I don't really understand, Ellen. Because it doesn't really frighten me."

Ellen shuddered. "That's just because you're a brave woman, Judith. But you should use the good sense God gave you and exercise a little caution too."

Judith nodded as if in agreement. "Ellen, I've noticed that you use the word 'colored' instead of the word that Burt and Hal and the others use. Why is that?"

She pressed her lips together and thought. "Well, I s'pose it's due to the way I was raised. Mama and Daddy didn't abide the n-word in our home. We got our mouths washed out with soap if we used it."

"Really? That seems rather extreme—for Mississippi, I mean."

"It was Mama who really hated that word." Ellen's voice grew slightly hushed as if she might be revealing some deep, dark secret. "And, to be perfectly honest, I think it might be because there'd been a coon in the woodpile."

"What?" Judith glanced over to Ellen. "What does that mean?"

Ellen giggled like a little girl. "Well, I never told anyone this, not even Burt, but it's possible my family has some colored blood in it—oh, just a little, mind you, but on my mama's side, I think."

Judith laughed. "Well, I'd be surprised if there were many Southern families who didn't have a little 'colored blood,' as you put it."

"Oh, now, dear, don't you *ever* let Burt hear you talking like that. And don't you *ever* breathe a word of what I just said to a living soul. I think I must've just been feeling a little light-headed after my scare in the driveway, talking like that to you. I don't even know what came over me."

Judith glanced at Ellen again, suddenly remembering her as a younger woman. Her dark, almost black, curly hair, her big brown eyes, how easily she tanned. Always a sharp, but attractive, contrast to her husband's fair looks. And then Jasmine had been just like that. It did seem possible they carried some African American blood. "It's okay, Ellen, your secret's safe with me. That might explain why your parents and siblings think the way they do."

Ellen frowned. "You know, Judith, I'd just as soon we didn't talk of this anymore. I never should've mentioned that nonsense to you in the first place. In fact, I'm certain it's not even true. Please, don't speak of it again."

"Right." She looked straight ahead. "It feels like it's going to be a scorcher today. I'm glad I got to give Aunt Lenore's garden a good soaking. Thanks for letting me do this, Ellen." She glanced at the clock. "And it's just barely nine. We made good time. And I picked lots of produce. Plenty to share with your neighbors, if you like. And do you suppose you might take some to Aunt Lenore? Those tomatoes look just fabulous. I'm sure she'd enjoy them."

"Oh yes. I'll see if I can't drop by there after church."

"Will Burt mind taking you, I mean, since he's got his meetings and all?"

She frowned. "Yes, that might be a problem. Maybe I'll have to sweet-talk Daddy into letting you drive me there, if you don't mind, that is."

"Sure. That'd be fine." *That'd be fantastic,* she thought. "And the ladies' luncheon is at noon?"

"Well, actually twelve-thirty—" She held up her hand. "Say, Judith, why don't you stop at the grocery store."

"Do we have time?"

"Sure, we'll just have to be fast. I noticed last night that we're out of ice cream, and Burt just hates the brand they carry at the general store. I planned to make a blackberry pie for dessert tonight, and I just can't bear the thought of blackberry pie without ice cream."

Judith offered to run in and get the ice cream, but Ellen decided she wanted to pick up a few other things as well, so Judith patiently wheeled the cart as she shopped. She noticed Adam's son Josh working on the cereal aisle putting boxes on the shelf, but she quickly looked the other way, afraid to even acknowledge him. It was nine-forty by the time she loaded the bag of groceries into the trunk of the car. "Are we going to make it to church on time?" she asked as she started the car.

"Oh, sure, we're fine. We'll just head straight there and I'll explain everything to Burt when we see him. He can't yell too loud in church."

"But we need to get that ice cream in the freezer so it doesn't melt."

Ellen made a face. "Oh, dear, I didn't think of that. Well, just drive fast, dear."

It was nearly ten when they passed through the security gates. "Shall I stop at the clubhouse so they can check me with their scanner again?" asked Judith. Adam had assured her that his device was mostly undetectable, but there were no guarantees.

Ellen waved her hand. "Heavens, no! Just hurry on home, and we'll put that ice cream in the freezer."

Burt was standing in the driveway, scratching his head with a grim expression, when they pulled up.

Ellen hopped out of the car. "Oh, it's all my fault, Daddy. I begged Judith to take me to the grocery store so I could get ice cream—"

"Good grief!" exclaimed Burt. "Well, get back in the car, we're late as it is."

Judith was already carrying the bag into the garage. "Shall I just put this ice cream in the freezer out here?" she called.

"Yes!" yelled Burt. "And hurry it up."

Within seconds they were back in the car with Burt behind the wheel and growling. "Women! Making us late to church just so you could go get some ice cream!"

"I'm sorry, Daddy." pleaded Ellen in her little-girl voice. "Judith warned me it was getting late, but I just insisted we needed it to go with my blackberry pie."

"Well, in the future maybe you should listen to Judith. At least she's got a good head on her shoulders."

Judith blinked in surprise, but could think of nothing to say in return.

The church service was held in the lodge, a large gymnasium-type building with a metal roof. Judith sat in the third row with the Morrisons and Hal was already there waiting for them. Ellen had hastily explained to her that a group of men, elders, took turns preaching on Sundays, and today it was Ed Burns's turn. And, she warned, Ed sometimes got a little carried away, but that the people liked his enthusiasm.

"A little carried away" seemed a gross understatement. Judith wondered if Ed Burns had studied under Hitler or Mussolini or the devil himself. His face grew tense and red as his voice became louder and he thumped his fist again and again on the podium. "WE are the *chosen people,* brothers and sisters! Look down at your hands! What color are they? White! Do you know why your

skin is white? Because *we,* my brothers and sisters, *we* are the true
children of Adam. Our roots are planted in the Adamite nation, a race
that has remained pure and unpolluted for more than seven thousand
years! Another name for this superior race is the Aryan Nation.
And that's who we are, brothers and sisters, the chosen people, the
children of Adam, the Aryan Nation. And we have every reason to
be proud of our heritage! Our roots are pure and undefiled just as
God commanded. Did you know that God's first commandment
to Adam and Eve was not to mongrelize the holy seed of God's
family. But right off the bat, Eve, *the woman,* was tricked by Satan.
And she mixed her precious seed with Satan's to beget the evil
Cain. And that's where all this trouble with races began, my
Aryan brothers and sisters. The Jews came from Cain, all other races
came from Cain. All of them children of Satan! Mongrels! Infidels!
Animals!"

At this point, Judith could bear to listen no more. Such hatred,
such venom, such complete and inexcusable ignorance! It literally
made her want to run out of here screaming or to throw up or to
hit someone. Well, Adam's wire would have to do her listening for
her, for she could stand it no longer. She closed her eyes to the
gaudy banners hanging down on the stark white walls, their ugly
words boasting of racial supremacy, love of nation, and the right to
bear arms...and then she closed her ears to the pulpit and instead
began to envision her good friend Eli, his warm countenance and
smiling face, his indomitable spirit, his love of God. Oh, if only she
could have joined his Bible study group this morning. She prayed
that it went well. She prayed for his safety. She prayed for the town
of Cedar Crest to be delivered from this evil influence.

Then she envisioned her best teaching friend at school,
Harmony Jackson, with her big, hearty laugh and the way she gave
the warmest hugs. Children would seek her out on the playground

whenever things went wrong, and she was always ready with a "happy hug," as she called them. Then Judith imagined all the children she had taught over the years, all their different little faces, all their varying ethnic origins. And she sent up a prayer for them, for their protection, for their happiness, for their right to live in a free society where all were truly created equal. And finally, to her huge relief, the service was over.

"Well, Judith, what did you think of that?" asked Burt as they made their way down the aisle.

"He preaches a powerful message," said Judith.

"Really gets the people stirred up," added Ellen as she linked arms with Judith. "Let's you and me slip out of here and wait in the car," she whispered.

Judith nodded, thankful to escape the lodge. Even the air in there seemed tainted with hatred and poison. But the interior of the car was hot, and so the two of them found a bench in the shade and waited for Burt to come out. As Ellen fanned herself with the program, Judith observed the people leaving the lodge. She didn't like to make generalizations, but many of them were older and had the look of lower-middle class—the kind of people who still wore polyester leisure suits, drove older American cars, and drank domestic beer; people who, under different circumstances, might have belonged to the VFW or maybe some philanthropic community club. And she'd never seen so many women carrying white purses and wearing white shoes in her life. Even Ellen had them. Was it some sort of uniform?

Mixed in with this older generation were a few younger ones. And a few families. She studied the younger women first. They all wore dresses or skirts, but not the sort of clothing you might see in an office or even where she taught. These dresses had more of a homemade look and all went well past the knee. And most of the women had long hair. Some wore it pulled back and some wore it loose. One woman even had hair that reached past the hem of her dress! The men mostly wore plaid or plain shirts tucked neatly into their jeans. And western wear seemed to rule with large belt buckles and cowboy boots. Although she did notice a number of pairs of army style pants and even a couple of camouflaged pants too.

She studied the expressions on their faces. Had any of them, like her, been offended by Ed's message? You couldn't tell to look at them. But then she was doing a pretty good job of hiding her disgust too. Just then she noticed a tall man step out the door. He vigorously shook hands with Hal as if they'd just met. And Burt was coming up behind them. The tall man had curly red hair and a full beard, and she guessed he might go by the name of Hank. And other than his height, he fit right in with the rest of the crowd.

"Oh, good." said Ellen, slowly rising to her feet. "There's Daddy now."

He walked over to the bench. "Say, Judith, do you mind driving Ellen home? I think I'll just stick around the lodge and visit until the men's lunch."

"Sure, that's fine."

"Now, don't forget that John Wagner's speaking tonight." he reminded her. "That's the man I want you to hear."

She nodded, at the same time wishing there was some way to escape it, but then remembered her wire. Perhaps there would be something of value to overhear. "Yes, I was planning on it. Will I get a ride with you?"

"Yeah. We'll go after dinner." He nodded. "You ladies have a good day."

Ellen made a grumbling sound when they reached the car. "You'd think he could've told us sooner that he'd planned to stick around. We could've been home putting our feet up by now."

"Are you tired, Ellen?" Judith started the car and waited a moment.

"Yes, this heat just takes it out of me. But I'm thankful we don't have too many days like this out here at the lake."

Judith cranked the air conditioning up. "I suppose you don't feel up to visiting Aunt Lenore then? I left some garden produce in the car just in case you did."

"Oh, heavens, I forgot all about that. I'd meant to ask Daddy..."

"Do you have to get permission to visit your aunt?"

Ellen's mouth puckered a little, as if she'd eaten something bitter. "No!" she declared. "I most certainly do not."

Judith suppressed a smile. "Would you like me to take you?"

"Yes. Take a right at the next intersection. The clinic is down that road."

"Clinic?"

"Yes. With all the older folks, we decided it was wise to have a clinic nearby. We don't have a doctor, but we do have a good nurse practitioner. And if you ask me, she's as good as any doctor. Plus, she's got connections with an MD in some nearby town, and he can even prescribe for her. It's a pretty good setup."

"And that's where Aunt Lenore's been staying?" Judith tried to keep her voice calm.

"Yes, Burt says it would be cheaper than a nursing home, and better care too."

"But doesn't she have insurance or Medicare or something?"

"I don't know. But it's also handier for us to keep an eye on her."

"Oh..."

"And don't worry, she has round the clock care. We even hired another health care person specially for her."

"But isn't that expensive?"

"I don't know about that." Ellen pointed. "It's that building straight ahead."

Judith parked right in front. "Do you want me to come in?"

"No, dear, you better just wait out here. I might really get into hot water if I took you in there. You know, what with security and all. And Burt's been very careful about not letting anyone disturb Aunt Lenore. She's been very frail these days."

"Yes, I understand. You stay as long as you like, Ellen. I don't mind waiting."

"Thank you, dear."

Judith studied the long, low building. One story, and it didn't look to be much bigger than a good-sized house. There were two sets of windows on each side of the front entrance. Perhaps they were patient rooms. Then she noticed the louvered blinds on the room to the far left flutter as if someone had just opened them. She peered to see what looked like Ellen's shape standing before them. That must be Aunt Lenore's room! Now, if only there were some way to slip in there and see her somehow. Judith leaned her head back and closed her eyes, sending up a prayer for Aunt Lenore, for her health and well-being, and she also prayed that she might get to see her old friend once again and help her if need be.

"There, that didn't take long." said Ellen as she opened the door.

"Oh!" Judith started. "I didn't even hear you walk up."

"Were you having a little catnap?" teased Ellen.

"Something like that," she said as she backed out the car. "It's already past noon, Ellen. Do you want to go home, or do you think we should just stick around for the ladies' luncheon?"

Ellen groaned. "Well, if we go home, we'll just have to turn around and come back."

"But you look tired to me."

Ellen nodded grimly and turned the air conditioner up. "No excuse for missing this luncheon. I'll tell you what. Let's go early, visit a bit, then we can eat quickly, and just leave a little early. How does that sound?"

"Sounds brilliant."

The luncheon was set up behind the clubhouse. About a dozen card tables and folding chairs were set out where they had full view of the lake. A stocky, rather bossy, woman named Betty was in charge, and Judith offered to help out while Ellen sat down at a table with a middle-aged woman named Karen—a potential recruit, Ellen had whispered in Judith's ear. The luncheon consisted of a variety of egg, tuna, and chicken salad sandwiches, Waldorf salad, a vast array of homemade desserts, and cold drinks. Judith's job was to stock the cooler of ice and cold drinks. Once that was done, she joined Ellen, who was furiously fanning herself with a paper plate.

"Maybe we should move you into the shade," offered Judith.

"What shade?" Ellen waved her hand around the tables all set up in the sun. "There is no shade." She blotted her brow with a handkerchief. "Well, at least the luncheon should be starting any minute now."

"How about if I get you a cool drink?" Judith listed the available drinks she had just stocked, all cans of soda.

"I don't like any of those fizzy drinks," said Ellen. "Can't you just find me a glass of water somewhere."

Judith went into the kitchen and filled a large glass with water, then she stopped by the cooler to plunk a few ice cubes in it.

"Bless you," said Ellen as she began to drink.

Soon the luncheon was underway, and Judith went to fill plates for both of them. But when she returned, Ellen looked extremely pale and said she wasn't hungry.

"You don't look well to me, Ellen," said Judith. "Let's get you out of the sun."

By now there was a thin sliver of shade next to the building, and Judith led Ellen with one arm, carrying a chair with the other, and sat her down in the shade. She handed her the water. "Here, you drink this up." Then she went back to get her own chair and their plates. But when she returned Ellen still looked bad. The main speaker, the wife of John Wagner, was just getting ready to speak. "Let's get you inside," commanded Judith, gently pulling Ellen from her chair and guiding her into the slightly cooler building.

"I don't feel so good," murmured Ellen as Judith eased her into a club chair.

"I think you're having heat stroke." said Judith suddenly. "We need to get you to the clinic as soon as possible." She ran into the kitchen and grabbed a tea towel, then soaked it with cool water. Then she helped Ellen back to her feet and slowly led her to the car.

"I feel woozy." said Ellen as Judith helped her into the car, placing the damp cloth atop her head.

. "Just lean back and relax, Ellen." said Judith as she quickly drove the car to the clinic.

By the time they reached the clinic, Ellen's eyes were closed and her arms hung limply by her sides. Judith dashed inside to get help. Fortunately there was a young man at the front desk, and he and Judith managed to get Ellen to an examining room where they laid her down.

"Our nurse practitioner is gone right now," said the young man. "But I'll get the nurse's aide. You stay here with Ellen."

Soon the man returned with the nurse's aide in tow. "We'll handle this now," she said. "Go ahead and wait out there."

Judith stepped out in the hallway, her heart still racing from the scare. Should she contact Burt? But how? Go back to the lodge? But she didn't want to leave Ellen on her own here either. She paced down to the other end of the hallway, still wondering what to do. And that's when she noticed an open door leading into a room on the right end of the building. Judith peered in to see Aunt Lenore's small face looking up from a hospital bed with safety rails raised on either side. Her eyes were open, and she appeared to be fairly alert.

"Aunt Lenore!" exclaimed Judith. "Is it really you?"

"Come here, child." Her voice sounded old and tired. "Come here where I can see you."

Judith stepped over to her bedside. "I'm so glad to see you, Aunt Lenore!"

"Is that you, Jasmine?"

"No, it's Judith. Remember me?"

She nodded. "Yes, yes.. Judith, of course. I thought you were Jasmine at first. But Jasmine's not with us anymore, is she?"

"No, Aunt Lenore, she died. Do you remember that?"

"Yes. And I think I shall join her soon."

"Are you terribly ill, Aunt Lenore?"

"They say that I am. But I'm afraid they're giving me medicine that makes me ill. I think they want to shut me up."

"But why, Aunt Lenore?"

"Because I know too much."

"About Jasmine?"

"About many things. Many things they want dead and buried. Including me."

Judith reached for her hand. "Maybe I can help you, Aunt Lenore. Maybe I can get you out of here."

Her old eyes lit up a little. "Oh, I do want to go back to my little house again."

"Yes!" said Judith. "You must come back. I've been keeping everything watered for you. And your garden is unbelievable.

Please don't give up, Aunt Lenore." Judith looked over her shoulder, worried that she'd be discovered any minute.

"Now, Aunt Lenore, what do you know about Jasmine? Can you tell me?"

"Did you find her box?"

"No, I've looked everywhere. But I couldn't find it."

Aunt Lenore closed her eyes as if trying to remember. "In my bedroom," she said. "On my dresser, inlaid mother-of—"

"What are you doing in here?" demanded the nurse's aide.

"Oh!" Judith jumped. "I heard a voice calling for help in here and I came to see—"

"This room is off limits."

"Water." said Aunt Lenore, as if playing along. "Thirsty.. .need water..."

"She only wanted a drink," said Judith innocently.

"Well, thanks." said the nurse's aide. "But I'll take care of it. Anyway, Ellen's recovering and wants to see you now."

"Ellen?" said Aunt Lenore.

"You go on now," said the nurse's aide. "I'll take good care of Miss Barker."

Thirty

JUDITH FOUND THE NURSE practitioner at Ellen's bedside, checking an IV while Ellen seemed to sleep soundly. "I'm Nurse Bryant." the tall, thin woman said. "And you must be Judith. Ellen said you brought her here."

"Is she okay then?"

"Yes. But it's good that you got her in here when you did."

"Was it heat stroke?"

"Probably more like heat exhaustion about to become heat stroke. But she's stabilized now. And I gave her a little something to calm her. She'll probably sleep for a couple of hours."

"But everything's okay?"

"Yes, her vital signs are stable."

"I wanted to tell Burt, but I wasn't sure how to reach him, and there wasn't anyone around to ask."

"Yeah, I got Tim, the guy who helped you get her in here, and he's letting Burt know what's up. I expect he'll be by any minute now."

"Oh, good. Should I just wait around here then?"

"Sure, have a seat."

Judith sat in a chair next to Ellen's bed. She studied

Ellen's features as she slept. Suddenly, she looked very old. Not as old as Aunt Lenore, perhaps, yet in some ways even older. Was it because she was so stuck in her ways, because she let Burt control her, because she'd compromised her childhood teachings to accommodate a man who was ruled by hatred and bigotry? Somewhere in her life, Ellen had given up on her own life and simply surrendered to the lies. It's as if she had almost ceased to exist, or had gone into some sort of emotional coma where she functioned like a wind-up robot, without thinking or discerning, just putt-putting along while Burt tossed out the commands. And perhaps that had made Ellen old long, long ago.

Judith considered Aunt Lenore. Although, she was quite elderly, she still had spirit and a bit of fire left in her faded eyes. Judith could tell she wanted out of that bed, and even though she was literally a prisoner here, she had never given up. Not completely anyway. And she had information to share. Something that was important enough to worry Burt. Perhaps something about Jasmine. If only Judith could think of a way to get back in there and ask more questions. She reached down to her midsection. The transmitter. Adam had been privy to every word spoken today. Suddenly she remembered that Aunt Lenore had said something about Jasmine's box. On her dresser. And then something about a mother of someone. What had she meant? Of course! The jewelry box! All along Judith had been looking for a larger sort of box, perhaps something made of cardboard. As a result she had just assumed that pretty jewelry box belonged to Aunt Lenore. And of course, it had inlaid mother-of-pearl on top. That's what she meant. Judith glanced over to Ellen, still resting peacefully.

She stepped out into the hallway, spotting the nurse's aide. "Excuse me? Is there a restroom I can use?"

"It's the door to the left of the front desk."

Judith went into the restroom. She turned on the fan and then bowed down her head, cupped her hands, and spoke quietly. "The box on Aunt Lenore's dresser that's inlaid with mother-of-pearl. That's Jasmine's box." Then she flushed the toilet. She had no way of knowing if he'd heard her above the noise of the fan, but she didn't want anyone else to hear her either.

Then she returned to Ellen's bedside to wait for Burt. After about thirty minutes Nurse Bryant came back to check Ellen's vital signs again. "She's looking good." she said as she released the air from the blood pressure band.

"Yes, her color's much better now." agreed Judith. She glanced at her watch. "Shouldn't Burt be here by now?"

"Oh, it's hard to say. These guys can get pretty wrapped up in their meetings."

Judith frowned. "Are you suggesting that he's more concerned with his meetings than his wife's health?"

Nurse Bryant's face remained blank. "You didn't hear me say that."

"How long have you been part of this group?"

The woman studied her for a moment. "I'm just an employee. They pay me good money to live out here 24-7, always on call. I keep my politics to myself. And I don't ask questions."

Judith nodded. "I see." She wanted to inquire about Aunt Lenore, and how Nurse Bryant could justify keeping an old woman here against her will, but thought better of it. No need to stir up undue suspicion right now. It was plain this woman's motivation was the bottom line—as she said, they paid her well.

Burt arrived at the clinic just after two. He seemed only mildly concerned, telling Judith that young Tim had assured him it was nothing to be concerned about, just a little overheating.

"Actually, the nurse practitioner said Ellen was on the verge of heat stroke," said Judith, her irritation showing. "And heat stroke can be deadly, especially to older folks."

Burt looked at her curiously. "Well, then, I should thank you for getting her in here like this. I didn't realize it was so serious. Maybe I should go have a word with Bryant."

"Yes, she might have some recommendations for Ellen. I would think she might need to take it easy. I'll be glad to help out while I'm here."

While Burt was speaking with the nurse, Ellen awoke and looked all around the room in surprise. "My goodness, where in the world am I?"

"It's okay," said Judith. "You had a little heat exhaustion, but you are going to be just fine now."

Ellen stretched a bit. "Well, I feel fit as a fiddle. That was a nice little nap I had. Did we miss the ladies' luncheon?"

Judith laughed. "Yes, but that's okay by me."

"And by me. Good grief, it was hotter than—"

"Hey, old girl," said Burt in the kindest voice Judith could ever recall hearing him use. "Feeling better?"

"Yes, I had a nice little nap."

He leaned over the bed. "Nurse Bryant says you were in a bad way, Ellen. I'm sure glad Judith thought to bring you in."

"Yes, our little Judith is a real godsend."

Burt smiled over to Judith. "Well, do you think you could get Ellen safely home whenever she's ready?"

"Of course."

"And don't worry about dinner tonight. You girls just take it easy. Hal and I will eat with the other boys."

Ellen smiled. "The night off, Judith. Imagine that."

"Yes," said Judith. "And you're going to take it easy and let me wait on you."

"Looks like everything's under control then." said Burt. Then he frowned. "But I guess this means you'll miss hearing John Wagner."

She feigned disappointment. "Do they make tapes of the meetings?"

He shook his head. "Nope. It's not allowed. But I'll see if he's brought some of his newsletters for you to look at."

"Thanks."

"You ladies have a nice relaxing evening." He nodded and left.

"Well, now wasn't he just the sweetest old thing." said Ellen. "Guess I ought to get sick more often."

Judith got Ellen home later in the afternoon and settled her down on the couch with a couple of magazines and a tall glass of lemonade. Then she puttered around in the kitchen, putting together a light dinner using the leftovers from the evening before.

"You really are a godsend, Judith," said Ellen as she set her now-empty plate aside. "I just don't ever want you to leave."

Judith smiled as she picked up the dishes. "Well, it's been a treat for me to spend time with you, Ellen. I appreciate your hospitality."

"Hospitality!" Ellen shook her head. "Look at you waiting on me. You call that hospitality?"

Judith laughed. "As a matter of fact, I do. See, you're making me feel right at home."

Ellen yawned. "Well, good. I don't know what Nurse Bryant put in that IV, but I can barely keep my eyes open."

"Why not just close them and have another little rest? She said you needed to keep resting and drinking fluids."

"Yes, that sounds like good advice. Just a little catnap."

By the time Judith had loaded the dishwasher, Ellen was snoring soundly from the couch. Judith walked over to the closed door that led into Burt's office. She suspected it might be locked, but was surprised to find it wasn't. She turned the knob and looked in. Was there any surveillance equipment going? She had seen nothing to make her think so, just the same she decided to be careful. She would enter on the pretense of looking for stationery to write a letter.

First she just stood and studied his office. Very organized, almost military like with two five-drawer file cabinets standing at attention on either side of a bulky metal desk. A mounted elk bull head looked sightlessly from one wall and a large buck from the other. She walked over to the desk. The only items on top were a desk pad, a pencil cup, a tray for correspondence with only one newsletter in it—*The Aryan National,* of course. No personal items of any kind and no computer. Maybe Burt felt he was too old to learn new tricks, or maybe he left such things to Hal and the other computer whiz kid that Ellen had mentioned. She was relieved to find his desk so sparse, now at least she had an excuse to open a drawer.

She took a deep breath and listened. Just the rhythmic sound of Ellen's snore and the hum of the air conditioner. She opened the top desk drawer, There she found normal things like paper clips, rubber bands, and spare pens, as well as a roll of stamps. She tore off one. Next she opened a side drawer. There she found a stack of paper and business envelopes. She took one of each. She opened the next drawer. There she saw an address book and lying next to it was a small black revolver, almost as if to threaten anyone who dared trespass.

She was tempted to simply close the drawer and retreat, but instead, she carefully removed the address book without touching the revolver. She set it on the desk and began to flip through until she reached the M section and there she stopped at the name Con M lightly penciled onto the last space in that section. Had this been Constance Morrison's phone number? She picked up a pen and wrote the number on the inside of the envelope flap then folded it back down. Of course, she knew Constance was dead, but perhaps someone else was still at this number.

She continued to flip through the book. And whenever she found a lightly penciled number, usually in the back part of the section, she would pencil it down, also on the inside of the envelope. Finally, she felt her nerve fading and she returned the address book to its place by the gun, then took her letter writing items upstairs to her room. There she wrote a quick note to her mother saying that if she actually received this letter she was to save the envelope and that Judith would explain everything later. Then she put the letter inside, sealed, addressed, and stamped it. This, she tucked into her purse.

She went back downstairs to find Ellen still snoring. Judith decided to go outside, hoping she could talk quietly to herself as she walked and this way share some discoveries with Adam. She had made herself memorize the phone number with Constance's name, just in case her envelope was lost. This she would repeat to Adam along with any other thoughts that occurred to her.

She spoke out loud, giving specific directions to the clinic, and exactly where Aunt Lenore's room was located. She described all the entrances and the windows, as best she could remember, and the people working there, even suggesting that the nurse practitioner might possibly be bribed. Or maybe not. She mentioned having seen Hank. She described where all the buildings were, as far as she knew, and where Burt and even Hal's houses were located.

"Okay, I'm sure a lot of this information is just meaningless." she said finally. "And I'm not even sure that you can hear me. But I guess I'm lonely and just need to talk. By the way, I hope Eli's doing okay. On one hand, I don't feel too worried, since everyone's pretty busy with these meetings, but on the other hand, what if these boys got all fired up after one of the speakers, like Ed Burns this morning, and decided to go out on a little mission of their own? What then? Can you hear me, Adam? Anybody? So, keep an eye on things, okay. Now, I'm almost wishing I was going to that meeting tonight. But not really. I mean a person can only stomach so much of their propaganda at a time. Signing off for now."

She walked down to the little dock on the lake. She slipped off her sandals and put her feet into the water, then she leaned back on the dock, still warm from the sun, and closed her eyes, and for a few minutes just daydreamed, pretending she were far away from the horrors and problems that surrounded her. The sound of the water gently lapping against a little rowboat was soothing to her jittery nerves.

"Hey there."

Startled, Judith sat up quickly and looked all around. "Oh, Hal. Where'd you come from? You scared me."

"Sorry. I didn't mean to. Burt's tied up with the meeting, but he sent me down here to check on you two. Everything okay? I heard about Ellen's little spell. That's too bad."

"Yeah, but she's all right. She was sound asleep when I left her. I just wanted some fresh air."

"Mind if I join you?"

"Not at all, pull up a chair, but watch out for the slivers."

He chuckled as he sat down on the dock. "It's sure been great having you around, Judith. I know how much Ellen loves having you here. Even Burt's hoping you'll consider staying on, maybe take that teaching position at the school."

"Well, you just never know." She smiled at him. This, she suddenly realized, might possibly be her best chance to collect some evidence—if he had any.

"So, how do you like it here?"

She shrugged. "To be honest, I have sort of mixed feelings."

"What do you mean?"

"Well, it's a beautiful place and all. But to be perfectly honest, I just can't shake the feeling that Jasmine lived here and that she was horribly unhappy during that time. And that kind of bothers me." She looked him right in the eye. "Forgive me if I've offended you, and I would never say this to the Morrisons. But I guess I thought maybe you'd understand."

He nodded. "Yeah. I kinda do. It's almost like she haunts me too."

She looked at him intently. "Yes, that's how I feel. And I just need to know what happened to her—before—I could ever consider settling down here. And, well, I hate to ask Burt and Ellen too much. I know it's distressful to them. And probably to you too. You were, after all, her husband." She looked right into his eyes again, pretending to see something there that she couldn't for the life of her imagine. A slight breeze from the lake ruffled his combed-over hair to expose the large, pale bald area on top. "Tell me, were you in love with her, Hal?"

He looked out on the water for a long moment, then finally shook his head. "You know, I really wanted to love her. And I remembered how pretty she was when she was in high school—I was quite a bit older than her, of course, but I knew her through Burt back then. And then when she came here to live, I think I believed I was in love with her— right at the beginning, at least. But it didn't take long before I realized that something was wrong with her. She wasn't the same Jasmine I'd known back in Mississippi. It was almost like she was already dead."

"Yes. That's just what Ellen said." She looked at him again. "But then why did you marry her, Hal?"

He shrugged. "Mostly for Burt, I guess." He puffed out his cheeks then slowly blew. "You see, Burt's been like a dad to me.

I think I'd do most anything for him. And when he wanted me to marry Jasmine, I thought he was handing me the world on a platter. Oh, I know it must seem pretty strange to someone like you, like an arranged marriage or something. But you know, those things can work sometimes. I know this other guy who lives here and he met his wife by mail. And they seem fairly happy. And it's not like my first marriage was any screaming success. So, I figured, heck, why not. I thought maybe Jasmine would change over time, get better, you know. But as it turned out, I didn't know what I was getting into."

"And what was that?"

He studied her closely, then continued. "Well, for one thing, I didn't realize that Jasmine had been forced into the whole thing, right from the start. Burt sort of made me think that she had agreed, like she actually wanted to get married. He explained how she'd been sort of messed up, but was ready to return to her family and live a decent sort of life. And he said that she was ready to get married to a respectable guy and have some respectable children and live a respectable life. And we talked about building a house and raising a family and all kinds of stuff."

"You and Jasmine talked about these things?"

He shook his head. "Me and Burt."

"Oh."

"Yeah, that was the main problem. Jasmine wasn't too involved. Basically, she just didn't want to be here. And I didn't really know what all was going on with her. I mean, all the stuff she'd been through. I still don't know the half of it."

"Like what?"

"Oh, I don't know. But she'd messed up real bad. Burt said she'd shamed her family. And he was holding something over her head. Kind of like he was blackmailing her or something like that. But he had power over her, and he could make her do whatever he wanted. Until the end, that is."

"The end?"

"Yeah, when she shot herself."

"And you're certain that she shot herself?"

Hal looked sharply at her. "What're you suggesting, Judith? You think somebody else shot her? Me maybe? Since it was my gun, after all."

"Nooo..." Judith sighed deeply. "I guess it's still hard for me to understand why she gave up on life. I mean, I've been through some pretty hard things myself, and I'll admit I almost gave up, but then I didn't." She didn't mention that it was Jasmine's very death that had brought her back from the brink of her own. But her purpose here was to keep him talking—any way she could.

"But you're a strong woman, Judith. Jasmine was weak. She'd given up on everything before she ever came here. I just hadn't known it."

"Did you feel bad toward Burt because of all this?"

"Well, to be honest, I was a little upset for a while. But then I don't really think he meant any harm. I'm sure he just thought that he was helping her, and me too, for that matter. But it's like Jasmine was already broken and couldn't be fixed."

"Who was the last one to see her alive?"

He pressed his lips together. "Well, at first I thought it was me. But it may have been Burt." He shrugged. "Doesn't really matter though."

"Yeah, I suppose not. But I guess I'm just curious. What makes you think it was Burt?"

"Well, something he said, I guess. I mean right after we found out."

"What did he say?"

"Something like he shouldn't have told her something."

He turned and looked at Judith. "But it's not like he really had anything do with her death. You know how you blame yourself when something like that happens. Like, I just keep kicking myself for leaving that stupid handgun out there. I'd forgotten all about it. I guess, if anyone's to blame, it should be me."

"So, you don't know what Burt told her then?"

He shook his head. "Probably nothing important."

"Who found her?"

"The kid next door. Poor kid. I heard it really shook him up bad."

"Oh my." Judith pushed her hair back with both hands, then took a deep breath. "Well, thanks for answering my questions, Hal. It really helps me to understand better. And to appreciate that you never meant her any harm."

He nodded. "Yes, that's exactly right. I never meant her any harm. And if I'd a known she was going to kill herself, I'd have tried to work things out with Burt or something."

"Work things out?"

"Well, like I said, he was holding something over her. I might've tried to talk him into forgetting about it, and just letting her go her own way—whatever that might've been. I mean, it didn't do anyone a bit of good having her here. Poor Ellen's been just crushed by this business. We all have. But I know that whatever Burt did, he did it for Jasmine's own good."

"Yes, I'm sure he did." She looked back toward the house. "I suppose I should go check on Ellen."

"You've been good medicine for Ellen. I sure hope you decide to stick around." He was smiling now.

"Well, you just never know. Thanks for sharing that stuff, Hal."

"Yeah, guess I'll get back to the meeting."

"You enjoying these meetings?" she asked as they walked toward the house.

He looked at her curiously. "Well, to be honest, I might not be as committed to all this stuff as some of the other guys."

"All this stuff?"

"Oh, you know. I guess I kinda go along with it mostly 'cause of Burt. Like I said, I'd do most anything for him."

"Would you break the law?"

He looked at her intently. "I might."

"Really?"

"Well, the thing is, some laws are completely ridiculous and just begging to be broken anyway."

They were at the house now, and she turned and looked him right in the eye. "Would you hurt or kill another person for Burt?"

He rubbed his chin. "Well, now, I might, if it was in self-defense or defending someone I care about. Or are you meaning would I go out and do a lynching or something like that?"

"Maybe that's what I mean."

His countenance grew dark. "Some things are better left unsaid."

"Have you ever seen a lynching?"

He frowned, his lips pressed together.

She knew she was getting out on a limb here, but somehow she couldn't stop herself from asking the next question. "Do you know anything about what happened to James Paxton?"

His eyes flashed. "What do you know about that?"

"Only what I've heard." She eyed him carefully. "That he may have died under some mysterious circumstances."

Hal rolled his eyes and laughed a forced laugh that sounded more like a snort. "That boy was living carelessly. He brought on his own death."

"Meaning he didn't have any help?" These words came out just barely above a whisper. And she couldn't believe she'd said it.

Now Hal looked seriously perturbed and Judith felt sure she'd gone way past the line. Suddenly her heart began to beat fast and her palms grew clammy.

"You ask some pretty tough questions, Judith."

She forced a smile to her lips, hoping to look coy and somehow throw him off her trail. "Well, Hal, how else am I supposed to get to know somebody better?"

He dipped his head and his cheeks reddened, just slightly as he cleared his throat. *"Okay* then, have a good evening and give my regards to Ellen. I hope she's feeling better."

Judith went into the house and stood before the kitchen sink, breathing deeply and trying to steady herself. She could hear Ellen still snoring contentedly in the living room. She turned on the tap water then looked down to see her hands shaking. For a long time she washed them in the warm water, soaping up again and again, and rinsing slowly. Then she filled a glass with cool water and slowly drank it.

Dear God, help me, she prayed silently as she wiped the empty glass across her forehead. Just get me through one more day undetected, and please, help me find some real evidence and concrete answers.

Ellen continued to sleep soundly, and then after the sun finally set, Judith decided to call it a day herself. First she opened the windows to allow the fresh evening air inside since it was cooling off nicely now, and then she draped a light afghan over Ellen and tiptoed off, slipping upstairs, where she took a careful, tepid shower, protecting the strange little device taped to her upper abdomen from the splashing water.

Once in bed, she opened Jasmine's little Bible again. Suddenly she wondered if she shouldn't have also given this book to Adam for clues. For somehow it seemed they were there, even if she couldn't quite grasp it. She remembered the curious verse she'd read last night, and decided to read it out loud now, for Adam's sake. First she announced that it was underlined in Jasmine's Bible and then slowly read it, feeling slightly ridiculous as she did. Then after reading, she fingered through some more pages and not much further along but in the same book of Matthew, she found some more verses, also underlined in pencil. So she read these lines aloud as well. *"Again, the kingdom of heaven is like a merchant seeking beautiful pearls, who, when he had found one pearl of great price, went and sold all that he had and bought it."*

Now, she mentally compared this Scripture to last night's verses which spoke of not giving things you treasured to those who didn't appreciate them. But this new verse was different in that it spoke of someone who found something of great value and gave up everything to attain it. She wondered if these two verses had anything to do with each other, or had they simply been ones that Jasmine had liked. She continued to thumb through the little Bible in search of more underlined verses, but to her great dismay found not a single one more.

As she heard Burt's key in the front door she snapped off her light and then whispered into her chest, "Good night, Adam."

Thirty-One

JUDITH ROSE EARLY THE next morning. She slipped downstairs while it was still quiet and started a pot of coffee. She wanted to be extra helpful today, making things go as smoothly as possible. And although they hadn't discussed it, she hoped this would be her last day at the lake. She wasn't sure how much longer she could last in this role she'd created and felt worried that her disguise might be wearing thin by now. But just the same she wanted to win their final portion of trust today and hopefully learn something really important and helpful.

"Morning, Judith." said Burt as he came into the kitchen.

"Good morning," she answered in a cheerful voice. "Would you like a cup of coffee?"

"That'd be nice." He sat down at the breakfast nook and folded his hands on the table. Clearly, this was a man who was used to being waited on.

"How's Ellen feeling this morning?" she asked as she set down his cup and spoon.

He reached for the sugar and stirred in two rounded spoonfuls. "She's feeling a little worn out still. I told her to go 'head and sleep in if she liked."

"Well, that's nice of you." She hoped her voice didn't convey the sarcasm behind it. She took a slow sip of coffee and then noticed that Burt was eyeing her carefully, almost suspiciously or so it seemed. She looked out the window, noticing the clouds on the horizon. "Looks like it's going to be a little cooler day."

Burt cleared his throat. "Hal tells me you've been asking a lot of questions, Judith."

She turned and looked at him, her eyes meeting his over the brim of her coffee cup. She held her gaze steady, cup still poised before her lips, and wondered how best to answer this accusation. That's what it felt like anyway. And for once she longed to somehow match that icy penetration of his cold stare. "Well," she began slowly, "as a matter of fact, I have been asking some questions." She lowered the cup and sighed.

"Care to explain why?"

She eased herself into the seat across from him and placed her cup on the table. She felt her heart beginning to pulse harder, and suddenly wondered if perhaps Adam or someone else was listening now. Could he hear her heart pounding? Would it interfere with his reception? And what if Burt suspected she was wearing a wire? She suppressed the sudden urge to reach for it, pat it, make sure it was there.

"Explain why?" She looked at him innocently. "I'm not sure I know what you mean exactly, Burt?"

"I mean, why are you asking all those questions about Jasmine?" His voice was flat and full of accusation now.

She suppressed the urge to scowl, angry at herself for trusting Hal last night. She should've known who held his allegiance. Here, she'd thought it was she who was gathering information, and as it turned out he was simply playing her for a little fool. It was time to think fast. "Well, as I told Hal, I'm still a little unsettled about a few things, and before I can seriously consider moving here or teaching at the—"

"Moving here or teaching?" Now this seemed to catch him slightly off guard.

"Well, yes. Didn't Hal tell you the full context of our conversation last night?"

"I'm not sure."

"Hal asked if I had any serious interest in relocating here. And I told him, quite honestly, that I was still a little troubled by Jasmine's death." She looked Burt right in the eye, hoping to convey the honest pain and sadness she felt about losing her friend. "And sometimes, it's almost like I can feel her near me. Like I can understand how miserable she was during the last part of her life. But what I don't understand is why. I mean, this is a beautiful place to live. She was close to her family. Can you tell me why she was so completely miserable, Burt? You were her daddy. Did you know what was troubling her? Because until I can resolve this thing about Jasmine, no matter how much I love Ellen and you, no matter how much you feel like family to me, I will never be completely comfortable here." She felt her voice grow louder. "Jasmine was like a sister to me. I loved her dearly. I just want to know what really happened. Did she really kill herself? And if she did, why did she do it?" She felt genuine tears in her eyes.

He nodded soberly, no longer appearing so affronted and full of accusation. "Well now, I suppose that makes some sense. I appreciate your honesty, Judith."

"But do you have any answers for me?"

"Don't know that I have the answers you want to hear."

"All I want is the truth."

"Well now, the truth comes in all sorts of packages."

"I just want the plain and simple truth, Burt. No fancy package."

"Okay then. First off, Jasmine did most certainly kill herself. Shot herself in the head with a Colt .45—Hal's gun, although I do not hold him responsible. The neighbor boy found her out back by the pond. The police will confirm that the wound was self-inflicted. Go and check them out if you like. But you want to know *why* did Jasmine kill herself? That's a question we've all asked ourselves over and over. You want to hear my version, Judith? Why I believe Jasmine killed herself?"

She nodded.

"Well, first off, as a young adult Jasmine chose to run off and rebel against her parents. She left home and went her own ways. And eventually her own ways got her deeply into trouble. She not only sinned against her own family, but she sinned against God and against her own race. And her sins brought her judgment and condemnation and ruin. And as her daddy, I tried to give her a second chance. I was willing to forgive her. I did my best to rescue my baby and bring her back here where she could be safe, where she could start her life over. All I wanted was for her to have the life that the good Lord intended her to live."

"A life that ultimately killed her?"

His eyes flashed with blue fire. "She killed herself."

Judith put her hands into her lap so he wouldn't see them shaking. "Hal said you were the last one to speak to her that day."

His jawline grew firm and she feared she had really crossed the line now. But to her surprise he answered. "Yes. I believe I was."

She paused, focusing; she wanted to soften her voice, warm her words a little, win an answer from him. "What did you say to her, Burt?"

His eyes narrowed now. "I told her to quit living in the past. I told her that her life was here with us, and that Hal was her legal husband, and that she better quit living in a dream world. I told her the past was dead and gone and done with."

She nodded slowly. "And did you feel that had anything to do with her taking her own life?"

He looked down at his hands wrapped around the coffee mug. She looked at his hands too, surprised at how old and wrinkled and almost fragile they looked. Yet those were the same hands that had once hunted and fished, and even whipped Jasmine with a long leather belt. She turned her gaze away and swallowed hard.

"This is hard to say, but sometimes I actually wish I hadn't said those things to her. Sometimes I think she might still be alive if I hadn't said those words. But I was only speaking the truth. I thought she needed to hear it, once and for all."

To her chagrined surprise, a part of her wanted to comfort this old man, so seemingly broken, bereaved of his firstborn daughter. And yet another part wanted to slap him hard, right across his wrinkled old face. Burt Morrison wasn't a stupid man; he had to have known that Jasmine was in a fragile state, that mere words from him could hurt—even kill her. And so she looked down at the table and said nothing.

"But even so," he continued, "we all gotta make our own choices in this life. Right or wrong, they're ours to bear, and when we stand before our maker, we, each one, stand alone."

Judith looked at him in wonder. Was he defending himself? Or making a confession? Or was it simply a plea? She couldn't tell. Still she said nothing, hoping her silence might encourage him to continue, filling up the spaces with his own words.

"And in the end, Jasmine made her own choice. She took the easy way out, leaving the rest of us here to pick up all her broken pieces." He took a long swig of coffee, then set down his cup with a thud. "And that's about all I have to say about that."

She nodded, smiling weakly for his sake. "Thank you, Burt. I needed to know."

He stood and walked over to the sink. With his back to her, he continued to speak. "You've been a real help to Ellen these past few days, Judith. I want you to know you're welcome here. And should you decide to stay, we'll treat you just like kin."

Her first response to his kindness was a sense of gratitude. This was followed by a wave of disgust as reality hit and she remembered what this man actually stood for and what it meant to be treated as his *kin.* Good grief, his very own daughters' lives had been ruined by his hatred, and now both were dead! How could he take himself seriously in his invitation to be "part of the family"? Although her hands still trembled, she controlled her countenance, willing her expression to be flat with no show of emotion. Then she took a deep breath, deciding to smooth things over. For she must keep him open to her. "I really appreciate that, Burt. It's been such a comfort how you and Ellen have been like family to me. You make me feel right at home here."

"What's that?" chirped Ellen happily as she stepped into the kitchen wearing a bright pink bathrobe. "Sounds like I'm missing out on a good little chat."

"Good morning, Ellen," said Judith in a cheerful voice. "Burt was just saying that I'm welcome to stay on here at the lake."

"Why, of course you're welcome, honey doll. I won't be able to bear it if you leave us. Now promise me you won't, will you?"

"Well, how about if I get you a cup of coffee first?" she offered, turning away to avoid the bright hopefulness in Ellen's eyes.

"Coffee sounds fine, but don't you go being evasive with me. You *are* going to stay with us here, aren't you, Judith?"

Judith turned back around and gave her the brightest smile

possible. "Like I said, Ellen, we'll have to see. There are some things I have to take care of first. It's a very big decision for me."

Ellen wrapped her arms around her. "Oh, I know, dear. And I'm just certain you'll make the right choice. Just you make sure you choose to come back to us!"

Judith laughed even as she tried to unobtrusively back away. She didn't want Ellen to feel her wire. "Oh, Ellen, you make it hard to say no."

"Good. That's just what I was hoping. Now, how 'bout a cup of that coffee?"

"You ladies want to go to the parade this morning?"

"Parade?" repeated Judith.

"Yes, don't you remember the Fourth of July parade?" asked Ellen. "Why, you and Jasmine used to dress up like all sorts of things just so you could participate."

Judith smiled, "They still have that?"

"You bet," said Burt. "We march in it every year."

Judith felt her stomach twist at the idea of a bunch of white supremacists marching down Main Street. "You march too, Ellen?"

"Oh no, I just watch." She looked at the clock. "If we get a move on we can probably get us a good spot out in front of the Timber Topper where we can get us a little snack if we like."

"You sure you feel up to it, Ellen?" asked Burt. "You were a little under the weather yesterday."

She waved her hand. "I'm fine. Just keep me in the shade is all I ask."

❦

BURT ALLOWED JUDITH TO drive Ellen into town to secure a good seat. And at half past nine they had their lawn chairs set up in a shady spot right outside of the Timber Topper. Judith had planned ahead and brought a thermos of lemonade. She didn't want Ellen wilting in the heat again. But the way it was suddenly clouding up, she wondered if her precaution was necessary.

"You know what sounds good to me right now." said Ellen as she dug into her purse for money, "is a cup of coffee and a Danish. You suppose I could twist your arm to go in there and get us some?"

"Sure." Judith took the money and reluctantly entered the crowded café. To her surprise she saw Josh Ford, Adam's boy, chatting, or perhaps flirting, with Katie Miller, who was standing behind the cash register. Katie had a big smile and appeared to be enjoying Josh's attention. But when Judith walked up her smile faded and she whispered something to Josh, who turned around to look. But when he saw Judith, he seemed somewhat confused.

"Hi," he said, staring at her curiously.

"Hello," she answered coolly, turning her gaze to Katie. "Could I get a couple cups of coffee and a Danish, please?"

"Yeah, just a minute." And she disappeared back into the kitchen.

Josh continued looking at her, then finally spoke in a hushed voice. "I saw you in the store yesterday with that woman." Then he glanced outside the window. "Looks like you're still with her." He shook his head. "I just didn't think you were really like that."

"Yeah, well, I guess you can't always go by what you think, now can you?" She looked him right in the eye, trying to appear as cold and intimidating as she'd seen Burt do. For the less Josh knew about her, the safer he would be. Better to offend him right off and get it over with.

"Guess not." He turned away in what appeared to be sincere disgust. And even though she still knew she was acting, it hurt deep inside like the real thing.

"Here's your order," said Katie in a stony voice. "That'll be $4.85."

Judith laid a five on the counter, picked up her things, and walked away.

"Oh, wow," she heard Katie say sarcastically. "Thanks for the tip."

Judith looked straight ahead and made her way out the door. But even as she did, she noticed a table filled with some women from the lake smiling her way. "Hey, Judith," called the woman who'd organized the ladies' luncheon. "How's Ellen doing today?"

"Oh, she's just fine now. Got a little heat exhaustion, is all."

"Well, good that it's cooling off today then," she said. "We gonna see you out at the big picnic this afternoon?"

Judith nodded. "You bet."

A heavyset woman hopped up from their table and opened the door for her. "There you go, Judith."

She smiled brightly. "Thanks."

"Oh, there you are," said Ellen. "I think the parade's about to start."

The parade didn't seem anything like what she remembered from childhood. If anything, it was more like a white supremacist celebration. To start off there was the horse brigade from the lake. In the center of the first row came Burt, his hand steadying a United States flag that flapped in the breeze. Ellen waved and called out to him, but his gaze remained directly forward, almost as if he were leading his group into a serious battle. Hal carried the Oregon state flag, and a man called Jerry bore a flag that didn't look all that different from the Confederate one, but now Judith suspected this flag must represent their little colony at the lake. Next came a fairly large group of marching men wearing camouflage uniforms, carrying rifles, and waving a banner that bore the name of a national gun organization.

Following this was a float of sorts, really pretty tacky, with a bunch of the lake kids dressed up like pioneers or cowboys. Their sign read: "Remember our Forefathers." But it galled Judith to see the children looking so happy and cheerful. She would've preferred it if they'd been stone-faced and somber, as if they'd been forced into this, although she knew they hadn't. And they were, in fact, having a pretty good time. But then, why shouldn't they? This was probably one of the merrier days in their rather gloomy little lives. And besides, what child didn't enjoy a parade? Suddenly, she simply felt sorry for them.

Then came some of the older men, obviously veterans, and all wearing a variety of uniforms. Their banner said, "We Fought for Our Freedom—We Won't Give It Away!" After that came a number of old classic cars and pickups, nothing too spectacular. Several pickups displayed Confederate flags, and various slogans were draped over the sides of the vehicles, "White Pride" seeming to be the general favorite. And then there came a short lapse, and it looked as if the parade was over.

"What's that down there?" called someone from the sidewalk as he pointed down the street.

"What the—" yelled another.

Judith craned her neck to see a small group slowly coming their way. There appeared to be only about a dozen of them and they were dressed in regular street clothes, but carrying a white banner in front of them. But as the marchers drew closer, she could see three tall African American men walking amid them, right in the front row. And in the center marched Eli Paxton!

Thirty-Two

SHE FELT HER HEART pounding in her throat as she watched
Eli and the others steadily approach the area where the spectators
were situated. What in the world were they doing here? Didn't they
realize the danger? Why would Eli, of all people, blatantly invite
this kind of trouble? The small crowd of spectators grew hushed as
the marchers drew closer. And now several people emerged from the
café to get a closer look, among them Josh and Katie.

"Go home!" yelled an onlooker suddenly, his voice cutting
through the stunned silence. "Go back to Africa!"

Judith felt a very real shiver run down her spine. *Dear God,
please protect them,* she prayed in silent desperation. Now she could
clearly read the banner they carried. "Prayer Changes Things—Let's
Pray for Unity."

"Oh my goodness." gasped Ellen as realization hit. "What in
heaven's name?"

"Go home, you animals!" yelled an older man. "We don't want
your kind here!"

Just then, Josh Ford pushed through the small crowd. He stepped right
out into the street and suddenly joined the slow, deliberate stride of

the protesters. Then Katie Miller, following his lead, grabbed his hand and marched right beside him. *Bless you both,* thought Judith. *But please, God, protect them.* Now she could also see Martha Anderson, cane in hand, and several other women, all about her age, slowly walking with an expression of sheer determination carved into each face. The women all had a similar look to them, and Judith guessed them to be friends. And there was old Dr. Warner and his wife, marching in the second row.

With the initial shock over, the heckling began to increase. And the air was tangibly charged with open hatred and bigotry. Still, the brave marchers continued on. Over the derogatory shouts from the onlookers, Judith could hear the marchers singing "We Shall Overcome" just like in the old nonviolent protests from the sixties. It amazed Judith that the community of Cedar Crest had remained so backward for all these years.

Oh, how she longed to stand up and join the marchers right now, to raise her voice in song with theirs! What would it matter to end her charade? Perhaps her mission out at the lake was completed anyway. Why not just announce her true allegiance here and now, with the whole world of Cedar Crest looking on? But then, what if there were something more for her to uncover out at the lake? If not about Jasmine, perhaps about James. Her eyes darted across the small crowd of angry spectators, growing more indignant and hostile by the moment. Where was Adam Ford right now? Did he have his people on hand for this potentially volatile situation? And what about all those rifles just up the street? Could the FBI, or whomever, possibly handle it if serious trouble erupted here? What if Burt and his bullies outnumbered them?

Just then, someone from the sidewalk threw a large Coke cup, smacking Eli midthigh. It splattered, then fell to the ground in a dark, wet puddle. Without missing a beat, Eli continued to march. Now a few other onlookers began to throw things too. Food items, beer cans, beverage containers, and even a couple still-burning cigarettes.

And then suddenly, as if out of nowhere, a camera crew appeared and with video cams rolling, began to instantly film the entire spectacle, catching the ugly words, the thrown items, the sneering faces—as well as the patient countenance of the peaceful protesters, a sharp contrast to their opposition. Judith spotted a man in a neat sports jacket over by the hardware store. She couldn't remember his name, but she knew she'd seen him before on NBC news, and now he was speaking quickly and loudly into a microphone and camera, as if he were describing the whole nasty event in vivid detail. Now Judith wanted to stand up and cheer. But instead she remained firmly rooted to her chair, publicly humiliated that once again, she was sitting on the wrong side of this critical issue. She felt Ellen's arm tugging at her. "What should we do, Judith?" Ellen's eyes were wide with fear.

"I think we should—"

Suddenly shouts were heard from up the street where the earlier parade marchers had headed just minutes earlier. It appeared as if word of the protest had reached them. Although Judith couldn't see them yet, she clearly recalled their guns and wouldn't be surprised if they were actually loaded.

"We better go inside the Timber Topper, Ellen," said Judith. And although she hated to miss a moment of what was now transpiring, she quickly rose from her chair and helped the older woman into the café. "I'm going back out," she explained as she situated Ellen at a table with a couple of the older women who seemed oblivious to what was happening, "but you better stay here."

Judith went outside and stood with the crowd, unsure of why, or what she might even do if real trouble broke out. Would she risk blowing her cover? Of course she would, how could she not? Just then several policemen appeared. They wore riot helmets and carried large billy clubs in their hands. And they planted themselves squarely in front of the marchers, legs spread, hands on hips, blocking their way. A barricade.

"Do you have a permit to march in this parade?" demanded the captain.

"I didn't know we needed a permit." said Eli, taking a step forward.

"Stop right there!" barked the captain, raising his club in a threatening way.

"Look." said Eli in a calm voice as he held up both hands, palms forward. "We are unarmed. This is a peaceful protest."

One camera was focused in on the captain and one on Eli. "Get outta my face," the captain snapped at the cameraman, waving his club.

"Freedom of the press," called the cameraman without budging an inch.

The captain turned his attention back to Eli. "You folks are marching without a permit. That's breaking the law. I could take you all in for this."

"Did all the other marchers have permits?" Eli asked calmly.

The captain didn't answer. And Judith could tell by his face that they didn't. She'd wager that not one single permit had been issued for today's parade.

The young man to Eli's left took a step forward. "Do the other people in the parade have permits?" he repeated in a firm but calm voice.

"Shut up, *boy!*" yelled the captain.

"What's going on here, Arlen?" asked Gary as he

approached the barricade. He had led the camouflaged troop, the ones carrying rifles.

"We got us some illegal marchers," said the captain from the side of his mouth.

"Need any help keeping these varmints under control?" asked Gary. He shifted his rifle and eyed Eli in a condescending manner.

"You haven't answered our question," said Dr. Warner in a loud, clear voice. He stepped forward to stand next to Eli and the other young man. "Did everyone else here have a permit to participate in the parade today?"

"Now, you don't even live here no more, Doc," said Arlen in a hostile voice.

Gary stepped closer to Eli and the two young men that Judith now felt certain must be his college-aged sons. "And you boys don't live here neither. Y'all got no right to march in this here parade." He took another step toward them and spit out a nasty racial slur, jutting his chin out as if inviting them to fight back. But they simply stood there, staring evenly back at him, not even flinching.

"Hold on there, Gary," warned the captain. "This here is police business."

"Well then, do something about it, Arlen!" yelled the man standing next to Gary. "These coons are ruining our parade. Why don't you just arrest them all and be done with it?"

Eli began to speak. ""We've only come here today because we, and a number of other people, are praying for change in Cedar Crest. We want to see acceptance and unity restored to this town—"

"Shut up, boy!" yelled Gary, raising his gun as if he meant to use it.

"Gary," warned Arlen in a quiet voice. "Put that thang away."

Just then, Judith spotted Adam, across the street and about a block down, standing off by himself and leaning against a street sign. He had a ball cap pulled low on his brow and he was hunched over as if talking into a cell phone or something like that. Hopefully, he was calling in for reinforcements.

"Y'all better go on home now," Arlen told the protesters. "You've had your fun and games, now go on home with ya."

"You never did answer our question," said the young man again, slightly louder this time as if to make sure everyone else could hear. "Did the other people in the parade register for permits?"

"Look!" said Arlen. "I'm telling y'all to disperse and go home, do ya hear me?" He stepped forward, slapping his billy club in his free hand. "Now, if y'all wanna make trouble, I'd be more'n happy to take y'all in and book you."

"Book us on what?" asked the other young man who'd been quiet until now. He stepped up next to Eli. "We've broken no law."

"You don't have no permit!" Arlen snarled, his face just inches from the young man. "And if you don't leave right now, I'm taking y'all in. Ya hear me?"

The young man held out his wrists as if inviting the captain to cuff him. "Well I'm not leaving, so I guess you'll have to arrest me."

Arlen made a sour face. "Boy, why don't you just go back to wherever it is you came from. We don't need your kind here, and I sure as heck don't want you down at city hall defiling my jail."

This made several people laugh, tossing out more nasty comments, and telling the protesters to go home as well as some other unsavory places.

But one by one, the other marchers all stepped forward, including young Josh and Katie, and each held out their hands, wrists together, as if they too were waiting to be cuffed. Even

Martha and her lady friends, although it was plain to see by their wide eyes that they were a little frightened by this possibility. But just the same, Judith admired them more than ever. She wished she could stand among their ranks. And then, to her complete surprise, a few others began to step out from the sidewalk. Not people from the lake, but people she had assumed held similar views. But then they walked out onto the street, joining the small group of protesters, quietly taking their places all around them. And then, as if to show their actual support, each of them held out their wrists to be cuffed as well. Judith estimated there to be about forty people out there by now.

Arlen was clearly flustered by all this. He turned and looked at his men, calling a couple uniformed officers over to him. Then the three put their heads together for a short consultation lasting several minutes, before they turned and faced the protesters.

"Fine," said Arlen, "have it your way then." He and the other two policemen pulled out the handcuffs. Arlen loudly told the whole group that they were under arrest and then proceeded to recite their rights. First he handcuffed Eli. Meanwhile the other two policemen cuffed the two young men. Then each of the officers shoved their cuffed man ahead of themselves, and they began to walk toward the police station just a couple blocks down the street. The crowd cheered in victory, hurling more cruel and racist words to their backsides. Judith felt tears burning in her eyes as she watched Eli and his sons being led away, their heads still held high as they walked.

"Wait!" called Dr. Warner loudly. "What about the rest of us?"

"Go home!" yelled Arlen over his shoulder. "The party's over. And this entire crowd has exactly five minutes to disperse!"

Once Eli and his sons were out of sight, the onlookers began taunting the protesters still standing in the street, calling them all sorts of names. But the group ignored them, talking among themselves as if concocting some sort of plan. Then all together, they moved off the street and began walking away toward the other end of town. Judith sent up another prayer for them, for their safety and for divine wisdom. She looked back over to where Adam had been standing only to find him gone. How she longed to talk to him, to tell him she'd had enough of her charade, that it was time for her to quit this thing, but he was nowhere in sight. Well, surely he and his people would be watching out for Eli and everyone else. Surely, he'd been calling for some outside help.

"Where's Ellen?"

She turned to see Burt, no longer on his horse. "She's in the Timber Topper," answered Judith meekly.

"Good. Go and get her and let's go home."

Home? She shuddered as she went back into the café. She had no desire to return home with them. But how could she get out of this? "Burt's here, Ellen," she said woodenly. "It's time to go."

A plan occurred to her as they walked toward the car. "Say, Burt," she began. "Maybe you could drop me by to pick up my car. That way I could follow you back to the lake, but you wouldn't have to take me back home tonight."

"Oh, aren't you going to stay the night with us?" asked Ellen. "I hope you didn't let that little display out there bother you, dear. Once we get back to the lake, everything will be just fine again. We'll have our little picnic celebration, and then a wonderful fireworks display."

"Yes," said Judith as they climbed into the Cadillac. "But wouldn't it be easier on you two if I just brought my own car?"

"No," said Burt abruptly as he turned on the engine. "It's best if you just ride with us, Judith."

She swallowed. Everything inside her said to put an end to this charade right here and now. But suddenly, she remembered Aunt Lenore back at the clinic. Perhaps, with all the day's festivities, she could slip in and have another conversation that might be used as evidence. And what about her promise to get the old woman out of there? Perhaps with everyone distracted with their activities…or perhaps Judith was simply being foolish. She wondered what Adam thought of this whole thing. He'd suggested that problems might develop. Who knew what would occur after this little display in town today? She'd seen the angry looks on the men's faces as Eli and his group stood their ground. She didn't think men like Burt and his friends would take something like this lying down. Then it occurred to her, this might be her best chance to get some information from Burt as well.

"So, what did you think of all that, Burt?" she asked from the backseat as he drove toward the lake.

"Hmph." He shook his head. "I think those boys don't know what they're getting themselves into."

"What exactly are they getting themselves into?" she asked innocently.

"Trouble."

"You mean by being arrested?"

He laughed, but it was mean and cynical. "That's probably the least of their troubles right now."

"So do you think they're in danger?"

"What d'you think, Judith?" he snapped as he turned onto the highway.

"Well, to be honest, I think they might be safer in jail than out on the streets."

He laughed again, only more quietly this time. "You really think so?"

"Are you saying they aren't safe in jail?"

"Oh, you two," said Ellen. "Can't we talk about something more pleasant?"

"But I'm curious about this," persisted Judith. "What do you think will happen to those—" she clinched her teeth— "those *boys?*"

"You know, I think I'm getting too old for all this," said Burt.

"Too old for what, Daddy?" asked Ellen.

"Oh, I don't know."

"But what do you think will happen to the ones in jail?" Judith couldn't force herself to say "boys" again.

"I'll just say this, Judith, I wouldn't want to be the one responsible for their safety, is all."

"So, you really do think they're in danger?"

"Why do you care?" His voice was sharp now.

"I'm just curious." She tried to make her voice sound light and excited, like she was enjoying this whole thing. "Don't you think it was pretty smart for Arlen to come up with that business about not having a permit?"

Burt sniggered. "Yeah. Gotta hand it to ol' Arlen, he was thinking fast on his feet today. Permits, that's a good one!"

"Yeah, I've just never seen anything like this happen before. It was pretty exciting, kind of like a movie. I wonder what'll happen next."

"Well, I 'spect that's up to Gary and his boys. No telling what they might do when they get riled like that."

"So you've seen things like this happen before?"

He nodded, his eyes sparkling with excitement. "Oh yeah."

"Wow. That was pretty interesting, I mean, watching the big showdown."

"Yeah, well, we got to keep them boys in their place. Let 'em know who's boss. That ringleader boy used to live in this town. One of them Paxton boys. But I don't know where them other two boys come from. But you see, this is just the thang. You let one of 'em in and they all start pouring in—just like some nasty disease, spreading like the plague. Same thang's happening all over this country. We're just a crawling with foreigners. And it's up to folks like us to put a stop to it."

"But how do you put a stop to it?"

"By drawing the line."

"But what if they step over it?"

"That's when things can get a little rough."

"Has it ever gotten rough around Cedar Crest before? Or are you just talking about back in Mississippi?"

He was turning off toward the lake now. "Well, mostly things stay pretty quiet around here, but we've had us a few wild nights when we had to get tough."

"Yeah," she said eagerly. "I heard about that time with that Paxton boy. That must've been one of those times."

The car grew quiet now. "Who told you 'bout that?" Burt's voice was like ice.

She swallowed hard. "Oh, I don't recall for sure, Burt. Maybe it was Hal."

"Hal knows better than to be shooting his mouth off like that." The guard at the gates waved their car through and the Dobermans chased after them, barking loudly.

"Oh, I don't remember for sure if it was Hal or not. Anyway, isn't it common knowledge around here? Didn't someone set up that whole thing, making it look like an accident?"

Another quiet pause. "Well, I'll say this—there's accidents and then there's accidents. But it's time you learned that there's some things we just don't talk about, Judith. And that is one of them. You understand me?"

"Well, sure. If you say so. I was just so interested." Then she decided to try Ellen's tactic and use a little-girl voice. "I'm sorry, Burt. I didn't mean to upset you."

"Yeah, well, if you're going to live out here you better start learning how to keep your mouth shut."

"Oh, Daddy," said Ellen, shaking her head. "You don't need to talk like that to her. Judith is a smart girl, but she's just curious, is all. She don't mean no harm."

"Well, okay then, but I think she's heard plenty for one day. Some things are better left unsaid, if you know what I mean. Just you rest assured, Judith, we vow to protect our own around here. And that includes you. So you've got no cause to worry about your safety."

She wished she could believe him.

Thirty-Three

BURT WENT STRAIGHT TO his office when they got home, and Judith joined Ellen in the kitchen, helping her make the lemon meringue pies.

Although she couldn't decipher the words, Judith could hear Burt ranting on the phone as she juiced lemons. "Burt sounds pretty upset." she said in a matter-of-fact tone.

"Yes, it's just such a shame you had to witness all that nonsense in town," said Ellen as she separated an egg. "And here I was just feeling so hopeful that you might really stay with us out at the lake, but now all this has to go and happen. I sure hope it won't change anything."

"Oh, don't you worry," reassured Judith. "What happened in town won't affect my decision one way or another." She smiled, at least that was the truth. "I was just curious about how they would handle it now."

"Well, I don't usually trouble myself with such things." Ellen cracked another egg. "Because before you know it these little incidents just blow over and you can forget that anything unpleasant ever happened."

She wondered just how much Ellen had been forced to forget over the years. And had she really forgotten everything? Or were things just buried deep down inside of her, things like the memory of broken family ties, lost daughters, and who knew what else? It seemed a high price to pay in order to hate.

"Is this enough?" asked Judith, holding up the glass measuring cup of lemon juice.

"That looks fine. Now, how would you like to whip these whites while I check on those pie crusts?"

"I've got to go to a meeting." said Burt abruptly. "And I 'spect it'll take most of the day, so don't look for me at lunch."

"What about the picnic?" asked Ellen.

"It's still on. Judith can drive you both down to the clubhouse at four."

"Oh, goody," Ellen clapped her hands like a child. "I was hoping that silly old thing downtown wouldn't spoil our picnic. And how about the fireworks?"

"Yes, Ellen," Burt scowled. "The fireworks are still on. Nothing has changed. We'll have the picnic as scheduled, and then fireworks will begin shortly after sunset."

She clapped her hands again. "Oh, this will be such fun, Judith."

"I can hardly wait," said Judith, striving for enthusiasm, but feeling more drained by the moment. "I'll bet the fireworks look beautiful over the lake."

"Oh, they do. They truly do."

"See you girls at four then." Burt peered into the kitchen. "You bringing them pies to the picnic this afternoon?"

"Well, of course, silly," said Ellen playfully. "What'd you think I was gonna do with them?"

He grinned. "Save 'em all for me?"

"Oh, you'll get yours, Daddy," she said with a sly smile. "Now, you better get along with you before they send out a search party."

After a light lunch, Ellen went to take a little catnap but Judith felt more like a cat on a hot tin roof. Finally she decided to go for a walk; after all, no one had said she couldn't. The clouds had burned off by now, and it was turning out to be a fairly nice day. Not quite as hot as the previous, but fairly warm just the same. She tried to enjoy the calm serenity of the clear blue lake and the tall evergreens all around, but somehow they just looked flat and unappealing to her. Sort of like a faded picture postcard of a place you never really wanted to visit in the first place. With no real purpose, she began to walk toward Hal's house and then on past it, toward the edge of the new development. She wondered if Jasmine had ever walked along here before. Somehow, she suspected she had.

Without really paying much attention, she just kept going through the rough of the meadow. And after awhile, a dirt road of sorts appeared off to her right and she decided to follow it and see where it went. After about twenty minutes of fast walking that led her into a wooded area, she realized that the road turned sharply and headed straight toward a gate in the tall security fence. Unlike the front gate, this gate appeared to be unguarded with no dogs in sight, but she felt fairly certain it would be solidly locked. It must be the fire exit that Ellen had mentioned. Judith turned around and began to head back toward the house. She scanned the horizon as she emerged from the trees out into the open again. Had anyone observed her walking out here, all alone? But she saw nothing unusual. Besides, she figured, everyone must be fairly busy about now. Women putting the finishing touches on their picnic meals. Men at their stupid meeting. She wondered what was going on at Burt's meeting today. Just the same old thing, or were they getting themselves all worked into a lather over Eli and his demonstrating friends? Suddenly she touched the transmitter on her upper abdomen. She'd almost forgotten she was wearing a wire. Was there any important information she might dispatch to Adam while she had this unusual bit of solitude?

"I don't know if anyone is listening out there or not." she began in a feeble voice. "I mean, I do realize there's all kinds of trouble breaking loose all over the place. But for what it's worth, I've just found the west fire exit. The dirt road starts about a hundred yards, I'd guess, after you go past the last house in the development. I think they'd planned to connect it to the existing road, so they probably line up. Anyway, I walked pretty quickly on it for about twenty minutes, then into the wooded area west of the lake, and then the road took a sharp right turn and headed directly to a gate which I'm sure is securely locked. But I didn't see any guards or dogs over there. In fact, it's all rather quiet and deserted on this side of the lake." She walked along for a while then added, "I sure hope everyone is okay out there. I'm trying to figure out a way to see Aunt Lenore again today. I'm thinking maybe during the picnic festivities, if I can sneak off for a few minutes. Or maybe during the fireworks tonight. I thought maybe I could head over there and pretend to be sick or something. I'm not really sure yet. It's probably a dumb idea. But I'd like to do two things. First off, I'd like to reassure Aunt Lenore that there are good people out there who know what's going on with her, and that we're going to get her out somehow. We are, aren't we? Next, I'd like to see if she can tell me anything that can be recorded for evidence. But most of all I'd just like to get her out of here. And it just occurs to me now that I'll be driving Ellen to the picnic today, so that could mean that I'd have the car keys. Maybe, just maybe, I could try to get Aunt Lenore out and make a break for the fire exit. Okay, okay, I can just hear you now, Adam. You're probably yelling and screaming at me not to take such foolish risks. But I'll tell you what. I'm getting pretty darned tired of just sitting around, waiting for someone else to do something. You have no idea how hard it was to just stand helplessly by today watching all that crud going down in town. And I just hope you guys are keeping a close eye on that jail, because according to Burt, Eli and his sons—I assume those were his sons—anyway, they're not safe in there. So you guys better be watching them like a hawk." She angrily kicked a stone with the toe of her tennis shoe as she walked along. "Man, I just wish I knew what was going on right now!"

Ellen was already up and in the kitchen when she walked into the house. "Oh, there you are, dear. I was getting a little worried. Where were you?"

"Sorry, I took a short walk. I needed some fresh air and exercise. I think I've been sitting around too much lately."

"That must be from spending too much time with us old folks. Well, at least you should have some fun at the picnic today. They have a horseshoe tournament and baseball games and, well, all sorts of things."

"Shall I start putting that green salad together now?" asked Judith as she washed her hands at the sink.

"Yes, all that produce from Aunt Lenore's garden will make a wonderful salad."

"Say, I forgot to ask, Ellen, how was Aunt Lenore when you took her those things from her garden?"

"Oh, she seemed all right, I guess."

"Do you think she'll be able to go home soon?"

"I meant to ask Burt about that, but so much has been going on lately, I guess I plum forgot."

"Oh, that's okay. I was just wondering."

Before long, they had the picnic basket all packed and ready to go. "I think I'll just run upstairs to freshen up a bit before we leave," said Judith.

"Yes, good thinking. I'll do the same."

Judith looked around her room. She'd already packed her things, hoping that she might talk Burt into taking her home after the fireworks tonight, but somehow she thought that was highly unlikely now. And yet the idea of spending one more night out here at the lake made her want to literally pull out her hair and scream. What if she just couldn't take it? What if she fell apart and confessed everything? How much longer could she be strong? She shot up another quick prayer for help as she picked up her purse. What choice did she really have anyway? What choice that wasn't foolish or dangerous? She looked around the room again, wishing she were seeing it for the last time when it occurred to her—what if she did get her chance to escape tonight? What might she take now that wouldn't be noticed? Suddenly she picked up Jasmine's small Bible and tucked it into her purse. Then she carefully tore out and rolled the sketch of the bed and quilt, and slipped that down the side of her purse too. Finally, she combed her hair and put on some fresh lipstick, then went downstairs.

"All ready," she announced as she picked up the picnic basket.

Ellen handed her the car keys. "Well, off we go then."

Lucky for Judith, numerous vehicles had already filled the closest parking spots near the clubhouse, even Burt's pickup had taken the one space reserved for the Morrisons. "How about if I drop you off at the door, Ellen?" she suggested. "Then you won't have too walk so far."

"Thank you, Judith. That's right thoughtful of you."

Judith stopped the car in the front of the clubhouse and waited for Ellen to climb out. "I'll park the car and be right back," she called. Then she drove toward where the lodge and the clinic were located, going as far as she could without appearing overly conspicuous. After parking the car, she pocketed the keys, and carried the picnic basket over to the clubhouse. Hopefully, Ellen would be so distracted with today's activities that she'd forget about the keys.

No sooner had Judith set the basket down on a table, when Ellen came rushing over to meet her. "I just signed you up for the horseshoe tournament," she said breathlessly. "And Ed Burns is to be your partner."

Judith blinked. "But I.. .I don't even know how to play horseshoes."

"Oh, that's okay. Most of the women don't. That's why we partner everyone boy-girl, you know, so that everyone gets a fair chance."

But Ed Burns, Judith thought with horror. Of all people to be partnered with, she had gotten the horrible Ed Burns, the racist creep who'd gone on and on about white supremacy just the day before.

"I'll just go set these things out with the rest of the food," she said, masking her irritation. "You go find a nice shady place to sit, and I'll join you in a minute."

All the women in the kitchen seemed consumed with what had occurred in town this morning. Some speculated on what might happen next, and some complained that the world would soon fall completely apart while others made some nasty insinuations about how their "menfolk were gonna turn things around." Judith just hurried to put her food items away and get out of there quickly.

"Oh, there you are, honey," said Ellen as soon as Judith got outside. "They've already been looking for you. It's your turn to go play horseshoes right now."

"But I really don't know how—"

"Now, don't you worry, little lady," said Ed as he took Judith firmly by the arm. "You'll be just fine." He led her to one end of the horseshoe pit and then briefly explained the rules. "The gals stand down here and throw their horseshoes down there to where the fellars stand, and then we throw them back. That's about all there is to it. And someone else keeps score. So all you gotta do is try to get them two horseshoes right into that box down there." He pointed. "Ya see? Hopefully close to the peg."

She nodded, avoiding eye contact. "I'll try, but I can't make any promises."

The woman next to Judith introduced herself as Sue Biggins. "Don't you worry, kiddo. Nobody takes this game too seriously." Then Sue began to throw. The first shoe landed right into the pit and the second throw struck the metal spike and made a loud twang, and everyone cheered wildly.

"It's a leaner!" yelled Sue's partner from the other end.

Sure, they don't take this seriously, thought Judith as she stepped up and prepared to sling her first shoe. This whole silly thing seemed moronic and ridiculous, especially in light of all that was going on here, as well as in town. Why, here she was playing a stupid game of horseshoes! With irritation, she heaved the horseshoe with all her might and then watched in horror as it went straight up into the air and then back down again not even halfway to the other pit. She groaned as she heard some suppressed snickers from the spectators. "I knew I couldn't do this!" she exclaimed. She held up her hands helplessly. "Send in the replacement before it's too late."

Just then she felt a hand on her back and turned around to see a giant of a man standing right behind her. "Here, little lady, let me give you a couple pointers," said the tall, bearded redhead. "First off, you need to just relax a little." He took her throwing arm and swung it slowly back, cradled in his own. "See? Just like this." Then as he showed her the rest of the throw as he spoke quietly in her ear. "Clinic. Tonight. Nine-thirty."

She nodded mutely.

Then in a louder voice he spoke, "Okay, you see? Just follow through on your throw with your hand. Now then, that's about all there is to it. You understand?" A few onlookers laughed.

"Yes," she said with a confident nod. "I think I got that." Then focusing all she had on making a good throw, she drew back her arm then swung it forward, releasing the horseshoe at shoulder height and following through, or at least so she hoped. And to her amazed surprise it sailed right into the pit and made a twanging sound of its own. The crowd cheered once again, even louder this time.

"It's a ringer!" yelled Ed.

She turned and winked at Hank. "Thanks, I needed that." She repeated his words in her mind. *Clinic. Tonight. Nine-thirty.* And when her turn came to throw the next shoe, it also landed in the box. Slowly her confidence grew. And throughout the game, she focused her thoughts on Aunt Lenore and how she hoped Hank would help her to get her out tonight. She smiled to herself as the men took their turns. Somebody must've been listening to her little speech on the transmitter today after all!

To her dismay, she and Ed actually made it to the third round of the elimination tournament, but finally Hank and his partner Betty beat them. She shook both their hands. And as she shook Hank's, she said, "Well, I guess it's only fair that the guy who gave me the best horseshoe throwing tips should beat me."

He winked. "Just don't you forget what I told you, little lady."

She joined Burt and Ellen to eat their picnic dinner, and Burt congratulated her on making it into the third round of the tournament. "I lost out during the second round," he confessed. "But that's because my partner wasn't pulling her weight."

"Oh, Daddy," said Ellen in a hushed voice. "You better be quiet or poor old Janet Myers will hear you and feel bad."

"Well, if I'd known our Judith here was such a ringer, I'd have asked her to be my partner."

"Maybe next time," said Judith with her brightest smile, determined to carry out the rest of this day without the slightest reason for suspicion. There's no way she wanted to risk whatever scheme Hank had in mind.

"I think that redheaded fellar likes you, Judith." said Ellen with a sly smile. "He seemed to enjoy giving you those pointers."

Judith laughed. "Well, they sure did work. And I appreciated his help."

"His name's Hank Rollins, and he seems to be one of our more serious recruits," said Burt as he forked a bite of pie. "By the way, Judith, he's not married."

"You two!" scolded Judith. Then she glanced over to where Hank was still playing horseshoes. "But I'll admit he is kinda cute." She figured it wouldn't hurt to play along, just in case she and Hank were discovered together before the night was over.

"And not a bad horseshoe player either," added Burt. "You see the muscles on that guy's biceps? I'll bet he's a good arm wrestler too."

"Where's Hal?" asked Judith, suddenly realizing she hadn't seen him all afternoon.

"He's got some business to attend to," said Burt in a curt tone. "He'll be by later."

Judith took a bite of potato salad. She hoped this business had nothing to do with Eli and his sons. But then she remembered what Hal had said about not caring for some of the more violent elements of this business. Of course, he'd also said he'd do anything for Burt, including breaking the law. She sent up another silent prayer.

As the afternoon moved into evening, the men began to break out the beer. It was the first time she'd seen anyone actually drinking out at the lake, and it troubled her. The mere idea of alcohol, hotheads, and firearms all at the same party left her cold. And to her dismay, it appeared that Hank was among those imbibing. He'd no sooner sat down with Burt and a few others than they handed him a beer, and he popped the tab and took a big swig. But then, she reconsidered it, how would it look if he'd refused? He needed to appear to be one of the good old boys. And he was such a big guy, surely one beer wouldn't affect him much. Now he and Burt were laughing loudly as if in some sort of conspiracy, then they nodded her direction and laughed even harder. She turned away, as if embarrassed, but felt actually glad. This might be easier than she'd imagined. Burt seemed to be playing right into their hands by egging Hank along. He'd probably just chuckle to himself if he noticed her and Hank slipping away during the fireworks. But hopefully, no one would notice.

The evening air began to chill a little as the sun dipped down into the trees on the west side of the lake. "Ellen, I saw a blanket in the picnic basket," said Judith. "Want me to go get it?"

"That'd be nice, dear." Ellen nodded and smiled. "And would you be a darling and see if you could beg me a hot cup of coffee from the kitchen?"

"Of course. I'll be right back."

When she returned she took care tucking the blanket snugly around Ellen's shoulders before she handed her the coffee. And then she did something that surprised even her. She bent down and kissed Ellen right on the cheek.

"Why, thank you, dear," said Ellen, beaming. "Whatever was that for?"

For a moment, Judith wondered herself. Was it a Judas kiss, the last show of affection before the final act of betrayal? But then

she knew that wasn't the purpose. She knelt down by Ellen's chair
and looked directly into her eyes. The light was fading fast now,
but she could still see how pleased Ellen was by this attention—her
eyes sparkled with a childlike happiness and suddenly Judith felt
torn. "Ellen, I just want you to know that no matter what happens,
I really do love you."

"Oh, I love you too, sweetie." Ellen patted her hand
warmly. "You've just been a real godsend to me, dear. You have
absolutely no idea."

Judith stood. "I think I'll go get my sweater. That breeze off the
lake is getting a little nippy."

She went back to the car and got her sweater and her purse,
this time leaving the car unlocked. Just in case. Then she returned
and sat down next to Ellen again. It was after nine now and the
fireworks would begin shortly. She looked around as the crowd
began to settle down on lawn chairs and blankets, getting ready to
enjoy the big show. Burt was still sitting with his buddies over by
the dock. She didn't see Hank's tall form anywhere in sight. Perhaps
that just meant he was getting whatever it was all ready. At least she
hoped so. Hopefully he wasn't having any trouble. She sent up
another silent prayer.

She figured it would take about ten minutes to walk over to
the clinic and she didn't want to leave too soon. Didn't want to
give Ellen too much time to get worried about her. Someone by the
dock played a tinny sounding rendition of the national anthem on a
cassette player and then the show began. After about ten minutes,
Judith checked her watch by the light of an exceptionally bright
explosion. Then she waited another minute or so for it to quiet down
before she leaned over and whispered to Ellen. "I need to use
the restroom, then I think I'll pick up a cup of coffee. Can I bring
you anything?"

Ellen waved her hand. "No, dear, I'm fine."

Then with heart pounding in rhythm to the crackling fireworks, she went inside the clubhouse as if to use the restroom. Thankfully the building was empty. She silently let herself out a side door, then began her short trek over to the clinic. It felt weird walking in the pitch-black darkness and then suddenly having the entire sky explode into colorful light. It was like being in a war zone with bombs going off. She began to walk faster now, wondering what she would say if someone found her out here right now? Perhaps that she was sick and on her way to the clinic for help. But then how would she explain why she'd come on foot? And all alone?

Just then she heard another set of footsteps behind her. They steadily matched her own. Deep inside of her, she knew that someone had spotted her. She knew with conviction that she was now being followed. With shaking hands, she grabbed her stomach and broke into a fast run. Her excuse would become true. She *would* be sick. She felt certain she was about to throw up, maybe even pass out! But what if they tried to examine her at the clinic? What would they do when they found the wire?

Oh, God, help me, she prayed as she ran blindly through the dark.

Thirty-Four

DEAR GOD, CAN YOU see me down here? It's awful dark, but Miss Molly say you can see in the dark. I'm real scared, God. Real scared. I heard Carmen talking on the phone just now. She be saying, "Yeah, she all yours, you just pay me the money first, then I won't never tell a soul I gave her to you." That's when I snuck out the front door, real quiet like. I didn't even have time to get my backpack, I just thought I better get outta there before it be too late. I went down to Miss Molly's 'cause she always say she will help me. And I need help now. But she be gone! Now I don't hardly ever remember her being gone before. Where'd she go, God? She be coming back soon? What'll I do, God? Keep hiding down here in this cruddy old box back in this nasty, dirty laundry room? Carmen always be saying there rats down here—that why she never do no laundrying. But Miss Molly say she just be a lazy slob, and them rats be more afraid of us than we be of them. But I ain't too sure 'bout that, 'cause I be feeling mighty scared right now.

Just yesterday, I be thinking 'bout this Aunt Constance somebody that Carmen told me 'bout. I be thinking Carmen liked this Aunt Constance person, and she say only 'cause of her she still keeping me round. So I ask Carmen 'bout this aunt I ain't never heard nothing of before and don't even remember and she get all weepy and say, "Constance was my best friend." So, I ask her, "Where is Constance now?" Then Carmen look at me, and I be thinking she almost looking like she like me a little. And she say, "Your Aunt Constance be dead, Pearl She died when you was just little. Don't you remember her?" I just shook my head. It figures. Just when I think of an aunt that might get me outta here and back to my mama, I find out that she be dead. What's up with that, God?

But right after that Carmen start getting herself all in a huff, saying my mama a liar and a cheat (but I know she's not) and saying she gonna fix my mama and she gonna fix me and she gonna get herself some money and she gonna get Larry back. And I be a thinking (but I keep them thoughts to myself) you wanna get Larry back? You crazy, girl. Larry be bad news, and you best just let that man go and hope he never come back. But Carmen ain't too smart. Miss Molly say she too messed up to know up from down. And I think Miss Molly be right.

Dear God, why do everything have to be so sad and hard for me? My life ain't nothing like them people I see on Miss Molly's TV set. They all wear nice clothes that match, and they laugh a lot. They got themselves family and nice houses to live in with pretty things all 'round. But me, I gotta sit down here in this stinky old cardboard box with spiderwebs and them nasty ol' rats creeping all around everywhere. Now what be fair about that, God? I don't mean no disrespect, but it seem to me you not doing your job just now. Seem to me you be sleeping or something. Wake up, God! Wake up and take care of your little Pearl. I need help, God, and I be thinking you the only one can help me. Wake up! Please, wake up!

Thirty-Five

AS JUDITH RAN DOWN the dark street, the night sky-exploded with flashes of brilliant light, followed by loud booms that echoed in her chest. Knowing that each blast of light exposed her every step, she decided to change direction, hoping to throw off her pursuer. In the next moment of darkness, she dodged around a pickup and turned her course toward the lodge. She paused for a split second, to catch her breath. But the footsteps were still coming her way. She knew she couldn't lead her pursuer to the clinic and risk exposing Hank. So in the next explosion of light, she changed direction again, heading back down toward the lake this time, hoping to appear as if she had a purpose, but then she stumbled over something and fell to the ground, landing hard on one knee. She scrambled in the darkness, her knee throbbing in pain as she tried to stand. But before she got to her feet, a pair of hands grabbed her by the shoulders.

"Stop!" he hissed as he pulled her up. Suddenly, she felt the world spinning around, and she feared she might actually faint as the dark sky burst into light again. But by the glow of bright orange sunburst overhead she could almost determine his features. Or else she was hallucinating.

"Adam?" she gasped, tears now streaming down her cheeks. "Is it you... what are you..."

"Shhh!" He pulled her with him toward the shadows of a darkened building, then gently brought her close to him, whispering, "Are you okay?"

At this point, she collapsed into his arms and began to sob. "Oh, Adam, I... I can't go on... I can't take this anymore. It's too... too hard."

She felt one hand stroke her hair, the other gently pat her back as he held her close. And despite all that was going on around her, she actually felt safe. "It's okay," he said in a soothing voice. "You're doing a fantastic job, Judith. Just like a pro. We're really proud of you. You've managed to get some good information on tape. Some things that will really help our case."

She pulled back and looked at him in surprise. "Really?"

He nodded, then took out a handkerchief and wiped her wet cheeks. "Yes. You've been totally amazing. I'm sorry it's getting so complicated right now, but there's a lot going down. And we really need you to hang in there. Do you think you can continue?"

She nodded slowly, taking in a ragged breath and wiping the tears from her cheeks. "Yeah. I... I think so." But her hands still shook uncontrollably. "I'll try. I really will." She stood up straighter now. "I'm sorry about falling apart like that. I was just so terrified. Actually, I still am."

"Yeah, we all are." He took her by the arm and gently guided her along. "We've got to get you to the clinic now. Hank and a buddy are getting Aunt Lenore out as we speak. But we've got some other problems brewing that we've got to deal with tonight. So we're really hoping you can drive yourself and Aunt Lenore out of here right now. Do you think you can do that, Judith?"

Her knees felt wobbly as she walked, and she clung more tightly to his arm. She didn't want to continue being strong anymore. She wanted someone else to take care of her. "I... I don't know. I thought Hank was going to—"

"We desperately need Hank right now, and every other hand we've got here as well. Things are starting to break loose, and it's getting dangerous, Judith."

They were on the back side of the clinic now, close to the parking area. "I want to do this, but I just don't know if I can," she whispered. "I desperately want out of here, and I want to help Aunt Lenore, but—"

"We don't know what might happen before the night is over," said Adam in a hushed voice. "We've learned of a group that's planning a hit on the jail after midnight. They're hoping to teach those Paxton boys a lesson, but at the same time some of the men, especially Burt and Hal, suspect the BATF are here right now and they're trying to get their boys together on that. By the way, you were right about Hal's guns—he has gotten some of them illegally." Adam glanced around the corner then continued. "But if all that isn't enough, we've also got a faction of members and new recruits who believe the world's coming to an end—they can be the most dangerous of the lot because they get all paranoid and trigger happy and ready to hole up with their families in those big bunkers out behind the lodge. It sounds crazy, but this place is like a powder keg right now. And we gotta get you and Aunt Lenore out ASAP, you understand?"

"But what about the others?"

"Others?"

"You know, the women and children and—"

"We'll do everything we can to keep this place from blowing sky high. We plan to make some arrests and hopefully defuse some situations before they get out of hand. But it's anyone's guess what could happen before the night is over."

She noticed someone going out the side door now. "Is that Hank?" she whispered.

He glanced over his shoulder. "Yes. Let's wait until they get her all loaded safely in and then slip over. By the way, you were right about that nurse practitioner too—she's not one of them. All we had to do was tell her who we were and she lit out of here with no questions asked." He glanced at his watch. "Okay, this is the plan. I'll get you ladies to the gate, but you're on your own after that." He reached for her hand now. "Don't worry, Judith, you'll do just fine. I know you can do this. I'll start the engine just as they begin the grand finale of the fireworks. All that noise should provide us with about five minutes where I can really drive loud and fast. Hopefully by the time this thing ends we'll be almost over to the new development."

"But how can you—"

"An alternate route." He peered over to where two men had completed loading what appeared to be Aunt Lenore into the back of a Jeep. "Come on, let's go."

Within seconds, Adam and Judith were in the front seat, windows opened, waiting in silence for the grand finale to start. And just as quickly, Hank and the other man disappeared out into the night. Judith peered around to see poor Aunt Lenore, wrapped in blankets and buckled snugly into the seatbelt. "Are you okay?" asked Judith, but the old woman only nodded, her face a mask of pale fear.

Then just as the noise began, Adam started the engine and took off straight into the woods behind the clinic. He drove over lumps and bumps for what seemed like ages but was actually only several minutes, then cut back onto the main road, but quite a distance past the clubhouse now. He drove as fast as the curving road allowed.

Judith could barely breathe as he careened around sharp corners, but somehow the Jeep managed to stay upright and on the road.

"Okay, now just keep going straight, slightly to your right," she told him as he came to the end of the development road.

"Hold on," he yelled, not slowing as he hit the rough ground.

She clung to the dashboard with one hand and pointed with the other. "The road's straight ahead." she shouted above the din.

"Looks like the party's over." Adam spoke loudly as he gripped the wheel and continued driving fast. "It's possible that someone has noticed our lights from the other side of the lake by now."

"Will they follow us?" she asked as they finally hit the dirt road and turned into the protection of the wooded area.

"They might try. But, don't worry, there's plenty of other things to distract them."

"I see the gates ahead!"

"Hold on, ladies!" Adam yelled. "I'm busting right through!"

"Are you sure—"

But it was too late. She closed her eyes as she heard the loud crash. But when she looked up they were on the other side of the road, and Adam was already pulling the Jeep to a stop. "You take it from here, Judith. Drive straight to my house and Pops will take care of everything." He peered into the backseat. "Hang in there, Aunt Lenore. You'll be home safe before long."

"Thank you." Her voice came out in a hoarse whisper.

"Be careful, Adam," warned Judith. "I'd like to see you again."

He grinned. "Right back at you." Then he took off running back toward the lake.

Judith gunned the engine and took off in the direction that she hoped was toward town. She drove fast—faster than she'd ever driven before. But as she drove she prayed. This time out loud so Aunt Lenore could hear. After a few more minutes, she saw the road that led to the main entrance of the lake, and her heart began to pound even harder. What if they were coming after her right now? What if they chased her? Where would she go? What would she do? She prayed again. Just then she noticed a glowing orange light off to her left. She looked over to see what looked like more fireworks, only lower this time. As low as the treetops. Was there a fire out at the lake?

"Oh, God." she prayed with fervor, "please, take care of Adam and Hank and the others—and please, protect Ellen—"

"Ellen?" said Aunt Lenore from the backseat.

"Yes," Judith called over her shoulder. "Ellen's back there." She didn't mention the strange glowing light she'd just seen. Hopefully it was just more fireworks. But somehow she didn't think so. It was too low. Too orange. She continued driving nearly eighty miles an hour until she reached the edge of town. Then, not wanting to draw attention to herself, she slowed down. And finally, after what seemed like hours, she pulled into Adam's quiet driveway. She leaped out of the car and over to Aunt Lenore's door. Jerking it open, she looked at the old woman's face. "Are you okay, Aunt Lenore?"

She leaned her head back and sighed wearily. "I've been better, dear."

Judith smiled and unbuckled the seatbelt. "Wait here while I get Jack to help us."

She ran up to the door and began to pound, wondering what she would do if Jack wasn't here. But thankfully, he opened the door. "Did you bring Miss Barker?" he asked.

"Yes," said Judith breathlessly. "She's in the car. Can you help me?"

They soon had Aunt Lenore settled on the couch, and Jack made a pot of tea as Judith sat with the perplexed old woman, reassuring her that everything would be okay now. "I know that ride must've been an awful ordeal for you," said Judith as she stroked her wrinkled hand. "I'm so sorry we had to do it like that. But we needed to get you out of there quickly."

"It's all right, dear." Aunt Lenore shook her head sadly. "I'm just glad to be out of my prison cell."

"Did it feel like that?" Judith looked into her eyes.

"I was afraid I would die there, Judith." She sighed and leaned her head back, looking fragile and helpless in her pale pink nightgown. "But I was trying to hang on."

Jack set a wooden TV tray before them, then returned bringing them each a steaming cup of tea. "Did you see Adam then, Judith?" he asked eagerly as he sat down across from them.

"Yes. He had to go back to the lake and help out." She took a sip of tea, wondering if she should mention seeing what she feared was flames in front of Aunt Lenore. There seemed no sense in upsetting the old woman further.

Jack leaned forward, placing both hands on his knees. "Things might get ugly over there tonight."

Judith studied him curiously. He seemed like such an ordinary old guy in his plaid shirt and dungarees. "Just how much do you know about all this, Jack?"

He sat up straight and grinned. "Well now, Adam tried to keep it from me, but I've got my own ways of finding things out. I know how and when to listen." He nodded back towards the bedrooms. "Got me a citizen's band radio too."

Judith smiled. "Well, I'm glad you were here to help us."

"When can I go home?" asked Aunt Lenore weakly.

"Well, ma'am," Jack pressed his lips together. "That all depends. But you'd better plan on spending the night here tonight. We'll be cozy, but we've got room aplenty. We need to wait until Adam gives us the all clear signal before we make any moves."

He slapped his palm across the forehead. "Good night, I almost forgot—I'm supposed to get that Jeep in the garage." He stood quickly. "Judith, if you ladies are finished with your tea, you could go ahead and get Miss Barker all settled into the bedroom at the end of the hall, the one on your right."

Aunt Lenore set down her empty cup. "I'm afraid I'm still rather shaky on my feet, Judith. Can you help me?"

"Of course. I'm sure you've become weak from being bedridden for so long." Judith helped lift her to a standing position, then wrapped an arm securely around her waist. "You're light as a feather, Aunt Lenore. I could probably even carry you."

"Don't you even think of it." But she leaned into her as they walked. Judith could hear the old woman taking quick, short breaths.

"Let's just take it easy," said Judith as they moved slowly down the hallway. "I'm sure it'll take you a day or two to get back into gardening shape."

"My garden..." Aunt Lenore sighed.

Finally, Judith got her into the small room and seated on the twin bed against the wall. "I'm guessing this is Jack's grandson's room," she said as she moved a skateboard away from the bed. Then she slipped off Aunt Lenore's hospital slippers and helped her to lie down. "His name is Josh, and he's a very nice boy."

"Josh," repeated Aunt Lenore as she leaned back into the pillow. "I hope he doesn't mind giving up his bed tonight."

"I'm sure he doesn't."

Aunt Lenore sighed heavily and closed her eyes. "Don't know why I should be so tired now, seems all I've done is sleep lately."

"Well, you've had quite a night. Just rest up and hopefully you'll be back in your own house by tomorrow."

She opened her eyes again. "But just in case, Judith, there are things I should tell you." She shuddered. "Just in case I don't wake up."

"Oh, Aunt Lenore."

She held up a withered old hand. "Please, let me speak."

Judith sat on the edge of the bed and took Aunt Lenore's hand in hers. "Okay, but just don't wear yourself out too much."

Aunt Lenore took a deep breath as if thinking, perhaps arranging her thoughts. "It was that day when you came to see me, Judith, that I realized how badly I had let our dear Jasmine down."

"But how?"

"By not finding out what had happened. So I went into the spare room and got out her box." Aunt Lenore peered over at Judith. "Have you seen her box?"

"The jewelry box with mother-of-pearl?"

Aunt Lenore nodded.

"I saw it, but I thought it was yours. I never opened it."

"Well, it was that very day that I opened the box. And that's when I saw those photos. And at last, I understood." She took in a breath and exhaled slowly. "And that evening, Ellen called me. She was checking up on me."

"They'd just returned from Mississippi?"

"Yes. And well, I just let her have it. I told her I knew all about Jasmine—that I knew everything. I told her that she and Burt should be ashamed of themselves for treating their own daughter like that. I told her that they were the ones to blame for her death, and that I wouldn't have been surprised if Burt had pulled the trigger himself." She groaned and closed her eyes now.

Judith stared in wonder. "And what did Ellen say?"

"She hung up on me."

"Oh."

Aunt Lenore opened her eyes again. "But Burt and some other man came over that night. Ellen wasn't with them, of course. And they bullied me until I thought I might have just keeled over and died right then and there. In fact, I got a little breathless and light-headed. And then they told me I was sick and that they needed to take me to the hospital." She scowled.

"Yes, I came to see you at the care facility, and I had no idea what was up then. But the next day they wouldn't even let me in. And after that you were gone, and I didn't know where you were."

"They were hiding me away. Trying to keep their dirty little secrets silent."

Judith looked down on the pale, wrinkled face. "Oh, Aunt Lenore, I hate seeing you so worn out like this. I worry about your health. Why don't you just sleep for now, and you can tell me the rest when you're stronger."

"Yes, dear. That sounds wise." Judith stood. "I'm glad you're safe now." "Thank you, dear. Thank you for your help." Just as Judith turned out the light and closed the door, Jack stepped out of his room. "Judith," he said in a hushed but urgent voice. "I've been listening to my radio and it

sounds like they've gone completely nuts out at the lake." "Oh, dear. That's what Adam was predicting." "Sounds like the whole place is ablaze right now. They've called in the forestry firefighters and everything. I

heard it all on my CB."

"Do you think the fireworks started the fire?" she asked.

"I noticed what looked like flames within minutes after the fireworks show had ended."

jack frowned. "Maybe, but I don't know. I heard a

couple guys on the radio saying it was another Ruby Ridge.

They said someone blew up an arsenal, and it's like a war zone in there."

"You're serious?"

He nodded. "Sounds like trouble. Bad trouble." Judith swallowed hard. "Is there anything we can do?"

He frowned. "I wish there were. But Adam gave me strict orders to stay here and protect you two women. Now all we can do is just pray and wait."

"You're supposed to protect us? Do you think we're really in any danger?"

"Maybe not. But you never know."

"Jack, where's Josh right now?"

He shook his head and grimaced. "Stubborn boy—he's with those folks who've been meeting with Eli Paxton of late. Now, don't get me wrong. Ain't nothing a matter with what Eli's trying to do in this town, but I just worry about Josh hanging around the jail all night long."

"He's in jail?"

"No, he and the other protesters, as well as a bunch of media folks and civil rights people—well, they're all down there at city hall keeping a vigil of sorts until the prisoners are released."

"So, Eli and his sons are still locked up?"

"Yes. As ridiculous as it seems, they are. But their lawyer is here and he's madder than a wet hen about the whole dirty business. But that crooked police captain says that since it's a holiday they don't have the right person to process the bail and get them released until tomorrow."

"Release them?" Judith laughed at the irony. "They had no right to arrest them in the first place. Nobody else had a permit for that stupid parade."

"Yeah, that's just what everybody thought. But unfortunately for the Paxtons, the police won't do nothing about it until tomorrow. Their lawyer threatened to get the governor down here, but Josh said he decided to hold off since this is turning out to be a real media event. Did you know we were on national news tonight?"

"No, but that's great. Exposure like this might help to make the people in this town think for a change. So will the whole group spend the night down there at city hall?"

"Yeah, some of the older folks will take shifts so they can get some sleep. But they've got all kinds of camp gear and food, and I think they're having a pretty good time of it, in spite of everything. And it sure does help having those news media folks around. The place is starting to look like a three ring circus with vans and satellite dishes all over the town. Come to think of it, I suppose the protesters are safer than anyone else right now."

"Well, that's a relief."

"But this fire business has got me worried, Judith. I wish I knew what was going on in there. If only there were some way to be in touch with Adam."

She felt the wire and transmitter still taped to her abdomen. "Guess my wire's no help with this."

He shook his head. "No, I'll bet they've all got their hands pretty full right now. And even though I'm sure Adam's called in for reinforcements, you just never know how these things can go. Those hothead militant types can be totally unpredictable. I've heard that they've always had this crazy idea that the government is gonna come in there and get them some day, so just as soon as they get the slightest whiff of trouble they can go completely nuts, holing themselves up with enough weaponry to start World War III."

"Oh, dear." She bit her lip as she remembered Hal's room full of firearms. How many others had stockpiled such things?

"Well, you just keep on saying your prayers."

She nodded soberly. "Of course." Then she remembered Jasmine's box. "Say, Jack, do you think it would be okay if I ran over to Aunt Lenore's for just a little bit tonight? There's a box over there. I told Adam about it—on the wire, I assume he was listening—but I don't know if he's had a chance to go over and get it yet. It belonged to my friend, Jasmine, and according to Aunt Lenore it contains some sort of clues as to what happened to Jasmine."

"Well, why don't you check his office first, just in case," he suggested. "To be honest, I'd really rather not have you running around in the dark on a night like this. I've got everything locked and bolted right now, and even so I'm feeling a little uneasy about your and Miss Barker's safety."

"Sure. I understand."

Jack opened the door to Adam's office, then waited as Judith glanced around. It didn't appear quite as orderly as before, but then he'd been pretty busy lately. She looked across his cluttered desk, then over to the shelves against the wall, and then finally to a narrow table over by the window where she finally spotted the familiar box. "That's it, Jack!" she exclaimed.

"Well, I don't s'pose it'll hurt any for you to have a little look-see. Adam's been so busy, I seriously doubt he's had a chance to do much with it yet."

She picked up the box and fingered the inlaid top. "It's pretty. It's amazing to think how this actually belonged to Jasmine. That she actually held it in her hands and placed things of importance inside."

"Do you want some time to yourself with it?"

She looked up at him, tears already building in her eyes. "Do you mind?"

"Nah, I want to go keep tabs on my radio anyway."

"Thanks."

"Go ahead and make yourself at home, Judith. I doubt, especially considering all you've been through, that Adam'll mind much." He chuckled as he closed the door.

Thirty-Six

JUDITH SAT DOWN IN Adam's leather desk chair, leaned back, and slowly opened the box. On top was a yellow film processing envelope with the name Jasmine Phillips penned on the front flap and the date from more than a year ago. So her last name had been Phillips. Judith remembered the pretty ring set. Her married name perhaps? She opened the envelope, almost reverently, and removed a stack of glossy color photos. They appeared to be mostly shots of preschool-aged children at a birthday party. She slowly thumbed through the candid photos of kids and balloons and crepe paper in what appeared to be a nicely landscaped backyard with a slightly sloping green lawn, surrounded by beautifully blooming rhododendron bushes, until she came to one with only one child looking pensively at a large cake with four burning candles. She was a pretty little girl with light brown skin and a soft looking halo of dark, curly hair. She had a look of intelligence in her sparkling eyes. Judith flipped the photo over to see the words "Pearl Marie, fourth birthday" penned on the back. She continued to the next photo. This one also had the birthday child, as well as a pretty woman smiling next to her. Jasmine!

Judith stared at the photo in wonder. She knew it was Jasmine, had to be Jasmine. But it looked nothing like the Jasmine in the two photos that Hal had given her just a few weeks ago. Yet this was Jasmine as Judith would have imagined her, happy and smiling and looking as if life had treated her fairly well. She flipped to the next photos— more shots of children playing.

Then she came to a photo with Jasmine, the pretty child, and an attractive African American man. She flipped it over to see the words "Daddy, Mama, and Pearl" written on the back. Judith turned the photo back around and studied the face of the man. So this was Jasmine's husband. He had a warm, friendly smile and sincere-looking eyes. And the threesome looked incredibly happy. Jasmine's left hand was visible, resting over the shoulder of the man, and on it was the expensive ring set that Judith had found hidden behind the sink. She looked to see the man's left hand, and it too was visible, just barely, resting on the sofa arm. He also wore a platinum band, for all purposes suggesting a marriage that was real and vital just over a year ago.

So what had happened? Judith quickly looked through the remaining photos, more candid shots of the children at the party: Pearl blindfolded and swinging a stick at a pretty piñata, kids eating cake and playing games, some shots with a few other adults mixed in here and there. And Judith couldn't help but notice that there was a pleasant mix of cultures present, and all looked well dressed and somewhat affluent. And the photos that showed interior glimpses of the house revealed that whoever lived there had plenty of money and good taste, too. She flipped the processing envelope back over and saw the name "Flash Fotos, Edmonds, WA" printed across the top. Was that where Jasmine had lived? And if so, where were the child and the father now? And did they have any idea what had become of Jasmine?

Judith felt that too familiar lump burning in her throat again. And she felt her heart breaking for her dead friend. Jasmine had not only had what appeared to be a loving husband but a beloved child as well. And it wasn't too difficult to imagine what had torn this little family apart. Burt had told Judith how Jasmine had messed up her life, and Judith had simply assumed that he meant with drugs or something equally harmful. But of course to Burt, marrying an African American man would surely have to be the very worst sort of blunder possible. Certainly, he would rather see his own daughter dead than married to someone from a differing ethnic background. And for a moment Judith felt thankful she was nowhere near Burt Morrison right now, for she had no idea what she might say or even do to him. Right now he seemed more evil than the devil himself. She felt a real and violent wave of hatred growing inside her. If there was serious trouble at the lake tonight, she hoped that he'd be caught in the very worst of it; she even hoped that he'd be killed. And, worse yet, she hoped he'd die a slow and torturous death. Even though these dark and gruesome thoughts shocked her, she couldn't help hoping this miserable man would have to answer this night for all the harm he had caused.

And then, at the same time, she also hoped he'd live long enough for her to lash into him, to yell and to scream and to hurt him deeply for the ways he had hurt and betrayed his own daughter. And how responsible was he for her death anyway? Like Aunt Lenore said, he might as well have pulled the trigger. And perhaps he had. For how could Jasmine have given up like that? How could she have killed herself knowing she had this beautiful daughter and husband waiting for her somewhere? And why would she have let her father bully her into marrying Hal when she was already married? Or was she?

Judith wiped the tears with the back of her hands and began to pace back and forth in Adam's small office. Instead of finding any answers or comfort in these photos, she only found more disturbing questions. Haunting questions. She went back to the box still sitting open on Adam's desk. Surely there must be something more. Something with real answers.

She looked inside to see a small hair barrette with a little white lamb on it. Probably Pearl's. A keepsake perhaps. There was also a large heart-shaped locket with a diamond set into the front. She opened the locket to see what appeared to be a tiny wedding photo of a smiling Jasmine on one side and the man on the other. She flipped it over to see the words "Two Hearts Become One" and a date of almost eleven years earlier engraved on the back. So, they had been married.

Beneath these items she found an envelope with the name "Pearl" written simply on the front. The back was sealed. It seemed odd that it wasn't for both Pearl and the father, Mr. Phillips, or whatever his name might be. But only Pearl's name was on it. Judith considered opening it, but then stopped. It seemed wrong to read a deceased mother's letter to her only child. And yet, if she didn't read it, she might miss some important clue. And then how would she ever get this letter to the child? She wondered what Adam would do? She wondered what had he thought when he saw the strange contents of this box? Or had he been too consumed with all the other troubles brewing at the time? Then she wondered, how was he doing right now? Was he okay?

She sank down into his chair once again and tightly closed her eyes. True to her promise, she began to pray once again. This time she prayed with desperate determination and fervor she'd never known before. She prayed and prayed, losing complete track of the time, until a soft tapping on the door brought her back into the world.

"Judith?"

She looked up. "Yes, Jack."

"Everything okay in here?"

She nodded. "How about everything everywhere else?"

He frowned. "I don't know, but it sounds pretty bad to me. They've called in the National Guard. It's turning into a horrible mess."

She sighed. "I've been praying."

Jack slumped down into the chair across from her. He ran one hand through his gray hair, making it stand out in rumpled tufts. "Guess that's about all we can do."

"You look exhausted, Jack. Maybe you should try to get some sleep."

He stubbornly shook his head. "Nope. Can't sleep. Not with things like this."

She looked at the clock. It was past 2 A.M. now. "What a mess hatred makes of things."

"Yeah, people like that ought to be taken out and shot."

She looked at him curiously. "You really think so?"

He shrugged. "Well, I dunno. But when your kid's in danger, you tend to think like that, you know what I mean?"

"Yeah. I've had some pretty nasty thoughts myself tonight. In fact," she wondered if she could even admit it out loud, "I think if I'd had the opportunity, I could've almost killed a certain man, myself, tonight."

"Really? You don't seem like the violent type, Judith. But you said 'could've'—does that mean you wouldn't do it now?"

"I don't know for sure. Maybe." She clenched her fists. "I'm still furious. And I feel like I hate him. I mean, *really, really* hate him. I've never felt such deep hatred before, not for anyone. And the weird thing is, I just spent three days in his home, acting as though I was part of his family. But it's strange, because I don't really hate his wife. Although I sure don't feel very good about her right now."

"You talking about those Morrisons?"

"Yeah. My friend's parents. I feel pretty certain her father destroyed her life. I'm not sure how much he actually did himself, but I do believe he's morally responsible. The whole thing makes me absolutely furious. And yet I've been sitting here praying just now. At one point, I actually asked God to spare *all* the lives of everyone out there. Now, where did that come from? Because earlier I was sincerely hoping that Burt Morrison would be killed, and even that he'd suffer horribly before he died."

"That seems understandable, under the circumstances."

"But maybe it's not right."

"Well, the Bible does tell us to love everyone, including our enemies—it also says to pray for them. But sometimes I have a pretty tough time with those kinds of things, especially times like right now when I think certain enemies could be putting my own boy's life in serious danger."

"I know what you mean."

"And, to be perfectly honest with you Judith, I have no desire to pray that God will protect the likes of Burt Morrison or any of his extremist buddies. I'd just as soon see them all burn in the lake of fire." He rubbed his chin.

"I know exactly what you mean, Jack, but at the same time, I also realize how these awful emotions are making me feel absolutely sick inside—sort of like I'm being poisoned or something. It makes me feel kind of hopeless and dead. Do you understand what I'm saying?"

"Maybe so. But just the same, I don't think I can be praying for my enemies' safety tonight."

"I know." She thought a moment. "Maybe we just need to pray that God will deal with them in his own way."

Jack brightened a little. "Yeah. That's a good idea, Judith. I think I could do that. I'd sure like God to deal with them. Of course, I'd like him to deal with them the way I would, by knocking their narrow-minded, bullheaded noggins together. But then he's God; he probably knows what's best. Yeah, I think I could pray for him to deal with those hateful fools in his own way." He stood and punched a fist into his open palm. "In fact, that's just what I'm gonna pray."

"You sure you don't want to get some sleep, Jack? You might be all worn out before morning. And who knows what tomorrow will bring?"

"Nah, I won't be able to sleep. I might lie down for a little while, but I'll keep my ears tuned into the CB. How about you? You've got dark circles growing under those pretty eyes of yours. Maybe you should go rest a bit."

'T don't think I can sleep right now either. But I might lie down on the couch."

"Yes, you do that. And if you hear anything—anything at all, you come running and get me. I got a gun and I'm a pretty decent shot if I do say so myself."

She took in a quick breath. "Oh, let's hope we don't need a gun."

"Best to be prepared." He headed back to his room. "But I'll be praying too."

"I think that's our best defense." She carried Jasmine's box back into the living room and sat down on the couch, pulling one of the blankets they'd used for Aunt Lenore over her. She looked down at the box in her lap, then closed her eyes and tried to imagine Jasmine. Not the hopeless, defeated Jasmine that she'd been imagining during the past several weeks, but instead she imagined a vibrant, alive, and happy Jasmine—like the one in the birthday photo.

"What do you want me to do now, Jasmine?" she whispered

under her breath. Then added, "Please, show me God." She sat in the dimly lit room, her legs curled under her, almost afraid to breathe, as she waited. And then it came to her. Three simple words. She didn't hear the words audibly, but she sensed them deep within her soul.

Find my Pearl.

Suddenly, she remembered the verses underlined in Jasmine's old Bible. The one about not throwing your pearls before the swine, and the other about the man who sold everything to purchase the pearl of great worth. Of course, these were meant to be clues. And she had found them. And even the mother-of-pearl box was a clue in itself. For, of course, Jasmine was the mother of Pearl. And perhaps it was up to Judith to find this little lost Pearl and get this letter to her. And suddenly, she felt no guilt about reading this letter. It was as if it were meant to be read by her. As if, it would lead her to Pearl.

She carefully opened the envelope and slipped out the two thin sheets of stationary. She recognized the paper, just like the ones she had stolen from Burt's desk when she'd written down the phone numbers in Washington. And perhaps those numbers would even help her to locate Pearl and her daddy now. Judith's hands trembled as she read the words written by her dear friend's own hand.

My dear, sweet Pearl,

First off, let me say how much I love you. I have missed you more than I can say with words. You are Mama's special angel, you know, my own little Pearl. And I know it is your birthday today, and you are five years old. I wish I could be with you. And I hope it won't be long. But just in case, I am writing this letter. And I will leave it safely with my aunt. And if anything happens to me, I will pray that you will get it somehow.

I want you to know that I would never have left you if I'd had any other choice. But I had no choice, my love. You are too young to understand everything that has happened, my sweet. But there are things you need to know. Most of all you need to know how much your daddy and I love you.

But you also need to know that your daddy is gone now Angels have taken him away and we won't see him again until we join him up in heaven. And you may hear stories about how a bad man killed your daddy, and these stories are true, but you need to remember that God is bigger and stronger than that bitter old bad man. And even though that bad man killed your daddy, he couldn't hurt your daddy's soul. And your daddy is safe with God now. No one will ever hurt him again. Not ever.

Judith had to stop reading now for her eyes had filled with tears, and she didn't want them to fall on the letter and ruin it. She set the letter aside and wiped her tears on the rough woolen blanket. But hard sobs continued to puH on her. So Jasmine's husband had been killed. Poor Jasmine. But were the words "'bitter old man" referring to Burt Morrison? Had he actually taken it upon himself to murder Jasmine's husband? Or perhaps he'd hired someone else to do it. She picked up the letter again.

The next thing I want you to know, little Pearl, is that your Aunt Constance tricked me when she took you away. She said it was to protect you from someone in our family who is very wicked. And at the time, I was so frightened and desperate that I believed her. I even gave her lots of

*money to take care of you until I could come for you. But
I didn't know that she was being controlled by someone
else. Someone who had power and money and wanted to
take you away from me. Someone who tells me everyday
that unless I obey and stay here that you will be hurt. And
I don't want anyone to hurt you, and so I stay here in my
prison. But even though I miss you, I am glad that you
are still alive. And everyday I pray that someday I will
figure out a way to escape this place and find you.*

*You are the only thing that keeps me alive, my sweet
Pearl. Knowing that my life keeps you safe and sound
gives me the strength I need to face another day. And I
pray that whoever has you will see what a wonderfully
smart and beautiful little girl you are. I hope they are
taking very good care of you, baby. I pray that they are.
And someday, I know we will be back together again.
And someday, a long, long time from now, I hope that you
and me and your daddy will all be back together too. But
until I see your pretty face, always remember that I love
you, my sweet I will always love you—forever!*

All my love,
Mama

Carefully, Judith refolded the letter, placed it back in the
envelope and back in the box. She put the other things back too, then
closed the lid with a dull thud and held the box close to her. Fresh
tears were streaming down her face again. She leaned her head
back against the couch and took in a long, ragged breath. How could
a person survive such sadness?

Suddenly, she remembered Jasmine's words about how it
was Pearl who kept her alive from day to day. But if that were so,

why had she suddenly decided to give up? To take her own life? Had she finally reached the end of her strength, or become too depressed to continue? Was it possible that she had received news that Pearl was no longer alive? That might surely prove to be her final straw. And what if Pearl were dead right now? And if she were dead, where had those three words come from? *Find my Pearl.* They had seemed so real just a moment ago. In fact, they still did. And yet...

She closed her eyes and tried to pray for wisdom and understanding. Asking God if those three words had come from him or were simply created from her own imagination. But she felt her own exhaustion creeping in on her, and before long her words and thoughts became jumbled until she could no longer focus on the meaning. She felt herself surrendering to a restless sleep.

Thirty-Seven

SHE AWOKE AT THE sound of footsteps coming toward her. It took her a moment to remember where she was, but then she looked up to see Jack going into the kitchen. "What time is it?" she asked groggily.

"Sorry, didn't mean to wake you." Jack looked at his watch. "It's not quite six, but I thought I'd make some coffee."

She jumped up. "Oh, dear, I'd better check on Aunt Lenore."

"Don't worry. I just looked in on her, and she's sleeping soundly. Might as well let her rest."

She followed him into the kitchen. "Have you heard anything new, Jack?"

He shook his head as he filled the coffee carafe. "Nothing too specific anyway. Sounds like the fire's being contained though. And they're saying it was fireworks related after all. But you can't be too sure who's putting a spin on what."

She glanced through the kitchen window and across the backyard to where Aunt Lenore's house sat. "Do you think it's safe to go back over there? I don't have anything but the clothes on my back right now, and I'd like to take a shower and clean up."

He grew thoughtful as he measured out the coffee. "I hate to let you out of sight just yet, Judith, least 'til I hear something from Adam. But you could take a shower here, and I'll bet you might find a fresh shirt in Adam's closet. Or I can loan you one of mine." He grinned. "Although you might prefer Adam's selection better. And I doubt that he'd mind much considering the circumstances. Do you mind?"

"No, I understand. I just wish he'd call or something."

"You're not the only one."

Judith took a quick shower, thankful that at last she could remove the wire, then slipped on a clean gray T-shirt that she'd found in Adam's closet. It was the first thing she'd seen there and hadn't wanted to dig around too much. As it turned out it was a Trailblazers' shirt—her favorite pro basketball team. She smiled as she tucked the well-worn shirt into her jeans. Hopefully, Adam wouldn't mind.

She peeked into Josh's room to see Aunt Lenore sitting on the edge of the bed now, tentatively placing one bare foot on the floor. "Here, let me help you," said Judith, moving swiftly to her side. "You don't want to push this at first." She slipped the hospital slippers onto her feet. "Just take it slow and easy. Allow yourself time to build up your strength."

"I'm sure you're right, dear, but just being out of captivity makes me feel stronger somehow." She stood and leaned on Judith, then took a step. "Just help me to the bathroom, please."

After visiting the bathroom, Judith walked Aunt Lenore out into the living room and got her settled on the couch. "Would you like some breakfast?" she offered.

"I've already started some oatmeal," called Jack from the kitchen.

"Oatmeal," said Aunt Lenore with a small smile. "That sounds just lovely."

"How about some juice to go with it?" called Jack.

The old woman nodded. "Yes. That would be nice." She sniffed. "And is that coffee I smell?"

"Can I get you a cup?" asked Judith.

"Oh, would you, dear? I haven't had coffee in ages."

Judith joined Jack in the kitchen. "I think she approves of the menu." she said with a smile. She poured a cup of coffee and took it to Aunt Lenore, setting it on the TV tray still there from last night. Then she returned and got out the orange juice.

"How about you, Judith?" Jack asked as he filled a bowl with steaming oatmeal. "Can I interest you in some breakfast too?"

"I don't feel a bit hungry." She poured a glass of juice. "I don't even think I could eat right now."

"Well, maybe just some toast then."

"Okay I'll take this out to Aunt Lenore."

"Tell Jack this is good coffee," said Aunt Lenore as Judith placed the oatmeal and juice on the tray.

Judith returned to the kitchen and poured herself a cup of coffee. "This waiting just makes me feel so antsy. Isn't there any way we can find out what's happening?"

Just then the doorbell rang and Judith jumped, spilling the hot coffee down her hand. She looked at Jack. "Who do you think that is?"

"Stay back while I check and see." He quickly opened a pantry and pulled out a rifle.

Judith stared at the gun. "Do you really think—"

"You never know. You ladies stay back."

She watched as he went over to the front window and peered through the crack in the drapes. "Oh, it's just Hank," he called, relief evident in his voice. He laid the gun on the floor and went to unlock the door. "Hank," he said warmly, "come on in. You're just in time for breakfast."

Hank stepped into the room with his cap in his hands. "Morning, ladies," he said politely as he followed Jack into the kitchen. Judith went in to join them.

"Just coffee for me, Jack," said Hank as he sat down in a kitchen chair.

"Well, spill the beans, son." said Jack eagerly as he placed a full mug in front of him. "What's going on up at the lake? We're dying to hear the whole story."

Judith sat down across from Hank. "Yes. How's Adam?"

Hank frowned. "Well, that's what I've come to tell you."

Judith swallowed hard then glanced at Jack. His countenance seemed to shrivel. She felt the same. "What is it, Hank? Please, just tell us."

"Well, we don't know anything for sure except that he's missing."

"Missing?" Jack had a slight look of relief.

"How long has he been missing?" asked Judith.

"Well, we began making arrests right after the fireworks ended. Surprisingly, it was going nice and smooth at first, relatively speaking, that is. Our men began apprehending some of the men real quiet like as they were heading towards home. And Adam was with some of the guys who were making arrests at the lodge— some of the men, including Burt Morrison, had planned an emergency meeting after the fireworks show. But then that danged fire broke out on the east side, just behind the lodge, and well, it got a little crazy about then. And a few people got hurt. No fatalities that we know of. At first, we thought it was an effort on the militia's part to throw things off. And, of course, they assumed we were the ones trying to burn them out. But as it turned out, it really was just the result of a misfired bottle rocket. But by then we'd already called for our reinforcements that we'd had standing by outside of the compound. A good thing as it turned out, since we had a few unexpected surprises before the night was over. And then the wind had picked up, and at one point we thought the fire was going to just burn the whole danged place down to the ground."

"So you lost track of Adam following the arrests at the lodge?" Jack was trying to piece this together. "When things got crazy, as you say?"

"Yes, it was actually about the time our reinforcements began arriving, I think. There was some shooting going on and people were running all over the place."

"Was Burt Morrison arrested?" asked Judith.

Hank nodded soberly. "He's in custody as we speak."

"Good."

"How about Hal Emery?"

"Yep. All totaled I think we arrested about fifty men. Of course, some charges may not stick, but it was the best way to defuse the situation before it got out of hand."

Judith sighed. "So what happens to the rest of the people?"

"Well, there will be some tax evasion investigations and probably some property foreclosures. It's a real rat's nest out there. We've had them under investigation for some time, but had to play it out real careful to avoid another disaster. Plus, these people aren't your normal rednecked bigots. These guys have had access to money and power and they've played their hands real careful and smart. Well, sort of. This whole Fourth of July celebration with a loosening of security proved to be just the opportunity we needed to get in." He looked at Judith. "And it helped having you in there too. A lot of your tips turned out to be right on. And some of those tapes will be used for evidence. Thanks for your help."

She nodded. "Yes, but what about Adam? Do you think he's okay? Is he in danger? Is anything being done to find him?"

"Yes," said Jack urgently. "What *about* Adam?"

"We've got a search party going on right now." Hank shrugged. "Time will tell."

"So, how's the atmosphere in the rest of the town?" asked Judith. "Is it safe to leave this house?"

"Sure," said Hank. "I think everyone who's any real threat is pretty much locked up right now. Plus, this place is crawling with Feds who are keeping an eye on things. It'll probably take at least a week or two to sift down and wrap things up around here. But you can expect a lot of changes."

"That's a relief. Then maybe I can get Aunt Lenore settled back into her house today." Judith frowned. "I just wish we knew what was going on with Adam. Is this a normal thing? Do FBI guys just go missing like this? Don't they have some way of checking in with each other?"

"Well, yes. And I suppose that's what's troubling us most. We haven't heard a word from him."

Jack just shook his head and stared down into his cup. Then finally he looked up. "Well, I know my son, and if anyone can make it out of a tough situation, it's Adam Jackson Ford."

"Right," said Hank. "And now I better go. I've got some paperwork to do."

"Thanks for the report," said Judith in a flat voice, not feeling nearly as confident as Jack.

Not long after Hank left, Judith cut through the backyard over to Aunt Lenore's and opened up the house. Then she got out her car and drove around the block to the front of Adam's place, where she eventually helped Aunt Lenore outside and into the car.

"Did you realize that you were so close to home last night?" asked Judith as she drove back around the block and pulled into Aunt Lenore's driveway.

"I had no idea where I was at. But I knew I was in good hands." Aunt Lenore looked out the window and shook her head. "Goodness, you should've just let me walk home."

Judith forced a small laugh. "Well, I don't think you're quite ready for that yet."

After getting Aunt Lenore settled into her house, Judith went outside to quickly water the garden and check on things. She even peeked over the gate to see if she could spot Martha anywhere, but saw no sign of her. When she returned to the house, she found Aunt Lenore happily puttering in her kitchen.

"Oh, it feels so good to be home." she said as she filled the teakettle.

"But you still need to take it easy." warned Judith. "Let me help you with that."

"No, dear, it's like I've always said, the more I can do for myself, the longer I will last."

"Okay." But Judith stood close by just in case. Finally the teakettle began to whistle and Judith persuaded Aunt Lenore to sit down and allow her to make the tea.

"Here you go," said Judith as she placed the pot on the table and sat down across from her. "Shall I pour?"

"Yes, that might be wise for now. I suppose my hands are still a bit unsteady."

Judith filled both their cups. "I went through Jasmine's box last night."

Aunt Lenore nodded, then took a sip.

"And I know about Jasmine's daughter and husband."

"Yes. Pearl. Such a pretty little girl, isn't she?"

"Yes. Did you know that Jasmine's husband was killed? Probably murdered?"

Aunt Lenore set down her cup and looked at Judith. "I was afraid it was something horrible like that. When I first saw those photos, I remembered the frightened look in Jasmine's eyes when she visited me before. And I suspected that Burt may have done something barbaric and unconscionable. And it just sickened me. That's when I had that awful conversation with Ellen."

"Ellen..." Judith said the word yet felt no feeling.

"Do you think Ellen is all right?"

Judith shrugged. "Probably shaken up. Although she's pretty good at convincing herself that nothing has happened."

"Poor Ellen."

At the moment, Judith felt little if any sympathy for Jasmine's mother. She could hardly believe how she'd allowed herself to grow so close to her in the past few days. And now she no longer cared whether she ever saw the woman again or not. "But what about Pearl?" she asked.

Aunt Lenore's brow wrinkled.

"I mean, do you think she's still alive?"

"I just don't know, dear." The old woman sadly shook her head. "I just don't know."

"Well, I mean to find out." Judith stood. "I've asked Jack to come over here and check on you while I'm gone. First I'm going to go out to the trailer where Jasmine killed herself—I mean, *if* she killed herself. I'm still not absolutely certain. And after that, well, I'm not even sure what. But I'll let you know."

"Good for you, Judith. Do everything you can. If that child is alive, we need to find her. I'll be praying for you, dear."

Judith bypassed the downtown area, taking the quickest route to the trailer. She figured Main Street might be a traffic snarl anyway, what with all the media people and protesters, and she had no intention of being slowed or possibly sidetracked from this mission. Although, she didn't know for sure what her mission was, or if anything she might do could make a difference. Perhaps it was simply her own need to stand and look upon the last place where Jasmine had been alive. She parked her car outside the gate and looked around. Hal had already mentioned that they had kept the guard dogs at the trailer site shortly after Jasmine's death, but then had moved them back to the lake after things settled down. However, the No Trespassing sign was still posted. But ignoring the sign, she climbed over the fence and walked right in. Let Hal or anyone else try to stop her now! She walked slowly up the rutted gravel road toward the seedy-looking trailer. The rusted metal siding had once been aqua and white, but now was faded and old. She climbed the rickety wooden steps and tried the front door. Naturally, it was locked, and she stood there for a long moment, fists clenched, staring at the warped door with peeling paint as a fresh surge of anger filled her like the culmination of all the waste and devastation that a generation or more of lies and hatred and bigotry had brought. How many people had been hurt? How many lives ruined? Lost?

"Why?" she shrieked as she lifted her foot in the air and then punch-kicked the door with a strength she'd never known she possessed. To her utter amazement, the door burst open. With heart pounding, she walked into the front room of the trailer and stared. She had expected to find filth and squalor, and felt shocked and slightly disappointed to see a rather orderly little habitat. Shabby perhaps, but neat. She took in a sharp breath, the mildew-tainted air was stale and heavy. Then she glanced around to take in a sagging brown couch pushed up against the wall with an end table and lamp on one side. On the table, a cup and saucer, nothing fancy, just a plain white cup with blue cornflowers on it.

She picked up the empty cup and looked at it. Had Jasmine

sat here and drank a cup of tea or coffee perhaps? And why did that seem so strange? She set down the cup and looked around the room. The small kitchen was to her left. And, although it was rundown and shabby, the counter-tops were clean. She looked in the cupboards, but other than a few old-looking staples and an assortment of mismatched dishes, they were mostly empty. The refrigerator was empty. She turned and went to the other end of the trailer and looked into the bedroom. Other than a couple of neatly folded blankets in the corner, this room was also empty. She looked into the tiny bathroom and saw that it too contained nothing out of the ordinary, and other than a couple towels and soap, it too was mostly empty. She went through closets and discovered a heavy jacket with empty pockets, a pair of old rubber boots, and a few hangers.

Jasmine's time spent here had been under some pretty sparse living conditions. But perhaps this place, off by itself, had somehow felt like a haven to her. Perhaps it was a place where she could think undisturbed. Judith paused to listen to the birds singing outside. This trailer did seem to have a quiet air about it. And she could almost imagine Jasmine sitting there on the old brown couch, thinking, perhaps even praying, and drinking her tea. Perhaps she'd been trying to think of a way to escape her prison, to rescue her child.

Judith turned and went outside, breathing deeply of the fresh air. She walked toward the back of the property. Wasn't there supposed to be a pond back here somewhere? She pushed her way through some overgrown brush until she finally caught sight of the reflection of water. The pond, almost completely surrounded by blackberry bushes, also had a number of cattails and lily pads growing there, and was actually rather pretty in a wild, unkempt sort of way. She noticed a log laying across a slightly cleared out area near the water's edge. It looked the perfect bench for sitting and thinking. And so she sat down on the log and gazed out across the green-tinged water, and began to think. *What was going on that day, Jasmine?* she asked herself. *What was it that made you give up on life? Or did you?*

"Hey!" called out a gruff but young sounding voice. "What're you doing there?"

She looked up to see a boy's face peering at her from behind the blackberry bushes. The same boy she'd met when she'd first come to Cedar Crest.

"Hi," she called in what she hoped was a friendly tone. "I'm just sitting here thinking about my friend Jasmine. Do you remember her?"

He pushed his way through the bushes, cursing as he snagged himself on thorns. "Of course, I remember her. She was my friend too."

Judith stood and extended her hand. "I'm glad you were a friend to her. She needed a friend. My name is Judith. Jas mine and I grew up together as kids, but then we lost touch."

He shook her hand. "Yeah, well, I'm Matt."

"Nice to meet you, Matt."

"So what're you doing here then?" he asked again, as if he owned the place.

"Just thinking, I guess. Trying to figure out why she gave up on her life."

He shoved his hands in his pockets and looked down at his grubby tennis shoes. The abrupt gesture seemed to suggest something, and Judith studied him carefully. She remembered the last time they'd spoken, and he had seemed to be frightened.

"Do you know Jasmine's dad?" she asked.

He shrugged, then kicked a pebble with the toe of his shoe. "Yeah, sure, everybody knows Mr. Morrison."

"Did you know that he's been arrested?"

The boy looked up. "You kidding me?"

"No, it's the truth. A bunch of people from the lake have been arrested. Did you know that some of those people were involved in some pretty bad things—some illegal things? And now they're getting into trouble for it."

He looked at her skeptically. "Are you making this up?"

She shook her head. "It's the truth." She looked back over the pond. "And I know that something was terribly wrong with Jasmine—something between her and her father. And I think he may have hurt her—a lot."

"Yeah." Matt's eyes narrowed as he bent down and picked up a rock then chucked it into the center of the pond. "Her father was a real jerk."

"Did you spend much time talking to Jasmine?" Judith watched as the circular ripples from the tossed rock grew bigger and wider, finally reaching the muddy edge of the pond.

"Sometimes." He turned and looked at Judith. "Jasmine was real good at listening—not like most grown-ups."

She nodded. "Well, I'll bet she was glad to have you for her friend."

"Yeah. Maybe so." Then he pressed his lips together and shook his head. "But I wasn't a very good friend."

"Why not?"

"'Cause I couldn't help her. I couldn't protect her.. ."

"Protect her?"

He scowled. "From him."

"Her father?"

He nodded then shoved his hands back into his pockets and looked over his shoulder, almost as if getting ready to leave.

"Were you around that day when she died?" asked Judith

quickly, not wanting to lose this opportunity to talk.

He nodded again, but this time his chin quivered slightly.

"Did you see it?"

Now he shook his head vigorously. "No. But I heard it."

"The gunshot?"

He nodded, slowly this time.

"Who do you think shot that gun, Matt?"

He looked up now, directly into her eyes. "I know that Jasmine shot the gun, but it was her daddy's fault."

Without any show of emotion, Judith just slowly nodded now, as if this bit of news were no surprise to her. And perhaps it wasn't. "But if you didn't see it, how can you be so sure?"

"Because he'd been here earlier, then left. But first he said mean, ugly things to her. And he made her cry. And then she just sat out here all afternoon and just cried and cried and cried. I tried to talk with her, but she couldn't talk no more. Not even to me. All she could do was just cry. And I know it's 'cause of what he told her."

"What did he tell her, Matt? Did you hear?"

"Yeah, I heard it all right. He called her these really mean, nasty names, and he told her that she better start acting right. Then he told her that her mongrel was dead. I don't know what he meant by that. But that's what got her all upset. She started hitting him and asking him if he was telling her the truth. And he told her that God didn't want her mongrel baby alive no more and that she was dead. That's when Jasmine just started crying and crying. And then Mr. Morrison got in his truck and left."

Judith felt tears in her eyes again. "Thank you for telling me this, Matt. Now I think I finally understand things better. Do you think you could tell this story again? I promise that no one will hurt you if you do."

He shrugged, but she could see the fear on his face. "I dunno.

My dad might get mad."

She nodded. "Well, I understand. But maybe we could have someone talk to your dad and explain some things to him that would help him to see why you need to tell your story. You said you were Jasmine's friend. I'm sure she'd be glad to have you tell the truth for her."

He nodded, his chin firm. "Well, I'll think about it."

"Thank you."

"Uh," he looked up at her curiously, "what's a mongrel baby anyway?"

"There's no such thing, Matt. That was just Mr. Morrison being incredibly stupid and mean. Did you know that grown-ups can be dumber than kids sometimes?"

"Yeah. I knew that." He glanced over his shoulder. "Well, I better get back."

"Thanks again, Matt."

He took off the way he'd come, grumbling as he made his way through the brushy briars again. Judith sat back down on the log and allowed the tears to flow once more. This time for Jasmine and little Pearl and Jasmine's husband. What a senseless and tragic waste, but perhaps they were together now. And yet it seemed so unfair. *Dear God, why?* she asked. *Why did this happen? How can anything good come from such great loss?*

Suddenly, she remembered how she had judged Jasmine so harshly, questioning why her friend had chosen to take her own life, why she had given up so easily, so completely. Judith had compared her own situation to Jasmine's, thinking how she'd lost a husband and child, and how her situation had been so much more hopeless than Jasmine's—as if she'd had an excuse to give up. And yet, even at that grim moment, it had been Jasmine's death and circumstances that had brought Judith back to life. And eventually to God.

And yet, now, to arrive here—this hopeless, desolate place.

To fully understand now how Jasmine's losses and grief had truly been so much greater than her own. So much worse. Far, far worse. There was simply no comparison. For Jasmine's very life had been stolen from her by the hand of her own father. A man ruled by hatred—the father of lies. It was just too much to bear. Judith could hardly stand it herself. It's as if all hope had been, by one foul breath, extinguished from her.

Oh, God, she prayed, please, help me. Help me to survive this thing. Help me to trust you in spite of such evil.

And then, she heard a rustling noise—someone walking through the nearby brush again, not from Matt's house this time, but from the direction of the driveway. She hunkered down and listened in silence, holding her breath in fear as the sound of heavy steps grew closer, coming directly toward her. Hank had said that Hal and Burt were both securely locked up. But were they?

Thirty- Eight

"JUDITH?" CALLED A MAN'S voice. Neither Hal's nor Burt's; it
sounded almost like Adam Ford.

She stood up and yelled hopefully, "Adam?"

In the same instant, he appeared, pushing the branches aside
to make an opening in the brush. He stepped through and smiled.
"Hey, I found you!"

She rushed at him, throwing her arms around him in relief.
"Oh, Adam, I'm so thankful it's you! I was scared witless that it
was someone else—" Then, aware that she was gushing, she pulled
herself away from him. She looked up, still amazed that he was here,
actually standing before her. "You made it out! You're alive!"

He laughed. "Of course I'm alive."

She felt her cheeks flush with embarrassment. "I know, I
know...I probably sound slightly hysterical. It's just that I didn't
know if.. .well, you know.. .sometimes..."

His face grew serious. "You mean, sometimes people die."

She nodded, aware now that she still had traces of tears on her
face. She brushed the wetness off with her hands, then forced
a nervous smile. "I'm just so relieved you're okay. Does Jack

know?"

"Yes. He's the one who told me you came out here to look around the place. Find anything interesting?"

"Oh, Adam!" She pressed her hand to her mouth. "I don't even know where to begin. It's just too horrible— awful— unbelievable!"

"Okay, just slow down. Take it one step at a time." He helped her to sit back down on the log. "Take a deep breath and relax. There's no hurry. Just start at the beginning."

She paused to focus her thoughts. "Did you ever have a chance to look through Jasmine's box?"

He nodded. "Just barely, but I haven't been able to do much since then. Although I did put a tracer on the name of the town on the photo envelope, and for the Phillips family. It didn't take long to find out who they were. Pretty tragic. Jasmine's husband, Dr. Steven Phillips, was a surgeon. He was killed, reportedly a gang-related shooting downtown, but the ballistics report revealed the bullet was a 30-30, probably from a rifle in other words, not your typical gang-banger type of firearm—"

"Burt carries a hunting rifle in the back of his car." Judith shuddered. "For emergencies, he says."

"Yes, I know. We've already confiscated the weapon. It uses the same caliber bullets, which isn't all that uncommon for a rifle. We'll run further tests though."

"Do you think he did it?"

"Possibly. But even if he didn't, we won't rule out the possibility that it might've been one of his buddies."

"Suddenly, this whole thing seems so unreal to me. I mean, there I was, just staying at their house, and of course, I was suspicious about Burt and everything but to really think that Burt Morrison might be an actual cold-blooded murderer—his own daughter's husband." She bit her lip. "It's too much to take in."

"With this new evidence, for what appears to be a definite hate crime, we're now able to demand an autopsy of that Paxton boy who died in the car wreck back in the late seventies."

"James."

"Yes. Eli has already signed the necessary papers."

"Eli?" She looked at Adam. "Is Eli okay?"

"Yes, all three are being released today. The governor was flown out this morning to make a public apology. The media is having a heyday with this whole thing." He chuckled. "As it turns out, that's just how Eli and his sons had planned it. He's one smart cookie. And a good man too."

"Yes. He's pretty amazing." She took a deep breath. "Did you see the photos of Jasmine's little girl, Pearl?"

"Yes. And I noticed the letter, but about that same time I had to take care of something a little more urgent, and since I already had someone checking on the family, I figured it could wait."

"It sounds like Pearl may be dead." She stared out at the pond.

Adam slammed a fist onto his knee and cursed. "How do you know?"

"I think it might've been Burt. Or if not him, perhaps one of his good ol' boys. The kid next door, Matt, witnessed a pretty incriminating conversation with Burt and Jasmine— just before Jasmine shot herself."

"So now you actually believe she killed herself?"

She nodded sadly. "Yes, I suppose she did pull the trigger. But I'm certain her father pulled the strings."

"Well, if it's any consolation, you can be pretty certain that Burt Morrison will never be free to walk the streets of Cedar Crest again."

She shook her head. "He was never free, Adam. He lived in a

prison of his own design. A prison built with hatred and lies and racism."

"Do you feel sorry for him, Judith?"

She turned and stared at him. "No! Not at all! Right now, my biggest fear is that I might actually turn into the same sort of hateful person myself, only different I suppose. Because the truth is, I hate Burt Morrison so much that I can almost feel it seeping through my pores right this moment. In fact, I'm really thankful I don't own or even know how to use a gun. And I'm thankful he's locked up. Because I've never felt such strong, vengeful feelings in my entire life. Not even when I lost Jonathan or Peter. And I think hearing that news about Pearl today was just about the last straw for me." Her stomach knotted as she felt tears burn in her eyes again. "Burt Morrison is an absolute monster!"

He nodded. "I can understand how you feel about him. But I'm curious, how do you feel about Ellen Morrison right now?"

She shrugged and looked down at her dirty tennis shoes. "I'm not even sure. Sort of indifferent, I guess. And it's weird, because just a day ago, I think I really, truly cared about her. I honestly did. But now, in light of everything that I know, well, I think I could almost hate her too."

He set his hand on her shoulder. "You've been through a lot, Judith."

"Not nearly as much as Jasmine."

"No. Not nearly as much as Jasmine. But I think she'd be proud of what her blood sister did for her."

She looked up. "You really think so?"

He nodded.

She thought about that for a long moment. Was it possible that Jasmine knew what Judith had tried to accomplish? Would she appreciate her efforts? She closed her eyes and sighed deeply.

"I think you're overdue for a good, long rest, Judith. Your work here is done."

She shook her head. "Not quite. I think there's still one more thing that Jasmine would like me to do—something I need to do."

"What's that?"

She swallowed hard, wondering if she could even speak the words. "I need to confront her father."

Adam said nothing.

"Do you think that's stupid?"

"No, not at all. I think it's very brave of you, but are you sure you're up to it? Maybe you should give yourself some time to rest and perhaps think this whole thing over a little."

She shook her head. "No. In fact, I'd like to do it as soon as I can." She looked at him hopefully. "Is it even possible?"

His brows lifted slightly. "Well, I think we can work it out. The state police have stepped in to man the Cedar Crest police station. Believe me, those good ol' boys are either locked up or on temporary leave of absence until a full investigation is complete."

"So, I can see him then? Today, do you think?"

"May as well get it over with." He stood suddenly, and grabbing both her hands, gently pulled her to her feet. "Mind if we listen in too?"

"Not at all." She laughed sarcastically. "Maybe we'll get a full confession out of him, although I seriously doubt it. Burt Morrison knows how to watch his words."

"Well, you managed to get some fairly incriminating comments from him on tape yesterday. Good work."

"Thanks. I wasn't sure it would be worth much, but I tried."

He held the branches aside as they passed through the brush. "How about if you follow me in your car?" he suggested. "And on the way over, I'll call in and see if I can make the necessary arrangements."

"Sounds good."

When they passed the trailer, Adam paused a moment. "Say, Judith, you didn't by any chance kick that door open, did you?"

She nodded sheepishly. "I was feeling a little angry at the time."

"Whoa, girl. Guess we better not get you too riled then."

"I think I can control myself now."

She followed his pickup into town, noticing the letters on his license plates. DBS—or Don't Be Stupid, as he'd once told her. "Don't be stupid." she reminded herself again as they pulled in behind the police station to park. "Dear God." she prayed, "please help me not to be stupid. Help me to keep my anger under control. But please, help me to speak the truth to that man." Suddenly she remembered part of a Bible verse about "speaking the truth in love." Yet at the same time, she felt *love* was out of the question. Under these circumstances, she'd be doing well if she could simply manage to control her anger, not to mention keep from falling completely apart. She hated the idea of Burt Morrison witnessing her getting upset or crying. It might make him think he'd won. So, she determined, she would remain strong and in control, at least on the outside. Perhaps, with God's help, and for Jasmine, she could do this thing.

"Well, it's all set." Adam slipped his cell phone back in his pocket as he closed her car door for her. He looked at her with concern in his eyes. "Are you absolutely certain you want to do this, Judith?"

She nodded firmly. "Yes. That is, unless it'll harm anything you're doing. I mean, as far your investigation or the " prosecution's case or whatever. I don't want to mess anything up in that regard."

"No. If anything, it'll probably help us. By the way, Judith, you need to know that Burt's not aware of the role you played in all this. He may still think of you as his friend. How you handle *that* is entirely up to you."

"The charade is over," she declared as he unlocked the back door to city hall. "I plan to lay my cards on the table."

"Good. Just so you know." He placed his hand on her back as he guided her around a corner. "It's this hallway to the left. We'll have to get clearance first."

"Thanks," she turned and looked at him. "I know it's your job, Adam, but I appreciate your letting me do this."

"Yeah, sure." He smiled down on her. "By the way, cool shirt."

She looked down at his Blazers' T-shirt. "Yeah, I thought you'd like it."

After a few minutes, Judith was taken to a small room with a one-way glass window. And there, sitting on the opposite side of a metal table, was Burt Morrison. He wore a gray one-piece jail uniform that seemed to suit him. His hands, resting on the table, were cuffed. He eyed her with one brow slightly cocked as she entered the room, almost as if he were somewhat amused by this visit. Her heart began to race as the door was closed and locked behind her. *This is for you, Jasmine,* she thought as she sat down in the chair across from him. "Hello, Burt," she said in a crisp, businesslike voice.

"Where's Ellen?" he demanded gruffly. "I thought she'd be here with you."

"I don't know where she is. I haven't seen her since last night."

"What are you doing here then?"

"I wanted to talk to you, Burt. About Jasmine."

"We've already talked about that. There's nothing more to say."

"You're wrong, Burt. I have something to say."

His eyes narrowed a little, and he made a grunting sound. "Well, hurry it up then, Judith. Let's get this nonsense over with."

"Why?" she asked him sharply. "You got someplace you need to be right now?"

His eyes flashed angrily, but this time he said nothing.

"I know what you did, Burt. I know that you killed Jasmine's husband—"

"You don't know nothing—"

"I know you were there. I know your rifle matches the one that was used. I know that you hated Jasmine's husband simply because the color of his skin wasn't—"

He slammed both fists down on the table. "She did it to spite me! To humiliate me! She was selfish and willful and rebellious and just look where it got her!"

"Look where it got you, Burt! Jasmine was your own daughter—your own flesh and blood! How could you have done that to her? How could you have murdered her husband, taken her only child, and then used this power to force her to marry a man that—"

"I'm her father." His voice was cold and hard now; his eyes like ice. "The Bible teaches that children are supposed to respect and honor their parents."

"The Bible also says that we are to love one another."

He hit the table again. "Fathers are s'posed to teach their children to respect their elders. Children are s'posed to obey their parents!"

"What about Ellen's parents, Burt? You didn't want her to respect and obey her parents."

"That was different!" he snapped. "I done right by my family. I brought my children up in the way they should go, and—"

"Now they are dead, Burt! Constance and Jasmine are both dead! That's what your hateful ways gave to them. Death!"

"They brought on their own deaths, both of them, by being rebellious and sinful."

"But what about the others, Burt? What about Steven and James and poor little Pearl?"

He shook his head, rolling his eyes as if she were some foolish child who would never get it—never fully understand such grown-up things.

"You were responsible for their deaths, Burt, weren't you?"

He said nothing, but his features became like granite.

"And, sure, you may not have pulled the trigger when Jasmine died, not like you did with her husband, but you killed her when you informed her that her child was dead. You knew that little girl was all Jasmine had to keep her alive, and then you crushed her hopes when you took even that from her." She leaned forward and looked him right in the eyes, no longer afraid of his evil. "How does it make you feel, Burt, to think you murdered your own grandchild? How does it make you feel to know that you killed your only chance to carry on your name, your line of descendants? How does that make you feel inside?"

He stared at her with a hardened, even gaze, then spoke in a low yet lethal tone. "I didn't kill that kid, Judith, but I wish to God that I had. That blasted mongrel would be better off dead." He stood now and continued in a louder, more venomous voice. "And for your information, I don't want my line continuing—not if it's gotta go through some worthless, mongrel, half-breed!" He beat his bound hands on the table again. "Better that my line is dead! And that's all I have to say about that! And I hope to God that I never see the likes of you or your kind again!"

She stood too, though not quite ready to leave. "You know, Burt, I used to look up to you. Back when I was a little girl, with no daddy of my own, there was a time when I thought you could almost walk on water. Of course, it didn't take long to learn otherwise. And now I think it's just a horrendous shame that you took all the goodness that God tried to give you, and you allowed your hatred and your racism to ruin and poison everything until in

the end you're left with nothing but ashes and death and shame."
She shook her head. "Despite what you may think you've done in
the shadows, someday it'll all come out into the light. Someday
you will answer to God for all the atrocities you have done."

He said nothing, just looked at her as if she were deranged.

She walked toward the door, then paused. "And, I can't believe
that I'm even saying this next thing, Burt, but the Bible teaches that
we're supposed to pray for our enemies." She looked at him right
in the eyes one last time. "I'll be praying for you." Then she turned
away from him and waited while Adam quickly unlocked the door.

Her hands and knees shook uncontrollably as she stepped out of
the claustrophobic-sized room and into the hallway, but she held her
head up.

"You okay?" asked Adam with concern.

She looked at him and nodded, her chin quivering. "I think so."

Then he gathered her into his arms and held her close for a moment.
"You were absolutely great in there, Judith. Really great! We were
all just blown away as we listened in the other room. One guy even
suggested that you should assist with the prosecution."

She stepped back and fought to regain composure. "No thank you! I
think I've had enough of this whole nasty business for now." Then she
shook her head as if to clear away the jumbled emotions and thoughts.
"But Adam?" she said suddenly. "Did you hear what he said about
Pearl? Did he say what I thought he said?"

He nodded. "I think so."

"Do you think Pearl is still alive?"

"Sure sounds like it."

"I've got to find her!"

"I'll put everyone available on this right now."

"And I've got some phone numbers I copied from Burt's address
book—they're in my purse. They might be helpful."

"Good. I'd try to get Burt to tell us of the child's whereabouts, but after hearing him go on about wanting the poor little girl dead, it seems a fairly useless pursuit. But at least we can be fairly sure that she's alive now."

"Yes!" said Judith, amazed at the sense of hope that had suddenly returned to her. "She's alive!"

He led her toward the same office he'd occupied that first day she'd met him. "Come on in here and give me those phone numbers."

"Is this still your office?" she asked as she sank into a chair.

"Sort of, but not really." He took out a pad and quickly began to question her, listing everything they knew about young Pearl Marie Phillips.

Judith dug in her purse until she found the fake letter she'd written to her mother. She carefully opened the envelope to reveal what she'd written on the inside of the flap. "I should go and get that letter from Jasmine too," she said, "the one she wrote to Pearl. She mentioned something about Constance in her letter, that somehow she'd been involved in taking Pearl. Maybe we can track down all of Constance's old connections up in Seattle and figure this out."

"Right. Why don't you go get it. I think there's enough information here to get the wheels rolling again. And who knows, maybe after your final pep talk Burt will decide to cooperate."

She shook her head. "Don't count on it. He's a hard and bitter man."

"Oh, yeah," said Adam, as if just thinking of something. "About Ellen..."

"Ellen?"

"Yeah. I should probably tell you."

She felt the tiniest twinge of concern, yet her voice remained flat. "What about her?"

"Well, you know how I went missing earlier this morning?"

"Yes, Hank told us and we were pretty worried. What happened?"

"Well, it was about 4 A.M. when things finally started to settle down at the lake, our reinforcements had arrived, and most of the arrests had been made. The forest fire was still going pretty strong, but there were firefighters and the National Guard on hand, and everyone was being evacuated. It was a hopping place out there. Anyway, I was over on the west side of the lake at that time, and I saw this person out in a rowboat, out beyond the dock by the Morrisons' place. It was pretty smoky so I couldn't see more than an outline, and naturally, I thought it was one of the men, someone we'd missed trying to make an escape. So I ran down there, slipped into the lake, and swam out to see who it was. Of course, that's why I lost communication— getting all wet like that. Anyway, to my surprise, it turned out to be Ellen Morrison. But she was completely hysterical, crying and praying and talking to herself like she'd really lost her mind. And, to be honest, I felt pretty sorry for her. Maybe it was because of you and the things you'd said about her, I don't know. But I knew I couldn't just leave that poor old woman out on the lake like that. Who knew what she might do?"

Judith nodded. "Yes, she's not the most stable person in the world. And she told me once that if there ever was a fire, she'd just get in the rowboat and row out to the middle of the lake. I can imagine how upset she must've been."

"Yes, and with the fire still out of control, she must've been terrified. But when she saw me swimming toward her, she got so scared that she stood up right there in the boat and acted like she was going to run—who knows where! And, of course, she capsized the boat, and then I had to rescue her and get her back to the dock, then back inside her house where we could both dry off and warm up. By then I had told her I was a good friend of yours, and that I'd come out looking for you because I was concerned for your welfare. Well, that calmed her right down. But then she was all worried about you because you'd disappeared so suddenly. So I pretended to do some calling around and then finally told her I'd located you and that you were safe and sound at Aunt Lenore's house."

"So is she still out there at the lake, all by herself?"

"No." He paused as if unsure how to say the rest.

"Where is she then?"

"Well, she pleaded with me to take her to Aunt Lenore's house too. She said she didn't want to live out at the lake anymore. She said it was getting too hard. I don't know how much she'd seen, or if she'd been around when Burt was arrested or not, but I think she kind of knew what was going on. She asked me to run upstairs before we left; she wanted me to get a quilt off the bed for her. So I did. And I noticed your bags were still up there, so I grabbed them too. They're at Aunt Lenore's."

"Thank you."

"I didn't know what to do with Ellen. And she kept begging me to take her over to Aunt Lenore's house. I hope that's okay with you."

"Well, it's Aunt Lenore's house, not mine. How did *she* seem about the whole thing?"

"She actually seemed quite glad to see her niece. And Ellen just hugged Aunt Lenore like a long lost friend and then started bawling like a little girl. It was actually a rather touching reunion. Both women seemed genuinely happy."

"Interesting." Judith nodded, trying to take all this news in. "Well, I'll go get that box and the letter and then I'll get right back to you."

"Yeah, and who knows, maybe we'll get lucky and discover something helpful before too long."

"I'll be praying for a miracle," she said as she picked up her purse. "And you know, I've become a firm believer in the power of prayer."

"You and me both."

Thirty-Nine

JUDITH RETURNED TO ADAM'S house for the box and letter, then called him on the phone to read what few details of information she could find in Jasmine's letter. "Should I go ahead and bring this over to you now?" she offered.

"No, there's no hurry to see it right now. Of course, it's important evidence and you need to keep it safe. But we've got enough information to keep the search for our lost Pearl going strong. And I've already gotten a few good tips from the phone numbers you wrote down. I think the trail is starting to reveal itself."

"Great, keep me informed." She paused for a moment. "And if it's at all possible, I'd really like to go up to Seattle when Pearl is found. I mean, I realize she might have some relatives on her father's side who'll want—"

"Steven Phillips was a foster child. He was in and out of numerous homes while growing up. Amazingly, he turned out to be one of those rare, miraculous stories where the kid who comes from nothing grows up to make a huge success of his life."

"Oh." Judith sighed. "That just makes the ending seem all the more sad to me."

"I know what you mean."

"So our little Pearl doesn't have any living relatives—at least that we know of?"

"Just the Morrisons."

She groaned.

"That is unless blood sisters count as something..."

"Do you think?" She felt her hopes rising. "Oh, Adam, do you really think it's possible? I'd give anything to raise Jasmine's child for her." Tears were building in her eyes again. "Oh, what can I do? Who can I talk to? Oh, Adam, honestly, I'd do *anything* to have that dear child. And, I swear, I would love her as my very own. I really would!" She was crying now. "I'm sorry, I don't mean to get all emotional on you again—I suppose I'm just tired."

"I'm sure you are. We all are. Tell you what, Judith. You promise me that you'll lie down and take a nap, and I'll see if I can get some help on this. I happen to have a good friend who works in children's services up in Washington state. In fact, she owes me a favor or two. Let me see what I can do." He paused. "But Judith, don't get your hopes too high. I mean, we haven't even found the little girl yet. And, well, you just never know."

She swallowed hard. "I know. I just appreciate anything you can do. And I have a lot in my savings, Adam. I'm sure I can cover whatever cost might be involved. I don't care what it is. And if not, well, I'll take out a loan. But I want her, Adam! I want her like I've never wanted anything in ages. I just really sense this is meant to be."

"Yeah, I think it's pretty obvious. But do as I said, Judith. Get some rest. Stay in my room if you like. I just saw Josh, and he's on his way home now and pretty zonkered. I told him all about you and your role in this whole business. So don't worry about him treating you like a traitor anymore."

"Thanks, Adam. I'm looking forward to explaining some things to some other folks too."

"And don't worry about Eli. I got to know him better last weekend, and I told him a little about what you were up to. I knew he could be trusted with it."

"That explains why he just looked away when he saw me riding in the car with the Morrisons. He didn't react or anything."

"He's a good guy."

"I sure hope he sticks around this crazy town."

"I think he's planning on it."

Judith wanted to say she hoped Adam would stick around as well, but it seemed pretty presumptuous on her part. And so she just said, "Good-bye."

After a good nap in Adam's room, she awoke feeling more alive and refreshed than she'd felt in ages. The house was quiet and still, and she suspected both Jack and Josh were catching up on their own rest after their previous sleepless night. She felt slightly uncertain about going next door to Aunt Lenore's—not sure if she were ready to face Ellen yet. But unfortunately her bags were over there. She knew she had no choice. She wrote Jack a quick thank-you note which she left on the kitchen table, then slipped out the back door and across the yard, praying with each step. She had no intention of hurting Ellen, and yet, she could no longer play the part of adoring friend.

She tapped lightly on Aunt Lenore's back door, but when no one answered, she used her own key to quietly let herself in. These women were probably resting too. It seemed everyone had been stretched to the limits by last night's activities. She walked quietly through the kitchen and then spied her bags in a corner of the living room. She tiptoed over, and just as she bent down to pick them up, heard Ellen's voice.

"Is that you, Judith?" She lifted her head to look up from where she was resting on the couch.

"Yes," whispered Judith. "I didn't want to disturb you or Aunt Lenore. I'm sure you're both exhausted after all that went on last night."

Ellen sat up and rubbed her eyes. Her white hair stuck out in tufts, giving her an even more helpless appearance. "Oh my, wasn't that the most horrifying experience."

"Yes. It was pretty bad." She set her bags back down and turned to face Ellen. "I saw Burt today."

"You did? Well now, how is he doing?" her voice sounded artificially bright and cheerful.

Judith frowned. "You do know that he's under arrest, don't you, Ellen?"

The older woman nodded soberly, but her expression was unclear and hard to read. Was she troubled? Confused? "Yes, I know all about that, dear."

Judith went over to the couch and sat down beside her. "And how does that make you feel, Ellen?"

She looked down at her hands, folded neatly in her lap, then shook her head. "Well, I don't rightly know." She turned and peered up at Judith. "How do you feel about that, dear?"

Judith felt her brows raise with wonder. How did she feel? What an odd question, and why should it matter to Ellen anyway? "Well, to tell you the truth, Ellen, I feel relieved."

Ellen slowly nodded, as if trying to take this bit of news in. "Yes, dear, I think that's how I feel too."

"Relieved?"

Ellen smiled, sort of a sad smile, but a smile all the same. "Yes, dear. You see, it was bound to happen. I always knew it was bound to happen one day."

"Are you saying that you *knew* that Burt would get arrested?"

"I suppose that's what I'm saying."

Judith stared at Ellen with a fresh sense of horror. Had Ellen known all along? Had she simply pretended ignorance? Was it possible that she had been aware of what had happened to Steven Phillips and James Paxton, and who knew who else? Had she simply sat silently by while her husband and his buddies went out and committed these atrocious hate crimes? And if so, Judith was unsure that she'd be able to keep her opinions to herself. "So, have you *always* known what Burt's been doing?" she asked, not bothering to conceal her aggravation.

Ellen blithely nodded again, and now Judith wanted to shake her and scream and even slap her. But instead she took in a deep breath and simply asked, "Why didn't you say anything to anyone about this?"

"Well, I just figured it was his business, and I thought the IRS would catch up with him sooner or later anyway."

"The IRS?"

"Yes, dear." Ellen patted her hand soothingly. "I know it must sound just horrible to you, but Burt didn't believe it was constitutionally right to pay taxes. And, whether it was right or wrong, I just kept my mouth shut about the whole thing."

"And you think *that's* why he was arrested?"

"Well, of course, dear. I knew that they'd catch up with him one day."

Judith wondered how much she should tell her just now. How much could Ellen handle? Maybe it would be best to take it slowly, one step at a time. "Ellen," she began carefully. "There's more to Burt's arrest than tax evasion."

"More?" Ellen frowned.

"Yes. There are some other charges—very serious charges against Burt. Things that relate to racism and hatred. Do you know anything about these things, Ellen?"

"Well, I know how the boys get all riled up sometimes, and then they have their little meetings, and I know how they talk real big and rough and all. But I don't think anything really came of it. Not really."

"Well, you're wrong, Ellen. Some very serious crimes have been committed—crimes that are directly linked to Burt and some of the other guys from the lake. And *that's* why Burt's been arrested."

Ellen looked honestly shocked now. "Oh, my!"

"And it's possible that Burt will be locked up for a long, long time."

"Oh, dear!"

"And, I'm sure they'll need to question you as well, Ellen. Will you be able to cooperate with them?"

"Well, of course..." Her chin had begun to quiver. "Certainly, I'll tell them whatever I can recall. Although it won't likely amount to much. Burt says I've got the memory of a fly."

Lucky for Burt, thought Judith. "Well, I'm sorry for all you've been through, Ellen, but I'm afraid it's not over. And I won't lie to you. The truth is I'm not sorry that Burt's been caught. I'm glad. I think he deserves to be punished. And there's something else I need to tell you—actually there are several things. Do you want to hear them now, Ellen? Or would you rather wait until you're more rested? I know this is a lot for you to take in right now."

She seemed to consider this, then nodded. "Yes, dear, I think I'd like to hear everything there is to hear right now, if you don't mind."

"Well, first of all, I have to confess to you that when I came out to your house, I was looking for evidence in regards to Jasmine's death. I suspected that Burt had dealt unfairly with her, and because Jasmine and I were close friends at one time, I wanted to find these things out for her sake. So I want you to know that I was acting as something of a spy during my visit with you. But, you see, it was for Jasmine that I did it."

Ellen patted her hand again. "I understand, dear."

Judith blinked. "And, well, there's more to tell you. I have discovered some things about Jasmine's previous life that may be somewhat worrisome to you. But I think you need to know the truth. How you deal with these things is up to you, but I want you to understand."

"Certainly, dear. I want to know everything there is to know about my Jasmine."

"Well, first of all, Jasmine was married to a brilliant man who was a surgeon—"

"A surgeon? A doctor? My Jasmine was married to a doctor?"

"Yes, and it seems they were quite well off and living very happily. They even had a child. A little girl by the name of Pearl."

"A little girl? Pearl? I have a granddaughter?" Ellen's face glowed with happiness. "Oh my, this is the most wonderful news! But where is my granddaughter? Where is this brilliant doctor?" Then her face clouded over. "But I'm confused now. If Jasmine was married to a doctor, how could she have been married to Hal? Oh, dear me, she wasn't a bigamist, was she?"

"No, Ellen. She was a widow. You see, her husband was murdered."

Ellen's hand flew to her mouth. "Murdered? Oh, my goodness! Jasmine's husband was murdered?"

"Yes."

Ellen's voice broke as she spoke. "But.. .but.. .what about the little girl? Pearl? Oh, dear, was she murdered too?"

"No, we think Pearl is still alive. In fact, we have people looking for her right now, as we speak."

Ellen shook her head in confusion. "Oh my. This is all so

bewildering. Jasmine's husband was murdered? Then why in the world did Jasmine leave her little girl behind and come here to stay with us?"

"Because Burt forced her." This time Judith reached over and took Ellen's hand. Just then she noticed Aunt Lenore slowly shuffling toward them. "Do you want to join us, Aunt Lenore?" asked Judith hopefully. "I'm just telling Ellen about Pearl now."

Ellen looked up, her jaw dropped in surprise. "You mean Aunt Lenore knows about my granddaughter too?"

"Yes, dear." said Aunt Lenore as she carefully lowered herself into the rocker across from them. "I know all about her."

"This isn't going to be easy for you to hear, Ellen," said Judith. "But we have reason to believe that Burt was involved in the death of Jasmine's husband. And we also know that he arranged to have Jasmine's daughter kidnapped from her."

"Kidnapped? My Burt?" Ellen looked from Judith to Aunt Lenore then back again. "Oh no, Burt would never do such a dreadful thing...his own granddaughter kidnapped? Why that's completely ridiculous—"

"Ellen," interrupted Judith, "Jasmine's husband was African American."

Ellen's hand flew up over her mouth and her eyes grew wide. "You mean... are you saying that my daughter married a colored man?"

"Ellen, from what little I've heard, Jasmine's husband, Steven Phillips, was a successful surgeon. He was respected in his community, and I have reason to believe he was a wonderful husband and father. And if Burt hadn't interrupted their lives with his hatred and ignorance and who knows what else, well, I'm pretty sure that Jasmine and her little family would still be happy and thriving and alive."

Tears now flowed down Ellen's pale cheeks. "You... you really think my Burt killed that man and kidnapped that child?"

"What do you think, Ellen?" asked Aunt Lenore sharply. "What do you think Burt Morrison would do if he found out that his very own daughter had married a black man? What do you think?"

Ellen sobbed uncontrollably now, holding her hands over her face as if to suppress the horror. "I know...I know... I know..." Finally, her hands slipped down and she stared straight ahead with a blank expression. Then in a quiet yet horrified voice she spoke. "I *know* what Burt would do."

Judith put her arm around Ellen's shoulders. "But it's not your fault, Ellen."

Ellen's hands clenched into fists, and she turned to face Judith with red-rimmed eyes. "But I should've known better," she seethed. "I should've seen this coming. I never should have let things go so far. I should've protected my children from him." She looked down into her lap again. "I was a bad mother. I let Burt push me around too much. I let Burt push us all around. I never stood up to him. Not one single day in my entire life. I never said a word. And look where it's got us." She began crying again.

This time Judith just sat there in silence, simply letting Ellen cry. She glanced uncomfortably over to where Aunt Lenore sat rocking across from her. Judith raised her brows as if to question what she should do, how she should proceed. But Aunt Lenore simply nodded her chin, dipping it down slowly, as if to say, it's all right, just let her cry. And so she did.

After several minutes, Ellen blotted her eyes with what was now a very soggy handkerchief and turned to Judith. "Where is my granddaughter?"

"We're not really sure, Ellen."

"But you said someone is looking for her?"

"Yes." Judith wondered how to say this, "And there's something else you should know, Ellen. You see, Pearl has no living relatives on her father's side. And I have asked my friend to look into the possibility of me having her—I mean to adopt and to raise her as my own child."

"You would do that? You would take her in as your own?"

Judith's eyes flashed with anger. "You mean because her skin is of a slightly different hue? Do you actually believe that could stop me from loving her, Ellen? The fact is, it would probably only make me love her more. That combined with the fact that she is Jasmine's daughter! I know I put on a good show while I was staying out at the lake, but that's all it was, Ellen. Just a big show!" Her voice grew louder. "The truth is, I've got friends of all kinds, different races, religions, ethnic backgrounds. And color doesn't matter to me in the least. I believe God made us all different because he saw the beauty in it. And I wouldn't care if Pearl were green or purple or spotted! It just doesn't matter to me! Do you understand that?"

Ellen was leaning back now, her eyes widened with stunned silence, and Judith realized that she had actually been yelling. "I'm sorry for shouting," she said in a quieter voice. "But as you can see, this is something I feel quite passionate about. And if it's at all possible I *will* adopt Pearl, and I *will* raise her as my own daughter. And I *will* do all I can to help her to remember her mother."

"But what about a grandmother?"

"I'm sure my mother would be honored to be Pearl's adopted grandmother."

"But what about me?" Her voice sounded like a little girl again.

"Are you saying that you could be a loving grandmother to a child of mixed race?"

"But she's my baby's baby."

"Yes, Ellen." Judith's voice softened. "She was Jasmine's beloved Pearl." She reached over to her nearby bags and lifted up the jewelry box, removing the packet of photos. "Would you like to see her picture?"

Ellen nodded, eagerly reaching for the photos. One by-one, she examined them all, fresh tears spilling down her face as she did. Finally she slipped them back into the envelope. "She's a pretty little thing."

"But what about her skin color?" asked Judith, closely observing Ellen's response for any sign of negativity.

Ellen glanced over to Aunt Lenore and smiled a little smile. "I already told Judith about how our ancestors had a little mixed blood." Then she giggled. "Well, I think our little Pearl will fit in just fine. Don't you?"

"But what about Burt?" asked Aunt Lenore, her head cocked to one side.

"Well..." Ellen fingered her limp handkerchief. "I don't 'spect we'll be seeing much of Burt."

"And how does *that* make you feel?" asked Judith.

"I'm...I'm not completely sure. But it might be just as well since right now I'm feeling mighty vexed at that man." She sighed heavily. "It might be just as well that they've got him locked up."

Just then, the phone rang, and Judith jumped to answer it.

"Hey, Judith, you're there," said Adam, his voice bursting with excitement. "You won't believe this!"

"What?"

"I think we've located your lost Pearl."

"Are you serious?"

"Yes. And I just gave this woman a call—trying to sound her out, you know, and you'll never believe it, but she thinks I'm responding to some ad she ran in the paper. It sounds like she was planning on selling Pearl to the highest bidder or something equally moronic."

"You're kidding!"

"No she sounds like a real nut case to me."

"When can we leave?"

"I've got a flight booked for 3:50. Can you make it?"

"Yes. I'm on my way."

Judith hung up the phone and scooped up her bags. Halfway to the door, she turned and cried out, "They've found Pearl!"

"Wonderful!" Aunt Lenore clapped her hands together.

"And I'm on my way to get her." Judith paused to throw her purse over one shoulder.

"You'll bring her back here, won't you?" asked Ellen.

"Ellen, are you sure you can handle this?" Judith paused with her hand on the doorknob. "I refuse to risk hurting this child again—not for you or anyone."

"But she's my own flesh and blood," pleaded Ellen. "I swear to you I will do nothing to hurt her."

"I think we can trust Ellen," said Aunt Lenore with reassurance. "You just go and bring that baby back here and let us show you how much we can love her."

Judith smiled. "I'll see what I can do."

"And we'll be praying," promised Aunt Lenore.

"Yes, we will," echoed Ellen.

"Good. I'm sure we'll need it." Judith paused by the door. "I'll let you know as soon as I can how it goes."

Forty

DEAR GOD, YOU DONE heard me after all, didn't you? I know that now, and I'm real thankful you be a good listener even when I thought you weren't. Now, I know I didn't say that just right, with good grammar and all, like Miss Martha next door to Grandma's keep reminding me I should do. And I be trying, God, but it be hard when you used to a certain way—like how that ol' mean Carmen used to talk. But Judith say that in time I will forget all about them old days, and before long I'll learn to talk just like the rest of my new family and friends. And she told me that my mama and my daddy both talked with good grammar so that it should come natural to me before long. And so I be hopeful—I mean, I am hopeful. See, I am trying, God.

And speaking of Judith, God, I have to tell you that when I first saw her—when she come downstairs with Miss Molly and find me hiding in my cardboard box down there in that smelly old basement, well, my first thought was that my mama had finally come and got me. Why, I just jumped outta that box and spread my arms and cried out, "Mama!" And she just grabbed me and hugged me and started crying and everything. But then later on she told me that she wasn't really my mama, but that she loved me and she loved my mama and that they were like sisters—closer than sisters. In fact, she told me how they made a promise to always be true to each other and that they poked their fingers and became real, live blood sisters. She even showed me the place where they did it right underneath the big maple tree. And she told me that makes her like a blood relative to me. And I like that. Because I love her, God.

And even though I'm real sad that my mama be dead, I mean, that my mama is dead, Judith told me that my mama's up there in heaven with you and my daddy and that they are real happy up there and that they look down on me and they smile with pride. And, as it turns out, Judith's got her some family up there too. She's got a husband and a little boy who was just a little older than me when he died. She says one day we'll all be together, but until then we gotta love each other and all our other good friends down here.

And, let me tell you, I got me some good friends, God. Like there's Uncle Eli. Judith said he's been her friend since they were just kids. And he's got two great big boys. And I'm sure you know Uncle Eli real good 'cause he talks to you all the time. He's going to be starting a church real soon too. We saw the building he's going to be using, and we all met there last week to pray that you would bless it real good. And I'm sure you will. And then there's my Grandma Ellen and Aunt Lenore. They're both real nice and make really good cookies and things. And I even have another Grandma and Grandpa that I just met a couple weeks ago. They live right next to the beach, and they're real nice too. So I got all sorts of folks to love me now. Why, I feel just like those people I used to watch on the TV set—you know, the ones with all the family and friends and smiling faces. Only this is for real!

And here's something else I gotta thank you for, God. It's almost fall now, and I get to go to kindergarten in a real school! It's the same school that my mama and Judith used to go to when they were just little girls. And Judith is going to be a teacher there. She say that way she can keep her eye on me. And I like that.

But here's the thing I really want to thank you for, God:

Today, Judith adopted me as her very own little girl. We went in and signed all the papers that makes it really real. Adam went with us too. He's a really cool guy, and I think he loves Judith. He's the chief of the Cedar Crest Police Department, so he's really important and he makes everyone in this town obey the law. But he's really nice to me.

So, now that I'm all adopted, I asked Judith if this means I should start calling her "Mama." She said that she would love it if I did, but that it was up to me. And now I'm wondering, God, is it right for me to call her "Mama"? I mean, I can barely remember my real mama, but I don't want to make her feel bad. And seeing that you're right there with her, maybe you know what's right to do. But I do love Judith, God, and I'm real thankful you helped her to find me. She told me that it was all because of you and my mama that we're together now. And I told her about all those times when I was praying to you and sometimes I wondered if you were even listening. But you were listening, God. I know that now.

After Judith adopted me, we went to a party that Miss Martha planned for us to celebrate. And it was just like a birthday party (although my birthday is really in April) but everybody there gave me presents and all sorts of things. And it was really fun. I felt just like a real, live princess. And then when it was all done, Judith gave me another present (and that's after she already gave me something). But she gave me a real pretty box that used to belong to my mama, and a necklace that my daddy got for her a long, long time ago. And some other things. Keepsakes, she called them. She said she also had a letter from my mama that I can read when I'm older and know how to read, which shouldn't be long because between Miss Martha and Judith

I already learned my letters and can even sound out some easy words like dog and cat and nap.

So anyway, I'm thinking right now God, that it's okay for me to call Judith "Mama" too. I'm thinking my mama up there with you must love Judith just as much as I do. I'm thinking she must be awful glad that Judith came and found me. So, I think I'm gonna do it, God. I'm gonna go tell Judith right now that I want to call her "Mama"!

Thanks for listening, God. I know now that you always be listening—no matter what it might seem like sometimes. I love you, God! Amen!

Dear Reader,

I KNOW I HAVE taken you on a journey that's not been exactly light and easy. Yet I thank you for joining me. I realize this story tackles some difficult issues, but my goal was to present them as honestly as possible. For, you see, this story was inspired from real life—a tale I felt compelled to tell. And I pray I have handled it well.

Some of you may have been surprised and naturally dismayed to learn that Jasmine actually did take her life. But I encourage you to remember Jesus' warning about judging others (even in fiction). We, as the observers, can plainly see that Jasmine was deceived (by her own father) and actually believed the lie. As a result, she lost out on what was dearest to her (reuniting with her only child). But we need to remember such tragedies do happen in real life. And unless we've walked in another's shoes and fully experienced her hopelessness and pain, how can we ever fully understand her struggles?

Perhaps the best lesson we can learn from Jasmine's death is that we should never give up—never lose hope that our Father in heaven can redeem anything. He always has a better plan for our lives. Judith brings this home to us in the way she begins the story imbedded in her own hopelessness. But then, as a result of her. dear friend's death, she is pulled back into the land of living—and eventually finds hope.

So, once again, I thank you for reading *Blood Sisters*. And I pray that God will use this story in an extraordinary way in your life.

May God bless you and keep you and shine His loving light upon you!

Melody Carlson
Melody Carlson

Also from Melody Carlson:

HOMEWARD

ONE

FROM THE CORNER OF her eye, Meg noticed the flashing blue light in her rearview mirror. She glanced down to check the speedometer and exhaled an impatient breath. Just what she needed—a nice welcome home. She pulled off the freeway, tires skidding in the loose gravel.

The patrolman sauntered up. "Howdy, ma'am," he said with a slight drawl. She greeted him and wondered why some people in southern Oregon sounded like they were from Texas. And why was it that highway patrolmen all seemed to have mustaches?

"License and registration, please," he said. Rain coated his plastic-covered cowboy hat, dribbling down the brim and straight into her car. He obviously had no concern about the damage water could do to leather upholstery. She fumbled with her billfold, then handed him her card and registration with a forced smile.

"Sorry, Officer. You see, I haven't had this car for too long, and I'm still getting used to the cruise control." Not completely true, but worth a shot. Meg smiled again.

"Uh-huh. Nice wheels," he murmured, then moved to the front

of her Jaguar to copy the plates. A semi rushed past, spewing a dirty, oily spray onto the sleeve of her silk blouse and into her car. She clenched her teeth, but forced another saccharine smile as the patrolman returned to her window. Maybe there was still a chance he would go easy on her.

"Thing is," he began evenly as he handed her the ticket, "fancy cars like this smash up just the same as any ol' junker. Sometimes worse. I see you're from San Francisco; maybe you didn't know these roads are extra slick up here today. We hadn't had a drop of rain for two weeks. Unusual for March. But I clocked you at eighty-six."

She muttered a cold thanks, with no hint of a smile this time. He tipped his dripping hat and returned to his car. She stared at the name printed neatly across the top of the ticket—*Alexandra Megan Lancaster*. Someone else's name. The *Alexandra* part was from her grandmother, something she'd once been proud of.

Suddenly her chest tightened with the urge to scream. Not over the stupid speeding ticket; no, that would be too simple. This unwelcome rage was vaguely familiar, but it surprised her just the same. She had worked so hard all these years to forget such tiresome things. Was she inviting it all back now, simply by returning?

In another lifetime, she had promised herself she would never return. But this was not the time to dredge up old memories. That would only send her back to San Francisco, and she wasn't ready for that. She needed a break to clear her head, and perhaps it was time to clear up some other things as well. Or at least to try. So she pulled back onto the freeway and decided to blame it on Jerred. Fair or not, it really was his fault that for the first time in nearly twenty years she was going home—at least the closest thing to home she had ever known.

To distract herself, she thought about Jerred. Had it been only two years since he had stepped into her life? It seemed like longer. But then she had just turned thirty-five when they met. How she had celebrated that milestone. Only thirty-five, and at the top of her field. She had carefully played the corporate game and climbed high in the San Francisco advertising firm. And her reward had been a luxurious office with a private bathroom and an assistant who was somewhat efficient. It was all she'd ever hoped for. Wasn't it?

She considered the brief spell in college when she had fantasized about a more creative career: she'd live in a loft in some interesting part of the city and pursue photography or maybe journalism. But she had quickly returned to her senses, reminding herself that such thoughts were probably just carried over from her unconventional upbringing. And by the end of college, money had become important. With bills to juggle and loans to repay, the field of advertising offered the financial security she longed for.

When she first hired on with Montgomery and Tate, she had thought perhaps she'd stay on until her finances were in line, but it didn't take long before she acquired an appetite for the things that money could buy. It was the first time she'd ever worn designer labels and real Italian shoes. And Meg liked being around people who had money. Even more, she liked the power that accompanied that money. It seemed to surround and insulate those who had it. Working twelve-hour days hardly fazed her because she came to believe it was her ticket into their world, a world she had only viewed by pressing her nose to the window.

Then the "golden boy" joined his daddy's firm, and Mr. Montgomery asked her to work with his son—to show him the ropes, so to speak. She'd been somewhat flattered, yet understandably cautious. This upstart wasn't going to pilfer her job. But Jerred Montgomery, with his impeccable manners and boyish charm, quickly won her trust and later—she grimaced at the triteness—her heart. How had she been such a fool? She should have known better. For starters, he was almost ten years younger than she. Why hadn't she recognized that red flag? But Jerred always assured her that "age was a nonfactor." And Meg knew she looked better at thirty-five than ever.

They'd gotten engaged on a picture-perfect New Year's Eve. Jerred's parents had invited them to Lake Tahoe for the holidays, and there was snow on the ground and stars in the sky. She immediately started planning a summer wedding, but then Jerred moved it back. First October, then Christmas—he always had another reason to postpone it. She was patient, turning her energy back to work, making her future father-in-law happier—and richer. Meanwhile, Jerred assured her that being together was what counted. Unfortunately, it didn't count for anything last week. That was when she discovered he was having an affair with his twenty-something secretary, Tiffany.

In her more honest moments, Meg could admit she'd known it even before Tiffany. In some ways, Tiffany provided Meg with the perfect excuse.

Mr. Montgomery had been so kind and fatherly about the whole thing. It only made it harder. The Montgomerys were a fine family, and she once hoped they would become the family she'd always longed for. Meg didn't actually tell Mr. Montgomery about Jerred's part in the breakup, but when he so quickly consented to her month's leave of absence with no loss of position or benefits, she felt certain he knew. Just the same, he made her promise to return as soon as possible. "We don't want to lose you to Crandale permanently," he told her with a kind smile.

Meg frowned as she turned off the freeway toward the coast. Suddenly, it seemed a pretty dismal choice—Crandale or Jerred.

It was Meg's sister, Erin, who had given her the final nudge. The note was actually three months old, something Erin had slipped into a Christmas card, and Meg had only skimmed it at the time. But right after the trouble with Jerred, Meg went on a full-scale cleaning binge in her tiny apartment. She discovered the wrinkled note underneath her sofa. Then suddenly, as she reread the part about her grandmother's deteriorating health, it seemed the perfect excuse. It would allow her to escape San Francisco for a couple of weeks and thus avoid some messy confrontations.

Meg had not warned her sister of this impending visit. She seldom wrote to Erin, and in almost twenty years never phoned her. This sparse communication was Meg's stipulation a long time ago. She originally gave Erin her address with the clear understanding that Erin would never mention it, or their infrequent correspondence, to the rest of her family.

This severing from the family had been important to Meg. And she liked the anonymity—at first. It made her feel free. Jerred had once questioned her lack of family connections, so unlike his close-knit clan. But then his family wouldn't have understood hers, and that had been one more reason to keep them closeted.

The rain stopped, and directly ahead, above the ridge of a fir-covered hill, opened a slit of clear sky so bright it almost hurt her eyes. Meg dug in her purse for sunglasses. The sunlight illuminated the lush fields, creating an almost unreal shade of green. Every leaf and blade of grass seemed to leap out. It was one of her favorite scenes—the rain-washed countryside backdropped by a leaden sky and then spotlighted by the sun. If only she had a camera handy, she would shoot this panorama over and over until she got it just right.

Meg opened the window and let the fresh air blow in. The cool, wet smell reminded her of childhood. How many times had they trekked off to the coast in their rickety old Volkswagen Bug during spring break? Of course, it was only after she and Erin had spent days of strategic pleading and begging to entice Sunny to "please take them to Crandale." Living on a college campus in the radical sixties had seemed less than ideal to Meg, but for some reason Sunny seemed to thrive upon the unrest and would have never considered giving up her professorship in the University of Oregon's art department.

Meg's refuge came in the form of Grandpa's house. They had always called it Grandpa's house. Everyone knew the house belonged to Grandpa and the dress shop belonged to Grandmother. As a child, she never questioned the carefully divided ownership within her grandparents' marriage, or even the nontraditional roles they both lived so naturally. But then nothing in Meg's family had ever been what "should be." Sometimes she imagined she was Alice, living on the other side of the looking glass, where everything was backwards.

At Grandpa's house there seemed to exist some magical element, and Erin and Meg always had high expectations when they went there. Maybe it was because Grandpa truly loved children, or maybe it was just the comforting familiarity of the small coastal town. The two girls spent every vacation moment in Crandale while Sunny took classes and finished graduate school and then started teaching. Grandpa always did the cooking, fixing special dishes they never saw at home. The little cleaning that was done in the big old Victorian house was done by Grandpa's hand as well, but it never bothered Meg that there were cobwebs in corners or that you could write your name on the dusty end tables. Because the best part of staying at Grandpa's was being outside.

Grandpa's grandfather had purchased the several hundred acres right after the turn of the century. He named it Briar Hedge because there was a slight rise between the property and the ocean where a long, thick wall of wild blackberries had grown profusely. Those particular blackberries had been removed long ago, but there were always more than enough blackberry patches to be found close by. The real purpose of Briar Hedge was cranberries. And Meg's favorite thing as a child was to help Grandpa in the cranberry bog. He always made sure a pair of big rubber boots was waiting for her. And when they made the trip into town for supplies, he always let her drive the old truck down the beach road.

Maybe going back wouldn't be so dreadful. Why had she put it off all these years? Sure, some ugly things had been said at Grandpa's funeral, but that was almost twenty years ago. The accusations had been cruel and hateful, spoken in the heat of anger. Some by her, some not. But Grandmother could be dying now. It was time to forgive and forget. Perhaps this would help the old woman go in peace—even if it meant Meg's taking the brunt of the blame. She knew Grandmother would gladly allow that. Besides, it might be worth taking the blame if it would help her avoid that debilitating feeling of guilt, the kind she'd experienced after Grandpa's death.

Meg turned off the main road when she saw the old sign before her. It looked just the same as in the old days, only now it was freshly painted in bright, cheerful colors: *Welcome to Crandale, Home of the Cranberry Carnival.*

She hoped the sign was right. Would she really be welcome?

About the Author

MELODY CARLSON IS THE bestselling author of more than 200 books, including the Diary of a Teenage Girl series. She has won various awards for her writing, including the Gold Medallion and The Rita Award, which was won for Homeward. She and her husband divide their time between the beautiful Cascade Mountains and the coast of Oregon. Writing is both her work and passion.

Made in the USA
Lexington, KY
15 October 2013

A Day in the Life of a Television News Reporter

WILLIAM JASPERSOHN

A Day in the Life of a Television News Reporter

Little, Brown and Company

BOSTON   TORONTO

By William Jaspersohn

A Day in the Life of a Veterinarian

How the Forest Grew

The Ballpark
One Day Behind the Scenes at a Major League Game

A Day in the Life of a Television News Reporter

FIRST EDITION

Library of Congress Cataloging in Publication Data

Jaspersohn, William.
    A day in the life of a television news reporter.

    1. Television broadcasting of news — Juvenile literature. 2. Rea, Daniel J., 1948–
— Juvenile literature. I. Title.
PN4784.T4J37   070'.92'4 [B]   80-26203
ISBN 0-316-45813-9

HOR

*Published simultaneously in Canada
by Little, Brown & Company (Canada) Limited*

PRINTED IN THE UNITED STATES OF AMERICA

Preface

NEWS! NEWS! NEWS! We are bombarded by it, flooded
with fresh information daily. Pick up a newspaper, flick on a
radio, and out it pours: news. In the case of television, night
after night, its newscasters virtually troop into our homes.
And we welcome them — the superstars, Walter Cronkite,
Barbara Walters, John Chancellor, and our own favorites
from local stations. Indeed, no matter what our feelings about
the medium may be, few would deny that television has become the most popular and powerful source of news in
America.

Who, then, are these news gatherers whom we invite into
our homes night after night? What do they do all day? How
much work goes into airing a single nightly newscast? What
kind of person is drawn to this field that has been so watched,
studied, and criticized in recent years?

In search of answers to these questions, I contacted the
management of WBZ-TV in Boston, Massachusetts, and inquired if I might watch one of their reporters at work. They
agreed; and because I knew and admired his work, I asked to
be introduced to Dan Rea.

Luckily for me, Dan consented to be the subject of this
book. I began going out on stories with him in the late summer of 1979. I discovered that, like me, Dan was a baseball
fan, lived and died with the fortunes of the Boston Red Sox,
jogged, played tennis, liked seafood. We quickly became
friends. Throughout our travels and through all my endless
note- and picture-taking, what impressed me most about Dan
Rea — and still impresses me — was his professionalism. He
cares about his job, does it well. I hope that that fact shows
in this book.

I'd like to take this opportunity to thank Dan for his splendid cooperation and help, and to thank also everyone I worked with at WBZ news. I owe a particular debt of gratitude to Sy Yanoff, WBZ's manager, who said yes to this project; and to Ann Finucane and Jolan Schmauss, who were my liaisons with the newsroom. Many thanks to Jack Feeley, Richard Bevilacqua, and Wayne Moores for allowing me to photograph on the roof of the Hancock Tower in downtown Boston; and to John Carroll and the staffs at the Front Page in Charlestown and Memory Lane restaurant in Manchester, New Hampshire, for their kind hospitality and friendship. Ward Rice, as always, worked his wonderful darkroom magic, printing the photographs for this book; Pam — bless you for being — was and is always a guide and a comfort; and Andrew consented to delay his arrival into this world long enough for his father to finish this book.

Finally, love to my brother Ron, to whom this book is dedicated.

TELEVISION REPORTERS lead exciting lives. On any day they may find themselves assigned to interview famous people, or to travel to distant news sites, or to report on major fires and other disasters. Since news stories can break at any time, TV reporters often lead suspenseful lives, too, never knowing when or where their next assignment will be.

Dan Rea loves the reporting life. He's a news reporter for TV station WBZ in Boston, and his regular assignment, or *beat*, as it's called, is the city itself.

Usually Dan works from 3:30 to 11:00 P.M., but sometimes his day starts earlier.

At ten o'clock on a warm August morning, Dan is awakened by a phone call from the assignment desk at WBZ. Dan gropes for the ringing phone; he is tired. Two nights ago he worked twenty-four hours without sleep, covering a story about a plane crash on Cape Cod, and he still hasn't caught up on his rest.

Could he come in early? asks the assignment editor. A reporter is out sick today, and the news department could use some extra help. Could Dan maybe come in at noon?

"Sure," Dan replies, and hangs up the phone.

He dozes till nearly eleven, then showers, eats, and dresses in a rush. He is already wondering what his day's assignment will be as he drives the five miles from his apartment to the station.

You don't necessarily have to go to college to become a television news reporter, but for those who do, there are schools with courses in broadcast journalism throughout the United States.

Dan Rea didn't study broadcast journalism in college. Instead, he majored in English at Boston State College, and then earned a law degree from Boston University. While he studied law he wrote a regular political column for the *Boston Globe*, and later he hosted a call-in talk show on current events for WBZ radio. He discovered he liked broadcasting — indeed, had a flair for it — and not long after graduating from law school, he began reporting for WBZ television. Today he is regarded as one of the best TV reporters in Boston, and his news stories are seen five nights a week by hundreds of thousands of viewers throughout New England.

When he arrives at the station, he usually stops and chats
with Fred, the security guard at the main door.

There is always mail in Dan's mailbox at the end of the hall. Often viewers write to say how much they liked the way he covered a certain story, but sometimes letters are critical. Dan reads all his mail, but his busy schedule often prevents him from answering every letter he'd like.

As always, the newsroom is a hive of activity when Dan arrives. Typewriters clackety-clack, phones ring, people mill and shout — to an outsider it might seem bewildering. But in

fact, everybody here has a special job, and somehow five times a day it all works. Their energy works. The news is gathered and aired.

Two men oversee all this bustle: the assistant news director, and his boss, the news director. The news director hires
workers for the newsroom, oversees its budget, and controls
the general style and makeup of the news shows. The assistant
news director makes more of the day-to-day decisions about
what news stories get aired, but both these men are Dan
Rea's bosses.

The person who organizes the news stories into a complete news show is known as a *producer*. The producers of the three evening news programs, where Dan's reports appear, are Pam Kahn, Pat Kreger, and Ken Tucci. Since time is limited during a news show — each show lasts only a half hour or an hour — one of the producers' main jobs is making sure the time in each show is properly used.

While Dan checks his mail, several reporters who work earlier shifts have already gone out and come back with their day's news stories. Peter Mehegan types a story about a bank robbery that occurred early this morning, while Gail Harris reads a piece she has written about noise pollution near Logan Airport. Walt Sanders, meanwhile, uses a stopwatch and a machine called a *video playback* to time some videotape footage he will use for a story about nuclear power plants.

Like any newsroom, WBZ's is equipped with machines called *Teletype terminals*, which print news stories from all over the world. These terminals are watched mostly by the hosts of the news shows, the *anchors*, but Dan and his fellow reporter Andy Hiller enjoy reading the stories, too.

Dan is pouring himself a glass of soda when the assignment editor, Jerry, calls him over to the assignment desk.

"I just heard a call over the police radio," says Jerry. "The police have just raided a warehouse in Jamaica Plain, and it sounds as if they found some stolen goods."

"Any arrests?" asks Dan.

"Haven't heard," says Jerry. "But I think we should check it out."

"Could make a good story," Dan agrees.

"Okay," says Jerry, "here's the address." He slides Dan a small slip of paper. "I've called a cab for you," Jerry continues, "and there'll be a cameraman at the warehouse when you arrive. Now, this may be a big story or it may not. But once you've shot some film inside the warehouse and interviewed the police, give me a call. Let me know what you've got."

"Do we want something for the six o'clock news?" asks Dan.

Jerry nods. Dan pockets the slip of paper, grabs his jacket off his desk, and off he goes to cover a story about a police raid in Jamaica Plain.

He picks up a fresh reporter's note pad from the stockroom, then steps into his cab, which is waiting by the back door. Reporters at WBZ travel by taxi to many story locations. Dan finds cabs good places to think about stories and take notes; and luckily, the station pays the fare.

Fifteen minutes later the cab cruises up to the Jamaica Plain address, and Dan finds himself alone in front of a three-story warehouse. It is quiet. Dan's footsteps click on the pavement as he walks to the warehouse door, rattles it, and finds it locked.

Undiscouraged, he follows an alley along the side of the building and makes his way around back.

There, he finds his cameraman, Dick Felone, already
shooting footage of the warehouse. The device Dick uses is
a 16-millimeter-film camera that comes with a microphone
and can record sounds and pictures simultaneously. Since TV
reporters tell their stories with pictures as well as words, the
cameraman is an extremely important member of the news
team. Dick is one of WBZ's veteran cameramen, with more
than sixteen years' experience in the field.

Filming a wide area is known as *spraying* in camera lan-
guage, and once this job is done, Dick and Dan walk to the
warehouse's rear entrance.

Soon, other reporters, for radio, newspapers, and television, begin arriving at the warehouse. Like WBZ's, their assignment desks, too, are equipped with shortwave radios, and that is how they first got word of the police raid.

At first, the police detectives, who are inside the warehouse, ask Dan and the others to wait outside for a few minutes. Then Boston Deputy Police Inspector Anthony DiNatale, who is in charge of the case, steps out to brief the press. He tells them the raid occurred at approximately eleven o'clock this morning, and that stolen goods worth more than $250,000 were discovered. He will answer questions later, he says. For now, he tells the cameramen that they may film inside, but asks everyone to promise not to touch anything because the crime lab is still dusting the stolen goods for fingerprints. Everyone promises.

Deputy DiNatale then says, "You're welcome to step inside, gentlemen."

Everyone enters the warehouse, eager to see the thieves' hideout.

Sure enough, just as the deputy said, there are the stolen goods. "That sports car alone is worth forty-five thousand dollars!" someone whispers. Elsewhere, there are skis, ski boots, a boat, a camp trailer, radios, power tools — all allegedly stolen from stores and homes and hidden here. Even to an untrained eye it looks like the work of professionals — people in the business of stealing things and selling them for profit. But when you're a reporter you must withhold quick judgments. Dan draws no conclusions until he can talk with Deputy DiNatale.

Dan looks around carefully and takes notes of what he sees, and meanwhile, Dick films everything in the warehouse. What Dick is doing is *overshooting*, that is, shooting more film than necessary. That way, he knows Dan will have enough film with which to assemble his story.

Once the filming is done, Dan and the others step out into the sunshine to interview Deputy DiNatale.

Before they can write their stories, good reporters must have answers to five basic questions: Who? What? When? Where? and Why? Now, Dan knows the *what* of this story: the stolen goods. He knows *when* the police raided the building: at eleven o'clock this morning. And he knows *why* the raid happened: because Deputy DiNatale says the building has been under surveillance for a long while. Now Dan asks the deputy if the police know *who* stole the goods, and the deputy replies that he's not at liberty to say. But he can say that the work is that of professionals, and arrests are expected soon.

Dick films this interview. Then, when his questions have been answered, Dan thanks the deputy, and he and Dick leave.

As always after he's finished at a story location, Dan uses the camera car's portable shortwave radio to call Jerry at the assignment desk and tell him what kind of report to expect.

"KCG eight-three-nine: this is seven-seven-five-two."

"Come in, seven-seven-five-two."

"We're through here at Jamaica Plain," radios Dan; he describes what's in the warehouse. "I think we should plan on showing maybe a minute of film while an anchor does a live, voice-over reading of the story."

"Do you have a filmed interview?" asks Jerry.

"Yes," replies Dan, "with the police deputy. That'll be part of the minute."

"What about arrests?" asks Jerry.

"Forthcoming," answers Dan.

"Okay," says Jerry, "sounds good. I'll tell the producer to give your story a minute. See you in fifteen?"

"See you in fifteen," says Dan. "Over and out."

Dan now rides back to the station in the camera car with
Dick Felone. Once back, he heads directly for his typewriter
while Dick rushes the film to the station's film laboratory for
processing. The film is run through ten different chemical
tanks, and is developed and ready to use in twenty minutes.

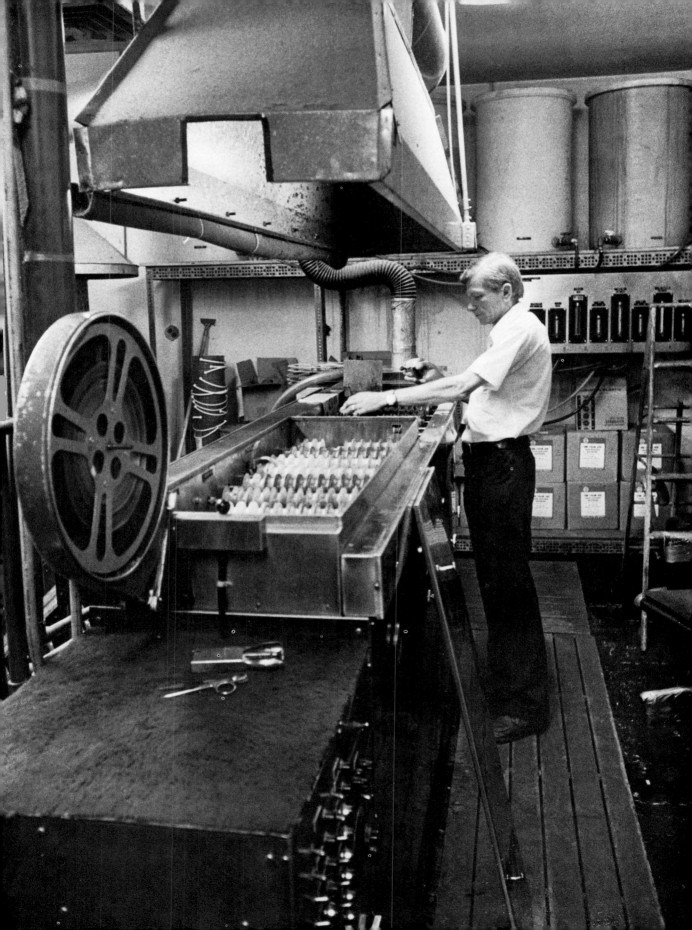

Meanwhile, from the careful notes he took at the warehouse, Dan writes his story of the police raid. Good reporters must know how to write fast and clearly, and Dan says that for him the hardest part of writing is finding an opening, or *lead line*. Once he has that, he says, the rest of the writing comes quickly.

Now he curls his fingers over the typewriter keys and writes: BOSTON POLICE RECOVERED A QUARTER MILLION DOLLARS IN STOLEN GOODS TODAY AT A JAMAICA PLAIN WAREHOUSE. . . .

And *that* will be his lead line! He begins typing his story.

While he does this, the film editor, Jack, receives Dan's film from the film lab. Jack checks the film for flaws, then waits for Dan so the two of them can choose the right scenes for the warehouse story.

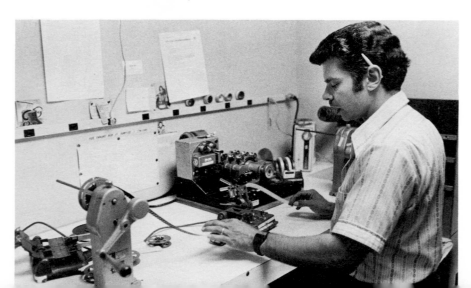

Twenty minutes later, Dan finishes his script, which he hands to the six o'clock news producer, Pat. She in turn will discuss the stolen-goods story with the assistant news director, who will agree it should appear in the beginning, or *A-section*, of the show.

Dan now goes to the editing room to choose a minute's worth of film for the words he has written. In just a few hours, both words and film will be broadcast to hundreds of thousands of viewers throughout New England.

Crime stories aren't the only kind of reporting a TV reporter does. At any time, day or night, he may be called on to cover a fire or other catastrophe.

Once Dan was awakened at 5:00 A.M. to cover a fire that had broken out on a pier in the Charlestown area of Boston. Amid the blare of the fireboats' horns and the pall of smoke, he interviewed Boston Fire Captain John Collins, who, unlike some people Dan interviews, is always cooperative, and answered all of Dan's questions. Luckily, the blaze injured no one.

The news events most frequently covered by TV reporters are meetings of one kind or another. At least once a week Dan can expect to be present at some meeting hall in Boston, taking notes, listening, and watching. Since a reporter can't possibly describe *everything* that happens in a meeting, he and his crew try to capture its main ideas, or *essence*. Before entering a hall Dan always asks himself, "What is this meeting for?" then tries to answer his own question.

Meetings can get emotional. Once Dan covered a meeting of a group called Fair Share, who were worried about reports that the oil companies wouldn't have enough heating oil for Boston during the winter. They questioned representatives of a major oil company, who tried to explain why heating oil was scarce, but many people remained worried, and some were angry.

Another common source of news for any reporter is a press conference. These special meetings for reporters are designed to give them information and answer questions about particular newsworthy topics. When Pope John Paul II announced plans to visit Boston on a tour of American cities, the Boston Catholic Archdiocese organized a press conference given by Humberto Cardinal Medeiros, which Dan attended. Cardinal Medeiros answered Dan's and other reporters' questions about the Pope's visit, then unveiled a model of the altar the Pope would use to celebrate Mass on the Boston Common.

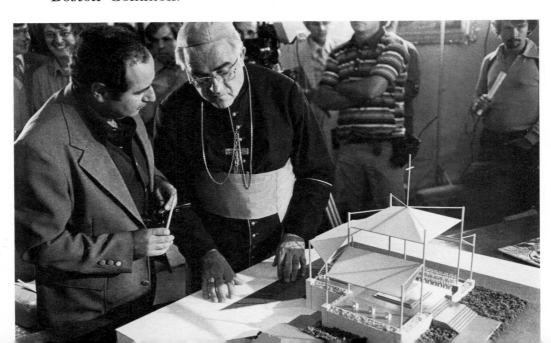

 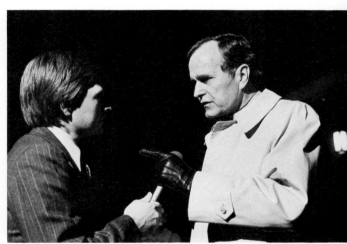

There are always news-making people to interview. Dan's favorite times are election years, because then he gets to interview all the presidential candidates. Sometimes these interviews can be difficult. Candidates usually don't have much time, so you must ask your questions as quickly and clearly as possible. Dan says that doing interviews has taught him that even famous people are human beings. "I'm not in awe of them," he says. "As a reporter, I can't be. In journalism, there's no place for hero worship."

For most of these occasions, Dan works with a two-man camera crew, who record his stories on videotape. While one person operates the video camera, the other receives the sound and picture signals on a videotape recorder. Videotape is perfect for television news because unlike film it doesn't need developing, and any sounds and pictures it records can be played back immediately. The only drawback is its cost. A single video camera, for instance, costs $50,000. Still, the station owns six of them.

It also owns four vans, each of which is outfitted with $100,000 worth of broadcast equipment.

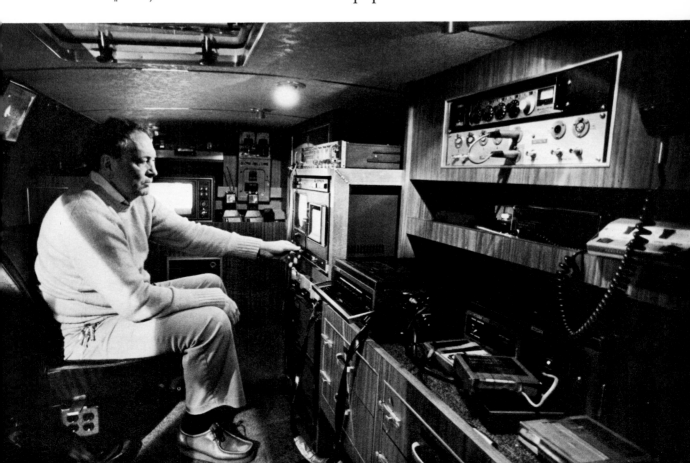

Using the van and its equipment, Dan and his crew can do what are known as *live shots*. Sound and picture signals are beamed as microwaves from a special dish on the van to an antenna atop a tall building. The antenna throws the signals to WBZ, which in turn broadcasts them to its viewers. Since all of this happens in microseconds, it means that Dan can report news "live," on the scene, instantly, as it happens.

Once he did a live shot from the Boston Common on Pope John Paul II's upcoming visit. The station cued him when to go on the air through an earphone he wore, and as he reported, he could watch himself on a special TV set called a *monitor*.

Dan likes live shots because going on the air live is challenging and fun. Dan foresees a time when all TV news will be introduced live by reporters at their story sites throughout the news broadcast.

Even now Dan always covers the Boston city elections live.

Once while Carl Yastrzemski of the Boston Red Sox tried for the three thousandth hit of his career, Dan reported live from Fenway Park for two nights. That was really exciting! Dan asked Yaz if he felt he was under much pressure, and Yaz said yes, but he tried to block it out when he went to bat. Dan thought Yaz looked tired but surprisingly relaxed. He wished Yaz good luck, and Yaz smiled and said, "Thanks," and Dan watched the game from up in the press box.

Surely the biggest live shot for Dan — and for the other reporters at WBZ — occurred on the day Pope John Paul II came to Boston. Dan was assigned to the rooftop of a building overlooking Boston Common, where the Pope would celebrate the Catholic religious ceremony known as the Mass. At dawn, many hours before the Pope arrived, Dan began reporting live.

At 7:00 A.M. police unlocked the Common's gates, and people who had been waiting all night began to stream in.

As the hours ticked by, Dan kept in touch with the station by telephone, or *land line*, as TV people call it. To keep track of the station's coverage at the airport and along the route the Pope's motorcade would take, Dan and his crew had their own TV monitor on the rooftop.

Finally, at four-thirty in the afternoon, ten hours after Dan delivered his first report, the Pope's motorcade came into view. Even non-Catholics were moved to applause by the sight of this gentle man.

The Pope almost seemed to wave to Dan and the crew as he passed below.

Dan got help describing the Mass to the TV audience from a friend and local priest, Father Richard Cunningham.

It poured rain during the Mass, but none of the quarter
million people on the Common seemed to mind.

News stories like the Pope's visit are perfect for television because there's so much to show and report. But unfortunately, says Dan, such stories just don't happen very often. So on days like today, Dan finds himself phoning sources — that is, checking for news tips from people he knows around the city.

Then he stops by the news studio to chat with Mel Robbins, WBZ's courtroom artist. Since cameras aren't always allowed while law courts are in session, artists like Mel are hired to do paintings right on the scene. These are paintings he did at a trial this morning, he tells Dan. Trying to paint portraits in a courtroom isn't easy, he says, because the subjects never seem to sit still.

Five o'clock. If Dan were anchoring the five-thirty news show, as he sometimes does when one of the regular anchors isn't in, he'd be in the men's room now, putting on his makeup. And then, perhaps with Shelby Scott, he'd be sitting in the studio, anchoring the news under the hot studio lights.

But all the anchors are in today, so instead, he and Charles Austin, who is WBZ's crime reporter, go to their favorite diner, the Pig and Whistle, for supper.

When they return to the station an hour later, Dan checks in at the assignment desk with the night assignment editor, Susan, who has a story for him, an intriguing one. The Teletypes are reporting that the one and a half million members of a national labor group called the United Auto Workers staged a protest today. They all stopped work for a few minutes to send postcards to the President and to their senators and congressmen, protesting the high cost of gasoline. At most factories throughout the nation the workers lost pay for the few minutes they took filling out the cards. But at an auto plant in Framingham, a town near Boston, workers filled out the cards and then, instead of going back to work, they all went home.

"They walked off their jobs," says Susan. "They're the only auto workers in the whole nation who did that. I phoned some of them, and they say the night shift may do the same thing."

"So we should be there in case they walk out," says Dan.

"Exactly," says Susan. "I've got a crew all lined up for you. The night workers are scheduled to fill out their postcards at seven-fifteen. If you could be there before then, in case they do walk off, you could find out why."

Dan promises Susan he will phone her the minute he has the story.

Dan's crew, meanwhile, has already packed van #3, known as the Eye-Three, and they're ready to go to Framingham. The crew consists of Art Donahue and Tom Rehkamp, two of the youngest cameramen at the station. Like many in their department, they both learned their jobs at smaller TV stations, then came to WBZ. To work full-time as a cameraman at any station, you must have a first-class communications license, which is issued by the federal government. And to get that license, you must show you understand TV electronics by passing a series of tests. Both Art and Tom have their first-class licenses. But each will tell you that the tests were very, very hard.

Everyone is ready, and a minute later, Dan walks out the door, and off he goes with Art and Tom in the Eye-Three van to Framingham.

Framingham is an industrial town, twenty miles west of Boston, whose chief industry is automobiles. Several American car companies have assembly plants there that employ many people in the area.

All the wage earners in these plants are members of the United Auto Workers labor union. Now, Dan knows about labor unions from his experience as a newsman. He knows they are formed to gain better wages, hours, and working conditions from companies for their members. He knows union members walk off their jobs only when they feel they have good reason to. So why are the workers at this one plant in Framingham walking off their jobs today? That is what Dan must find out.

At seven o'clock, fifteen minutes before the workers are scheduled to fill out their postcards, Dan and his crew arrive at the assembly plant. A guard gives them permission to enter the factory grounds.

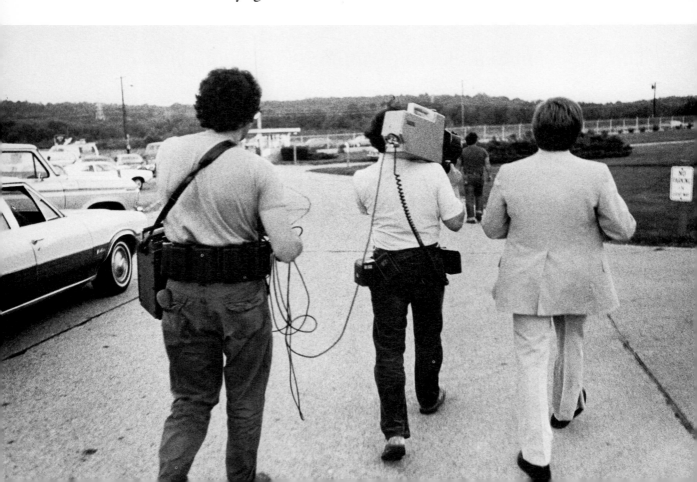

Art and Tom begin by using the video camera to "spray" the parking lot and factory area.

Then, without warning and ten minutes sooner than expected, the workers come out the door. They are walking off their jobs — fifteen hundred of them! Dan yells to Art and Tom, and with equipment clacking, they rush to interview the workers.

"Will you stop and talk on TV a minute?" Dan asks the workers. They brush past silently, unwilling to talk. But then one does stop, and Dan asks why he is walking off the job. The worker explains that he wants to show the members of Congress that they haven't been doing enough to control oil and gasoline prices. If these prices keep climbing, he says, it's going to hurt the auto industry. And that will hurt him and his fellow workers.

Dan stops another worker. "You're going to lose a half day's pay."

"It's better to lose a half day's pay now," says the worker, "than to be paying the price we're paying for gas and oil. It's ridiculous. They [the President and Congress] have got to do something. Maybe this might help. I hope it does."

Dan interviews more workers, and their answers are roughly the same: they are walking off the job to show Congress and the President they are fed up with the high price of gas and oil.

Now Dan, Art, and Tom hurry down to the gate to video-tape the workers driving from the plant. It is a loud and lively scene. Horns honk, workers shout, engines roar. Tom turns up the volume knob on the videotape recorder to capture this rich mix of sounds.

Art even lugs the camera up on the roof of the van and mounts it on a three-legged stand called a *tripod*. Cameramen are always searching for the best angle from which to shoot their subjects. This rooftop position gives Art a perfect view of the workers' departure.

Then Dan climbs up through the hatch to the roof of the van to do a *stand-up* for his story's ending. Stand-ups are simply views of the reporter talking into the camera, and they're mainly used for introducing or summing up a story. Dan has been thinking about what the workers at this plant have done today, and now he tries to sum it up quickly and with the help of Art's camera:

DAN
(*Gripping microphone, staring into camera*)

The automotive workers in Framingham both today and tonight had two separate messages for the politicians in Washington: one for them to *read* . . .

(*Dan holds up a copy of the postcards the workers filled out*)

DAN
. . . and one for them to *see*.

(*Camera pivots away from Dan to show the workers in their cars, driving off the job*)

DAN'S VOICE
(*As the cars whisk by, below*)

From the General Motors plant in Framingham, Dan Rea, TV-Four, Eyewitness News.

"Great!" shouts Art. "Good stand-up!"

"Was the sound okay?" asks Dan.

"Sound was fine," calls Tom from down below.

Dan is pleased. He now has shots of the factory, the workers walking off the job, the interviews with the workers, the cars leaving, and the stand-up. Like most stories, this one feels like a giant jigsaw puzzle. And now it's coming together. The pieces are falling into place.

"We all through?" asks Art, folding up the tripod.

"Not quite," answers Dan. "I'd like to talk about the walkout with an official from the United Auto Workers and a representative from the car company."

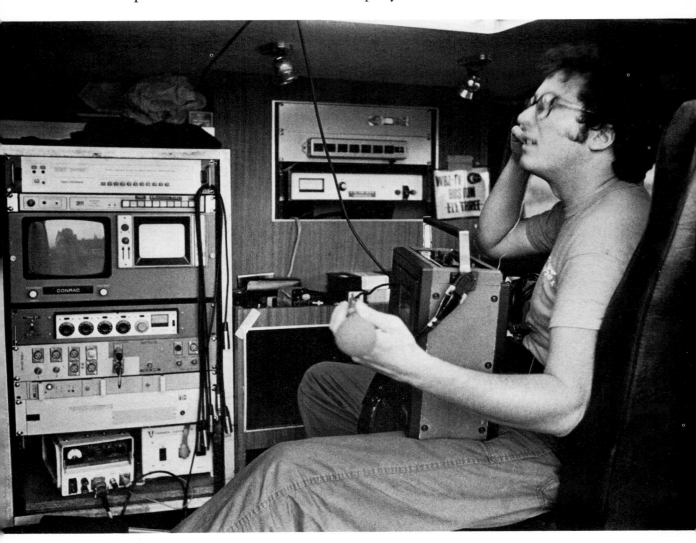

Both people, it happens, are back at the factory and quite willing to talk. The United Auto Workers official says he's surprised by the walkout. He didn't expect it, it just happened.

"Fifteen hundred people walked out spontaneously?" asks Dan.

"Exactly," replies the United Auto Workers official.

The car company representative says the workers shouldn't have been filling out the postcards on company time.

"What will happen to those who walked out?" asks Dan.

"They're in violation of their contract," the company representative replies. "Anyone who participated in the walkout will be docked pay according to the amount of time they lost."

Art and Tom record these interviews. Since it's dark now, Tom lights the scene with a portable light called a *frezzy*, whose power comes from a battery belt pack.

And then he has it: Dan has the story. He drives off in the van with Art and Tom, and at a land line outside Framingham, he stops to phone Susan at the assignment desk.

"Good news," says Susan. "NBC in New York just called, and wants to use your report on the walkout for tomorrow morning's 'Today' show. Can you stay late tonight and put together a separate videotape for them?"

"Sure can," says Dan; then he says good-bye and hangs up the phone.

During the forty-minute van ride back to the station, Dan starts writing his story about the walkout. This isn't easy, because the ride is so bumpy, but writing in this kind of situation is what Dan does five nights a week. By the time the station comes into view, he has written practically the whole story.

He dashes across the garage and throws off his coat and goes quickly to work.

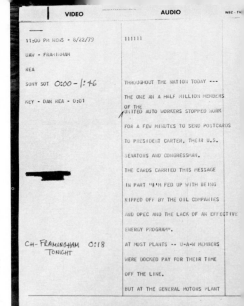

First he types the story, using a special paper that makes six copies at once. The paper is divided down the middle, and on the *video* side Dan types what will be *seen* by the viewer; on the *audio* side, what will be *heard*.

The finished product is a *script*, and he hands five copies to Pam, the eleven-o'clock-news producer, and keeps one for himself.

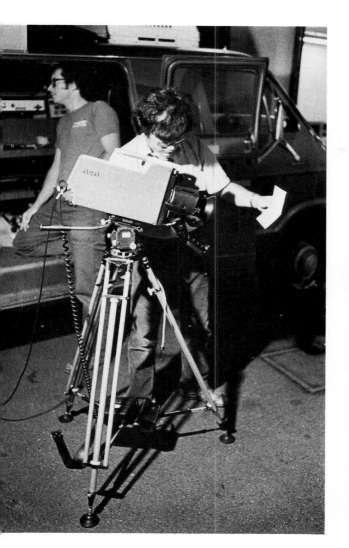

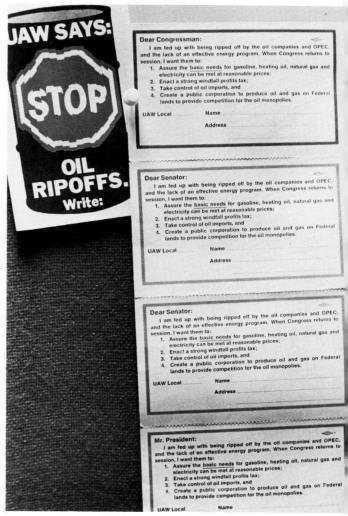

Art and Tom, meanwhile, are out in the back parking lot, shooting close-ups for Dan of the United Auto Workers' postcards. Like the rest of Dan's story tonight, these shots are recorded on a videotape cassette, which is rushed to Dan the moment the shooting's over.

Once Dan has all the tape cassettes, he begins editing his story in a special booth with Rory, one of the videotape editors. Editing, in this case, means choosing scenes from all the footage shot at Framingham, then stringing those scenes together so they will tell the story of the walkout.

Dan stands watching the monitors while Rory operates two videotape machines. When Dan sees a scene he wants from the first machine, Rory punches a few buttons and records the scene on the second machine's blank cassette. They keep doing this — choosing scenes, punching buttons, stringing the scenes together — till the connected scenes start to look and sound like a finished story.

Sometimes Dan uses a microphone to add voice-over commentaries to different scenes. But his favorite part of editing is choosing scenes and sounds, and blending them to make the viewer feel he is right there at the story.

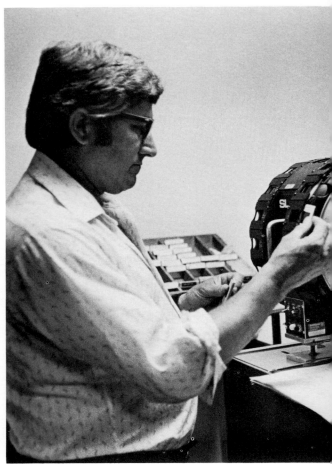

As soon as Dan finishes editing his story, Rory takes the edited tape to the electronic news-gathering room, or E.N.G., where it is wound to its starting point and stacked with other tapes for tonight's news broadcast. During the program Rory will play the tapes one by one as their turns come up.

The rest of the technical staff is busy, too. One technician, Ron, loads a special projector called a *film island* with slides to

be shown on tonight's news. Another technician, Carol, types the words that will appear on the screen on a device known as a *Chiron*. The Chiron is a fascinating machine that stores words, numbers, and diagrams electronically until news time. When a slide or word is desired during a broadcast, it is "punched" on the air by Bill, the technical director, in a special control room called *B-booth*.

 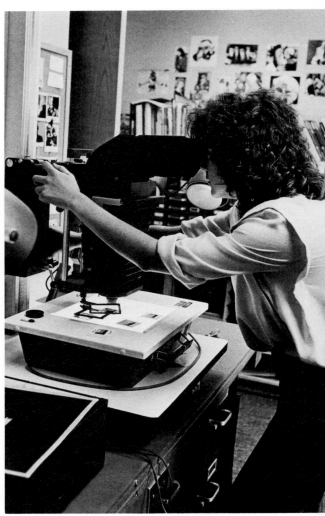

One of Dan's favorite departments is *graphics*, which produces most of the pictures, maps, and charts that appear on the air. From the slide file, the graphics director chooses a slide she needs enlarged, then photographs it with a special close-up camera.

A minute later the enlarged picture is ready, and the graphics assistant glues it to a piece of heavy matte board, then labels it with special stick-on letters.

Since details don't show up well on home TV screens, maps must be made clear and simple.

In their offices in the newsroom, a half hour before news time, the anchors, Tony Pepper and Jack Williams, are putting together the stories they will read tonight on the air. Both Tony and Jack worked in every phase of news broadcasting before becoming anchormen. Jack even built his own radio station as a boy of thirteen. What is their advice to someone who wants to go into television news? "Learn to read and write," says Tony. "And learn to enjoy these skills as you practice them." Jack agrees, and adds, "Get a tape recorder and talk into it. Understand your voice as a tool of communication."

Meanwhile, WBZ's sportscaster, Roger Twibell, prepares his segment of the news show, too. People often wonder if going on the air makes broadcasters nervous, but Roger says no, though he does get keyed up.

Bruce Schwoegler prepares the weather report. Bruce is a university-trained weather scientist, or *meteorologist*, and his office at the station is packed with all kinds of weather-reporting equipment. A computer terminal, into which Bruce types a code, feeds back weather data from any part of the world, while facsimile machines hand him weather maps and satellite pictures. And if it is raining or snowing anywhere in New England, a radarscope pinpoints the spot.

Bruce says that just a short while with these machines gives
him enough information to talk about the day's weather for
hours. Weather news is important, he says, especially during
storms, because unlike much news, weather affects us all.

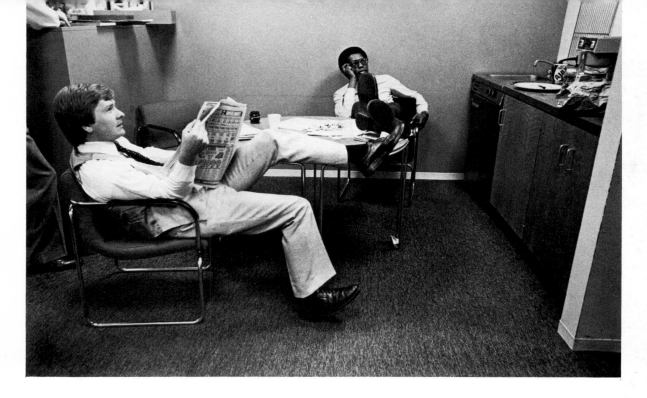

Dan can relax now, put his feet up, and read the paper, because it's the production staff's turn to move into full swing. As the scripts come in from Dan and others, they are checked by the director, Fred, who oversees the actual broadcast of the eleven o'clock news.

Then a production assistant *rips* the scripts — that is, he separates each of the six copies and sorts them into piles for the anchors and others.

Once that's done, the assistant tapes the pages of one of the scripts into a single long sheet so it can be fed into a special machine called a *TelePrompTer*, used during the broadcast.

In the studio, technicians are making hurried last-minute adjustments of the lights and the set. Only ten minutes remain until air time.

You always know when it's ten fifty-five at WBZ because that's when Tony and Jack walk down the hall from the newsroom to the studio. At one minute to eleven, the floor director, Bob, shouts, "Places everybody!"

Tony and Jack clip on their microphones.

Then: "Thirty seconds!"

"Fifteen seconds!"

The prerecorded theme music starts to play.

Bob counts the last ten seconds on his fingers for everyone, and a prerecorded voice introduces Tony and Jack, and Bob gives the signal, and it happens. It finally happens. The news broadcast begins.

The most active place in the station at news time is B-booth. That's where the technical director, the director, and the producer all sit, controlling the flow and action of the show. All four cameras in the studio can be switched off and on from B-booth. When the director, Fred, who's watching the monitors, sees a certain camera's picture he wants shown, he calls out its number, and instantly Bill, the technical director, punches a button, switching that camera on the air. Meanwhile, the producer, Pam, keeps track of the show's time with a stopwatch. News shows always have more stories than can be reported in a half hour. So when Pam sees the show running late, it's her job to cut some of the lesser stories.

Up behind B-booth, a separate engineer controls the sound, or audio, portion of the broadcast.

All the sound and picture signals from the show travel by wire from B-booth to a place in the station called *master control*. From there the signals are whisked up WBZ's huge transmitting tower, which is two hundred feet tall, and broadcast to viewers throughout New England.

And who do those viewers see? Well, Tony Pepper, for one. Only, Tony can't see them. Instead, he looks straight into the lens of one of the four studio cameras, which cost $100,000 each, and reads his reports from the TelePrompTer mounted on top.

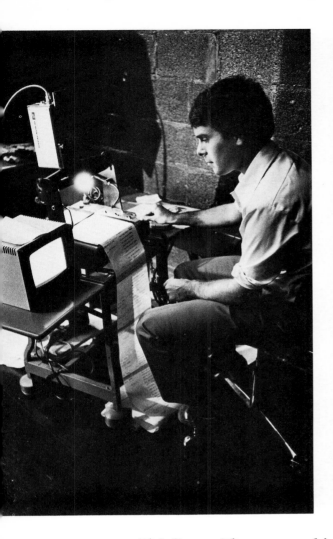

TelePrompTers are used in all the big news studios. In one corner of the WBZ studio, the production assistant runs the specially mounted TelePrompTer camera, which feeds pictures of the script he taped together earlier to the TelePrompTers themselves.

TelePrompTers help anchors maintain good eye contact with their TV audience, but Dan has learned from his anchor experience not to read from them exclusively. "You must follow the script in your hands, too," he says. "Otherwise, if the TelePrompTer breaks down, you're sunk!"

Another tricky part of anchoring, Dan and others say, is following the floor director's hand signals. WBZ's floor director has signals for practically everything, including when the anchors should take a phone call from B-booth.

Dan and Charles Austin usually watch the nightly news
show together on a TV set up behind the assignment desk. At
five past eleven, as Charles and Dan watch, Dan's videotaped
report on the auto workers' walkout is aired. Dan says that
even after five years of reporting, he still finds the experience
of seeing himself on television a little strange. "Especially," he
says, "when you know that at that very moment hundreds of
thousands of others are watching, too!"

The rest of the news show goes without a hitch, and at eleven thirty-one the studio empties.

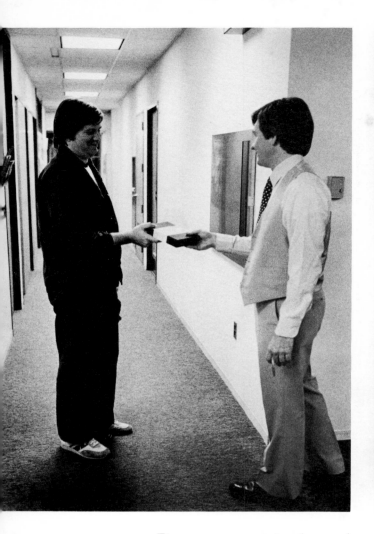

Dan now goes back to the editing booth with Rory to re-edit his Framingham report for NBC's "Today" show. As an affiliate of NBC, Dan's station always supplies it with news stories of national interest. Dan himself has had past stories on the "Today" show, and on other newscasts throughout the country.

At 1:00 A.M., thirteen hours after he came to work, Dan finishes the newly edited tape and hands it to a member of NBC's Boston office. The NBC man will transmit the tape by telephone line to New York, where it will be aired nationally on the "Today" show to ten million viewers.

Dan can now file his scripts of today's stories. His working day is done.

And the day has been exhilarating. Dan has looked inside a thieves' hideout and witnessed the walkout of fifteen hundred workers who were protesting a problem — energy — that faces us all. But more important, Dan put together news reports about these events — reports that informed many hundreds of thousands of people throughout New England. In the course of one year, Dan will file some six hundred reports, each one timely, informative, and different.

Now he strolls through the empty newsroom, slightly tired, but oddly happy.

"Sleep," he murmurs.

He must go home and get some sleep.

He never knows when he'll be called on to cover a story.

Or where he'll be reporting from next.